"What the devil were you trying to do? Kill yourself?"

Startled by the intrusive demand, Selena opened her eyes and saw the captain peering down at her with concern. His heavy brows were drawn together in a frown as they had been earlier that day, just after he had kissed her. He was shirtless now, as well, the wet, powerful muscles of his arms and shoulders gleaming in the moonlight.

Feeling those sinewy muscles ripple beneath his damp skin as his naked chest pressed against her, Selena couldn't help but remember how brazenly she had responded to his kiss. And then a sudden thought struck her. Avery wanted a virgin bride, did he?

Her slender jaw hardening with resolution, Selena met Captain Ramsey's gaze directly. "Captain," she said very clearly, even though her voice was husky with tears, "I would like you to make love to me."

Dear Reader,

The new year is here, and not only are we bringing you some terrific new books to read, we also have some very exciting news in store. In fact, it's *so* exciting that I don't think I can wait before delivering it. Next month we're going to be bringing you *four* Harlequin Historicals every month instead of only two. Your enthusiasm has been so great and your welcome to our authors so warm that we couldn't resist answering your requests for more top-notch historical romances every month. In months to come, favorite authors such as Heather Graham Pozzessere, Patricia Potter, Bronwyn Williams, Lynda Trent and more—as well as talented new authors we've found for you—will be coming your way. I hope you can't wait to read all the Harlequin Historicals we'll be bringing to you in the months and years to come.

But let's not forget this month, when Caryn Cameron and Nicole Jordan bring you New Year's reading to delight and entertain. There's always something good going on here at Harlequin Historicals!

Leslie J. Wainger
Senior Editor and Editorial Coordinator

Moonwitch

Nicole Jordan

Harlequin Books

TORONTO • NEW YORK • LONDON
AMSTERDAM • PARIS • SYDNEY • HAMBURG
STOCKHOLM • ATHENS • TOKYO • MILAN

Harlequin Historical first edition January 1991

ISBN 0-373-28662-7

MOONWITCH

NICOLE JORDAN

is out to prove that whoever said engineers were unromantic is totally wrong. With several sizzling historical romances now in print, she's certainly made her point. Nicole, who has a degree in civil engineering, started writing to "add some creativity to my life," but what began as a hobby has now become her driving passion.

In memory of
VICKI SAUNDERSON POWERS
for her courage and love of life

Chapter One

Antigua, British West Indies 1819

The crew of the American schooner spilled from the Jolly Tar Tavern and swarmed up Long Street, a laughing, rough-and-tumble throng of seamen. Their good-natured hoots and cat-calls carried on the ever-present sea breeze and drifted through the shuttered windows of the white weatherboard buildings that lined the street. The clamor even dared invade the offices of Ignatius P. Foulkes, Solicitor, where Selena Markham sat consulting the prestigious founder of the firm.

Momentarily diverted by the noise, Selena paused in mid-sentence to glance beyond the solicitor's balding head toward the window. But since she heard no cries of "cane fire," the warning that every sugar planter dreaded, nor a mournful proclamation of "ship down," a lament Selena dreaded even more, she resumed her discussion of a subject she found highly distressing: the problem of her stepmother's continued extravagances.

"I had hoped," Selena confessed, "that you could suggest a solution. Edith became rather...abusive when I refused to raise her allowance on quarter day. Yet I had no choice. She continues to spend far more than the plantation can support. And now this! This time she has gone beyond extravagance. To put the house up for security... I must do something. I cannot allow her to lose our home to a moneylender."

The solicitor fingered the gold timepiece that hung from a fob at his rather massive girth and eyed her thoughtfully. He was surprised by her vehemence; Selena could tell by his expression. No doubt she was lacking her normal reserve, though she knew she appeared cool and elegant as usual, dressed as she was in a sprigged muslin gown and a narrow-brimmed gypsy bonnet that hid much of her silver-blond hair.

"I understand entirely," Ignatius replied with the familiarity of a family friend, "the difficulty of your position, my dear. I well know how...headstrong your stepmother can be."

Headstrong was far too nice a word, Selena thought with asperity. Grasping, shrewish, perhaps even vicious. Those were all more appropriate descriptions of Edith. Since Edith's marriage to Thomas Markham seven years before, Selena had made every effort to live in harmony with her stepmother. Through the years, she had developed a means of dealing with Edith, one which consisted primarily of ignoring the situation and not allowing herself to respond to the barbs that frequently annoyed and sometimes wounded her. She had continued the habit after her father had passed away, for she felt that respect for his memory made it her duty. This time, however, Edith had gone too far.

"It seems," Ignatius observed in answer, "that Mrs. Markham means to force your hand."

At that unnecessary remark, Selena felt a surge of impatience. She leaned forward, her fragile features becoming set and earnest. "Precisely. But you know as well as I that the income Papa left Edith is more than adequate to keep her in style—although it won't begin to cover the lavish expenditures she has been indulging in lately. The emeralds alone cost nearly two thousand pounds."

Pursing his lips in a frown, Ignatius shook his head slowly. "I'll think on it, my dear, but I'm afraid you have no legal recourse. Your father left you the land, but Mrs. Markham has clear title to the manor house. Of course, you can purchase the mortgage from her creditors—"

"At a usurious rate, no doubt!"

"Yet the cane crop has been good this year. You could probably afford it."

Selena clasped her gloved hands in her lap, trying to contain her frustration. "I have nearly four hundred people to provide for, Mr. Foulkes, not to mention purchasing a new set of rollers for the south mill and a cistern for the curing house. Given free rein, Edith would just as soon bankrupt the plantation! Even my father had little faith in her judgment where money was concerned."

When Ignatius merely nodded in sympathy, Selena sighed bitterly. "Of course, I might purchase the house outright, but what would I do then? I could hardly ask Edith to leave, for she would have nowhere to live. Besides, what kind of monster would that make me?"

The solicitor's response was interrupted by a rough voice directly outside the window.

"My blunt's on the cap'n!"

"I say Tiny will settle the question once an' fer all!" came the shouted reply.

The disturbance was impossible to ignore. Ignatius raised his great bulk from behind his desk and flung open the louvered shutters to look down at the street. At once, the blazing Caribbean sunlight streamed into the room, creating a glare that would have made any person not inured to the brightness and heat of the islands wince.

But Selena had grown up there so, though anxious to continue the conversation, she rose from the leather wing chair where she had been sitting and joined the solicitor. To her left, Long Street rose steeply from the docks of St. John's Harbor. Beyond was a striking view of turquoise waters dotted with fishing ketches and feluccas. The harbor was only deep enough to accommodate drafts of five feet or less, so the hundreds of seafaring ships that docked at Antigua each year had to anchor across the island at English Harbor, the headquarters for the British naval fleet in the Caribbean.

Looking to her right, up the hill, Selena caught sight of a boisterous crowd of perhaps thirty men dressed in the blue jackets and canvas trousers of sailors. They were loudly making their way up the street toward the courthouse, bearing two of their numbers on their shoulders.

Ignatius harrumphed in disapproval. "That is the crew of the *Tagus*, if I'm not mistaken."

"The *Tagus*?" Selena asked, following the retreating crowd with her gaze.

He nodded. "An American schooner of four hundred tons. Put in today." The solicitor emitted another sound, which resembled a grunt. "See the man they are carrying, the one with the chestnut hair? That, my dear, is Captain Ramsey. Even for an American, such behavior is disgraceful in a man of authority. I expect the governor must be relieved to claim no connection."

Selena recognized the name then. The American captain shared the same last name with the governor of the Leeward Islands, Major General George Ramsay, although the spelling was different. She remembered her father, who had been a close friend of the governor, remarking on it.

Curious to at last glimpse the man who had so often been the object of such fierce interest among the ladies of the island, Selena leaned forward. The captain's back was turned toward her as he was borne away by the laughing, jeering crew, but even at this distance, she could tell that his dark chestnut hair was thick and waving. He appeared as tall and muscular as she had heard him described, though not as powerfully built as the black-haired giant who shared his swaying throne.

Kyle Ramsey was a regular visitor to Antigua, she knew—*regular* meaning one or two times a year. Whenever he was on the island, he stayed at the home of one of his friends, an absentee planter who owned a plantation on the leeward coast, near her own. To Selena's knowledge, half the females of her acquaintance had pursued Captain Ramsey at one time or another. He was accepted in the finest homes, but generally he avoided island society, preferring the company of his rowdy crew.

Indeed, it looked as if Captain Ramsey had joined his men in partaking rather freely at the grogshop down the street. He was making as much noise as any of them, his deep timbred voice raised in song as he thumped his airborne companion heartily on the back.

When Ignatius turned away in disgust, Selena withdrew from the window. She was disappointed, however, when the solicitor returned to their discussion of Edith Markham, for he informed her that there was little he could do.

"I greatly regret, my dear, that I couldn't be of more help. Fortunately, though, you will shortly have a new home. When is the happy occasion to be?"

Selena found it hard to repress a sigh at the thought of her engagement. "We haven't set a date yet. It seems somewhat callous to marry so soon after Papa's death."

Ignatius presumed on the familiarity of his long acquaintance to shake a fatherly finger under her nose. "It has been nearly two years, my dear. You don't want to lose Mr. Warner by delaying longer. You're past the first blush of youth," he pointed out, his kindly tone taking the sting from the words.

Selena declined to respond as she gathered up her reticule and parasol, well aware that at four and twenty she was considered almost an old maid. It wasn't that men found her unattractive. She possessed an ethereal kind of beauty: a tall, slender figure; hair that was more silver than blond, as pale and fine as corn silk; and light blue eyes that seemed gray in certain lights. Nor was it that she disliked the idea of marriage. Her first engagement had been to a British naval officer whom she had loved with all the ardor of her eighteen-year-old heart. Their love had survived the ravages of war with America but had ended in tragedy when her betrothed's ship foundered in a storm off Dominica.

She hadn't completely recovered from her loss when Thomas Markham's yacht had gone down in the same hurricane that laid waste to much of Saint Lucia. That calamity, following so close on the heels of the first, had left her with a fear, not of storms, but of ships.

After a lengthy period of mourning, she had accepted the suit of the wealthiest planter on the island. The Honorable Avery Warner was a widower twenty years her senior and a member of Antigua's House of Assembly.

Selena wasn't in love with Avery, but she greatly respected his ability as a legislator and his skill at managing his vast holdings, and while she sometimes chafed at Avery's highhanded conduct toward her, she was willing to honor her father's wishes. Thomas Markham had favored the match and had often expressed his desire to see her settled with such an estimable gentleman for a husband. In any event, marriage was the expected course for well-bred young ladies. And in marrying Avery, she would finally become mistress of her own home—without a harping stepmother to contend with.

Remembering Edith, Selena found herself fighting the urge to clench her fists. Instead, she extended a slender hand to the solicitor while struggling to maintain the quiet air of authority that had stood her in good stead when managing her vast sugar plantation.

"Thank you for your time, Mr. Foulkes," she said, forcing a smile. If he couldn't help her, she would have to find a solution to her problem herself. She rarely opposed her stepmother, for Edith usually came out the winner in any open confrontation. But in this instance, it was her family home that was at stake—her one link to the father and mother she had lost. Even if it would no longer be her home after her marriage, she didn't intend to let Edith sell it to strangers.

Ignatius seemed to understand her predicament, for he gave her a look of condolence as he took her hand. "Of course, my dear, if any ideas occur to me, I'll let you know at once. Shall I escort you somewhere, or is your servant waiting downstairs?"

"Samuel is meeting me at the milliner's with the carriage."

"Very well, then. I shall see you at the ball tomorrow evening and beg a place on your dance card—if you will indulge an old man."

Selena agreed with a strained smile and allowed the solicitor to show her out. As she descended the wrought iron stairs, a cooling sea breeze tugged at the neat coil of pale hair beneath her bonnet, loosening a few strands to wisp around her face. Impatiently she restored them to their proper place, then opened her parasol to shield her face from the harsh glare of the May sun as she made her way up Long Street toward the milliner's shop.

She had only gone a short distance when she heard the chorus of cheers and wagers coming from the yard of the old arsenal across from the courthouse. There seemed to be some kind of brawl taking place, for she could see the rowdy crew of the *Tagus*. They had formed a large ring around the yard, and their gestures and shouts indicated they were deriving great enjoyment from the spectacle.

As she moved closer, raising the skirts of her blue muslin gown slightly to avoid the dust, she could see what held their attention. Two men were engaged in a hand-to-hand combat—a strange combination of fisticuffs and grappling. Selena recognized the black-haired giant she had seen earlier and knew by the shouts that his name must, ironically, be Tiny. The other man was Kyle Ramsey.

Captain Ramsey might be the smaller of the two, yet he was powerfully built, tall and perfectly proportioned. His shoulders were a yard wide and molded bronze, while his narrow waist tapered to lean hips and long, muscular legs that only added to the impression of limitless strength. Both men had stripped off their shirts and boots, and their glistening, rippling muscles provided a brazen display of sheer male virility.

Selena had been raised under a strict code of deportment and knew better than to linger, but the sailors' excitement was contagious. She paused to watch, standing well back from the crowd.

It wasn't a brawl so much as a contest of strength, she realized. The two men circled each other warily, then suddenly charged. They came together with a thud and bounced apart, neither able to gain the advantage by knocking the other off balance.

The captain got the best of the next encounter, managing to duck the giant's flailing fist and land a blow in Tiny's rock-hard belly, then dance away out of range. Grinning, the captain issued a jovial taunt to the giant. "You're slipping, lad," he called amiably. "You'll want to aim lower next time."

His teeth flashed white against his bronzed complexion, and as he stood there poised for combat, all taut muscle and lean power and pulsing strength, Selena studied him. His overwhelming masculinity tugged at some deeply rooted feminine instinct that her engagement didn't give her the liberty to acknowledge. Yet she could understand quite well why the captain had aroused the ladies' interest. His sheer size and vitality was fascinating. He moved with litheness and grace for all his imposing height and powerful physique, and there was a lust for life about him that was extremely appealing.

Her gaze moved to Captain Ramsey's face. It too was attractive. Roughly carved, it had a high forehead, heavy eyebrows, lean cheeks creased by laughter and a strong chin. The next moment, that same chin received a blow that made the captain stagger backward.

When Tiny followed through with a lunge, wrapping his massive arms around Ramsey's waist, the captain nearly fell. But he saved himself at the last moment by thrusting one booted foot in front of the giant's, sending Tiny catapulting face first into the dirt.

Tiny let out a roar and leaped to his feet for the next assault. His face contorted with determination as he lowered his huge head and came at the captain with the force of a battering ram, gathering speed all the while. The blow hit the captain in the midriff, making him grunt and double over as he was propelled backward.

The combined weight of the two men parted the crowd in front of Selena. Tiny stumbled and lurched forward to land spread-eagled on the ground, while the captain's momentum carried him backward to where she was standing. He fell with a thud at her feet and lay there sprawled on his back, not moving.

Selena knowing full well that a lady ought not be seen on the street among such rabble, knowing also what was expected of her as the future wife of a prominent gentleman on the island, disregarded both the conventions of society and the wishes of her betrothed and bent over the captain, her blue eyes full of concern.

She was close enough now to see that his rugged features were weathered by the sun and wind. The laugh lines around his eyes were nearly as prominent as the heavy brows and the cleft in the strong chin. Then his eyes opened, and she could see they were hazel, flecked with green and ringed with gold. Those deep-set eyes assessed her frankly, taking in her cool, quiet beauty.

"An angel," he murmured appreciatively. "I've died and gone to heaven."

His speech was more drawling than her own clipped tones but held a definite hint of a British accent. Knowing he was American, Selena wondered about it as she searched his face for signs of pain. "Are you hurt, Captain?" she asked gently.

A laughing gleam filled his hazel eyes. "Mortally wounded. I'm sure to need ministering."

She liked the humor that glinted behind those eyes, yet it made her realize that her concern was misplaced. It would take far more than a fall to topple this Viking of a man.

The captain shook his head as if to clear it, then, with a groan, got unsteadily to his feet. Selena took a hasty step back as she found herself confronting a sleekly muscled chest that was lightly furred and glistening with sweat.

His nakedness disturbed her almost as much as his overwhelming physical presence. She was tall herself, but Kyle Ramsey towered over her. Next to his powerful body, she felt as slender as a cane stalk.

He stood there swaying, whether from exertion or any spirits he had imbibed, she couldn't tell. He staggered a little then and reached out for her, putting a large, callused hand on her shoulder to steady himself. Worried that he would fell her without even intending to, Selena lifted her gaze to Captain Ramsey's face. He was regarding her with a mournful expression that she was sure was feigned.

"You mean to send me back into battle unattended?" he asked in his deep-timbered voice before trying to sweep her a bow. "I beg one of your favors, fair lady. A handkerchief for luck? Or perhaps your parasol. I'll wager that would come in handy... applied upside Tiny's head."

Amused in spite of herself by his high spirits yet disliking his attempt at flirtation, Selena raised a full, arching brow at him. "It would be highly improper, I'm afraid, Captain. I also think that you should remove your hand from my shoulder before I find yet another use for my parasol."

The roguish glint that must surely be what had charmed half the females on the island made his hazel eyes dance with amber lights. "So you mean to be unaccommodating? Then I see I'll have to claim my victory kiss now."

She should have expected his next move, especially after his warning. But she was accustomed to men who accorded proper respect to gentlewomen, if not out of chivalry or a sense of honor, then because they feared British justice on the island. The Englishmen of Antigua tended to be highly protective of their ladies and not the least hesitant to see transgressors clapped in the stocks for the slightest offense, especially Americans, whose presence was merely tolerated.

Selena was quite unprepared, therefore, when Kyle grasped her arms and hauled her against his naked chest, his hands gentle and controlled, yet unyielding. Nor did she have time to protest before he lowered his head and found her generous mouth with his own wide, hard one.

The kiss was brief, little more than a meeting of lips, yet before it ended, she felt him stiffen slightly, as if he had found something surprising. And when he lifted his head, she saw that he was frowning down at her, his heavy brows drawn together as if in puzzlement. Dumbfounded, Selena returned his golden gaze, shock holding her motionless.

He didn't release her but continued to stand there, appraising her. "I must be more foxed than I realized," he muttered rather huskily. "I felt the ground shaking."

Selena stared at him wide-eyed, having lost the power of speech. When she remained silent, his hands tightened on her arms, and with inexorable strength, drew her rigid, corseted body even closer.

He wasn't entirely drunk, she realized as his lips met hers again, though he tasted of rum. The alcohol further dazed her senses. Or perhaps it was the musky odor of sweat that was making her so dizzy and pliant. Or the distinctively clean scent of his skin, a salty freshness that reminded her of the sea.

Neither of her betrotheds had ever affected her in such a manner—leaving her breathless and trembling. Nor had they ever kissed her the way Kyle Ramsey was doing, with his mouth open against hers, his tongue parting her lips to probe and explore.

His strong hands moved up her arms to her slender shoulders as he kissed her in an almost leisurely way...deeply, thoroughly, filling her mouth with his tongue, gliding his long fingers along her delicate jawline to tangle them in the pale tresses that framed her face beneath her bonnet.

Her hair, never willing to stay pinned at the best of times, started to slip from its moorings, yet oddly, Selena didn't care. She felt the wildest urge to respond to his overpowering maleness, to the warm animal magnetism that radiated from him. She was vaguely aware of the crowing and catcalls coming from his men and that sometime in the past few moments she had dropped her parasol, yet still she stood there pressed against Kyle Ramsey's hard, half-naked body, submitting to his kiss, her gloved fingers actually clinging to his corded forearms—until finally, reluctantly, he released her.

Her composure shattered, Selena stared up at him, wondering at the amazement she saw on his rugged face. Then, like a great hound shedding water, he shook his head, as if to clear his muddled senses.

The movement brought Selena to her own senses. She felt a slow, painful blush rising to her face as she realized she had allowed a half-dressed, loutish sea captain to kiss her on the streets of St. John's in full view of a crowd of coarse sailors and who knew what townspeople.

With quiet deliberation Selena drew back her gloved hand and struck the captain across the cheek. It wasn't precisely what she wanted to do; it was what good breeding and a lifetime of training compelled. Nor did her blow seem to hurt him much, for even though Captain Ramsey reached up to rub the offended cheek, he grinned down at Selena, the creases in his face deepening into slashing masculine dimples.

"It was worth it," he said provocatively before bending to pick up her parasol. He was still grinning as he handed the blue confection to her. "I'll have to win now. I can't let such a victory kiss go to waste."

He spun around then to bellow, "Tiny, lad! Where are you hiding? Prepare to be soundly trounced!" leaving Selena to stare after him, her cheeks flushed in embarrassment, her customary serenity totally destroyed.

As Tiny showed himself and the contest got under way once more, the crowd of gawking sailors returned to their sport. Selena, her face burning with shame, made an attempt to restore order to her sagging coiffure while she glanced around quickly to see who else had witnessed the incident. She saw no one she recognized, yet she was certain word of her scandalous behavior would soon spread. Antiguan society was small and close-knit, and very little happened that wasn't discussed and analyzed and judged.

Raising her parasol, this time to hide her scarlet cheeks, Selena turned away and quickly crossed the street. She greatly regretted not having gone directly to the milliner's. Avery would be upset to learn what had happened, of course. He would consider her behavior unworthy of her birth and breeding, as well as his position in society. Yet Selena dreaded more what her sharp-tongued stepmother would say—especially since she had no defense for her actions. She hadn't protested Captain Ramsey's barbaric assault on her lips, and what was more shameful, she hadn't much wanted to.

She was still considering what explanation she would give when she reached the milliner's shop on High Street. Her Negro groom, Samuel, wasn't waiting with the gig as she had directed, but it was early yet and she still had her errand to complete. As she was about to enter the shop, however, an elegant black-and-green curricle clattered up the street and came to a halt beside her. The equipage was drawn by a matched pair of bays and driven by her betrothed, Avery Warner, with a young black slave perched up behind.

Avery was a tall, middle-aged gentleman, distinguished looking rather than handsome, with dark hair graying at the temples. At the moment his stern features were set in an unsmiling expression as he regarded Selena. "Might I take you up with me, my dear? It is unbecoming for you to be walking the streets unattended."

Selena felt herself flushing at his public censure. "That won't be necessary, Avery," she replied woodenly. "Samuel will be along in a moment, and I have some shopping yet to do."

"But I insist. I cannot have my future wife behaving in a manner that is less than circumspect. It will give rise to gossip."

"I'm surprised you think it proper for us to be seen together without a chaperon!"

Avery's brows drew together as he shot her a surprised look; Selena rarely spoke sharply to anyone. "I rather think a chaperon is unnecessary, my dear," he said in mild reproof. "This an open carriage, and we are affianced, after all. I am simply concerned about appearances."

Selena pressed her lips together. It was a bit late for Avery to be concerned about appearances, for she had already lent herself to gossip with a vengeance.

"And of course," he continued in a more tolerant tone, "I am thinking of your safety, as well, Selena. I passed a throng of ruffians fighting in front of the courthouse just now—the courthouse, no less—and not a justice in sight. I was disgusted, I can tell you. Such conduct is disgraceful. Rabble like that should be clapped in jail and not be free to roam the streets. I intend to take it up with the council at the first opportunity."

She should have told Avery then about her encounter with the "rabble" and their bold, roisterous captain, she knew. But she couldn't bring herself speak of it, not in the middle of the street with the bright-eyed black groom overhearing her every word. Besides, Avery would learn of it soon enough. And perhaps by keeping silent she would be avoiding an even greater scandal. Avery was sufficiently aroused just now to demand the captain be brought to justice, and she didn't think Captain Ramsey's offense was serious enough to warrant a jail sentence.

And so she murmured a noncommittal reply. When Avery insisted on waiting for her so that he could see her home, she gave in gracefully and hastily completed her shopping. She was carrying a bandbox when she left the shop. Avery consigned it to the groom, who stowed it behind the seat, then handed Selena into the curricle, informing her that he had sent Samuel on ahead.

As they left St. John's, with its Georgian weatherboard buildings and scattering of coconut palms, they turned south onto a narrow road of crushed coral, following the ridge of a hill. From that vantage, Selena had a good view of the warm, wind-washed island.

On her right was a luminous expanse of jewel-blue sea, shading to lighter green as it met the reefs that ringed Antigua and filled the numerous coves and inlets along the coast. The leeward side of the island was sheltered from the full force of the trade winds, so that the waves of the Caribbean lapped easily at the dazzling white sand beaches—unlike the eastern shore, which had no defense against the wind-driven rollers of Atlantic.

Before her stretched a gently rolling landscape, covered by low scrub and verdant fields, and beyond, in the distance, rose Boggy Peak, the highest point of the generally flat island. Except for the slopes of Boggy Peak and the cultivated gardens of the vast plantation houses, Antigua was nearly bare of trees, for there were no major rivers and no dependable water supply, leaving the inhabitants at the mercy of the occasional drenching showers and whatever water they could collect in cisterns and catchments. The lush stands of sugarcane were nearly gone, as well, for the harvest was almost over. Even so, the island shimmered a verdant green.

Selena's thoughts were centered on the harvest when Avery politely inquired about the errand that had brought her to town.

"I needed a toque bonnet of a particular shade," she prevaricated, offering that excuse rather than mentioning her trouble with Edith. "I shall be wearing a new gown tomorrow evening."

"Ah, yes, the lieutenant governor's ball. I'm sure you will look charming, my dear. But surely you could have sent a servant to fetch it."

"Perhaps."

"Well, in future it might be better if you were accompanied by a maid, or wait till I am free to escort you."

Selena raised her chin with a touch of defiance. Avery's request was reasonable, perhaps—in her mother's day, gently reared females never appeared on the streets of Antigua without being veiled—but Selena had been accorded the freedom of the island since she could first sit a horse. If Avery meant to curtail that freedom so severely before their marriage, her responsibilities as a planter would be difficult to carry out.

"I went to see Mr. Foulkes, if you must know," she replied. "It concerned a business matter that could not be delegated."

"I suppose you are referring to Edith's extravagance. Oh, yes," Avery added when Selena glanced at him in surprise, "I'm aware that she mortgaged the house to buy a king's ransom in jewels. An extremely foolish venture, considering the size of her income. I hope you don't intend to come to her aid."

"I don't know that I have much choice. She could lose the house if she can't redeem the debt."

"Let her lose it."

"Avery, it is my *home* we are speaking of."

"You will have no need of it when you marry me, my dear. That is another reason to avoid delaying the ceremony any longer. I should like to be in full command of the plantation before autumn planting. Not that you haven't done an admirable job of managing, particularly for a woman. But your father never intended for you to retain control, rather, to turn it over to your husband. And I'm certain you will be relieved to have such a burden lifted from your lovely shoulders."

Selena bit her tongue to keep from saying something she would regret, and Avery reached over to pat her hand in an avuncular fashion. "I shall speak to Edith, my dear. I expect I can persuade her to consider your feelings about the house and to abstain from any more reckless expenditures."

By this time Avery's curricle was drawing up before the house that so concerned Selena—a single-story, stone construction, cooled by a raised basement and louvered outer galleries and shaded by mango and silk-cotton trees. The arched overhangs of the galleries were supported by slim wooden columns and brightened by cascades of yellow cassia and golden logwood blossoms.

Despite her annoyance at Avery's lecture, Selena felt obliged to invite him in for tea. The interior was cool and elegant, decorated much like an English manor, with Aubusson carpets and Hepplewhite furnishings that her father had had shipped over from England years before.

Her stepmother wasn't home, Selena learned from the Negro housekeeper, and Edith still hadn't returned by the time Avery took his leave, promising to escort her to the lieutenant governor's ball the following evening. So Selena next saw her stepmother at dinner.

A petite and sultry brunette, Edith Markham scarcely looked like a grieving widow. Nor was she old enough to be Selena's mother. Only ten years separated them in age, but a vast difference existed between them in temperament and form. While Selena was sensitive and reserved, Edith was callous and outspoken. And while Selena was slender and pale, Edith was full figured and as dark as a Gypsy. They had never gotten along well, neither during the five years before Thomas Markham's death, nor in the two years since.

It never occurred to Selena that her stepmother might be jealous of her elusive beauty or her managerial talents. She only saw that Edith rarely lost an opportunity to undermine her confidence and belittle her efforts. So she wasn't surprised when during the soup course Edith immediately brought up the subject she had been dreading.

"I understand you made quite a spectacle of yourself this afternoon," Edith remarked, giving her an accusing stare. "Really, Selena, I feel I must take you to task. Your want of conduct is embarrassing me dreadfully. No less than three of my acquaintances commented on your scandalous display."

Selena stiffened at the rebuke, but she said nothing, knowing any argument would only make Edith more determined to be unpleasant. The best way to deal with her stepmother, she'd found, was to ignore her when possible and treat her with cool civility when not.

"If you insist on behaving so disgracefully," Edith continued, "I'm afraid I will have to ask you to refrain from visiting town."

"It won't happen again, I assure you."

"I should hope not! If you aren't careful, you will give Avery a disgust of you. I'm sure he is quite aware of your preference for seamen after you cut such a figure of pity a few years back, pining after that naval officer."

In spite of her determination to maintain her composure, Selena felt a painful flush rise to her cheeks; Edith had struck at her most vulnerable point—her lost love.

Edward had survived the war with America, for Selena had received a letter from him shortly afterward, full of plans for their impending nuptials and hope for their future life together. After learning that his ship had gone down in a storm, she had developed the habit of riding the long distance to English Harbor each day to inquire of the admiralty about incoming vessels, searching for news of her betrothed. No survivors of the downed ship had ever been found, yet without physical proof of Edward's death, Selena had found it harder to recover from her grief. Even after so many years, she would sometimes dream that the report had simply been a terrible mistake.

"I suppose," Edith commented in the silence, "it could have been worse. At least Captain Ramsey isn't a common sailor.

Rumor has it that he is every bit as wealthy as your father was. Though why any man would continue to captain a ship when he could enjoy the comforts of dry land is beyond me.''

"Perhaps he likes the sea," Selena suggested coolly.

Edith shot her an unfriendly stare. "If Captain Ramsey is wealthy enough to settle down, then as a gentleman he should invest in an estate."

When Selena made no reply, Edith left off eating her soup to give her stepdaughter a penetrating look. "Of course he will be staying at Five Islands. I suggest you keep well away from there, unless you mean to disgrace yourself entirely."

Selena's expression turned frosty. Certainly she owed it to her father's memory to treat Edith with polite deference, but filial duty only went so far. There was a limit to how far she could be pushed, and Edith had nearly reached it. "I hardly need your warning," Selena replied with chilling politeness.

Edith seemed to recognize the limit, for she finally dropped the subject and spoke of other things. Selena, her eyes quietly flashing, returned her attention to her soup plate and said little throughout the rest of the meal.

Perhaps it was Edith's scolding that made Selena so wide-awake and restless that night, or perhaps it was the mention of her lost love, or even the shocking kiss she had received earlier that day, but when she retired to her room, sleep wouldn't come. Drawing on a wrapper over her white muslin nightdress, she slipped through the French doors of her bedroom and onto the gallery.

A full moon shone brightly through the slats of the louvered jalousies, while a soft breeze caressed her skin and stirred her pale tresses. She hadn't braided her hair that night, and it hung fine and straight down her back, like a silver mantle. Resting her head against the cool stone of a gallery arch, Selena stared out at the shadows of a towering silk-cotton tree.

She should have been happy. It was crop season, when work was the hardest but spirits were highest for slaves and planters alike. The harvest had been good, not like some years when the lack of rainfall had resulted in barely enough output to keep the islanders from starving. And she was soon to be married. Avery might not be the essence of a young woman's romantic dreams, but he cared for her in his fashion and would make her a good husband. And she would soon be mistress of her own

home. She could leave behind the insecurity she had felt since
Edith had usurped her mother's place in Thomas Markham's
heart.

Yet an inexplicable heaviness weighed on her heart—probably, Selena thought, because she hadn't yet determined what
to do about saving her birthplace. It didn't help, either, that
her thoughts kept returning to that devastating kiss Kyle
Ramsey had given her. His rugged strength had made her feel
so very feminine, his earthy sensuousness, so very desirable.
No doubt *he* hadn't been affected by that embrace as she had
been. Captain Ramsey was the kind of man to whom kisses
meant little, the kind of seafaring adventurer with "a woman
in every port." By now he would have forgotten about it entirely.

Yet she couldn't forget. She kept remembering the hardness of his sleekly muscled body, the musky male scent of him
and the strange ache it had aroused in her, and kept wondering what would have followed his kiss if it hadn't had to end.
She had a general idea of what happened between men and
women, so she could imagine—

Abruptly, Selena shook her head. Such fantasies weren't
acceptable for an unmarried young lady, especially one of her
social standing, not when she was engaged to one of Antigua's leading citizens.

She raised her gaze to the horizon. She couldn't see the
ocean, but she could smell its freshness mingled with the exotic scent of tropical flowers. The place where Captain Ramsey was staying as a guest was only a short distance away. Five
Islands plantation, which got its name from the five small islands off the coast, was adjacent to her own land and near one
of her favorite coves. She went there frequently to bathe in the
sea. Not at night, of course, but in the early morning, before
the sun was hot enough to burn her white skin.

The plantation house at Five Islands was less formal than
her own, a low, rambling bungalow surrounded by spacious
verandas and towering coconut palms. Would Kyle Ramsey be
there now? Or would he have stayed in town and found a willing tavern wench to warm his bed?

Selena shrugged. She couldn't imagine why she was thinking this way. She would do far better to try to sleep. She was
turning toward her bedroom when she heard a sudden cry
coming from around the corner of the gallery. It was softly
uttered, as if someone were in pain but trying to hide it.

Greatly concerned, Selena went to investigate, her slippered feet making no sound on the slatted wooden floor as she moved along the gallery.

Around the next corner, on the opposite side of the house from her own bedroom, a light was shining from Edith's room. When Selena heard the soft moan again, she recognized her stepmother's voice. Worried, she hastened her footsteps, but when she reached the French doors of Edith's room, she halted abruptly, staring past the long, sheer curtains that billowed in the soft night breeze.

Edith lay sprawled on the huge master bed, still wearing the silk gown she had dined in, her face contorted with pleasure. Avery was lying on top of her, almost fully clothed, his body pumping between her legs while he held her arms stretched above her head.

Before Selena could move, he gave a final thrust, eliciting another muffled cry from Edith. "Be quiet, my dear," Avery ordered hoarsely, "or you'll wake the entire household."

His back was to the door, so Selena couldn't see his expression, but she could hear the annoyance in his tone. He shuddered once more, then withdrew abruptly and stood up. Pushing down the hem of Edith's disheveled gown to cover her gartered thighs, he began fastening the buttons at the front of his pantaloons. Edith's eyes opened then, and they were almost black with sensual pain.

Selena stood there frozen, trying to take in what she was seeing. When Avery carefully began brushing the marks Edith's slippers had made on his silk waistcoat and his dove-gray pantaloons, though, Selena gasped and took an involuntary step back, her appalled mind finally comprehending. She had known she couldn't demand fidelity from Avery, but to betray her with her own stepmother! In the very bed where she had been born!

Edith raised her head then and stared at the curtained windows for such a long moment that Selena realized her gasp must have been heard. She knew she ought to leave at once so that she wouldn't witness any further evidence of Avery's betrayal, but the nausea welling in her stomach kept her rooted where she stood long enough to hear Edith's next words.

"How can you marry that chaste little puritan?" Edith asked as Avery strode over to the dressing table chair, where his coat was draped. "Selena won't give you what I do."

With infinite care, Avery picked up his jacket and began examining it for creases. "Precisely because she is chaste, my dear," he replied in a bored tone.

"*And* because she owns the land you covet—don't deny it! If Thomas had left me the plantation, you would be marrying me."

"Gentlemen take virgins to wife, my dear, not wantons. You, Edith, are a complete wanton. Selena, on the other hand, is a lady. She hasn't a wanton bone in her body."

Selena took another step backward, digging her nails into her palms to keep from crying out her hurt and humiliation.

"You'll miss this when you are married," Edith declared irritably.

"I've told you before, I don't intend to give you up simply because I have a wife. I mean to have you both as well as the land."

Edith cast a glance at the windows then and smiled slyly, triumphantly. Selena turned away, stumbling, blinded by tears, knowing only that she had to escape her home.

Somehow she found her way to the stables and threw a bridle over the head of her favorite horse—a white mare named Pallas. They made a pale blur in the moonlight as they streaked through the night, heading for the sea. Sobbing with anger and pain, Selena bent low over the mare's neck, her hair streaming in a silver cloud behind her.

When they reached the quiet cove, the glittering waves of the Caribbean stretched out to infinity before them. Nearly blinded by tears, hardly aware of what she was doing, Selena flung herself from the mare's back and threw herself at the swelling surf, driven by a primal need for solace.

"What in blazes...?" a startled voice growled behind her just as the warm sea closed over her head.

She felt her slippers come off as she struck out wildly through the waves. The skirts of her wrapper and nightdress had entangled with her bare legs, making it difficult to stay afloat, yet when she heard a shout from that same masculine voice and then a splash, as if someone had dived in after her, Selena redoubled her efforts. She was too distraught to face her pursuer. She only wanted to be left alone.

In only a moment, though, she could tell that she was losing the battle; the sound of his powerful stroking was almost directly behind her. And then a hard arm threaded around her waist, jerking her back against an even harder chest.

"Stop it—unhand me!" Selena cried, flailing her arms as she sobbed with wounded fury.

"I'm not gong to watch you drown yourself," a deep-timbred voice grated in her ear.

She realized then that this stranger had feared for her safety, but she was in no mood to countenance a rescue from him. She tried to pry away the muscular arm and found that it was like prizing open a steel trap. All she could do was struggle helplessly as she was dragged backward through the surf.

When they reached the shore, Selena was kicking furiously and choking on all the salt water she had swallowed. Her captor hefted her from the waves and carried her like a sack of grain over one hip, but as he made to deposit her on the beach, her foot somehow got entangled with his long legs and he tripped, falling to his knees on the damp sand, swearing as he barely avoided crushing her beneath him.

Selena was still sobbing, her breath coming in shallow, quick gasps, but she managed to turn onto her back so that she could use her fists against his broad shoulders. "You!" she sputtered. The tall man who was sprawled half on top of her was Kyle Ramsey. Through a veil of bedraggled hair and tears, she could see the rugged planes of his face shadowed by moonlight.

"Damn it, be still," he ordered gruffly as she squirmed beneath his great weight. When she continued to push against his chest, he threw one muscular leg over her thighs and grabbed her wrists, holding her arms above her head.

His action only reminded her of how Avery had pinned Edith's wrists during their coupling. Selena quieted then, closing her eyes, tears streaming down her cheeks as she relived that horrible moment. Avery had betrayed her in her very own home, yet he still intended to marry her. *Gentlemen take virgins to wife, my dear.* And she was undoubtedly a virgin. He had vowed to have the Markham plantation, as well—

"What the devil were you trying to do?" she heard Captain Ramsey mutter. "Kill yourself?"

Startled by the intrusive demand, Selena opened her eyes and saw that the captain was peering down at her with concern. His heavy brows were drawn together in a frown as they had been earlier that day, just after he had kissed her. He was shirtless now, as well, the wet, powerful muscles of his arms and shoulders gleaming in the moonlight.

Feeling those sinewy muscles ripple beneath his damp skin as his naked chest pressed against her, Selena couldn't help but remember how brazenly she had responded to his kiss. And then a sudden thought struck her. Avery wanted a virgin bride, did he?

Her slender jaw hardening with resolution, Selena met Captain Ramsey's gaze directly. "Captain," she said very clearly, even though her voice was husky with tears, "I would like you to make love to me."

Chapter Two

Kyle stared at Selena, wondering if he had heard her correctly. He knew who she was now. His first mate had enlightened him about her identity and warned that there might be repercussions from his bout of drunken revelry; Miss Selena Markham had some rather high connections on the island.

Kyle regretted now the wicked impulse that had led him to kiss her earlier today in the street. She represented the worst kind of danger to a freedom-loving bachelor. Normally he steered clear of entanglements with females of marriageable age or any females who might place demands on him, preferring instead the more honest and uncomplicated relationships with women of a lower class and of lower expectations. It was safer that way, he had learned from experience. A brief encounter with a lonely young matron who needed consoling had left him shackled by bonds that could never be broken. He wasn't about to repeat that mistake.

Not that he could believe he was being asked to do so. "I didn't drink *that* much this afternoon," Kyle muttered under his breath, "and I'm entirely sober now."

"I want you to make love to me," Selena repeated quite firmly.

She was in the grip of some powerful emotion, Kyle realized, for he could feel her trembling. Involuntarily, he dropped his gaze to her mouth. It was a tantalizing mouth made to be kissed, generous, with a lush bottom lip that begged for a man's caress. It was what had made him behave like such a fool that afternoon, Kyle thought, remembering how soft and warm her lips had felt—and how amazed he had been at his enjoyment of them. That kiss had surprised him entirely; he

never would have expected the fierce desire that had shot
through him. She wasn't at all in his usual style. He liked colorful, buxom women—ones with no inhibitions and no pre-
tenses. Selena Markham was a definite contrast, with her
tresses of spun silver and scent like cool violets. There was little trace of that demure elegance now, but even dripping wet
and panting from exertion, she had a mysterious allure he
found hard to ignore.

"You don't know what you're asking," he said uncomfortably. "You're obviously upset, or I wouldn't have had to fish
you out of the sea."

"I know very well what I'm asking, Captain. And it isn't
particularly flattering for me to have to plead with you. After
the way you kissed me today, I wouldn't have thought you reluctant to continue where we left off."

Seeing the determination on Selena's fragile features, Kyle
frowned, feeling strangely disappointed. He had thought her
a virtuous female, in spite of her response to his kiss earlier.
But then, he had once made the same mistaken assumption
about her stepmother. The last time he had visited the West
Indies, Edith Markham had propositioned him before he had
been on the island two days. He had refused, of course, a refusal that had angered the sharp-tongued widow. And now her
very proper stepdaughter was offering herself, as well. Such
hypocrisy irritated him. Earlier, Miss Markham had slapped
him for daring to steal a kiss, but now that no one was observing, she was begging him to take to her as brazenly as any
strumpet.

"What must I do to persuade you?" she asked as she
reached up to wrap her slender arms around his neck. "Shall
I kiss you again?"

Kyle had the definite impression he had lost control of the
situation. And he didn't like where it was leading, either. He
didn't *want* to become involved with a hot-blooded young
hussy who was masquerading as a straitlaced lady of quality.
On the other hand, he wasn't a saint, and it had been quite a
few weeks since he had left England and the the red-haired
beauty who had warmed his bed. And he was undoubtedly
tempted by the warm, slender body beneath him. Oh, was he
tempted.

"I'll give you twenty pounds."

The offer startled him as much as had the one of her body.
"You're offering to pay *me*?"

"Do you want more? Fifty pounds, then. One hundred."

Kyle stared down at her a long moment before he finally shrugged. If she wanted it badly enough to pay him a hundred pounds, she could easily find another man to accommodate her. He didn't like to think of some drunken lout using her harshly. Come to think of it, he didn't like the idea of any man using her. She would be wasted on someone who couldn't appreciate her unusual beauty or give her pleasure in return.

"Two hundred pounds, Captain Ramsey."

"Keep your money, Miss Markham. I'll do it for free."

"Then what are you waiting for?"

Definitely suicidal, Kyle decided. "You want me to take you *here*? On the beach?"

"I didn't imagine you would be so particular."

"I'm not, but you're a lady, after all. I thought you might prefer a bed."

"Here will be fine."

Still he hesitated, while seawater dripped from his curling chestnut hair onto her pale cheeks, mingling with her tears. Yet there was a reason for his reluctance, he realized, studying her bedraggled appearance. There was something vaguely distasteful about making love to a woman who looked like a refugee from a shipwreck. He would feel, however absurdly, as if he were taking advantage of her.

When she tightened her arms around his neck, Kyle caught her wrists and held them away. "Not so fast. I don't like to rush things."

"Very well, Captain. But I would prefer that it didn't take all night."

Whatever happened, Kyle wondered, to sighs and endearments and sweet murmurings, the rituals every woman craved? Feeling annoyed by her cool impatience, he rolled off her and got to his feet. "I'm quite capable," he said curtly, pulling her up after him, "of entertaining a lady, Miss Markham. And I'm willing to lay bail you won't have any cause for complaint when I'm done."

With the ease of long practice, he divested Selena of her wrapper and tossed it onto higher ground, out of reach of the lapping waves, and held out his hand to her. When she seemed reluctant to take it, he wondered if she was going to change her mind.

Selena was indeed having second thoughts about her rash proposal. And she was very much afraid that if Captain Ram-

sey delayed any longer, she would lose her nerve. Revenge on
Avery was hardly an admirable motive, after all. And Kyle
Ramsey did look a good deal more intimidating when he was
towering over her in all his masculine glory. He was half-naked
again, wearing canvas breeches that were cut off at the knee,
but nothing else.

"What do you intend to do?" she asked warily, eyeing his
powerful, fluidly muscled shoulders and feeling a strange
fluttering in her stomach.

"I mean to wash you off. I don't want a mouthful of sand."

Selena wondered why he should be concerned about getting sand in his mouth, but she didn't allow herself to ask as
he led her into the surf.

The water was warm and welcoming, the gentle swells
sending her muslin nightdress swirling around her thighs. Kyle
waded out hip-deep and turned to her. Feeling his intent gaze
studying her face, Selena took a deep breath and waited.

His movements, surprisingly, were as gentle as the waves as
he scooped up a large handful to let it spill over her hair and
shoulders. The warm salt water ran between her breasts,
soaking the thin gauze covering once again, outlining shapely
peaks that were high and firm, fuller than her wraithlike slen-
derness indicated. When his gaze dropped to her breasts, Selena quelled the instinctive urge to cover them. She felt
indecently exposed without a corset and could feel her nipples
growing tight and puckered, whether due to the breeze blow-
ing off the sea or to Kyle Ramsey's warm regard, she wasn't
sure.

"Now your turn," he murmured when he finished his ministrations. His voice was suddenly husky, as warm and sensuous as the water he poured over her.

Realizing that he wanted her to reciprocate, Selena hesitantly complied, stretching to reach him because he was so tall.
Yet as she bathed him, rinsing the sand from the sleek muscles of his arms and shoulders, she found herself staring in
fascination at the dark sprinkling of hair that covered his
broad, bare chest. The slight furring narrowed as it reached his
flat abdomen and dipped below the waistband of his
breeches—

"You act as if you're afraid to touch me."

His observation brought color rushing to Selena's cheeks.
She *was* afraid to touch his powerful bronzed body, yet she was
also determined not to let Kyle Ramsey know it. "Of course

not, Captain,'' she said more breathlessly than she intended. Bracing herself, she dribbled a thin stream of seawater on his chest and reached out to brush the resultant droplets away, stroking him quite deliberately. The feel of him was just as masculine as she expected it to be, iron-hard flesh and sinews beneath damp, silky skin. But she didn't expect him to capture her slender fingers and imprison them against his naked chest.

Startled, she looked up to find Kyle watching her, a smoldering golden glow in his eyes. ''Come closer,'' he commanded softly.

Assailed by that same queer breathlessness, Selena obeyed, taking a single step toward him to close the distance. When Kyle slowly slipped an arm around her narrow waist, she found herself pressed against the full length of his big, splendid body, feeling his hard male contours, his heat.

He was still watching her intently as he reached up with his free hand to smooth a wet tress back from her face. ''Lord, you're beautiful in the moonlight.'' His thumb drifted lightly over her cheekbone, then moved to her lips and, with gentle pressure, urged them open.

She quivered.

He bent his head.

His mouth was just as warm and exciting as she remembered, and just as devastating. As his tongue probed for entrance, she opened fully to him, wanting his kiss, his possession.

She was hardly aware that his large hand was gliding upward over the filmy gauze of her nightdress, until she felt his fingers curl around her breast, cupping the swelling fullness. The resultant wave of heat shocked her; it raced through her body to settle as a throbbing ache somewhere between her thighs, in the very core of her womanhood.

''Captain—'' Selena gasped in halfhearted protest.

''Call me Kyle,'' he breathed against her lips. ''And I'll call you Seawitch.''

She could feel his deep voice vibrating through her body, just like the fierce need he was arousing in her. Involuntarily, her hands crept up the broad plain of his chest and curled around his neck.

He tasted her, dallying over the silky softness of her face while his thumb rubbed her nipple seductively, circling and teasing. The erect tip tightened unbearably under his light touch, while heat flared between her quivering thighs. When his long, blunt-tipped fingers closed over her nipple, plucking at the tight bud, Selena arched against him, her hands reaching up of their own accord to bury themselves in the thick dampness of his hair.

He stroked and caressed the aching peak, and by the time he had lavished the same erotic attentions on her other breast, Selena's fingers were clenched in his hair. Kyle drew back slightly then, and she was surprised to realize he had managed to unfasten the buttons at the throat of her nightdress. When he deftly slid the bodice down over her shoulders to expose her pale breasts, Selena shivered, not from the breeze that was caressing her damp flesh, but from the hot lover's gaze that was traveling the length of her.

She heard his quick intake of breath as his eyes fastened hungrily on her naked beauty, heard him mutter some unintelligible exclamation as he drew her against him again, and she braced herself for another shattering kiss. Yet he didn't kiss her. Instead, he bent to take her right nipple boldly into his mouth.

Selena couldn't stifle a gasp. That was what he had meant earlier, about the sand, she realized. But she hadn't imagined anything like this. He was suckling her breast, tormenting the nipple with his lips, massaging it in shuddering waves with his tongue. His possessive mouth created an incredible pleasure within her, making her feel weak and thoroughly helpless. Her legs were trembling, as if they might buckle beneath her, and when his searing lips moved to claim her other breast, she had to grip Kyle's shoulders to support herself.

It wasn't long before a whimper escaped her. Kyle raised his head and smiled in satisfaction. "I can accept impatience," he said, his teeth gleaming in the faint light, "as long as I'm the one you're impatient for." When Selena stared dazedly at him, he drew a languid circle around her nipple with one finger. "*Are* you impatient for me, Seawitch?"

"Yes." The husky reply seemed to be dredged from her throat. Yet it must have been what Kyle wanted to hear, for he chuckled as he stooped to catch her up in his arms and carry her to the shore. Embarrassingly aware that she had spoken no more than the truth, Selena felt her cheeks flood with color. She shut her eyes as he strode with her a few paces up the beach and kept them shut as he laid her down gently and stretched out beside her, his weight supported on one elbow.

He paused for a moment to survey Selena: her pale skin gleaming in the moonlight, her silver tresses spilling over her shoulders to accentuate the soft rise and fall of her breasts.

"No, not a Seawitch," Kyle murmured, pushing a silken strand of hair back from her face. "A *Moonwitch*." Then he bent and captured her lips again, while he moulded her breasts in his palms.

His hands were large and callused, vital and strong with life. As they gently stroked her, Selena stirred restlessly. The sand beneath her was heated, still warm from the Caribbean sun, but it was cool compared to the heat rising within her with each brush of Kyle's fingertips. In a moment, they were moving over the rest of her body, caressing, arousing, slipping beneath the hem of her nightdress to glide up a shapely thigh and search out the center of her womanhood.

Selena stiffened when she felt his hand between her thighs, then shuddered as his sensual fingers began exploring the yielding, warm folds of her flesh with sure mastery. Never would she have suspected that a man's hand on that part of her body could give her such fierce pleasure or that she would respond so brazenly. Her hips were moving of their own accord, as if an ancient, primitive force were controlling her, driving her on. She wasn't frightened, either, as perhaps she should have been when she felt his flagrant, rigid arousal pressing against her thigh, restrained only by the damp canvas fabric of his breeches. Instead, she arched against his hard, powerfully muscled body, hardly realizing that the soft whimpers she heard were coming from her own throat.

His own voice was none too steady when he broke off his kiss to whisper, "Who would have guessed you had such fire in you?"

As he unfastened his breeches and freed his rigid hardness, Selena opened passion-dazed eyes to stare at him. His rugged face was taut with desire, and she had the impression he was forcing himself to go slowly.

His hands were urgent but gentle still as they slid under the soft, full curves of her bottom and lifted her to meet him. "I don't know if . . . Moonwitch . . . it's been too long."

She had some idea what to expect and so braced herself against the invasion of her flesh. Yet she couldn't prevent a soft gasp as his maleness slowly began to fill her.

"Damn, but you're tight. You can't have done this often."

Kyle's ragged voice sounding so close in her ear startled her. Afraid that he might withdraw if he realized her innocence, she thrust her hips forward and at the same time slid her hands down his sinewed back to grasp his taut buttocks and pull him closer, then turned her face away to hide the pain that she knew had crossed her features.

She heard him grunt in surprise as she took him deeper. "Easy, lady," he rasped. "I don't want to hurt you."

"Please . . . don't stop."

"I couldn't . . . stop if I wanted to."

Those hoarse words were the last he spoke for a long time as he buried himself fully in her silken warmth, intent on giving pleasure as well as taking.

His movements were slow and controlled, as if he were forcibly restraining his great might, and Selena's pain gave way to a burning, aching need. He was incredibly tender for so large and rugged a man, she thought, feverishly running her hands over the flexing muscles of his back.

But it *had* been a long time since Kyle had made love to a woman. And the slender, writhing creature beneath him bore no resemblance to the cool, remote lady he had taken advantage of earlier. He felt his control snapping, like silken threads under too much strain.

His breath quickened against her throat as he surrendered to a primitive, powerful need. He drove into her more forcefully, more deeply, though still his instinctive care for the weaker sex kept him from being as rough as he might. In a moment his great body stiffened, then contracted, pouring into her with tremendous pulsing spasms.

As he collapsed on her, bathed in perspiration, panting, the hot, spiraling world that had caught Selena in its grip slowly faded, leaving her unsatisfied and unfulfilled. Her position was extremely uncomfortable, trapped as she was beneath Kyle's sleek, heavy body. Squirming, she wedged her hands against his powerful shoulders to keep him from crushing her further.

Weakly, Kyle pushed himself up on his elbows. "I'm sorry, Moonwitch," he said hoarsely. "It was too fast for you. I'll make it better next time, I promise."

"No."

He found her lips again and kissed her with repentant tenderness before Selena managed to turn her head away. "I said *no*. Once was quite enough."

Drawing back, Kyle peered down at her with a frown, trying to read the quicksilver light in her eyes. "Did I hurt you?"

Selena hesitated, considering his question. Her body was limp and aching and still throbbing with a strange sort of tension. But she *had* asked Captain Ramsey to make love to her, after all. And he had granted her request—quite thoroughly. At least thoroughly enough to prevent her wanting to repeat the experience. "No, Captain," she dissembled. "You didn't hurt me. Now, will you please let me up? I should like to breathe again."

For a moment she thought he might not comply, for he was studying her intently, his heavy brows drawn together in puzzlement. But then he untangled his body from hers and rolled off her, rising to his feet with the easy grace of a practiced athlete as he adjusted his breeches.

Selena rose more slowly, cautiously testing her weak legs to ensure they could support her weight. Acutely embarrassed now by what she had done, she avoided looking at Kyle as she fastened the buttons at her bodice with shaking hands.

"I will pay you in the morning," she murmured, brushing at the damp skirt of her nightdress, trying to wipe off the sand.

"Keep your money, Miss Markham. It was worth it." His tone sounded dry and somewhat biting as he came up behind her. "Besides," he breathed in her ear, "I haven't yet finished."

Somewhat nervously, Selena looked around for her horse. But then Kyle bent to lift her into his arms, and she suddenly found herself clutching desperately at the corded muscles of his shoulders as he cradled her against his naked chest. "What are you doing?" she gasped.

"What I should have done from the first. Take you to bed."

She struggled without success. "Put me down! I demand you release me!"

"Uh-uh. I don't like to leave a woman unsatisfied. I have my pride to think about, after all."

Selena glared up at him as he strode determinedly along the beach, noting that the slashing dimples had again creased the hard planes of his cheeks. He was finding this amusing! "Captain—" she began with strained patience.

"I told you to call me Kyle."

"Kyle, then. I have no intention of going to bed with you."

"Then we'll talk. I'm just the least bit curious why you were trying to drown yourself."

"I was not trying to drown myself! I was merely going for a swim."

"Sure. And I'm a mermaid."

Selena clenched her teeth. When she saw an imperial row of palms illuminated by moonlight, she realized he was taking her to the Five Islands plantation house. The captain carried her up a flight of steps and across a wide veranda into the house before setting Selena on her feet. She heard the clink of a glass chimney as he lighted a lamp, and when the flame flared to life, she could tell from the book-lined shelves and comfortable leather chairs that she was in the library.

But it was Kyle Ramsey who claimed her attention. She watched as he picked up a brandy decanter from a side table and poured a large measure into a snifter. He seemed not to mind that he was almost naked in the presence of a lady who was also less than fully dressed, but Selena was very much aware of it. Indeed, his towering, muscular grace was rather intimidating, and when he advanced on her, holding the glass, she found it hard not to shrink from him.

He offered her the brandy, but she shook her head. "Thank you, no. I don't indulge in spirits."

Kyle's mouth quirked at the corner, deepening his right dimple. "Drink it. It'll do you more good than the lime juice and water you ladies find so appealing."

When he stood there waiting, looking as if he wouldn't countenance her refusal, she accepted the glass and took a small swallow, nearly choking as the fiery liquid burned her tongue and throat.

"Now," Kyle said casually, "why don't you tell me what you were doing, charging into the sea like that? It didn't seem to me that you were intent on a moonlight swim."

Selena searched his face, reading only concern in his hazel eyes. "Perhaps I wasn't thinking very clearly, but I wasn't trying to kill myself. I was merely upset."

"Want to talk about it? I've been told I'm a good listener."

Oddly, she thought he might be right. He looked as if he might sympathize with her. But it wasn't something she could share with a stranger, even if she was in the habit of bearing tales.

"Thank you, Captain," Selena said, turning away to avoid his penetrating gaze, "but I am quite all right now. Truly. And I should return home. Someone may wonder where I've gone."

"God Almighty." The oath was breathed slowly, in a low tone. A large hand clamped down on Selena's arm and spun her around to face him.

Kyle's face was incredulous. "You were a virgin!"

Selena winced at the fierce accusation in his tone and the pressure of his grip. She returned his gaze mutely, wondering how he had known.

"There's blood on your nightdress," he ground out, answering her unspoken question. "Sweet heaven! That was why you were so—" He broke off then to eye her narrowly. "I think you'd better start explaining, Miss Markham."

Selena searched for a plausible reason. "Perhaps I cut myself, Captain—"

"Like hell you did!"

Selena swallowed hard. Kyle Ramsey might be an unrefined American; he might swagger and curse like a common sailor. But he was deceptively quick. She wouldn't be able to fool him with some halfhearted lie. Yet she couldn't tell him the truth. "Please," she said, stalling for time, "you are hurting my arm."

Kyle gave vent to a muttered oath, but he released her to stalk over to the brandy decanter. He poured himself a very generous amount as he grappled with the dilemma Selena Markham had presented him. If she wasn't so anxious to leave, he would have suspected a ploy to snare him as a husband. It wouldn't be the first time a lovely young innocent had insinuated herself into a man's bed with marriage as her object. But if rumor could be believed, Selena Markham was already betrothed.

Kyle shot her an unfriendly glance. "Lady, I don't know what your game is, but I don't much like it."

"I . . ." Selena took a deep breath, and, for one of the few times in her life, told a deliberate lie. "I wanted to learn about love."

"So you gave yourself to a *stranger*?"

Flushing at his disbelieving tone, she stared down at her bare feet.

"You're engaged to be married, aren't you? Why didn't you ask your betrothed to initiate you?"

"I . . . my reasons are my own, Captain. I don't think I am obliged to share them with you."

Kyle gave her a long, assessing look. How did she manage to look so cool and remote after losing her virtue to a man she had only met that afternoon? "What's your betrothed's name? Warner? I suppose now he'll be challenging me to pistols at dawn."

Selena lifted her gaze to his. "I don't intend to tell him," she said quietly. "And I would appreciate it if you would refrain from mentioning what happened tonight, as well."

"You can bet your sweet life I won't mention it! I'm not that much of a fool."

She stood there, silent. Kyle ran his fingers through his hair in a gesture of frustration. "Blast it, I don't have any experience deflowering virgins, or I would have realized at the time—"

"Please ... I don't hold you responsible. You merely did what I asked."

Glaring at her, Kyle took a deep swig of liquor. He didn't need this kind of trouble. He could have—and now it looked as if he should have—availed himself of any of a dozen willing females in St. John's, but oddly, after kissing Selena Markham that afternoon, he hadn't quite felt in the mood for the full-blown temptresses he usually favored. He had chosen instead to sober up from his afternoon revelries in solitude. And then Selena Markham had shown up, sobbing and looking like some wild wraith in the moonlight. And what had begun as an attempt at a rescue wound up as a seduction. *His.*

It had bothered him that she hadn't found pleasure in his lovemaking, but perhaps Miss Markham's inexperience explained her coldness. If he had known— But he *should* have known. Now he had more to worry about than getting shackled in marriage; he could wind up with a noose around his neck. *If* Warner didn't shoot him first.

Kyle took another gulp of brandy as he studied Miss Markham. She wasn't a fool; her eyes were bright with an unexpected intelligence he had recognized from the first. And she didn't look the type to try to make her betrothed jealous by dallying with another man. But then, he was unable to comprehend why she would even want to marry a man like Avery Warner. Warner was a self-righteous prig with an inflated opinion of his own importance. But perhaps Miss Markham was attracted by his wealth or his power as a member of the assembly council. Perhaps they had merely had a lover's spat, and she had found solace in another man's arms. It would serve Warner right to be cuckolded, Kyle reflected nastily, if the man had upset her enough to drive her away.

Realizing that his thoughts were futile, Kyle shrugged. The damage couldn't be undone. And as Miss Markham had so subtly pointed out, it wasn't his business. He didn't know if he could believe her promise of secrecy, but he wouldn't get any answers by browbeating her. One thing he did know, though: she couldn't stay here all night.

"I should take you home," he observed tersely.

"I can find my own way, Captain."

"Devil take it, I *said* I would escort you home!" He set his glass down on the table with more force than necessary, and as he relieved Selena of hers, gave her a critical appraisal. "Weren't you wearing a wrapper or something?"

Seeing the hard set of his jaw, Selena nodded, deciding it wiser not to argue.

"Come on, then," he ordered, taking her arm. "There'll be the devil to pay if you're seen here like this."

He found her wrapper lying in the sand where he had tossed it and her horse a short distance away, grazing on a patch of scrub grass. After helping Selena don the robe, Kyle lifted her onto the mare's back and vaulted up behind her. "Which way?" he said gruffly, not liking the necessity of such close proximity. He was having enough difficulty forgetting their moonlight coupling on the beach without being reminded by the warmth of her slender body or the pale hair that was drying in fine wisps and floating back to caress his bare chest.

Selena, too, was finding the closeness discomfiting. After giving directions to the Markham plantation, she lapsed into silence. She was riding sideways as modesty dictated, but in spite of her efforts to stay well forward, her left hip was pressed against parts of male anatomy whose existence she would rather not acknowledge. At least her rigid training stood her in good stead, allowing her to maintain an appearance of cool composure. In truth, she was struggling with shame and mortification, for now that she had time for calm reflection, she greatly regretted her rash behavior. Throwing away her innocence because of a childish desire for vengeance hadn't solved her problem with Avery. She would still have to deal with that when she returned home.

"Is this the place?" Kyle asked after a time, interrupting her thoughts.

Seeing the plantation house gleaming in the moonlight, Selena nodded. "Perhaps you shouldn't come any closer," she said, thinking of Avery. "You might be seen."

"Very well. Where are the stables? I'll put your horse away."

Selena thought about protesting, but the hard edge to his tone warned her he wouldn't brook a refusal. "Along this path," she replied quietly, "beyond a stand of mango trees. The second stall on the right."

Kyle halted the mare, then hesitated a moment, as if trying to decide what to say. Putting a finger under her chin, he turned Selena's face to his. "Look, Miss Markham, I'm sorry about what happened tonight. If I had known—"

"Please, Captain, I don't blame you in the least."

"Is that supposed to make me feel better?"

She gave him a faint smile. "Most definitely. You were quite . . . considerate."

She started to dismount then, but Kyle forestalled her with a light grasp on her arm. "Are you going to be all right?" he asked softly, searching her face.

"Yes," Selena murmured, uncomfortable with his scrutiny and with the gentle concern she saw in his hazel eyes. She slid from the mare's back and hurried across the lawn, knowing he was still watching her.

But when she had mounted the steps to the gallery and entered her bedroom, she froze.

In the faint light, she could see Edith Markham sitting in a damask wing chair, waiting, her dark eyes gleaming with malice.

Chapter Three

"I mean to have him," Edith said at once before Selena even had a chance to react.

"H-him?" Selena stammered, thinking of the rugged sea captain she had just left.

"Avery, of course. I intend to be his wife."

Selena lighted the lamp on her dressing table as she tried to collect her scattered wits. Why her hands should be shaking, she wasn't sure, but she clasped them together as she turned to face her stepmother. Edith had changed from her dinner gown and was dressed in a lime-green peignoir that clashed with the soft corals of the bedroom.

"Don't play innocent with me, my girl," Edith demanded when Selena stood there silently. "You came snooping and saw us together, didn't you?"

"I thought you were hurt . . . since you screamed. . . ."

"I've been seeing Avery since Thomas died. Usually we meet at Five Islands plantation, but since it was occupied tonight by that Yankee captain, Avery came here."

"Please," Selena said hoarsely, "I don't want to hear about it."

Edith surveyed Selena's pale face, taking in her unbound hair and disheveled nightdress. "I was never unfaithful to your father, if that is what concerns you."

It was some consolation, at least, Selena thought, feeling a little sick. Realizing she had better sit down, she crossed the room and sank down onto the edge of the bed.

"Avery only wants to marry you for the plantation, you know," her stepmother continued. "You were always such an ungainly child. He never would have noticed you if not for your inheritance.''

The accusation stung Selena, particularly since she suspected it was true. "Perhaps so," she replied with scarcely bridled anger, "but I didn't expect him to betray me in my own home!"

"Oh, come now, Selena, you can't be that naive. Avery is a man, with a man's needs. An overnice chit doesn't interest him. I must say, he couldn't keep his hands off me once I made it known I wouldn't spurn his advances."

The years of schooling her features into a polite mask around her stepmother were forgotten; the disgust Selena was feeling showed clearly on her face. When she didn't speak, though, Edith leaned forward in her chair, her sultry eyes narrowing. "I intend to be Mrs. Avery Warner before the year is out. And I won't let you stand in my way."

While Edith was obviously willing to fight, Selena felt the prize in question wasn't worth the battle. She wanted no part of Avery. Edith was welcome to him.

"You may rest assured," Selena returned with icy dignity, pleased to find that her voice remained almost steady, "that I won't fight you for him."

Relaxing back in her chair, Edith permitted herself a faint smile. "I am glad we understand each other, my dear. I shouldn't like to see you hurt."

"How very *kind* you are."

Edith's smile faded abruptly as she rose to her feet. "Don't push me, you wretched girl, or you'll find yourself without a home in short order. Much good your plantation will do you then!" In a swirl of lime-green chenille, she marched from the room, apparently not caring that the rafters shook as she slammed the door forcefully behind her.

When she had gone, Selena finally allowed her defenses to crumble; her shoulders slumped and she buried her face in her hands.

The next morning when Selena left the house, dressed in a lavender gown of jaconet muslin and a leghorn hat with matching ribbons, there was no sign that she had spent a sleepless night trying to come to a decision about her future course of action or that she was still trying to bolster the courage to carry out the wild plan she had conceived. But her delicate jaw was set with determination. Her stepmother had provoked more than her anger; Edith had aroused a long-dormant instinct for self-preservation.

When Selena reached the stables, her white mare was waiting as she had ordered. She mounted with the help of a groom, then rode out of the yard along the same road as the previous night, though at a much slower pace.

The island was gilded with sunlight and bustling with activity. The final cane stands were being harvested, and she passed dark-skinned field hands wielding machetes or driving heavily burdened mules toward the sugar works. Beyond, in the distance, Selena could see one of the two mills of the plantation—a truncated cone of stone whose great grinding wheels were driven by oxen rather than wind, as was the other.

The road split before she came to Five Islands Bay. Selena chose the fork that led directly to the sea, preferring to ride along the shore while she rehearsed the speech she had formulated during the sleepless hours of the past night. She found the cove quiet but for the gentle murmur of the surf. She might have paused to admire the dazzling vista of pale gold sand and clear, light green waves if she hadn't caught sight of Captain Ramsey farther up the beach.

He was standing calf-deep in water, looking quite at ease as he cast out a fishing line. He wore the same cutoff canvas trousers he had been wearing the previous night, and his sleek, sun-bronzed body was breathtaking against the backdrop of blue sky and turquoise sea. Poseidon surveying his realm, Selena thought, checking her horse abruptly as shameful memories came rushing back to haunt her.

To say that she was aghast at her recent behavior was an understatement. It seemed impossible to her now that she not only had allowed Kyle Ramsey to make love to her but had practically demanded that he do so. She had thrown away her virtue on a total stranger, and what was more, she hadn't even enjoyed it—at least not after those first few moments of breathless passion. Indeed, she had found the experience awkward and somewhat painful. Yet she was prepared to repeat that experience...under certain conditions. First, however, she would have to get the captain to agree to her proposal.

Forcing herself to ignore the fluttering in her stomach, Selena urged her horse forward. When she halted a few yards from Kyle, she could see he wasn't overjoyed by her presence;

he had half turned to watch her progress and was observing her with an extremely wary look in his hazel eyes.

"Miss Markham," he said, making the words more a question than a greeting.

Unexpectedly, Selena found herself the victim of an absurd attack of shyness. Up close, in broad daylight, his ruggedness seemed more pronounced, and the broad expanse of naked sinews reminded her rather forcefully of how his powerful body had felt pressed against hers.

She dropped her gaze, noticing as she did so the peels of several finger-size bananas and the skin of a large yellow mango lying in the sand. He must have carried his breakfast with him. She fixed her gaze on the fruit remnants as she tried to summon some semblance of her characteristic composure.

"Captain...I... You won't catch much this far in from the reef," she finished lamely, losing her nerve.

He studied her for an uncomfortable moment longer before he spoke. "I plan to take a ketch out later. But I don't expect you rode all the way here to advise me about the sport."

"No, I...I came to ask you a question." She hesitated.

"Yes?" Kyle prompted.

"I should like to know...if you would marry me."

"Good God." The words were exhaled slowly, but otherwise, he simply stared at her.

Somewhat heartened that she hadn't been refused outright, Selena went on. "Before you give me your answer, perhaps I should mention that my father left me a substantial inheritance. The Markham plantation has a thousand acres of prime soil, a modest size, perhaps, but highly productive. It's rare that we don't yield at least 350 hogsheads of sugar and 200 puncheons of rum in a year. My stepmother owns the house, however, so we would have to build one of our own—"

"Hold it, Miss Markham," Kyle interrupted, quickly raising a hand. "Just...hold it. Perhaps you'll forgive me if under the circumstances I don't know the appropriate response.... I expect I'm supposed to say that I'm honored but must respectfully decline your offer."

Selena raised her gaze then, her blue eyes searching his face. "The plantation is worth fifty thousand pounds sterling, Captain."

Kyle shook his head. It always took him aback, the way British aristocrats saw marriage as such a cold-blooded business arrangement. "You want me to marry you for your *money*, is that it?"

Seeing how one heavy eyebrow had shot up in surprise, she flushed. "No. . . . I merely thought a large dowry would make marriage to me more palatable."

"I already have one plantation too many, Miss Markham. I don't want the responsibility for another."

This was news to Selena, but she plunged bravely ahead. "You needn't worry about the responsibility. I'm capable of seeing to it on my own. I've done so adequately for the past two years, with the help of an excellent factor."

Kyle shook his head again dazedly. He should have rounded up his crew at first light and sailed with the tide, as his instincts had warned him. "I'm too old for you," he countered somewhat desperately, momentarily forgetting that her betrothed was a great deal older. "I must have a dozen years on you."

"How old are you?"

"Thirty-three."

"I have twenty-four years to my credit, Captain. So there are only nine separating us."

He took a deep breath, praying he would wake up and discover this was part of some strange dream. "Why are you so intent on marrying me? I thought you already were betrothed."

Uncomfortable with both the question and the penetrating look in his hazel eyes, Selena averted her gaze, fixing it on a row of towering palms farther down the beach. In spite of her prior intimacy with Captain Ramsey, he was still a stranger, and she found it difficult to discuss her present circumstances with him. How could she tell him about Avery's betrayal, about her humiliation?

Yet it would soon be common knowledge. Once she had called off the wedding, Edith would lose no time in becoming Avery's wife. And, Selena reflected, if the islanders already pitied her because she had lost one intended husband, how much more sympathetic kindness would she have to bear if they thought Avery had jilted her?

On the other hand, she could ignore Edith's threats and perhaps weather the scandal that would arise when she was forced from her home. But she had too much pride to marry Avery now. No, she would be reduced to begging before she'd become his wife.

She would have to deal with the consequences, though. Her life on the island would be intolerable—unless she already had a husband. She had thought Kyle Ramsey might be persuaded with the promise of a rich dowry, but she could see now that if he already had his own plantation, he wouldn't be so eager to gain hers. Yet she had little else to offer. There was no reason to believe she would appeal physically to a man of the captain's stamp. Edith had emphasized often enough that men desired a more buxom beauty and a more passionate nature than Selena seemed to possess. And Avery's tastes certainly underlined that.

Shifting her glance from the feathered palms, Selena gazed out over the pale green water of the cove. "I don't intend to marry Avery," she said quietly. "Recently I've discovered that . . . we wouldn't suit."

Kyle muttered something under his breath. After wading from the waves, he shoved the end of his fishing pole into the white coral sand before addressing her again. "Miss Markham . . . Selena, I doubt that you and I would suit any better. And as crude as this may sound, I'm afraid you have only one thing a man like me would be interested in—and it's a lot safer for me to find it at a tavern."

"I suppose . . . you spend a good deal of time in taverns, drinking and . . . wenching?"

He gave her a sharp glance. "No more than any other man," he retorted, not liking her to paint his character any blacker than he deserved. "I sometimes drink when I put in to port after a long voyage—though yesterday was something of a unique occasion. But the fact remains, I wouldn't make you a good husband."

"I could give you children."

Kyle sucked in another breath, his heavy brows rising in disbelief as he stared at her. "You do have a way of knocking a man between the eyes, don't you?"

It was early yet, and the morning was still relatively cool, but Selena felt heat flood her cheeks.

Kyle put his hands on his lean hips and regarded her with a frown. "Children, Miss Markham, are encumbrances in my line of work. Besides, I already have a family to care for."

"You're married?" she gasped, her startled gaze searching his face.

"No, thank God. But I have a gaggle of younger sisters who require my attention. The eldest has been looking after the rest since our parents died last year, but Bea is married with a baby on the way. She has her own family to think of. I've agreed to take responsibility for the girls. In fact, I'm bound for Natchez when I leave here. It might be years before I could return. I doubt that you would want an absentee husband."

"No," she said in a small voice. "But I could go with you."

Kyle gritted his teeth, trying not to feel as if he were kicking a lost puppy. Devil take it, how had he ever gotten himself into this situation? She looked as lovely now as she had in the moonlight, and there was no question that he had enjoyed her body. But that was a far cry from wanting to marry her. He had no wish to sacrifice his freedom, and he already had *one* obligation along that line. Someday he would have to legshackle himself in order to claim his son.

He shook his head. "I'm sorry, Moonwitch, but I'm afraid I'm not free to accept your offer. I have a duty I'm obliged to fulfill."

His tone suggested such finality that Selena turned her head away. It shouldn't hurt so much, being told she wasn't wanted, she thought. But she had done her best to persuade Kyle to accept her proposal. She couldn't force his consent. There remained only for her to extricate herself from this awkward situation as gracefully as possible.

"Very well then, Captain," she murmured, gathering the mare's reins in her gloved hands. "Thank you for your time."

Before she could turn her horse around, though, Kyle closed the distance between them and grasped the animal's bridle. When he looked up at her, Selena could see the green flecks in his hazel eyes and the crinkled web of laugh lines at the corners.

Yet he wasn't anywhere close to laughing now. He searched her face for a long moment, then reached up to gently touch her trembling chin with a long forefinger. "Moonwitch, if I were free...I really think I might be tempted."

She forced a smile at his gallantry but couldn't manage to answer. She was grateful when he released her horse's bridle and stepped back.

Kyle watched her ride away in silence. When she had disappeared, he raked his fingers through his chestnut hair in consternation, thinking of the reason he wasn't free. His son. A child he wasn't able to acknowledge. He loved the boy, fiercely.

He had never expected to feel that way about anything but the sea. Two years ago he would never have credited how profoundly he could be affected by a single dimpled grin from one small toddler. Nothing had ever claimed his heart like that before, not even his family. He had revered his parents, and he held his sisters in great affection, yet the bond between a father and son was stronger, deeper....

Kyle shook his head again in frustration. He couldn't marry Selena Markham. Not at the risk of losing his son. But he was determined not to let her impossible proposal cut up his peace or spoil his last days as a seafaring adventurer. There were too few of them left.

Snatching up his fishing pole, Kyle took two strides toward the swelling waves. Then abruptly, he turned back and hurled his pole down in the sand.

"Oh, hell!" he muttered, wondering how she had managed to make him feel like such a cad for refusing her.

Selena wasn't sure whether her fierce disappointment was due more to the captain's rejection or because she would have to deal with Avery and Edith alone, without even the comfort of a reluctant husband by her side. But she knew she needed to reflect on her options before she took any further steps to resolve her future.

It was unfortunate, therefore, that a proprietor of a large sugar plantation was frequently occupied by concerns of the estate. When she returned home, Selena found several problems to engage her attention and prevent her from dwelling on her own situation—chief among them the difficult birth of twins by one of her household servants. After spending the afternoon in the plantation hospital, where she provided support and encouragement rather than medical expertise, she barely had time to bathe and dress for the lieutenant governor's ball that was to be held that evening.

If she could have refused to attend the ball, she would have done so, for the thought of confronting Avery about his betrayal tied her stomach in knots. But she knew he would demand an explanation if she suddenly came down with a headache or some other feminine ailment, and she preferred to postpone their discussion till she had time to collect herself, or at least until they could be private.

She dallied over her toilette as long as possible, and when she was dressed in a high-waisted gown of ice-blue silk with an overskirt of silver tissue, and the blue-plumed brimless toque bonnet she had purchased in town the day before, she went to join Edith and Avery in the parlor.

Avery was pacing the floor impatiently. He looked distinguished in an elegantly tailored green coat and tall beaver hat, but his immaculate attire reminded Selena of his fastidiousness with Edith the night before, and she found she couldn't meet his eyes. When he complimented her on her appearance, she did manage to murmur an acknowledgment but she realized immediately that pretending nothing had changed in their relationship would prove a severe strain.

The carriage ride to the lieutenant governor's home was every bit as miserable as Selena had expected. She was quiet during most of the trip, although she occasionally forced herself to respond to Avery's comments while she tried not to shrink from his touch. It was a sheer test of breeding. Avery was sitting beside her in the barouche, and periodically he would take her arm or pat her hand as he discoursed on island affairs. Edith sat across from them in the forward seat, observing them with an expression that was at once smug and innocent. Selena was relieved when she could escape the close confines of the carriage and more relieved when Avery had to release her arm in order to progress through the receiving line.

Mounting the stairs, they moved along an open corridor that bisected the house and created a breezeway. Andrew and Elizabeth Thorpe stood to one side before a pair of stately louvered doors.

A planter by birth and avocation, Drew Thorpe was a handsome man with sandy-blond hair and a rakish mustache. His post of lieutenant governor was primarily honorary, since he was required to administer to island affairs only in the absence of the governor. His wife, Beth, was a rosy-cheeked brunette and a particular friend of Selena's. They were nearly the same age, although Beth had married at eighteen and by now had three children to her credit. Both Drew and Beth greeted Selena with unfeigned pleasure before allowing her to pass on to the drawing room, which was already filled to overflowing by some thirty other couples and the six Negro musicians who comprised the orchestra.

The white-haired governor, Major General George Ramsay, was also present, Selena saw at once. He seemed to take a great deal of space, for in addition to a stalwart figure, he had an intimidating air of command, derived from years of military service.

Avery ushered the ladies before the governor to pay their respects, then procured a glass of sherry for Selena while Edith paused to speak to an acquaintance. He was just remarking on the warmth of the evening when the gay conversation and laughter in the room suddenly lagged.

"I say!" Avery exclaimed rather loudly in the hush. "What the deuce is *he* doing here?"

Curious, Selena followed his glance to the entrance, where an extremely tall, powerful-looking man attired in elegant evening dress was bowing over Beth's hand. Selena felt herself flushing. She hadn't expected Captain Ramsey to be invited, or if he had, to attend. But he seemed to know the Thorpes rather well; Drew was laughing as he vigorously shook the captain's hand, and Beth was smiling up at her guest in delight.

"He," Avery continued in a deprecatory tone, "is one of the savages who made such a disgraceful display in town yesterday. A man like that should never be welcomed in polite circles. He does not belong."

Indeed, he didn't, Selena thought as she observed the captain. With his great height and sun-bronzed complexion, Kyle Ramsey appeared highly conspicuous, standing there breathing vigor and vitality. He affected the company like a fresh sea wind. Yet for once he was dressed appropriately...for once he was *dressed*, Selena amended to herself. His curling chestnut hair gleamed a deep burnished brown above a pristine white cravat, while his powerful shoulders filled his coffee-colored coat to perfection. A rugged Viking in gentlemen's garb, she reflected.

Selena wondered if he might be ill at ease in his formal attire, for the muscular grace she had noticed before seemed subdued by the formfitting coat, ivory brocade waistcoat and tight buff breeches. And once she saw him reach up to tug on his neck cloth as if it might be too confining.

But he must have known how to conduct himself at social functions—or at least how to charm the fairer sex. As soon as he entered the room, he was surrounded by half-a-dozen ladies who obviously knew him and were eager to renew the acquaintance. They were soon joined by several older gentlemen who no doubt had been pressed by their daughters into begging an introduction.

Captain Ramsey greeted them all with ease and showered on the ladies an attentiveness that couldn't fail to set their feminine hearts aflutter. When he happened to glance in Selena's direction, though, she edged back a pace, hoping to avoid his notice. She dreaded the prospect of speaking to the captain, and she dared not even think of their previous intimacy; she very much feared the hot blush that stained her cheeks each time she did would brand her as a wanton. Already the looks being cast her way—some sly, some sympathetic—made her aware that she was an object of gossip.

The small orchestra struck up the first dance then, and even though she was obliged to allow Avery to lead her out, Selena was grateful for the distraction.

After the set, she didn't lack for partners; she had known nearly every gentleman present for most of her life, and in spite of her engagement, she was a favorite among them. As the evening progressed, however, her spirits sank even lower. Kyle Ramsey never once sought her out. Indeed, it seemed as if he were avoiding her with as much determination as she was avoiding him. His disinterest carried a shaming sting. And even though no one was indelicate enough to mention her scandalous conduct of yesterday afternoon, Selena was quite conscious that it was being discussed.

By midway through the ball, she was fervently wishing the interminable evening would come to an end. Fearing she could no longer keep up the pretense of enjoyment while smiling and carrying on polite conversation, Selena declined the next dance by pleading fatigue. Making her escape, she settled herself in a chair in one corner of the room.

Beth found her there a short while later, half-obscured by a potted palm.

"Selena, dearest, whatever do you mean, hiding yourself away like this? I counted on you to partner my guests. Indeed, what can the gentlemen be thinking of to allow you to become a wallflower? You are always in such great demand. Never mind," Beth added, taking the seat beside Selena and arranging the pale, jonquil-colored skirts of her gown. "It will allow us to gossip. I haven't been able to get away all evening. My ball is a success, do you not think? Are you enjoying yourself?"

Seeing Beth's shining eyes and eager expression, Selena didn't have the heart to dampen her enthusiasm. "Indeed, I am," she dissembled. "And yes, your ball is a great success. I don't doubt it will be considered the event of the season."

"Do you truly think so? It was such a coup to have Captain Ramsey attend. Drew was able to persuade him, you know. But really, it is in the captain's best interest. Coming here tonight provides him with the opportunity to establish himself in the governor's good graces, and after that incident in St. John's yesterday— Oh, Selena, I *heard* what happened."

When Beth's declaration was accompanied by a sympathetic look, Selena realized her friend was speaking of Kyle Ramsey's very public kiss. Again she felt color flood her cheeks.

Beth squeezed her gloved fingers. "No one blames you—at least no one except the cats who have nothing better to do than gossip. I daresay every woman here is pea green with envy. Did Avery cut up stiff about it?"

"He . . . he hasn't mentioned it," Selena murmured, reflecting that she would need to be prepared for a scolding from him.

"Well, perhaps he doesn't know yet. I doubt anyone will be anxious to tell him. So, what was it like, Selena?"

Not following the rapid shift in Beth's conversation Selena stared at her blankly. "What was what like?"

"To be kissed by a man like that, of course. Come, you can tell me, your bosom friend."

Selena was extremely uncomfortable with such a question, yet she knew Beth wouldn't let up until she had given a satisfactory answer. "It was . . ." She paused, searching for an adequate description for that shattering kiss, yet one that wouldn't shock Beth. "Overwhelming," she finished lamely.

Gazing off into space, Beth gave a dreamy sigh. "I can just imagine. Perhaps it's fortunate that I'm a staid matron with a loving husband and three adorable children. There Captain Ramsey is now, waltzing with Marie. Isn't he magnificent, with those splendid shoulders and that rugged-looking face?"

"Beth!"

"Oh, pooh! You know I don't mean any slight to Drew. And don't tell me you aren't attracted to the captain, for I won't believe it!"

Selena followed her gaze to watch Kyle whirling a petite redhead around the floor. He *was* magnificent, exuding the kind of strength and masculinity that women found extremely appealing. And he looked as if he had perfected the knack of making a woman feel special; he was bending close to Marie, listening attentively and watching her with those gold-flecked hazel eyes. The same eyes that had smoldered so hotly the previous night.

Selena was discomfited by the warm rush of feeling that accompanied the memory. "What is Captain Ramsey doing here?" she said quickly. "On the island, I mean." It seemed incredible that she should have to ask such an elementary question after the intimacy she had shared with him, but she really had no idea what had brought him to Antigua. He couldn't be unloading his ship's cargo, for the Navigation Acts prevented the islands of the British West Indies to engage in trade with the United States.

"He's simply visiting, I fancy," Beth replied. "He comes here frequently, though he doesn't mingle much with society."

"But I've never seen him at a social gathering before tonight."

"He attended the Brindell's rout year before last, but you were in mourning for your father, if I remember. And yes, I know *some* people—" she gave Selena an arch look "—are saying the captain is a savage. But he must have some claim to gentility, or he wouldn't be accepted by British society. Drew met Captain Ramsey in London years ago and found him rubbing shoulders with the nobility. He's the intimate friend of a marquess, I understand."

"I suppose by 'some people,' you mean Avery."

"Just so. He was complaining to Drew earlier this evening about the 'riffraff' we had invited here tonight. I declare! Riffraff! But the unattached ladies, at least, are delighted to welcome the captain. And we *are* promoting international goodwill. Drew says the governor wants to improve relations with the United States.

"Besides, after that unfortunate incident in St. John's yesterday, something needed to be done. Americans are barely tolerated in Antigua as it is. That's why when Captain Ramsey called on us today to renew our acquaintance, Drew persuaded him to come to the ball—so he could soothe troubled waters. And now that Captain Ramsey has made his apologies to the governor for the disturbance, everything is famous. Indeed, the governor seemed to like him. I'm so pleased. It would be a shame if the captain were asked to leave the island."

Beth paused for breath. "I suppose I should attend to my guests. Do go and dance, Selena. You know the gentlemen will be disappointed if you continue to hide yourself away like this." When Selena murmured some noncommittal reply, Beth rose. But before she moved off, she spoke again. "Oh, I almost forgot. Avery was searching for you a moment ago. Shall I tell him where to find you?"

"Thank you, no," Selena said quickly. "I need a moment more to myself."

When Beth had gone, Selena remained in her chair only an instant longer before slipping through the French doors at the rear of the drawing room and onto the spacious gallery that wound around the house. Bright moonlight was filtering between archways of whitewashed brick to accumulate on the floor in silver pools.

Selena had thought the gallery deserted, so she was startled when she caught a flash of white out of the corner of her eye and heard the soft patter of feet. She turned in time to see a small, white-clad figure disappear down the wrought iron stairway that led to the garden. Having a good idea as to the identity of the apparition, she followed.

She found Beth's eldest child, five-year-old Colin, dressed in a nightshirt and crouched on the third step. With his crop of dark curls and rosy cheeks, he seemed the image of his mother, even down to the vivid facial expressions. Seeing the revealing look of guilt on Colin's cherubic face, Selena found it hard to repress a smile. He quite obviously had been spying on the company, no doubt attracted by the music and gay laughter and dancers in elegant evening dress.

He peered up at Selena as she stood at the head of the stairs. "You won't tell?" he said anxiously.

Selena shook her head. "Do you think I would be so shabby?" Colin looked visibly relieved. Selena could see the set of his small shoulders relax. "I suppose you were lonely," she added as she descended a few steps. "It isn't at all pleasant to be excluded from all the festivities. I'm lonely, too. Perhaps we should keep each other company."

When Colin promptly nodded, she sat down beside him, heedless of what the dust might do to her expensive gown. From that vantage, she could see much of the garden below. Beth had finally despaired of growing the kind of lawn that abounded in Britain, but her garden was laid out in the English style, with formal paths bordered by lime trees and swaths of native flowers. The delicate tropical fragrances filled the warm night. Selena was about to remark on the garden's beauty when Colin piped up.

"Did you see the cap'm?" he asked, the eagerness in his young voice unmistakable.

"The captain? Do you mean Captain Ramsey?"

"Yes, him. Papa said the cap'm was to come tonight. I hoped I should be able to see him. Papa says he has a great schooner and he sails over the sea and fights with pirates! That's what I will do when I am big. I will be a cap'm. I mean to have a giant ship. This giant," he explained, spreading his short arms out as wide as they would reach. "Papa said he would take me to the harbor and show me the cap'm's schooner...."

Selena wondered, as Colin's artless chatter continued, why Captain Ramsey seemed to be the sole topic of conversation this evening. One would think none of the islanders had ever seen a ship's master before—as if Antigua weren't the site of the largest naval base in the Caribbean.

Just then a footfall sounded behind her, interrupting her thoughts and causing Colin to break off in midsentence.

"Good evening," a familiar deep-timbred voice interjected into the silence.

Feeling her heartbeat quicken alarmingly, Selena turned her head to glance up at Kyle's powerful figure. She could understand how he might be viewed by a young boy as a heroic figure.

"Forgive me," he said slowly, "but I couldn't help overhearing my name mentioned."

Selena was dismayed by the effect his sudden presence was having on her pulse rate, but she was resolved not to let it show. "Colin," she murmured, trying to regain her composure, "I daresay the captain perceived your wish, for here he is, in the flesh. Captain Ramsey, may I present Master Colin Thorpe."

Colin's eyes grew very wide as he gazed up at Kyle, his cherubic mouth forming an O. But when Kyle responded to the introduction with a polite greeting, Colin abruptly scrambled to his feet and stood stiffly at attention. "S-sir!" he stammered.

"Colin is a great admirer of yours, Captain," Selena added. She hoped Captain Ramsey would understand such awe and be gentle, but after his earlier claim that children were an encumbrance in his line of work, she was afraid he might not.

"Is that so, lad?" Kyle flashed a broad smile, putting Selena's fears to rest. "I'll wager you do me too much honor, but I'm flattered nonetheless. Did I hear you say you want to captain a ship?"

"Yes, sir." The boy nodded earnestly, seeming to gather courage. "I want to fight pirates like you."

"Well, I've fought a few in my time, but it's dismal work and wretchedly hard, not the least exciting, the way I thought it would be when I was your age. But commanding your own ship—now that's a fine ambition."

"Cap'm . . . do you suppose . . . ? Could I go with you?"

Selena winced when she heard her own words echoed in the boy's request; she had made the same suggestion that morning and had been turned down. She was grateful when Kyle didn't refuse outright but cocked his head, appearing to give Colin's question serious consideration. "I should like to take such a fine lad with me," he said after pause, "but I'm giving up command of my ship. After this voyage I won't be sailing any longer."

His answer surprised Selena; she hadn't thought him the kind of man who would ever give up the sea.

"However," Kyle was saying, "my ships will still continue in service—"

"Ships?" Selena interjected curiously. "You have more than one?"

He glanced briefly in her direction, "I own several."

Colin's eyes grew round again. "And they are all yours?"

"Yes, lad," Kyle said gently. "And I'll still have plenty of acquaintances when I retire from the sea. I expect when you grow a little older, I can find you a berth on a worthy vessel—if you're still of the same mind, and if your father approves. Of course, you'll have to decide whether you want a military career or one in the merchant marine. There's money to be made in commerce, though some don't think making money is a gentleman's occupation."

"Oh, yes sir! How old, sir?"

"I beg your pardon?"

"How old must I grow?"

Kyle's expression remained sober, though Selena thought she could detect a gleam of laughter in his eyes. "Some apprentices sign on at twelve. You might do the same, only you would still have to complete your schooling. It can be arranged, though, so that you can study on board. It's what I did."

When Colin beamed, Kyle reached down to ruffle his mop of black curls. "However," he added with increasing sternness, "if you mean to become a seaman, the first and *most important* thing you must learn is how to obey orders. I expect your mama put you to bed hours ago, is that not so?"

"Aye, sir!" His rosy, round face breaking out in a sheepish grin, Colin raised his hand in a clumsy salute.

"No, lad, let me show you." Kyle reached down to take the small hand in his large one and demonstrate the proper method. "Aye, that's the way of it. Now lead the way to your bedchamber, and I'll tuck you in—before your mama finds you still awake and gives us both a tongue-lashing."

Nodding wisely, Colin climbed the two steps to the gallery and proudly took the captain's hand. But then he paused to glance over his shoulder. "Will you come, Miss Markham?"

Selena smiled. "I think perhaps I should stay here," she said gently. "Then if your mama happens to look for you, I can detain her."

Colin returned her gaze solemnly. "When I am a captain, you may ride on my ship."

Selena felt her heart melt. She hated the thought of riding on a ship, *any* ship, but she would cut out her tongue before she refused such a generous offer. "Thank you, my love," she replied softly. "I shall remember your promise."

As the footsteps—one pair booted and sturdy, the other slippered and light—died away, Selena sighed in the lonely silence. It was at times like these when she felt keenly what her life was missing. She would have liked very much to have a son like Colin.... But now it seemed she wouldn't even have a husband.

Feeling restless and despondent, she rose and made her way down the steps to the edge of the moonlit garden, where she stood gazing out at the distant horizon.

Kyle found her there a short while later—her shoulders drooping dejectedly, like a slender reed bowing before the wind. He thought he understood her misery. In the drawing room a moment ago he had observed her stepmother making a play for her betrothed husband, and the not-so-Honorable

Avery Warner responding to every blatant word of flattery, puffing out his chest like a stuffed peacock. It hadn't been difficult for Kyle to put the pieces together then or to understand why Selena had proposed to him this morning. And he could sense her distress now, even across the stretch of garden that separated them.

He ought to stay away, Kyle warned himself as he descended the stairs from the veranda. He knew enough about Selena Markham to realize she spelled trouble and more trouble. And yet he felt drawn to her quiet beauty. Her gown shimmered silver in the faint light, making her appear as tantalizing and elusive as a moonbeam.

Occupied by her own thoughts, Selena didn't hear his approach until Kyle was directly behind her. She started and turned, glancing up at him in alarm. She relaxed slightly when she recognized him. "Thank you," she said almost at once, "for being sensitive to Colin's feelings. That was kind of you."

Kyle shrugged. "I know how a boy dreams of the sea."

"Yet you seemed taken with him, not as if you viewed him an encumbrance."

He cocked his head, assessing her. "I like children well enough. I just never had much time for them in my line of work."

"Do you really mean to give it up?" she asked curiously as he advanced another step.

"Give what up?" The question seemed absent, but his deep voice stroked her like a caress.

Selena felt its impact even as she realized how intently he was studying her face. He was too close, she thought suddenly. Too close and too masculine. His potent virility made her feel entirely too vulnerable. "The sea," she replied vaguely, hardly remembering her question.

Kyle took one last step to close the distance, his gaze focusing on her lips. "I must."

Selena caught her breath. She could feel Kyle's warmth, could feel the vital power within him, indeed could almost feel again the bold thrust of him between her thighs. Sensations of unexpected pleasure flickered through her at the memory, making her quiver. She was powerless to prevent what she knew would happen next.

Slowly he reached up to run a slow finger along her lush bottom lip, tracing its curving outline. How, he wondered, could he possibly have mistaken her innocence before? She was so cool and virginal. His other hand slipped behind her neck, his touch light and sensual as he drew her against his hard body.

"You shouldn't...." she said breathlessly, reading the amber glow of his eyes as he held her.

"I know," he murmured quite seriously, and bent his head.

His kiss was just as devastating as before, each slow, probing thrust of his tongue stealing another measure of her resistance. For a full minute she could do little more than savor the taste and feel of his lips as they moved possessively over hers.

When he finished a thorough exploration of her mouth and allowed Selena to come up for air, she opened her eyes to find Kyle looking down at her, his heavy brows drawn together in bemusement. "You're too tempting by half, Moonwitch," he breathed, his voice quite husky now. "I don't know what it is you—"

"So!" The exclamation exploded the silence of the garden. "The gossip was true!"

Recognizing Avery's voice, Selena sprang back guiltily from her compromising embrace and turned to see her betrothed standing at the rail of the gallery. His fists were clenched by his sides, his face contorted with anger.

He stormed down the stairs and across the garden. "So!" he repeated, stalking up to Selena. "Edith was right. The minute my back is turned, I find you consorting with a sailor. My betrothed!" He seemed to have forgotten Kyle's presence entirely as he glared at Selena with fury. "Come away at once! I shall escort you home, where I will decide how to deal with this."

Although she was quaking inside, Selena faced him with outward calm. Now that the moment of confrontation was at hand, she was strangely relieved. She had now given Avery adequate reason to break off their engagement without bringing up his sordid affair with her stepmother or her own loss of innocence. She had only to get through these next few unpleasant moments...and the hundreds following when she would be required to face the censure and gossip and ridicule.

"No, Avery," she replied unsteadily, "you will *not* escort me home, nor will you decide how to deal with this. You may, however, consider our engagement at an end."

"I will not be played false!" he shouted, taking a threatening step toward her. Before she could move, he had raised his hand and slapped her across the cheek.

Selena was shocked more than hurt, but Kyle gave a snarl of fury.

"Why, you bloody—" Grabbing Avery's lapel, he let fly with a powerful fist. The blow lifted Avery off his feet and sent him catapulting into a hibiscus bush. Neither the yelp of pain he gave upon landing nor the groan he emitted as he tried to sit up was very dignified.

Kyle stood over him, his expression savage. "I ought to keelhaul you," he growled as he flexed his knuckles. "Get up, you scurvy bilge rat! I'm more your size."

Selena, who disliked any form of violence, was visibly shaken now. Yet Avery's double standards had incensed her. She stared down at him, holding one gloved hand to her smarting cheek, the other clenched in a gesture of defiance. "Play *you* false?" she jeered. "And just what do you call what *you've* been doing for the past year or more?"

"What does that mean?" Avery retorted, his tone guarded.

"It isn't something I choose to bandy about in public! And it hardly matters now. I don't intend to marry you. You won't be getting the plantation you coveted."

Avery stared at her. "But it was what your father wished."

"My father would have been the first to understand," Selena returned with icy civility. "If he had known you merely wanted the plantation, he never would have pressed me to accept your suit."

"I don't merely want the plantation. I want you, too, of course."

"Oh, yes, you require a 'chaste little puritan' for your wife!" Selena raised her chin, determined not to give Avery the satisfaction of knowing how his betrayal had hurt her. "Well, even if I were to marry you, you wouldn't be getting the virgin bride you wanted."

She sensed Kyle's sudden stiffening even before Avery's eyes narrowed in a sharp glance.

"*What,*" Avery demanded in a tone that had suddenly turned ominous, "*do you mean?*"

Selena checked abruptly, realizing that in her distraught state she had said more than she ought. Avery had read into her words exactly what she had meant. "N-nothing," she stammered, taking a step backward. "I only meant I wouldn't marry you."

Slowly, with effort, Avery climbed to his feet, his face darkening as he glanced from Selena to Kyle and back to Selena. "You little slut," he breathed. "You gave him more than a kiss, didn't you?"

Kyle took exception to the slur and raised a clenched fist, while Selena exclaimed, "No! Of course not!" with too much fervor.

They were all startled when Edith Markham spoke from the gallery. "Oh, Selena, how could you?" she exclaimed in shocked tones. "Bestowing your maidenhead on a common seaman!"

At the collective gasps that proceeded this statement, Selena's gaze flew to the veranda. Edith was standing at the head of the steps, observing the altercation in the garden, an expression of dismay pasted on her face. Beside her stood Governor Ramsay, Beth Thorpe and half a dozen of the guests.

Shock drained the blood from Selena's cheeks as she realized how complete her humiliation was. She heard Kyle curse under his breath, but she was too numb to do likewise, even if she had known the proper words.

"It's true, isn't it?" Avery demanded, taking a menacing step toward Selena. He was taking a second step when a lethal voice interrupted him.

"You lay another finger on her," Kyle warned, his tone low and deadly, "and I'll carve you into so many pieces you won't be fit for minnow bait."

Halting where he stood, Avery cast a wary glance at the taller man. Then his gaze sliced back to Selena. "Is it true?"

White-faced, Selena stared back at him. Her disgrace was total. To have both her betrothed and her stepmother question her virtue before the elite ranks of Antiguan society was nearly as damning as if she had paraded naked down Market Street. Her own position irredeemable, she could only hope to spare Kyle any further embarrassment.

And to do so, she realized, thinking frantically, she would have to absolve him of blame. Merely protesting that she hadn't lost her virtue to him would not be enough, for she wouldn't be believed, not with Edith prepared to assert otherwise.

She was still considering her limited options when Avery once again demanded if it was true that she and Kyle were lovers. And before she could answer, Kyle's patience snapped.

"Blast it, Warner, stop badgering her! Whether or not it's true hardly matters."

Turning then, his jaw set in a hard line, Kyle reached out to take Selena's slender, gloved hand in his own large one. He glanced down at her pale, startled face only once before again fixing his scowl on Avery. "There's a simple explanation for why you found us unchaperoned in the garden," he said, raising his voice for the benefit of the watching crowd. "This morning Miss Markham did me the honor of agreeing to become my wife."

Chapter Four

Unable to sleep for the second night in a row, Selena sat at her dressing table, slowly drawing a brush through her hair. The low-burning lamp beside her bathed her in a golden glow, highlighting the delicate lace trim of the wrapper she wore over her nightdress. She felt strangely calm now, despite the catastrophic events of the evening, despite the fact that she was now engaged to marry a stranger.

Captain Ramsey's announcement had rendered her speechless. She hadn't expected him to rescue her from a scandal that was greatly of her own making.

Selena's hand stilled as she remembered the shocked expressions on the faces of the guests, which Kyle's declaration had done little to mend. But then dear, kind Beth had stepped into the breach, scolding Avery for making a scene and spoiling her ball.

"Do calm yourself, Avery," Beth had insisted. "I know you are greatly disappointed to lose Selena, but this is no way for a gentleman to act." She turned to the governor with a bright smile. "Perhaps, sir, you would be kind enough to lead the company in a toast to congratulate Miss Markham and Captain Ramsey on their newfound happiness. Drew planned to announce their engagement at supper, but Selena wanted to speak to Avery first. It would have been extremely awkward otherwise. Although—" Beth shot Avery a disapproving look "—not as awkward as it turned out, I expect."

"You knew about this?" Avery sputtered up at her.

"Of course I knew. Indeed, my only surprise is that Selena waited so long to come to a decision. She realized during Captain Ramsey's last visit what a mistake she had made in agreeing to marry you, but Selena was just too noble to throw you over, Avery."

"Throw me over? Throw *me* over? I wasn't even aware she was acquainted with this . . . this . . . American!"

"Of course they are acquainted. They've known each other for an age! Good heavens, you don't believe Selena would allow herself to be kissed on the streets of St. John's by a perfect stranger? Anyone with eyes can see they are madly in love."

Kyle picked up his cue then, raising Selena's hand to his lips in a tender gesture. "Fortunately I finally persuaded Miss Markham to accept my suit."

"There!" Beth smiled with satisfaction. "Just as I said, a love match."

At that blatant falsehood, Selena felt her cheeks go from white to crimson. She felt as if she were being swept along by a tidal wave, as if there were no way to save herself from drowning. And yet Kyle had thrown her a lifeline. He was something to cling to.

As Beth turned to usher her guests inside, Selena glanced up again at Kyle. The lean, hard planes of his cheeks looked harsh and forbidding in the silver of the Caribbean moonlight; his jaw was set and rigid. He had spoken lovingly to her, but she was close enough to detect the underlying currents in his tone and in his body. He was seething with anger. And she had a strong suspicion his anger was directed at her.

He didn't want their engagement any more now than he had this morning, she knew. He was simply being chivalrous. But she was supremely grateful for his intervention in preventing a scandal—and grateful for his supporting hand beneath her arm during the next few hours as they received the hesitant toasts and questioning congratulations of the guests.

She would repay him for his kindness, Selena vowed now. She would be a good wife to him, a good mother to his children. She would be his helpmate, if she could. At the very least, she could continue to manage her plantation and keep that burden from his shoulders. Perhaps he would even want to learn how to become a planter. Kyle Ramsey was a seaman at heart, and even though he had expressed his intentions of relinquishing command of his ship, she had sensed his great regret. She might be able to help him adjust to the land, though, to help ease his pain at having to give up the sea.

And perhaps, Selena thought wistfully, they might even deal well together. They were not much alike, yet many couples began life together with less in common than she and Kyle shared. In spite of their differences, he was a man she could admire. He was compassionate, she knew, remembering his kindness toward Colin that evening and his gentleness toward herself the previous night. And he had honor, a sense of responsibility. The way he had protected her from Avery's physical threats, the way he had leaped to the defense of her reputation to save her from disgrace, proved how noble he was. He was honest, as well—to the point of bluntness—and his intelligence she had already noted. Even his rugged vitality was something she found attractive.

Perhaps if she worked at it, theirs could still be a good marriage.

By the time she had finished brushing her hair several hundred strokes, Selena felt she had regained a measure of her customary serenity. She was about to arrange the silken tresses into a braid when she heard a soft footfall behind her.

Selena turned quickly. The imposing figure of Kyle Ramsey stood just inside the French doors.

He was a towering masculine presence in her delicate bedroom. He had shed his cravat but otherwise was dressed in the same elegant evening clothes he had worn to the ball, the rich brown superfine of his coat molding his powerful shoulders, the tight buff stockinette of his breeches hugging his long, muscular legs. And he wore the same grim expression she had seen earlier, when she had left him discussing their upcoming nuptials with the governor while Beth and Drew Thorpe escorted her home. His rugged features were a mask of stone.

"C-Captain," Selena stammered, extremely uncomfortable with the dark way Kyle was regarding her, his gaze narrowed and assessing. Her hand crept to the throat of her wrapper. Her state of undress embarrassed her, despite the previous intimacies that had passed between them—or perhaps because of them.

The corner of his mouth twisted wryly in a gesture that was not quite a smile. "I presume our engagement gives me the right to speak to you privately."

"I . . . of course."

"Don't look so worried, Miss Markham. I don't intend to ravish you. That's what precipitated this mess, and I'm not fool enough to repeat it."

Selena didn't know what to say to his declaration, so she waited. Yet when Kyle took another step into the room, she rose quickly, not wanting to be at a disadvantage with him looming over her. His imposing height intimidated her, as did his grim look.

At her action he checked his stride, his hazel eyes sweeping over her muslin-clad form before returning to her face. "The governor wants the wedding to be held two days from now."

"Two days?"

"That's what I said." His biting tone carried anger and frustration. "Governor Ramsay seems to have appointed himself your guardian."

Selena eyed Kyle warily. He hardly looked overjoyed at the prospect of becoming a bridegroom. "My father was a close friend of the governor," she explained hesitantly. "I suppose he feels responsible for my welfare."

"Oh, he made that quite clear! Governor Ramsay threatened to confiscate my ship if I don't go through with the ceremony. He means to trump up charges and accuse me of trading illegally."

Selena had the disturbing feeling that something was terribly wrong; the captain wasn't merely objecting to the timing of their wedding. "You...don't want the ceremony to be held just yet?"

"I don't want it to be held at all," Kyle snapped. "But now it will be up to you to beg off. I've already tried and failed."

"I don't understand."

He sighed, running an impatient hand through his chestnut hair. "It's very simple, Miss Markham. When I announced our engagement this evening, I had no intention of wedding you. I planned to take you with me when I left here, though, so you could be spared the scandal. I'll settle you somewhere in the States, wherever you would like to live."

She felt as if a blow had been delivered to her midriff and had driven the breath from her lungs. "You," she said hoarsely, "want me . . . to become your . . . mistress?"

"Good God, no!" Kyle took a deep breath, trying to keep his tone calm. "I don't need a mistress any more than I need a wife. But I feel obliged to help you. In the States, you will have an opportunity to start over. You can build a new life for yourself there."

Selena stared at Kyle in shock, her eyes wide in her pale face. Her hands crept up protectively to cover her stomach as she tried to marshal her scattered thoughts. It would have been better, she realized, if he had never announced their engagement, if he had left her to weather the scandal alone. She might be branded an outcast on the island, but at least here she would have her few close friends to support her. With them, she could endure the slights and slurs, the whispers and jeers. But not in a strange land, with a strange people. Without even the support a husband, however unwilling he might be, would offer.

"No," she whispered.

"No? What do you mean, no?"

"I won't go with you."

A muscle flexed in his jaw. "Miss Markham...Selena, perhaps you don't understand. Governor Ramsay doesn't intend to let my ship or crew leave the island unless he's satisfied that you will be properly cared for. You'll have to be the one to persuade him. You can say we're to be married at my home in Natchez. You can use the excuse that my sisters want to be present for the ceremony. I've already explained that to the governor, but he wouldn't listen to me. He'll have to hear it from your own lips. That's the only way he'll allow the ceremony to be postponed."

Slowly, Selena shook her head. "No," she said again, quietly. "I won't go with you. You aren't required to marry me, but I won't leave my home to live alone, among strangers."

Kyle took a step toward her, clenching his hands. "Didn't you hear what I said? I can't leave here without the governor's permission, and he won't grant it unless you come with me!"

Selena raised her trembling chin. "I heard you, Captain. But I don't think you heard me. I won't go with you, not without benefit of clergy."

"I won't marry you! I can't."

Her eyes began to flash quietly. She would not beg him to wed her. Nor would she back down. "Why did you announce our engagement, then? Why couldn't you have let me handle it? I wouldn't have involved you."

"I was saving your reputation!"

"I didn't ask you to!"

They stared at each other for a long moment. Finally, Selena broke the tense silence. "I think you should leave, Captain."

Kyle ground his teeth. She was so lovely and demure in her lace-trimmed wrapper—cool and virginal and stunningly arousing. He could feel himself responding, a fact that only inflamed his anger. "I won't leave until this is settled," he returned darkly.

"Very well, I will speak to the governor tomorrow. Will that satisfy you?"

"And tell him what?"

"That we have decided we won't suit, of course."

"He won't accept that!"

"I'm sorry, but that is the best I can do. I won't go with you. Now, Captain . . . you may leave."

When she tried to sweep past Kyle to show him the door, his strong hand spun her around. "Devil take it, I don't want to marry you! Can't you get that through your beautiful head?"

He seemed enormous and very near. His powerful body emanated heat, matching the heat that was rising in her cheeks. "I don't wish to marry you, either," she returned with frozen civility. "The last thing I want is a barbarian for a husband!"

His eyes blazed with amber fire. "Barbarian? Lady," he warned, his voice rumbling softly above her like distant thunder, "I haven't begun to act the barbarian."

His hold on her arm tightened. Slowly, with menacing deliberation, he backed her against the wall. His grip wasn't overly painful, but the casual strength exerted in his fingers startled her.

"You don't want to be my wife," he said between his teeth, "I assure you."

His other hand rose to grasp her chin, but Selena turned her face away, eluding capture. When his hard fingers at last closed over her jaw, she gasped in alarm. "Please...don't hurt me."

Kyle stared down at her. He hadn't missed the flare of temper in her blue eyes, or the fright. "I am not," he gritted through his teeth, "going to hurt you. I've never hurt a woman in my life. But I mean to convince you to reconsider your decision."

His voice was hoarse with anger, his tone adamant. He wouldn't let her or the governor or anyone else deny him the chance to still win his son. He had acted instinctively earlier that evening. Even though Selena had borne the slurs and accusations with a touching dignity that had earned his admiration, her distress had been almost palpable. Seeing her in such straits had been more than he could bear, arousing in him a sudden need to protect and comfort her. But his kindness couldn't extend to actually marrying her. Not while Clay needed him. . . .

The target of Kyle's scowl, Selena fought the urge to cringe. His shirt was open at the neck, and she could see the corded muscles of his throat and the pulse that was beating furiously there. "Please . . . you're frightening me."

"Oh, famous. Cry foul. Plead feminine frailty."

"Well, I can't fight you! You're much stronger than I."

"It isn't fair, is it? But then neither is it fair to force me into marriage."

"I said you weren't obliged to marry me."

Kyle clenched his teeth in frustration. They were back to an impasse. Yet there had to be something he could do to convince her. Impatiently, he released her chin and shifted his grip to her arm, his fingers unintentionally brushing her breast. He was instantly aware of the contact. And so was she, he could tell by the furious blush that rose suddenly to her cheeks.

Selena attempted to ignore the effect of his unintentional caress. "Would you kindly," she uttered icily, clenching her own teeth, "remove your hands from my person?"

It was a supremely proper response, just the kind he would expect from a woman of her reserved manner and social standing. She would make the perfect wife for a cold-blooded aristocrat, Kyle thought nastily. She'd obviously been raised to be prim, restrained, ladylike. From the cradle, well-bred ladies like her were taught to hold the physical side of marriage in aversion. Perhaps, though, he could use her reticence to his own advantage.

"You don't want me to touch you, do you?" he demanded, deliberately running his fingers along the side of her breast, watching with grim satisfaction as Selena flinched. "Surely you know that as my wife, you would have to accept my attentions." He bent closer, his face dark and threatening. "Shall I show you how I would assert my husbandly rights?"

He lowered his mouth and assaulted her lips with a controlled expertise that left her gasping. His tongue plundered her tender recesses, thrusting deeply, shocking her with its arousing warmth. When Kyle finally raised his head, Selena's breasts were heaving in outrage and something else. Something very much like desire.

"You didn't enjoy my lovemaking last night, did you, Miss Markham?" Kyle goaded, his callused palm gliding down her throat to lie against the rapidly beating pulse at its base.

Still reeling from his devastating kiss, Selena hardly understood the question. His lovemaking? No, after his initial passionate advances, she hadn't enjoyed it at all. The act of consummation had been painful and rather undignified. If given the choice, she could happily live without it.

But that seemed to be precisely his point; she wouldn't be given the choice. He bent again to let his lips hover over hers.

"You will have to get used to this if you're my wife," he warned, his breath warm and dangerous against her mouth. "You'll have to be available to me whenever I want you."

Suiting action to words, he pressed his tall, wickedly muscular body against her slim one. A blaze of excitement and tension leaped through Selena, her reaction a purely primitive response, woman to man.... His body was hard and taut with sinew. She could feel its heat and vibrancy through her nightdress.

Helplessly, Selena stared up at him, two bright spots of color staining her cheeks.

His eyes smoldering, Kyle stared back at her. "Consider it, Moonwitch," he prodded, his fingers threading through the pale tresses that spilled over her shoulders. "As my wife, you'll be at my beck and call. I could take you anytime I please, anywhere I please."

If he was trying to destroy her resistance, he was succeeding. His voice had suddenly grown husky with sensuality, gliding through her like a hot knife through butter. As if he might follow his voice, he fitted their bodies together from chest to thigh. Feeling the male part of him vital and pulsing against the juncture of her thighs, Selena tensed with a mingling of dread and wanton longing.

Her rigidity only encouraged Kyle to pursue his course of persuasion. Again he bent his head, although this time he didn't kiss her. Instead his tongue flicked out to touch the corner of her mouth, sending a flame flickering through her to gather in the deep recesses of her body, between her thighs. As his lips trailed down the sensitive skin of her throat, Selena let her eyelids flutter closed.

"I would do this to you, for instance...." His large hand moved down her throat to cup the soft fullness of her breast, his thumb brushing her nipple, stroking until it stood rigidly erect. Selena was scarcely aware that the sharp gasp came from her own throat. "And this...." Kyle murmured. His other arm went around her, his fingers cupping her buttocks to bring her hips even closer to his. "I would take my pleasure of you at my leisure, whenever I wanted."

A shudder shook her body.

"I would waken all the passion in that lovely, untutored body of yours—" Kyle broke off suddenly, realizing his mistake. He could feel his body throbbing at the image his own words were arousing.

Mentally flaying his thoughts into obedience, he made a fierce effort to control himself. "I would make you moan for me, Moonwitch," he rasped against her silken throat. "I would make you scream with pleasure."

Selena believed him; the fire streaking through her loins was so fierce it made her tremble. Of their own volition, her hands crept to his powerful shoulders, and she let her head fall back, giving him full access to her throat.

But he only bent further, his lips seeking her left breast, his mouth closing over the taut nipple, hot and moist even through the layers of muslin. Powerless, wanting, Selena arched her body upward against Kyle's mouth.

Kyle groaned in response. This wasn't working. He was driving himself insane. He could feel sweat break out on his palms as he lost the battle for control.

Selena sensed his struggle. Through the heated dimness that had enveloped her mind, she heard him groan softly. His hoarse whisper dredged from his throat "Devil take it, I can't keep my hands off you."

With an abruptness that left her swaying, Kyle tore himself away. He stood there at arm's length, staring at Selena in the gasping silence as if seeing her for the first time, as if she were an apparition, his expression one of dismay, a look halfway between pain and pleasure.

She was glad for the support of the wall behind her back. Otherwise she might have fallen, her legs felt so warm and weak. Unsteadily, she fixed her gaze on his mouth, not comprehending why he had broken off their embrace.

Kyle hardly knew why himself as he looked at Selena standing there, wide-eyed and vulnerable and trembling. And lovely. God, she was lovely. He wanted her with a fierceness that took his breath away.

Marriage, he reminded himself, trying to regain some semblance of control over his throbbing body. That was why he couldn't have her. He would have to marry her then, and he couldn't do that and claim his son, too. He wanted his son more. Didn't he?

Kyle shook his head to clear his reeling senses. His strategy had backfired with a vengeance. He had begun by trying to frighten and threaten her and had wound up with his own resolutions threatened, instead. He had wanted nothing more than to carry her to her bed and take up where they had left off the previous night, to show her just what depths of passion could be found in her proper lady's body.

Perhaps, he thought disparagingly as his inner turmoil turned to self-scorn, he *was* the fool he kept insisting that he wasn't. He should never have gotten so near Selena, should have kept his distance. Hadn't his past encounters with her taught him that he had no self-command where she was concerned, that he couldn't resist her?

But not again. From now on, he would stay well away from her. He wouldn't lose control of himself again.

But there was still the problem of the wedding. Kyle clenched his fists, anger sweeping through him again as he remembered the governor's ultimatum. Fiend seize it, he would not be forced into marriage, not even to a woman as lovely and bewitching as Selena Markham.

He gave her a hard look, his mouth tightening as he stared at her softly heaving bosom and the tantalizing mouth that was still full and hot from his angry kisses. She might look fragile, but he was beginning to suspect she was as strong as steel inside. He wouldn't persuade her to change her mind.

But just because he would be required to go through with the ceremony didn't mean he had to go through with the marriage.

"Don't be concerned, Miss Markham," he rasped, his voice low and harsh in the silence, "that my barbaric display will be repeated. I don't intend to touch you again. This is one marriage that will never be consummated. The first thing I intend to do when we reach the States is to begin proceedings for an annulment."

He turned on his heel and stormed from the room, leaving Selena to stare at the sheer draperies that swayed in his aftermath.

Shakily, she raised a hand to her lips. A dozen conflicting emotions warred within her: anger, humiliation, wounded pride, regret.... She had truly wanted the opportunity to make this ill-fated marriage work. Her feelings were nebulous, chaotic, yet one stood out clearly: frustrated desire. She hadn't wanted Kyle to stop kissing her.

And she recognized another emotion: bewilderment. Bewilderment at herself. For amid her whirling thoughts was one that made no sense to her: Why was it that Kyle Ramsey's resolution *not* to touch her disturbed her more than his threat to have her at his every whim?

Chapter Five

They spoke their vows in the Markham garden, since news of Selena's marriage to Captain Kyle Ramsey had spread like a cane fire and neither the Anglican church in St. John's nor any house on the island was large enough to hold the many guests. Even on such short notice, most of Antigua's ruling class was in attendance, as were Thomas Markham's friends from the nearest islands. Owing to the governor, the higher ranking naval officers from English Harbor also had been invited.

The governor's hand could be seen at work elsewhere in the arrangements. The vicar had been persuaded to dispense with the reading of the banns, and a special license had been arranged. And from all over the Caribbean, gifts began pouring in.

Selena's own people had done their share, as well. Slaves had labored without ceasing, roasting pigs and preparing food for the celebration that would follow the ceremony. Even Edith had been surprisingly helpful, cataloging the gifts, supervising the kitchen servants and directing the construction of a makeshift altar in the garden.

A wedding on the island was always a merry occasion—an opportunity to socialize for the planters and their families, a holiday from labor for the slaves. But as Selena stood beside the tall, broad-shouldered stranger who was about to become her husband, she felt anything but merry. Tense, wary, desperate, better described what she was feeling.

She cast an uneasy glance up at Kyle. He was staring straight ahead, his jaw set and rigid, as he listened to the vicar pronounce the words that would bind them together until death's parting—or until he could be granted an annulment.

How odd, Selena reflected bleakly as she watched his grim expression, that the only people not enjoying themselves were the bride and groom.

Kyle had been right about the futility of attempting to cancel the wedding. Even so, she had tried—albeit not with much fervor. At first light she had sent Governor Ramsay a note, requesting an audience with him. And surprisingly, that distinguished gentleman responded to her request in person.

From the first moment, she realized her task would be difficult; when she broached the subject of her marriage, the governor assumed she meant to thank him for his efforts on her behalf.

"No, no, my dear," he said gruffly but with a fond smile. "There's no need to thank me. I wouldn't be doing my duty as a friend to your late father, or as His Majesty's loyal servant, if I failed to see this matter settled quickly."

Selena then asked if perhaps the wedding plans weren't going forth with unseemly haste, and when that brought no results, she allowed that she might be having second thoughts about marriage to the captain.

Governor Ramsay merely patted her shoulder in an avuncular fashion. "Nerves, my dear, nerves. All young brides have them. Better to get it over with at once, especially since we came a shade too near to having a scandal on our hands last night, what with Warner making a cake of himself. No, this will quiet the wagging tongues. A bit odd, perhaps, to be switching intended husbands at this late date, but not unheard of, nor regrettable, in this case. It would be different if the captain had no prospects, of course, but I've inquired at length into his background, and I'm satisfied. He's as wealthy as you can stare, and a gentleman, for all that he's an American and a sea captain at that. I liked the fellow, I must say. Besides, Andrew Thorpe vouches for him. Captain Ramsey will make you a fine husband—but you'd already come to that conclusion, hadn't you? A 'love match,' wasn't that what Mrs. Thorpe called it?"

Experiencing that same helpless feeling of being swept along by a too-powerful current, Selena had at last mentioned the captain's wish that his sisters be present for his wedding. But Governor Ramsay merely suggested that a second ceremony be held later for their benefit. He remained adamant that the arrangements would proceed as planned and wouldn't hear of a postponement, the captain's sisters notwithstanding. Her marriage to Kyle would take place the following morning at eleven o'clock in the garden.

Short of refusing outright to wed the captain and creating an even larger scandal than the one that had threatened last night, or disappearing from the island for an indefinite period—neither of which would guarantee that the captain could leave Antigua with his ship and crew intact—Selena had no choice but to accede.

When she had returned home from the ball, Edith had presumed to attempt to convince Selena of her good fortune. And for once her stepmother had seemed anxious to reconcile their differences. "You are angry with me now for pushing you into marriage with that American," Edith said, her tone conciliatory, "but you'll thank me one day. You and Avery were never meant for each other."

Selena was hard-pressed to keep a civil tone when she replied. "I am already thanking you," she said stiffly. "Indeed, you did me a favor, showing me what kind of man Avery is."

Edith had left the subject at that and returned to the task of organizing the festivities.

And so when her wedding day dawned, Selena allowed her hair to be dressed and her body to be bathed and perfumed. With the help of three maids and Beth, who had taken command of the bride since for once dear Selena didn't seem capable of making the simplest decision, Selena donned her mother's wedding dress—a wide-skirted gown of antique-white lutestring silk and exquisite Valenciennes lace. The beautiful gown sported vandyked sleeves and a long train, which could be caught up over one arm. A diaphanous veil cascading from a crown of pearls added to the appearance of fragility. Her only concession to color was a vivid red spray of bougainvillea blossoms, which she wore tucked behind one ear, an exotic contrast to her ivory gown and ivory skin.

She looked lovely, everyone said so. Everyone except her intended husband. He gave her a sharp and unfriendly stare when she came into view at the head of the gallery stairs. Selena was the only one who noted it, however, for all eyes were on her.

She was unable to quell the ache that his grim expression aroused in her or the sorrow she felt when she remembered her girlhood dreams of her wedding day. How different this was from those young dreams! She had always hoped to go to her future husband with love and joy in her heart. And instead...there was only anger and dread and regret. But somehow she managed to keep her own expression cool and serene as she descended the stairs on the governor's arm and took her place beside the captain.

Kyle, Selena amended in her thoughts as she listened to the droning words of the ceremony. She would have to cease thinking of him as "the captain" now that they were to be married.

Yet he still appeared every inch a captain, she thought, gazing up at him wistfully. The deep tan on his face above the pristine cravat, as well as his dark blue captain's coat, underscored his claim to the sea. His rugged elegance was extremely attractive, Selena thought absently before Kyle turned his head briefly to glance down at her. The hard gold light in his hazel eyes deepened as he repeated the vows in response to the vicar's prompting, promising to love and cherish her.

Embarrassed to have been caught watching Kyle so intently, Selena looked away, focusing her gaze beyond the vicar's shoulder, watching instead a small yellow bird flit across the garden. Not for the first time she was grateful for the cooling effect of the trade winds, for the breeze fanned her flushed cheeks as she promised in return to love, cherish and obey. But still she felt uncomfortable beneath the layers of silk and lace. The morning was sunny, the garden warm and bright, even shaded as it was by the gnarled silk-cotton trees.

In contrast, the slim gold band that Kyle slipped onto the third finger of her left hand felt cool to the touch. His lips were cool, too, as he bent and kissed her briefly on the lips. As was the smile he bestowed on her for the benefit of the governor and the wedding guests, since it never reached his eyes. And so were the words he spoke after they signed the documents that made their union legal in the eyes of the law as well as God. His voice was so low that only she could hear.

"I suggest, Miss Markham, that you use what remains of the day to pack your belongings and to make your goodbyes. We sail on the evening tide."

His announcement left her stunned, bereft of speech, so it was fortunate that Governor Ramsay chose that moment to congratulate Kyle on claiming the fairest pearl on the island. As the guests milled around them, Selena managed a faint smile, although with the tightness in her throat she found it hard to respond politely to their good wishes.

Finally Beth found her in the crush and pulled her aside, eyeing her with an odd look. "Selena, are you quite all right?"

"Oh, Beth...." Selena paused, knowing there was nothing her friend could do. She had brought this on herself. Indeed, she had expected to leave the island with her new husband, just not so very soon. "I expect I am overly warm," she prevaricated. "The heat..."

"It is rather close, with all these people. Here, take my fan, it should help. Perhaps you should change your gown, as well. You cannot leave yet, since you will have to open the dancing, but I shall accompany you back to the house after the celebration gets under way." Beth glanced at the throng of guests. "Good, Drew is directing the company toward the refreshments. It should be cooler away from the garden."

The crowd began to move then, toward the clearing beyond the garden. The wedding celebration—a sort of outdoor ball—was to be held there for the guests, but later in the afternoon, the plantation Negroes would hold their own ball there, and many of the gentry would stay. Such occasions—weddings and sugar harvests—were among the few times when blacks and whites mingled.

Selena was surprised when Kyle proffered his arm to escort her, until she realized he meant to keep up the pretense of theirs being a love match. No doubt, she thought glumly, he didn't want to jeopardize his opportunity to escape the island and the governor's authority.

When they arrived, the musicians were already playing a lively tune with fiddles and tambourines. The trestle tables that had been set out near a stand of mango trees were groaning with food, and servants were pouring tumblers of rum punch and sangaree for gentlemen and cups of watered lime juice for the ladies.

Selena found a cup being pressed into her hand as Beth whispered, "Look, the governor means to begin."

"Ladies and gentlemen—" Governor Ramsay raised his voice above the chatter and laughter of the crowd "—if you will, please join me in a toast to the happy couple. To a long and happy life!"

"Ah yes," Selena heard Kyle murmur as glasses were raised in salute, "'the happy couple.'" The bitterness in his tone was unmistakable, and when she glanced up at him, she caught the bright mockery in his eyes.

It wounded her, that look. More so because she felt guilty for her role in bringing matters to such a pass. She regarded him in silence, her gaze trapped by his, until he took her glass from her numb fingers and handed it to Drew.

"Come, my dear," Kyle invited as the musicians struck up a waltz. "I'm told we are to open the ball." He led Selena to the center of the clearing and into the dance, and when his gaze fell again to her face, surveying her somber expression, he bent to whisper in her ear, looking the picture of the devoted husband. "Smile, damn it," he said through gritted teeth. "We cannot disappoint these kind people, now can we?"

She flushed, which the guests mistakenly took for a maidenly blush, and pasted a stiff smile on her lips for the sake of appearance. She wished she could slip away from the crowd and the noise and the hostile, angry man who was whirling her around—she would give anything for a few moments' peace.

It was not so easy, however, for the bride to leave her own wedding celebration. When her dance with Kyle ended, Drew claimed her hand for the next. Then the governor asked for the honor, followed by the solicitor, Ignatius Foulkes. After that she lost count, but the list included several planters and naval officers and even two senior members of Kyle's crew.

Selena managed to keep up the charade of being a happy newlywed, though her face ached from the strain of smiling. Her left arm ached as well from the constant weight of her gown's train, and so did her head. She was worried about the future of her plantation and was anxious to discuss its operation with her factor.

But even her strained smile faded when the latest cotillion ended and her partner returned her to the sidelines, for she caught sight of Avery Warner moving toward her. She hadn't seen Avery since the altercation at Beth's ball, and she didn't want to see him now.

He appeared less distinguished than usual, in spite of his formal attire, for he was sporting an angry black eye, which Selena knew must be paining him. She had difficulty, though, finding the compassion to feel sorry for him, even when he approached her humbly, hat in hand, looking nervous and extremely uncomfortable.

"Mrs. Ramsey," he said stiffly, and Selena was mildly startled to realize that was her new name. "I should like to offer my sincere apologies for my behavior the other evening. It was unconscionable of me to strike you, and I ask your forgiveness."

His apology surprised her, but before she could reply, she heard a soft footfall behind her and realized Kyle had come to stand at her side. She felt the gentle touch of his fingers as he rested his hand possessively on her shoulder.

"Yes," she said distractedly, disturbed by the warmth of her new husband's fingers through the silk of her gown. "Of course, Avery. It was a trying moment . . . for all of us."

"May I offer my felicitations for your happiness, then? For both of you," he added with a sullen glance at Kyle.

"You may," Kyle responded for them both.

"Are you satisfied, then?"

The question seemed odd to Selena, but Kyle nodded brusquely. Avery made her a stiff bow before moving away and returning to Edith's side.

Kyle's gaze followed Avery's retreating figure, watching as Edith clung to the planter's arm. "You're well rid of him," Kyle said, letting his hand fall from Selena's shoulder.

She stared up at him, realizing what the two men had been talking about. "You demanded that Avery apologize to me, didn't you?"

The slight movement of his powerful shoulders could have been a shrug. "He owed it to you."

"Kyle?" she said quickly as he made to turn away. When he glanced down at her, though, she almost faltered, for that hard look still was in his eyes. "I'm sorry . . . about the way things turned out."

A muscle in his jaw flexed, but whatever he might have said to her was lost as Drew interrupted them with a jovial command to rejoin the company. "Come, you two lovebirds, you're missing the feast. Kyle, when was the last time you sampled our native island fare? There's baked fish still hot from the coals and roast pork that I vow will make your mouth water. And if you're truly adventuresome, you can try the pepper pot. . . ."

Selena sighed with frustration, knowing she had lost a prime opportunity to try to smooth things out between herself and Kyle. But she accompanied the two men to the tables.

As Drew pointed out to Kyle the native dishes that filled the calabashes or gourds, Selena helped her plate sparingly to some fish and fruit. After the stress and trials of the day, she had little appetite.

Which was just as well, since before she had finished her meal, the second phase of the celebration began, and Selena found herself surrounded again by well-wishers, the ebony-skinned people who worked her sugar plantation. They were all dressed in their best finery: the women wearing brightly patterned linen buoyed up by numerous petticoats, handkerchiefs around their heads and gold earrings and necklaces; the men in checked shirts and canvas trousers.

They swarmed around her, offering her smiles and felicitations, but they hung back from Kyle, skeptically eyeing the tall, powerful-looking man who was to be their new master.

Hoping to set them at ease, Selena began the introductions, starting first with the mulatto schoolmaster. Kyle shook his hand formally but raised an eyebrow at Selena, as if surprised that the plantation would have a school for slave children.

"Schools are a common practice on Antigua," she said in reply, "though not on some of the other West Indian islands."

Then she made Kyle known to Granny Sarah, who had been born in Africa some ninety-five years ago, to the best of anyone's calculations, and who cared for the fifty-odd children on the estate, the ones too young to labor in the fields. Granny Sarah, having lived too long to fear any man or master, squinted up at Kyle, and after a long scrutiny, beamed him a toothless grin.

"You trickify mon," she praised, her speech heavily accented by the island dialect. "You steal missy from Massa Warner when he not looking."

That made Kyle chuckle, which made the entire group relax, including Selena. It was the first spark of humor she had seen from him since that disastrous scene in Beth's garden.

Granny Sarah cackled in delight as she eyed Kyle's tall, powerful physique with approval. "You fine mon," the wizened woman pronounced. "You give missy fine children."

Her frankness brought a blush to Selena's cheeks. Involuntarily, she cast an embarrassed glance at her new husband and found his green-gold gaze assessing her. Selena's blush deepened at the measuring stare Kyle was giving her. But then she caught the ironic flicker in his eyes and realized he didn't plan for there to be any children. Trying to hide her disappointment, she turned away.

Yet as she continued the introductions, Selena thought Kyle seemed impressed both by her people and her management, and she felt a sense of pride, for she valued his good opinion. She was also inordinately proud to be able to present the rugged sea captain as her husband. He was, she decided suddenly as she watched Kyle converse easily with the plantation's chief driver, the kind of man her father would have wished her to marry, the kind of man who would accept responsibility for a vast estate and all the obligations that entailed, despite his own inclinations and preferences.

The music began again shortly, and Selena noted Kyle's surprise that it was a minuet. He watched with interest as couples paired off and began to dance with as much grace and correctness as any fashionable throng at any ball in England. The only striking differences, besides the dark colors of their skins, seemed to be the exotic flair of their dress and the presence of children, who laughed and ran about underfoot, chewing on short pieces of cane.

The ball became livelier when a Scotch reel was struck up, and livelier still as, some time later, the music progressed from British to Caribbean. Kyle listened attentively as the dancers raised their voices in chanting song, and the drums beat out a rhythm that was dark and primal.

Selena, who was intimately familiar with Antigua's customs and culture, found more pleasure in watching Kyle. She smiled to see him question one of the musicians about his musical instrument—an African *balafo*, which was made from pieces of hardwood of different diameters, laid on a row over a sort of box—and allowed herself to hope that his interest meant that he might be forming an attachment for the island that had always been her home.

When two maskers dressed in elaborate costumes took the floor to perform the whip dance, Selena felt she could safely slip away. She wanted to change out of her wedding gown and then consult with her factor about the future of her plantation. She left Kyle watching with fascination as one man chased and lashed at the other, who dodged gracefully just out of range of the wicked rawhide.

Beth caught her up as she reached the house.

"I thought you could use my assistance," Beth said somewhat breathlessly as they climbed the gallery stairs to Selena's bedroom. "You'll never manage those hooks and laces by yourself, and your maids are all at the celebration."

Selena smiled and clasped her friend's hand. "Dearest Beth, ever practical and kind as always. You've been a pillar of strength for me. How can I ever thank you?"

"You did the same for me when I wed Drew, if I recall." Beth gave her a sober glance. "I want you to be happy, Selena."

"Yes . . . well . . ." She fell silent, and so did Beth—for a moment.

Then Beth, who obviously felt a duty to bolster her friend's spirits, launched into a spate of praise for how smoothly the day had gone and kept up a flow of bright chatter as she helped Selena struggle out of the beautiful wedding gown.

As Selena bathed her face in water from the basin, Beth went to the armoire. "What shall you wear? The rose sarcenet would be extremely becoming."

"The burgundy-and-gray crepe, I think," Selena replied, patting her cheeks dry. "The one with the matching pelisse. It will be more appropriate for traveling. We are sailing this evening."

Beth turned to stare at her. "So soon! I expected you to remain for several more days, at least. Perhaps I should ask Drew to persuade the captain."

Selena shook her head. The governor could have obliged Kyle stay for a day or two longer, but she didn't wish to rouse her husband's anger further. "No, it is what Kyle wants."

"Well," Beth said brightly, "I'm sure you will find America very pleasant. Indeed, I fancy you will have a wonderful life. How could you not, with a handsome husband who adores you—"

"Beth . . . it isn't a love match. You know it isn't."

The look Beth sent her was full of sympathy and compassion. "Surely you're mistaken. I thought the captain seemed very taken with you. Perhaps he just doesn't want to admit his feelings."

"No," Selena said in a low tone, looking down at her hands. "Kyle doesn't love me." Her fingers tightened on the linen cloth in her hands. "Not yet. But he will. One day he will," she vowed quietly, realizing suddenly how very much she wanted it to be true.

But then she caught Beth's eye and was embarrassed to have confided so personal a thought, even with her closest friend. Briskly Selena completed her toilette and turned to Beth for help in relacing her corset.

"Will you be taking one of your maids with you to America?" Beth asked.

"No. I would enjoy the company, certainly, but their homes and families are here."

When she was dressed in the high-waisted burgundy gown with the pale gray sash, Selena glanced around the room that had always been hers and sighed. "I suppose I ought to begin packing."

"Why don't you go and join your new husband?" Beth said gently. "I can pack for you, and you can check later to see if there is anything I've missed."

"But the portmanteaus and trunks are in the storehouse—"

"I'm sure I can find someone to fetch them."

"And the portraits of my parents in the salon—I would like to take them with me. I doubt Edith will appreciate them as much as I will."

"I'll see they are carefully wrapped."

Selena gave a helpless shrug and smiled. "Very well, if you're certain...."

"I'm certain!" Beth exclaimed, and with a grin, gave Selena an impulsive hug. "Now go! Captain Ramsey no doubt is wondering what has become of you."

Selena was far more skeptical, but since she was anxious to find her factor and discuss how the plantation was to be operated in her absence, she pinned on an attractive hat that was bedecked with gray satin ribbons and made her way back to the clearing.

Her footsteps slowed, however, at the sight that greeted her. Ignatius Foulkes was sitting in a gig at the edge of the clearing, his portly bulk taking up most of the seat, while Kyle was preparing to climb up beside him.

Kyle paused when he saw her, one booted foot on a carriage step. He watched Selena warily as she approached, remaining silent when she reached them. When he offered no explanation as to their intention, Selena looked a question at the solicitor.

"The captain asked for a tour of the estate," Foulkes replied in his most formal tone, with more than a hint of disapproval.

"Now?" she said without thinking. Then realizing she sounded critical of Kyle, stammered, "I mean...the festivities are not yet over."

"I would like to see the property before we sail," Kyle said finally, "and that leaves very little time."

"Perhaps," Mr. Foulkes told Selena, "you would care to come?" He turned to address Kyle. "Mrs. Ramsey would better serve you than I, sir. She is more knowledgeable about her particular holdings and therefore better able to determine the fair market value."

"Market value?" Selena echoed, feeling a sudden sick dread in the pit of her stomach.

Ignatius nodded, his jowled face creasing in a stern frown. "Yes, my dear. The captain has not taken me into his confidence, but I rather fear he wishes to offer up the Markham plantation for sale."

Chapter Six

Selena paled at the solicitor's speculation. Reaching out, she grasped the edge of the gig to steady herself and looked up at Kyle with pleading eyes. "Please..." she said in a stricken voice. "Don't... Why are you doing this? To punish me?"

Kyle's eyes darkened in anger. "Perhaps, my love," he said carefully, with an undertone of grimness, "this is better discussed in private. Mr. Foulkes, would you be so kind as to allow us the use of your carriage for an hour?"

The solicitor looked from Kyle to Selena. But he must have felt this was a matter to be settled between the two of them, for he issued a terse reminder to Selena that he was at her disposal should she require his counsel, then clambered down and went off, leaving them alone.

"Get in," Kyle said through clenched teeth. When Selena merely stood there gazing at him in anguish, he grasped her arm and marshaled her into the gig. "I only just now began to entertain the idea of selling your plantation, Miss Markham. And certainly I intended to discuss it with you first before I made any decisions."

After settling himself in the leather seat beside her, Kyle took up the reins and turned the bay gelding toward the road. "And I am not," he insisted with strained patience, "intent on punishing you. You can't return here, but you'll be able to use the proceeds from the sale of the plantation to begin your new life."

Which didn't include him, Selena thought wretchedly. He hadn't said it, but the thought hovered between them and, if anything, deepened her despair.

"Look," Kyle said somewhat desperately, "I may not be a farmer, but I know enough to realize that an absentee landlord does no one any good."

Still Selena didn't speak, and Kyle's fingers clenched the reins in frustration. "Deuce take it! Why don't you say something?"

Selena took a shuddering breath. "What...would you have me say?"

"I don't know! Curse me or scream or threaten to haul me before the governor—anything but look at me like I've just murdered your favorite relative."

She glanced away then, looking down at her hands, remembering her foolish declaration that Kyle would someday come to love her. "You are right, of course," she said finally, in a small voice. "An absentee landlord wouldn't be at all desirable. It was just a shock.... I hadn't thought of selling...." Yet she should have thought. Everything had changed when she married Kyle.

"You knew you would be leaving the island," Kyle replied defensively, trying to see her face, which was partially hidden by the knot of gray satin ribbons on her hat.

"Yes."

"Look, Miss Markham—"

"Do you think," she asked, her tone becoming tight with anger, "you might bring yourself to address me by my given name? It seems rather foolish to be so formal now that we are married, even if you don't intend it to last."

He liked her better angry than when she got that wounded look in her eyes or when she retreated into cool civility. "Very well.... Selena. What I meant to say was that I wouldn't consider selling to anyone you didn't approve of. And in any case, we don't have to sell it at once."

"No. At once is better. The longer you delay, the harder it will be for everyone."

Kyle fell silent then, until he realized he didn't know where he was driving. "Where are we headed?"

She looked up with a start. "I beg your pardon?"

"You were going to give me a tour of the plantation."

"Oh, yes...of course." Selena roused herself from her despondent thoughts to direct him along a path to the left.

They passed several fields of cane stubble and shortly came upon the Negro quarters—a wide area that was cool and colorful, shaded by tall breadfruit trees and brightened by the purple and green of young mango leaves. In the clearing stood scores of good-size huts, most walled with wattle and daub, some of stone, all on stilts and all neatly thatched. Beside many of the huts were pens for poultry and livestock, and beyond, soaking up the sun, lay dozens of well-tended gardens.

"How many slaves does your plantation have?" Kyle asked thoughtfully as he drew the horse to a halt.

"Three hundred fifty-six, since Rose was delivered of twins the other day. But we employ more than fifty freemen, as well—factors, artisans, bookkeepers and the like."

He sat there a moment, looking around. Then he slowly shook his head. "I hadn't imagined it would be so big. It's a vast responsibility—to own so many lives. Not one I'm sure I like."

"But you're a plantation owner, too," Selena observed.

"Yes. But somehow I never thought of myself... Of course, my father owned slaves once he moved to Mississippi from England, but I put it out of my mind. I went to sea when I was twelve, a few months after my family moved there. It was easy to ignore the situation, for I didn't go home much."

She eyed him curiously. "You inherited your plantation from your father?"

Kyle nodded. "When my parents were killed last year."

"I'm sorry."

His mouth twisted. "For what? Because I inherited or because my parents died?"

"Both. You aren't happy about becoming a planter—"

"You've noticed?"

She ignored his sarcasm. "It's never easy to lose one's parents. Were you close?"

Kyle shrugged. "I don't suppose you could call our relationship close. I was young when I left home, after all. But I do miss them."

"Are you the eldest son, then?"

"I'm the only son. I have four sisters—one a few years older than I, the others much younger."

"I should have liked to have sisters," Selena said wistfully.

Suddenly realizing how personal the conversation was becoming, Kyle took up the reins again and urged the horse around.

As they passed more cane fields that were laid out in regular patterns, Selena explained that each year two-fifths of the land was planted and another two-fifths allowed to lie fallow.

The remaining acreage, usually the most fertile, was used as a provision ground.

"And just what is a 'provision ground'?" Kyle asked as they approached the buildings Selena said were the sugar works.

She gave him an odd look. "It's where we grow our food. We can't live on sugar alone, I'm sure you understand."

The rueful twist of Kyle's lips was almost a smile. "I don't suppose so."

"Everyone on the plantation has a garden plot, if he wishes, and two hours free at noon to work it. Most of the Negroes sell their excess produce at the market in St. John's."

"And do they get to keep the money they earn?"

"Of course they get to keep it. Most spend it on tobacco or trinkets or clothes. But some of the slaves save and eventually buy their freedom."

Kyle looked surprised at that, but they had reached the sugar works by then, so he didn't question Selena further.

She took him through one of the two sugar mills on the plantation, and he was able to see at close range the great iron rollers that pressed the cane into a pulpy mass she called bagasse. The bagasse was used as fuel to raise steam in the boilers, while the juice flowed into the rows of iron caldrons that lined the boiling room. They also toured the curing house, where the molasses was drained from the crystallizing sugar, and then the distillery, where scummings and treacle and lees were mixed with water and fermented into rum. By the time he came out into the bright sunlight, Kyle knew far more about sugar making than he had ever cared to know.

Still, he listened politely as his new bride explained how during the sugar season they usually worked late into the night, for Selena spoke with such enthusiasm that he could almost believe himself interested in whether or not cane needed to be pressed within a few hours of cutting to keep the juice from fermenting. He found himself watching her face and thinking how lovely it was and how much he preferred seeing it animated than saddened or distressed. She lost much of her reserve then. When Selena turned to him suddenly with a question, her blue-gray eyes bright, he blinked and was obliged to ask her to repeat it.

"The growing season here is opposite that in America, isn't it?"

Kyle grinned for the first time in several hours. "You're asking *me*? I hardly know the difference between a plow and a harvest. We grow cotton in Natchez, that much I do know."

"My father once experimented with cotton here but found it wasn't as advantageous economically as sugar. What kind do you grow? Green-seed or shrub?"

"There are different kinds?"

Selena eyed him with faint amusement. "You really aren't a farmer, are you?"

"I told you so," Kyle replied, giving a short chuckle. "My father, now *he* was a farmer. He never wanted to do anything else. But he was the younger son of an English squire, and his older brother inherited everything. He managed to scrounge together a few acres, but it wasn't enough to feed his family, so he moved us to America, looking for a better life. In Natchez land was inexpensive and labor cheap, and he already had relatives there. A cousin of his had purchased a big tract of land back when England owned part of what later became the Mississippi Territory."

So that was why, Selena reflected as she allowed Kyle to hand her into the carriage, his accent was more clipped than the Americans' usual broad drawl. Then she realized that he had actually laughed just now, and she slanted a glance at Kyle as he took up the reins. He was extremely attractive when he laughed, she thought, gazing at his rugged profile. His eyes danced with lights of amber and green, and the tiny lines at the corners crinkled.

"Is that where Natchez is located, the Mississippi Territory?" she asked, keenly interested about his home and family.

"Yes, except that Mississippi is no longer a territory. It recently became a state. Natchez is a few hundred miles north of New Orleans on the Mississippi River."

"And your sisters live there on your plantation?"

Selena interpreted the quick, measuring look Kyle gave her as a warning that her questions were becoming too personal. Not wanting to spoil his good humor, she didn't press him to share more about his family, as she would have liked. Instead, she began to tell Kyle about the celebrations that were held at the end of the grinding season, keeping the conversation impersonal, as she sensed he wished. They drove away, more in charity with each other than they had been since the night of their engagement.

It was as they were nearing the house once more that Selena grew silent. "Please, could we stop here a moment?" she said finally. "I must say goodbye to someone."

Kyle obliged, drawing the horse to a halt, though he was surprised that she had chosen to stop on a somewhat barren stretch of road.

"You needn't come with me," Selena added quietly when he made to descend. "I shan't be long."

He watched her climb down and then disappear up a small rise some distance from the road, where several tamarind trees grew. After a moment, though, he secured the reins and followed her, curious to see who lived there.

She was kneeling in the scrub grass, her head bowed. Kyle didn't need to see the two headstones to realize he was in a small graveyard or read the names carved there to know she was saying farewell to her parents.

He halted, regretting that he had intruded on her privacy, but before he could turn, Selena gave a sigh and rose. When she saw him, she smiled, but he could see how tremulous that smile was and how misty her eyes were.

Kyle gazed down at her with grudging admiration. This situation must be devastating for her, he realized suddenly; she was leaving everything and everyone she loved in order to face a new land and new way of life at the side of a husband who didn't want her....

If it wasn't for his son, Kyle thought with another twinge of regret, he might have been willing to give their marriage a chance. Having a planter's daughter for a wife would be a great benefit to him now. And Selena Markham was undeniably lovely, even if her figure was too slender and her manner too proper and restrained for his taste.

Suddenly he wanted to make her leave-taking as painless as possible. "Whom would you trust to run your plantation?" Kyle asked quietly, wanting to ease her mind. It was obvious how much she loved this land and its people.

Her tawny brows drew together in thought. "I hadn't really considered it. I always assumed Avery would take over the responsibility."

Kyle couldn't help the way his lip curled. "I wouldn't," he said carefully, trying to control his scorn, "sell a dog I didn't like to that man-milliner."

"I know you aren't overly fond of him, and I'm not ... particularly fond of him, either, after what happened.

But he has wanted the land for ages. And my father chose Avery because he values his people and treats them well. Honestly—" she reached out and placed a hand on Kyle's sleeve "—I've never seen Avery strike anyone before."

Kyle gazed down at her, watching the dappled shade play across her ivory skin. The shadows blended with the faint discoloration that smudged her left cheekbone. Unconsciously, he reached up to brush the slight bruise with his fingertips. Then abruptly, he let his hand drop, looking self-conscious even as his mouth tightened.

Selena felt somewhat self-conscious herself, especially when she realized she'd been considering a solution that she couldn't support with much enthusiasm. "I expect you could sell to Drew," she said after further thought. "He would see it was well cared for."

"Would he be interested?"

"He might have difficulty coming up with that much capital, but yes, his holdings march with ours, and I've heard him express interest in increasing the size of his plantation."

"I find that a much more palatable alternative. Very well, I'll speak to Drew when we return. The capital shouldn't be a problem. We'll offer him reasonable terms."

"Thank you . . . Kyle."

His broad shoulders lifted in a shrug before he glanced toward her parents' graves. "Then if you're finished here . . . ?"

"Yes," Selena replied, realizing he was uncomfortable with her gratitude.

"Can you be ready to leave by seven?" Kyle asked as he escorted her back to the gig. "I'll need to go aboard the *Tagus* shortly, but you should be at the docks by eight if we're to sail this evening."

"I will be ready."

"Good. I'll send a carriage to fetch you and your trunks."

"You needn't put yourself to so much trouble. Beth and Drew will drive me."

"It is no trouble," he insisted with somber courtesy.

Selena wasn't surprised to find that concerning the fate of her plantation, Kyle was as good as his word. As soon as they returned to the celebration, he took Drew aside and put forth their plan. And since Drew was pleased to more than double the size of his estate, they were able to announce to Selena's people an agreement on the sale of the Markham plantation and to consult with her factor about the transition of ownership.

Neither her slaves nor factor were overly surprised or unhappy about the arrangement, for Andrew Thorpe was known far and wide as a just and honest man and master. And although, her people said, they would miss her, it was to be expected that she would leave the island, for was not a woman's place with her husband?

Only Edith was not content with the arrangement. She held her tongue in public, however, and followed when Selena went up to the house to complete her packing.

"You should have sold the plantation to Avery," Edith said at once as she entered her stepdaughter's bedroom.

Selena glanced up briefly as she bent over one of her trunks. "You forget, Edith, that decision is for my husband to make."

"But you could have persuaded him! What will I do now? How am I going to live?"

"I'm sure the estate will continue to provide you the allowance Papa designated in his will."

Edith laughed harshly. "How can I possibly survive on such a mere pittance?"

"We have been over this before, Edith, time and again. Your allowance is no 'mere pittance.' Most people would consider themselves wealthy to receive such a regular income. You will simply have to learn to live within that limit."

"But I *can't*!"

Losing patience, Selena stuffed a protruding ruffle within the trunk and closed the lid with more force than necessary. "Perhaps you should sell some of your jewelry then, starting with the emeralds you purchased last week. The proceeds should keep you in style for quite some time."

"Sell my jewelry! Why, that's absurd."

"Then I suggest," Selena said, giving her stepmother a hard look, "that you marry Avery. You deserve each other, I think."

"You are acting out of spite! You are angry with me for taking Avery from you."

"On the contrary. I am quite grateful. I am also," Selena added more quietly, "grateful that you were discreet in your affaire with him. You could have caused a scandal to my father's memory, and for that I don't think I could have forgiven you."

"Is that your last word?" Edith demanded.

Selena glanced around the room, her gaze falling on the carefully wrapped portraits of her parents; Beth had been quite thorough in her packing. "Yes, it is," Selena answered softly. She felt a keen measure of satisfaction; it was only poetic justice that Edith would never have the plantation she'd coveted.

"You know," Selena added, meeting Edith's furious gaze once more, "it used to distress me that we were never able to become friends. I always wondered if there was something I could have done, could have said, to make you hate me less. Now I see how misplaced my worry was. You're so filled with greed and hatred, Edith, that I truly pity you."

Edith's jaw clenched. "Keep your pity for your new husband. He's the one who will need it, being married to you. You'll never be able to satisfy a man like the captain. Never!"

Selena winced. When Edith had turned and flounced from the room, she gave a sigh. It was a relief to know she would never have to deal with her stepmother again, but their discussion had left a sour taste in her mouth.

She closed the remaining trunks and went down the corridor to the morning room, where she was greeted with a loud squawk.

"Hello! Hello! Will you dance?"

Selena smiled at the vivid green-and-yellow parrot in the cane-constructed cage. "No, my fine fellow. I've had enough dancing for one day, thank you. I've come to take you with me. At least I shall have one familiar face to accompany me on my new venture."

Horatio tilted his head to one side, giving her what looked like a sympathetic look. But he couldn't understand, not really, Selena reflected as he set up a new chatter.

"Dance! Awk! Dance!" he cried, ruffling his feathers, and only became silent when she covered the cage with a dark blue cloth.

When she could delay no longer, she carried Horatio's cage out to the carriage where Beth and Drew Thorpe waited. They had insisted on accompanying her to the docks, for which she was grateful. She needed their comforting presence as she gazed for the last time on her beloved home. Even so, tears blurred her vision as she gave the gracious, galleried house one last, long look.

A boat was waiting to take her to the *Tagus*, her husband's large, schooner-rigged merchant vessel. She could see it lying in the harbor, looking sleek and fast with its tall, raking masts and graceful, billowing sails.

Her solicitor was at the docks, as well, and so was the governor. With a twinkling smile, Governor Ramsay bestowed his blessing on Selena and presented her with the proper authorization papers to give to Kyle, releasing the *Tagus* from the harbor.

Homesick already, Selena felt tears well in her eyes as she said goodbye to her dearest friends. But as she stepped into the six-oared pinnace, she made a determined effort to brush away her tears, and she fixed her gaze on the distant schooner that would carry her away from her island.

Kyle wasn't there to greet her when she awkwardly negotiated the rope ladder and stepped on deck, but his first mate immediately came forward with a welcoming smile. Selena remembered meeting Mr. Nathan Hardwick earlier that day at her wedding celebration. She had danced with him, too, she thought, recalling now his handsome features and dark hair. Tall and lean, he was several years older than she, yet he had a boyish look about him.

There was an unmistakable look of admiration in Hardwick's eyes as he gave her a gallant bow. "Good evening, Mrs. Ramsey. The captain ordered me to escort you below."

"Below?" Selena asked hesitantly, extremely reluctant to enter the bowels of the schooner. With her dread of ships, it was bad enough being on deck in the fresh air and fading sunlight.

"Yes, madam, to your cabin."

"May I not stay here?" She would feel more secure where she could still see land.

"Well..." The first officer looked uncomfortable. "The captain gave direct orders."

"Where is he? Perhaps I could speak to him and ask permission to stay."

"On the quarterdeck, ma'am, but I'm afraid he's busy at the moment. There was a problem with a tackle...."

Wondering where the quarterdeck was, Selena glanced about the schooner. Only the scents of tar and brine were familiar to her. She was standing at the bottom of a seemingly confused tangle of ropes, cables and spars, while far above her head the great masts swayed in gentle rhythm against the clouds. The ship creaked and groaned alarmingly at the motion, and Selena was hard-pressed to refrain from turning around and fleeing back to shore.

She didn't see Kyle, but it was not, Selena decided, noting the intense activity on board, an appropriate time to importune him. All around her, men scurried purposefully over the polished decks, seeing to the provisions—crates filled with chickens and barrels of salt beef and fish. Above, among the forest of masts and canvas, sailors swung from yard to yard, checking lines and raising sails.

At any event, her request to stay here would surely seem like cowardice to Kyle. He wouldn't understand her fear of ships.

So she allowed Mr. Hardwick to escort below. As they negotiated a steep flight of steps he called the companionway stairs, Hardwick offered to take the parrot's cage. Selena declined, though, feeling the need to cling to something familiar, even if it was only a bird.

She was given Hardwick's own cabin. When she asked in surprise if she wouldn't be displacing him, Hardwick, looking uncomfortable again, informed her that he would be bunking with the captain. The flush on his cheeks told Selena quite well that he thought the arrangements strange. Although it was quite common for married couples of means to sleep apart, this was stretching matters too far.

Yet Hardwick was obviously too well-bred to comment on it and too experienced a seaman to question his captain's orders. At his awkward explanation, Selena felt a flush rise to her own cheeks. It was mortifying, this public acknowledgment of their troubled marriage.

But she stiffened her spine and handed Mr. Hardwick the governor's documents. "Will you please give these to Captain Ramsey? And would you . . . ask him if I might speak to him—when it is convenient?"

Hardwick murmured an agreement and, with another brief bow, hastened from the cabin, closing the door behind him. Alone, Selena glanced about her warily.

There was a bed, she saw, built against one paneled wall, as well as a line of pegs for hanging clothes. Along another wall was a washstand with a commode and basin and a shelf that held a large lantern.

Selena hung Horatio's cage on a peg and pulled off the covering. He blinked and ruffled his feathers. "How do you do? How do you do? Awk!"

"Not very well, I fear," she answered with a rueful smile.

It was quite warm in the cabin, so she shrugged out of her pelisse. She glanced into the dark companionway, then went to the porthole window. From there, she could at least view part of the island. For a moment she watched a tern that was scooping up small fish from the bay. She tensed when there was a quick rap on the door.

It wasn't Kyle. Swallowing disappointment and frustration, Selena stood aside as her trunks were delivered by the giant she recognized as Tiny, then returned to the window seat. A few minutes later, she heard the creak of timber and mooring cables and the snapping of sails as they caught the wind. Selena tensed again as she felt the ship begin to move, clenching her fingers around the edge of the porthole.

She wanted Kyle, she realized with a vague sense of surprise. She wanted him to put his arms around her and calm her fears. Yet he was unlikely to offer her the comfort she yearned for. Or even companionship. This was her wedding night, but she would spend it alone.

It seemed like an eternity before Kyle finally came. He had changed out of his formal attire, she saw when she opened the door at his knock. He wore breeches and knee-high boots and a collarless shirt that was open at the neck, showing the corded muscles of his throat and a glimpse of his powerful chest. His sheer size and vitality made the cabin appear even smaller as he strode in.

"What are you doing down here in the dark?" he asked at once. "You should have had Hardwick light the lantern. I'll do it—"

"No, please.... I would prefer not to stay here."

Kyle's grim expression as he met her gaze boded ill. There was no trace of the momentary warmth or amusement she had observed earlier in the afternoon. "I would prefer not to have women on board my ship, either, yet I had little choice in the matter."

Selena's heart sank at his uncompromising antagonism.

When she remained silent, Kyle took the offensive. "I expect you aren't satisfied with the sleeping arrangements, but this is not a passenger vessel. I conduct most of my business in my cabin, and I don't see a reason to change it for the short time it will take us to make New Orleans." He had a much more pressing reason, of course; there was no way he could share a cabin with his lovely bride and still keep to his vow to maintain his distance. But he wasn't going to explain that to Selena.

Even in the dim light, though, Kyle could see the wounded look in her eyes. His jaw hardened in annoyance at the guilt he felt. "Don't you have anything to say, Miss Markham?"

Selena took a deep breath. "I don't . . . care for ships."

Kyle raised his eyes to the ceiling. "Why doesn't that surprise me?" he asked in a sardonic undertone. "We've yet to agree on much."

"They frighten me, if you must know. My father's ship went down in a storm."

That made him pause. "I'm sorry," he said finally.

"So did Edward's," Selena added, her voice a mere whisper.

"Who is Edward?"

"He was my betrothed."

"I thought Warner was your betrothed."

"Edward was my first."

"What do you do, collect men for sport?"

Even for a man with justification for being angry at the circumstances, it was a nasty remark. Kyle immediately opened his mouth to apologize.

But Selena drew herself to her full height, her tone edged with frost as she retorted, "There was one major difference. I *loved* Edward."

"Horatio loves you, awk! Will you dance?"

Looking startled by the squawked interruption, Kyle dragged his gaze from Selena and peered at the deepening shadows. "What is that?"

Selena hesitated, reluctant to disclose that she had brought another unwanted dependent on board. But she was grateful the bird had relieved some of the tension of the moment. She moved past Kyle to stand by Horatio's cage, as if to protect him. "'That' is a parrot."

"I can see what it is. I meant, what is it doing here?"

She didn't think it a propitious time to tell Kyle she had thought to give the bird to his sisters as a gift. At the moment, it was very unlikely she would even meet his sisters. "He is to keep me company," Selena said defiantly. Then, in a more conciliatory tone, "His name is Horatio—after Lord Admiral Nelson, who served on Antigua some years ago. The admiral also won the Battle of Trafalgar, in case you didn't know."

"I've heard of Admiral Nelson," Kyle said dryly, refraining from adding that any young English boy who dreamed of going to sea—and many American ones—knew by heart the exploits of England's hero.

"Are you going to tell me I cannot keep him?"

"Will you dance, love?" Horatio broke in.

A reluctant quirk appeared at the corner of Kyle's mouth. "No, you may keep him."

"Then," Selena asked, taking heart as his roughly carved features softened, "may I go upstairs?"

He glanced down, surveying her, and even in the dim light she could see the amusement flickering his eyes. "You're obviously as unfamiliar with a sailing vessel as I am with a plantation. On a ship, one goes up on deck, or above deck, not 'upstairs.'"

The hint of laughter in his voice relieved rather than annoyed her. "Above deck, then. May I?"

"I suppose so, under the circumstances—if you can keep out of the way of my crew."

"Of course."

As Selena moved to cover the cage with the cloth, Kyle indicated the parrot with an inclination of his head. "Do you mean to take Horatio with you?" he asked curiously.

"To be truthful, I'd rather not expose him to the rough language of seamen. He's very clever for a bird and is likely to repeat anything he hears."

"I'll warn my men to keep their salty tongues between their teeth."

"Oh, no, there's no need—" Selena began before realizing that Kyle was roasting her. "I shall keep Horatio out of their way and yours," she assured him frostily, her spine stiffening as she turned to don her pelisse as protection against the wind.

Belatedly remembering his duty as a gentleman, Kyle took the wine-colored garment from Selena and held it up for her. When she had slipped it on, he hesitated, his hands resting lightly on her upper arms.

"Moonwitch," he said gently in her ear, "you needn't fear the ship will go down. I haven't lost a vessel yet."

She glanced over her shoulder at Kyle, conscious of the intense physical awareness she felt at his nearness. Why was she so strongly attracted to him? He had treated her with little more than grudging tolerance since he had known her. "You don't think my drowning would be a fitting revenge for forcing you into marriage?"

She regretted the words at once, for Kyle's expression instantly turned grim again.

His hands dropped to his sides. "If you need anything, Hardwick is at your disposal."

What if I need a husband who cares for me? she thought despairingly. What if I need a friend to converse with, to share laughter and sorrow with, someone to love? But she said nothing.

Instead, she mounted the companionway stairs in the fading twilight to bid a silent and lonely farewell to her homeland.

Chapter Seven

As it turned out, the voyage wasn't quite as bad as she feared. The first night was the worst. Realizing she couldn't remain on deck the entire time, Selena allowed Mr. Hardwick to escort her to the officers' cabin for a late supper, where he tried to entertain her in Kyle's absence. After a brief stroll on deck, he persuaded her to retire to her own cabin.

Selena passed a restless night, starting awake every time the schooner rolled over a deep trough, but at least her preoccupation kept her from feeling too homesick. And she suffered nothing more than a minor queasiness from the rising and sinking with the motion of the ship. Thank goodness, Selena thought as she dragged herself from the bunk the next morning. If she had been susceptible to seasickness, she would have lost Kyle's respect entirely.

She had vowed to keep out of his way and not cause him or his crew any trouble, but she ran into a minor difficulty almost at once: the matter of her corsets. Unlacing was no problem, for she could reach the ties easily enough. But without a maid to help, she found it was impossible to tie the laces tightly enough to fit into her gown.

When a cabin boy brought her breakfast, she had to send him away, for she was still engaged in the struggle. Hardwick came a moment later. He called to her through the door, expressing worry that she might be ill, and his concern made her overcome her discomfort at being seen in such a state. Dressed in a wrapper, holding the lapels close together at her throat, Selena opened the door a crack.

"I'm not ill," she explained with a blush. "Indeed, I'm quite comfortable. It's just that I am having a slight difficulty getting dressed. I'm accustomed to the services of a maid, you see."

"Of course," Hardwick said kindly. "I should have foreseen it. I'll fetch the captain at once."

"That won't be necessary!" Selena protested. "I'm sure I can manage." But Hardwick murmured that this problem was in the captain's domain and disappeared along the companionway.

When Kyle arrived some moments later, he entered the cabin with extreme wariness. But his unwanted wife wasn't attempting a seduction, he realized as she carefully shut the door. Rather, she was embarrassed. Her cheeks were flushed the same pale coral shade as her wrapper.

"Hardwick said you needed me," Kyle remarked, his tone guarded.

Selena couldn't meet his eyes. "Do you suppose," she asked in a faltering voice, "that you might help me tie the laces of my corset? I can't accomplish it alone ... and I had no one else to ask."

Kyle, who had spent far more time helping ladies out of their corsets than in, stared at Selena. Her appearance was a striking contrast between angelic and wanton. Her pale hair, still tousled from sleep, spilled around her face, while the virginal way she was clutching at the throat of her wrapper suggested she feared he might attempt her virtue again.

Kyle greatly preferred her hair down to the severe style she frequently wore, but the sight, combined with quick rise and fall of her breasts beneath the frail muslin, aroused carnal feelings in him that he had no business feeling if he meant to seek an annulment of their marriage. Yet he couldn't think of a way to refuse her simple request without seeming churlish, not without admitting how fragile his control was whenever he was near her. Especially, he thought with a mental groan, when she was half-naked. Gritting his teeth, he nodded brusquely.

Selena, who still wouldn't meet his eyes directly, modestly presented her back to him. She was, however, quite aware of Kyle's scrutiny. It had sent her pulse rate soaring and nearly shattered what little composure she had been able to summon. Now she would have to yield what little protection she had. But it had to be done. Her body tense, she took a deep breath and let the wrapper slip off her shoulders.

Kyle, too, sucked in his breath. The loose corset covered her long, slender back with lace and satin, but Selena's smooth shoulders were completely bare and so was a vast amount of ivory skin. He realized at once that breathing was a mistake, for her scent—the scent of warm violets—filled his nostrils and made him want to brush aside the fine, silver-blond tresses and lower his lips to the curve of her neck. It was all he could do to keep his hands from sliding around her to fondle the ripe breasts that were being pushed up so provocatively by the stiffened fabric of the unlaced corset.

With a silent oath, Kyle forced such provocative thoughts from his mind. Bracing himself, he focused on the crisscrossing laces of the garment.

Her body was tense; he could feel it as he began his task. But so was his. And his fingers, which had tied thousands of knots during his long career at sea and mended even more sails, were unsteady. They slipped as he pulled on a delicate ribbon.

"Infernal things," Kyle muttered, trying to get a better purchase.

His voice was huskier than he would have liked—and huskier than Selena would have liked. It quivered down her spine like a caress. Tensing even further, she focused her gaze on the cabin porthole and tried to ignore how Kyle's long fingers felt as they brushed against her back. Her skin had turned into a trembling jumble of nerve endings.

When Kyle mumbled another oath, she cast a worried glance at Horatio. Yet she was less concerned that he might add Kyle's comment to his vocabulary than grateful for the distraction the parrot presented.

The silent Horatio was no distraction at all to Kyle, though; his fumbling fingers refused to do his bidding.

"Damn and blast it!" he swore as he tried for the third time to loop the ribbon ends into a simple bow.

"Awk! Blast it! Blast it!"

Kyle's head came up abruptly at the squawk. "No one asked your opinion," he growled, giving the parrot a darkling look. He turned that look on Selena when she caught her lower lip between her teeth. "I'm sorry!" he ground out. "I forgot that blas . . . that bird was there."

He tackled the laces again, wishing he was anywhere but there in the cabin with an eager-eared parrot and Selena Markham . . . Ramsey. Especially Selena. One part of him wanted nothing to do with her. Another wanted to punish her for bringing him to such a pass. And yet another—by far the greatest part—wanted to take her in his arms and awaken all the exquisite, undiscovered passion in that lovely body.

One thing he was certain, though: he couldn't take being in such close quarters with Selena for the entire trip. It would be more than a week before they reached New Orleans, and he was already aching for her like a callow schoolboy. What was worse, his condition would be obvious to any of his men, if not the lady herself, which meant that when he left her cabin, he would have to find a remote hiding place where he could cool off.

No, definitely he wasn't fool enough to repeat this torture day after day.

"I suggest," Kyle said tersely as he at last succeeded in strapping her into the feminine garment, "that from now on you leave off wearing a corset until we leave the ship. I don't have time to play lady's maid."

"Corset, awk! Horatio loves a corset!"

"Oh, dear," Selena breathed. Biting her lip, she glanced up at Kyle.

The look she gave him wasn't so much accusing as humorous—whether due to his woeful attempts at acting as maid or the parrot's ability to latch on to improper words, Kyle was in no mood to find out. At the end of his patience and restraint, he strode to the door and flung it open.

"I also suggest," he warned with quiet vehemence, "that you find a way to teach that bird to button his lip. I've heard tell that parrots make excellent fish bait!"

Kyle had thought he had solved the problem of his lovely wife by refusing to go near her, but his plight somehow only became more unbearable as the northeast trade winds carried them swiftly toward their destination. A four-hundred-ton schooner was only so big, and since Selena, with his permission, chose to spend the greater part of each day on deck, Kyle couldn't help but see her frequently.

He watched her from a distance without meaning to, his gaze frequently settling on the awning that his impassioned and adoring crew had rigged to protect her delicate complexion from the Caribbean sun. The sight often set Kyle's teeth on edge. His officers were leaping over each other to be of service to the lady—fetching her parasol or a cool drink, or whiling the time away by entertaining her with amusing stories of the sea. Tiny, the ship's massive boatswain, trailed at Selena's skirts like an overgrown puppy.

His own jealousy an unrecognized emotion, Kyle dealt with the enforced confinement by driving himself relentlessly, as if he could burn some of the anger out of his system. And at night he lay awake in his oversize bunk, restless and dissatisfied as he listened to his first mate's slow breathing issuing from the hammock that had been strung across the cabin. He was acutely aware that only a bulwark separated him from the beautiful young woman to whom he had been forced to give his name.

Despite Kyle's assessment, Selena was timid at first about making friends with his crew, but their consideration and eagerness to please, aided by her own wistful longing for companionship, overcame her natural reserve. It was an uncommonly lonely feeling not to be needed or wanted. At home there had always been some person or problem requiring her attention, and her relationships with many of the islanders were characterized by mutual affection. But on board the *Tagus* she felt useless and unnecessary and bored by her idleness. Often her gaze would stray to wherever Kyle happened to be working.

She had hoped their relationship would change for the better as they got closer to New Orleans, but he had only become more untalkative and morose, snapping at his men and making them wonder what had become of their jovial, high-spirited captain.

Except for a few terse comments in passing—required by politeness—Kyle hadn't spoken to her again. She was afraid to approach him herself or to inquire what he intended to do with her when they reached New Orleans, whether she would be on her own or if she would accompany him to Natchez while he initiated proceedings to annul their marriage.

So she only observed him from a distance, her attention captured by the solid play of muscle in his powerful, sun-gilded torso. In the heat of the afternoon, he often went shirtless and sometimes barefoot, wearing only the cutoff canvas breeches that hugged his lean hips in a scandalous fashion.

How he contrived to look so unkempt and rough and attractive at the same time was a mystery to Selena. She was becoming used to seeing him in his half-savage state, though, and used to seeing him perform feats with his ship that amazed and alarmed her for their danger and daring.

The first time he had gone up into the rigging, she had caught her breath. Kyle had given the order to trim the sails to a steady five knots and then proceeded to swing himself nimbly up into the shrouds. As he climbed hand over hand toward what Hardwick told her was the main royal and lost himself in the forest of billowing white canvas, Selena raised trembling fingers to her mouth. It seemed impossible that he could hold on, for though the bow of the ship carved purposefully through each successive wave, the vessel still dipped rhythmically, making the upper masts a precarious, swaying perch.

Hardwick, who had followed her uneasy gaze, merely grinned. "Don't concern yourself, Mrs. Ramsey. The captain was born at sea, for all that he claims to have spent his first twelve years on land."

It seemed to be true, Selena reflected four afternoons later as she watched Kyle. A storm was swiftly approaching, and already the sky was thick and gray. The wind whipping through the rigging made the topsails flap so hard that hearing was difficult, yet Kyle looked as if he were enjoying every minute. He stood at the helm, his long legs braced against the roll and sway of the ship, his face turned to the wind.

Selena saw him shout at Hardwick over the snapping canvas and creaking tackle. And at the mate's reply, Kyle threw back his dark head and laughed.

This was how she would remember him after they parted, Selena thought: laughing in the teeth of the wind, loving the sea in all its capricious moods, embracing life with joy. Here, he was in his element. Indeed, he was *like* the rugged elements: Free and untamed, raw, powerful.

This was where he belonged—not tied to the land. He was not a farmer. No matter how large or luxurious or comfortable a plantation, he would never be so at home as he was at sea.

And when, caught up in the exuberance of the moment, Kyle met her gaze and grinned at her, Selena was sure of it. She understood the excitement he found in the sea then, and for a heartbeat or two, she even shared the feeling. But only for a moment. During the past few days, she had come close to overcoming her dread of ships, but now the swelling waves flecked with whitecaps made her recall how she had lost two of her dearest loved ones to a hostile sea, and the increasingly choppy motion of the schooner renewed her fears.

She didn't want to return to her cabin, where she would be trapped if the *Tagus* were to sink, but as the thunderheads grew more ominous, Kyle ordered her below. Selena went reluctantly, for it was cold and dark down there; no braziers could be lighted during a storm, or even lanterns, Hardwick had explained to her, for fear of fire.

"Awk! Come to tea!" Horatio said in greeting, fluttering his wings.

Selena didn't have the heart to reply. There would be no tea, since the galley stoves would be cold.

As the afternoon wore on and the rain began, the conditions became worse. Bright veins of lightning briefly illuminated the cabin and the foamy, rolling seas beyond the porthole, making the intervals of darkness seem even blacker. Even the parrot provided little solace, since he grew silent except for an occasional squawk.

Shivering as she crouched in her bunk, Selena could imagine what the men were going through on the decks of the pitching ship. The pelting rain had become a downpour, and several times she was almost thrown from the bunk as a tempestuous swell lifted the schooner only to drop her with a sickening lurch. Minutes later, as the ship rode the crest of a wave, a gust of wind caught her sails and hurled her forward into the trough. When they sank so far down that Selena thought they would never come up again, she knew she couldn't stay below any longer, not in the dark bowels of a ship that seemed like a coffin.

Her stomach knotted with fear, she staggered and groped her way along the companionway and up the stairs, gasping as she pried off the hatch cover. The rain was cold and slashing, and it drenched her before she could pull herself up on deck, making a shambles of her bonnet and plastering her pelisse against her body.

Yet she breathed easier in the open. Laboring to replace the cover, she struggled to her feet.

The clap of thunder, which sounded like a cannon's roar, startled Selena less than the fierce fingers that suddenly gripped her arm. She looked up to see Kyle glaring down at her in the dim light, water streaming down his face in rivulets.

"Blast it, woman, what are you doing up on deck! Don't you know you could be washed overboard?"

She could scarcely hear him for the wind howling through the shrouds, but as if to prove his point, a shower of spray burst above the gunwale as the ship pitched to starboard. She would have fallen except for the powerful arms that came around her and pulled her close.

"Please," Selena asked, clinging to his shoulders, "I'm afraid down there in the dark." It was scarcely lighter here, but even the wretched cold and wet was easier to face than confinement below.

A muscle flexed in Kyle's jaw, and he looked as if he would refuse, until Hardwick, who had materialized in the teeming rain, shouted, "Maybe you should let her stay, Captain!"

"Please," Selena repeated.

Kyle relented. "Get her an oilskin and a line," he commanded Hardwick, before leading Selena amidships and settling her in the protection of a bulkhead, where she would be partially sheltered from the rain. He had shed his own oilskin in order to move more freely, but there was a rope tied around his waist, she noticed.

When Hardwick returned, Kyle lashed the thick cord to an iron ring, then secured it around Selena's waist. "Don't move so much as a finger!" he ordered as he draped the oilskin over her. "Stay here, where I can find you."

She nodded, but Kyle was already moving away, bent low against the wind and rain. If she lived through the storm, she would thank him, Selena vowed.

During the next hour, she spied him occasionally as he battled the elements; he seemed to be anywhere he was needed and to be doing the work of three men. From where she sat, she could just make out the helm, and when he was at the wheel, Selena fixed her gaze on him, drawing courage from watching him. It came as a vague surprise to her to realize how much she trusted him to keep the ship safe. She wondered if he was enjoying the battle.

He was not, in fact, for while he might relish a challenge, he took no pleasure in risking the lives of his men. Already he was calling on every ounce of skill he possessed to hold a course in the rough sea, continuously judging the sail needed to keep the *Tagus* close to the wind. Too little would have her floundering; too much would make her top-heavy and put her in danger of capsizing or shattering a mast.

Then the storm struck in its full fury, and the high waves that were battering the wooden hull threatened to swamp the ship. Having exhausted his limited options, Kyle sent two of his best tars above to reef the main topsail. When that did too little to reduce the risk of capsizing, Kyle himself went up the mainmast, along with Tiny, armed with an ax to cut away the main topmast.

Below, Selena watched the proceedings, her stomach churning, her heart in her throat. Kyle had ordered her forward, out of the way of falling timber or canvas, but she could see the small figures of the men high above her head, illuminated by shards of lightning streaking across the charcoal sky. It seemed that at any moment the wind that shrieked through the rigging would pluck them from their precarious perches, sending them plunging to the deck or into the sea to be swept away by the foaming breakers. Either way would mean death.

When the topmast finally gave way, Kyle was nearly caught in the tangle of ropes as it fell. A cry broke from Selena's lips as he clutched at a backstay to save himself, but the sound was drowned by the creaking of the mizzen topsail as it was ripped by the wind. The ship lurched oddly, and a spar crashed to the deck, but Selena's gaze was riveted on Kyle.

When she finally determined that Kyle wasn't going to fall and tore her gaze away, she saw Hardwick making his way aft to aid the helmsman, who had been directly beneath the falling spar. The first mate had discarded his safety line, and just as he crossed the open forecastle deck, a huge wave broke over the port rail, spewing a foaming cascade of black water down upon the ship. Selena stared with horror as he lost his footing and went down.

As seawater ran off through the scuppers, another flash of lightning showed her that Hardwick hadn't yet been swept over the side. He was curled against the railing, holding his ribs as if in pain.

It wasn't a conscious decision that made Selena leave the shelter of the foremast to go to his aid. She only knew that Hardwick was in no condition to save himself, and she at least still wore a rope.

The mountainous wave caught her when she was still two yards from him, propelling her across the pitching deck and knocking the breath from her lungs. Blindly, desperately, she made a frantic lunge at the direction she had last seen Hardwick, and when her fingers closed over wool, she wrapped an arm around him and hung on for dear life.

The rope jerked taut, jarring her whole body, and something hard and blunt rammed into her ribs, making her gasp in pain. But though she was near to choking as another fierce wave washed over her, she never relinquished her hold.

It seemed an eternity before the waves diminished and she heard someone call her name. She was pinned beneath something wooden and heavy, she realized vaguely, coughing up some of the seawater she had swallowed. And it hurt to move.

"Selena! Dear God, Selena!"

She wondered why Kyle was shouting at her. She didn't know what she had done to make him angry again, but she wanted to tell him she was sorry; there was far too much anger between them. Racked by a spasm of coughing, though, she couldn't catch her breath to form an apology or even a protest when Hardwick was pried from her death grip.

"Selena, are you hurt? Damn it, look at me!"

She opened her eyes to find Kyle kneeling beside her, his large body shielding her from the worst of the blinding rain, his fingers cupping her face. "Are you in pain?"

Not much, she thought, taking stock, except for the ache in her lungs from inhaling so much water and a dull throbbing in her ribs. She had lost her sodden bonnet, too. Selena shook her head, and the next instant she found herself in Kyle's arms, crushed against his chest. She couldn't breathe with her face pressed against his woolen coat, but absurdly, she didn't mind being smothered. It was far nicer than drowning.

"God, you gave me a fright," he croaked when he finally loosened his hold, a ragged note of relief in his voice.

"Hardwick?" Selena managed to ask.

Kyle glanced beside him, where Tiny was bent over the unconscious first mate. Hardwick's chest was dark with blood.

"He's alive, at least," Kyle shouted in her ear. "We'll take him below, but he'll have to wait till I can see to him. The worst is over, but I'm needed here, and I can't spare any of my crew."

Selena hesitated, turning to look at Hardwick. Even if the storm was abating, it would be some time before anyone was able to doctor the injured man. And she had tended enough wounds—from machete slashes to coral reef abrasions—to have a basic grounding in medical skills.

"I'll go with him," Selena said, although she knew that with the onset of nightfall the cabins would be pitch-black.

The smile Kyle bent on her was one of gratitude and approval, and it warmed her to her very soul. She would have braved the sea itself, she thought, if she could have been the recipient of another smile like that.

She caught her breath as Kyle helped her rise, wincing at the pain in her bruised ribs, but shook her head when he asked sharply if she needed medical attention herself. She was glad for his support, however, when she had to negotiate the wildly rolling deck again.

Taking care of Hardwick wasn't as bad as she feared, however. When Tiny had carried the unconscious man to Selena's cabin, he risked lighting a lantern, securing it to keep it from falling and setting the ship on fire. In the glowing light, she could see at once that Hardwick's wound wasn't fatal. Unlike hers, his ribs were probably broken, but the blood was only caused by superficial lacerations from slivers of wood.

She had Tiny strip off the wounded man's wet clothes and tuck him beneath a warm blanket, and when she was alone with her patient, she braced herself against the violent rolling motion of the ship and went to work removing the splinters and binding his chest with clean strips of cloth. She was glad to be occupied, for it prevented her from dwelling on the fate of the schooner.

Hardwick woke shortly afterward, not remembering what had happened after the first wave had hit him, and anxious, despite his pain, to return to his duties on deck. Selena alternately soothed and threatened, until she finally convinced Hardwick that he was in no condition to do battle and wouldn't be until his ribs healed. Then she managed to find him a bottle of rum when he asked for it, hoping it would ease the worst of his pain. He was pleasantly happy by the time Tiny came to check on him and was sleeping peacefully when Kyle entered the cabin an hour later.

Kyle listened a moment to his mate's quiet breathing, then glanced down at Selena. She was sitting on the floor beside the bunk, her knees drawn up, her arms wrapped around herself.

"You saved his life," Kyle said quietly. His tone held an odd note—of gratitude and pride and perhaps awe—that made Selena lift her face to him. Kyle drew in a breath. With her hair half escaping from its pins, she looked pale and bedraggled, even pitiful, as she huddled there, shivering. Something in his chest tightened.

"Selena," he murmured, sinking down before her, "are you all right?" Placing a gentle finger under her chin, he compelled her to meet his gaze. "What is it?"

"Would you..." Selena whispered, her teeth chattering, "do you suppose... you could hold me?"

She was still clothed in the wet pelisse and gown, he noted, and was chilled to the bone. But it was more than the cold that was causing her body to shake so. She was only now realizing, he guessed, how close she had come to death.

Wordlessly he opened his arms, and when she came into them, he could feel her body trembling. "There's nothing to fear now," he said gently, stroking her damp hair. "The storm is over."

"It wasn't the storm. I thought... you would fall. I was afraid you would be killed."

Kyle pressed his cheek against her hair. He had been afraid, too. Afraid that he had lost her to the sea. "Don't ever," he breathed, remembering that devastating moment when he had looked down to see that mountainous wave sweep over her, remembering the helplessness he had felt, "disobey me again."

"No."

Kyle repressed a smile, suspecting her docility was a measure of her fatigue.

"Come now," he urged, "we've got to get you out of those wet clothes."

He scooped her up and rose with her in his arms. Catching up the lantern, he carried her to his own cabin, where he settled her in a chair. When he had hung the lantern on a peg, he knelt before her. As he began chafing her cold hands, he saw she was watching him quietly with wide, expressive eyes that looked trusting and vulnerable.

He hesitantly raised her skirts to pull off her shoes and stockings and found she wasn't wearing slippers. Realizing that she had lost them in her heroic rescue attempt, he felt his heart flood with tenderness. Untying her garters quickly, he stripped off Selena's stockings and rubbed her shapely calves to bring the blood back. Then he unfastened the buttons of her pelisse, pushing it off her shoulders, and stood up, bringing Selena with him.

His gaze was drawn to her face, to her cold, trembling lips. Slowly, he bent his head, covering her mouth with his, warming her. He heard her sigh, and when he felt her arms tentatively reach up to rest on his shoulders, he deepened his kiss, thrusting gently into her mouth, warming her tongue with his.

When she shivered, he didn't think it was from the cold, but he left off kissing her to peel the wet, icy garments from her body. The chemise was last, and when he drew it over her head and she stood before him, pale and naked, he could see that gooseflesh covered every inch of her skin and that the nipples of her high, firm breasts were chilled and rigid.

His gold-green eyes darkened at the sight. Selena tried to cover her breasts with her arms, but Kyle caught her hands and pulled them away, scrutinizing her carefully for injury. In the lantern light he could see the bruises that shadowed the right side of her rib cage, and his mouth hardened. Gently, he reached out to touch the faint discoloration. Then, without conscious intention, his hand moved up to the curving swell of her breast, to brush a puckered nipple with one finger.

Her reaction was immediate; she gasped softly. Kyle heard her faint inhalation with satisfaction. Purposefully, he splayed his fingers, covering her ripe flesh and molding it against his palm.

Selena closed her eyes and shuddered, and Kyle realized with a surge of desire that her demureness and reserve hid a woman of passion, of courage. He wanted her. Wanted to fill his mouth with the taste of her breasts, to span that impossibly narrow waist with his hands and draw those inviting hips beneath him, to have those long, lithe legs wrapped around him.

The fierceness of his wanting startled him.

"You'd better get into bed," he forced himself to say in a voice suddenly grown deep and husky. Alone, now, please, he pleaded silently.

"Please," Selena breathed. She moved closer, seeking the haven of his arms and solace from the turmoil of her emotions. Kyle represented safety, warmth, security. His ruggedness made her feel so feminine, his concern so cherished and protected.

"Selena—" the word was a rasp "—I can't take much more of this. Any minute now I'm likely to forget I shouldn't be here, alone with you . . . like this."

"Please . . . don't go."

His arms went around her then, his hands tracing her curves without volition. "You should get some sleep." The words were jerky, gritted out between his teeth as he felt her flesh warming beneath his callused palms.

She tilted her head back to look up at him. "Where will you sleep?"

With you, his body responded. He tried to remind himself of his son, of how much depended on the successful annulment of this marriage, but her sensuous lower lip beckoned for his kiss, and he knew he was losing the battle.

He threw back his head in anguish, shutting his eyes tightly, but all he could think about was burying himself again in her silky sweetness. All he could see was the quiver of her tantalizing mouth urging him to kiss her into dazed insensibility.

Slowly, Kyle opened his eyes again, aware that the days of being around her, of wanting her, of self-denial and frustration had finally driven him beyond restraint.

"I know perfectly well," he said hoarsely, with his last vestiges of reason, "that this is insane." But his words were a mere whisper and were lost as he lowered his mouth.

Her kiss was tentative at first, as if she'd had time to reconsider what she was doing, but as his heat flowed into her, she seemed to relax a little. His tongue plunged into her mouth, seeking hers in a series of darting forays. He was determined to make her respond more fervently, to turn her shivers into shudders of pleasure. When finally her arms came up to encircle his neck, he urged her backward toward the large bunk.

He lowered her to the edge of the mattress, but instead of joining her, he knelt before her, placing his hands on either side of her waist. Selena tensed, watching him. She drew a quick breath as his hands slid upward to cup her breasts.

Kyle heard the soft sound and his eyes flared with golden flames. Slowly, he leaned forward to press his lips against her rib cage, his arousing fingers caressing her nipples. If he could manage it, he promised silently, she would experience the full depth of pleasure between a man and a woman before the night was over.

With exquisite tenderness, he kissed her bruises, letting his tongue flick out to touch her soft skin. She tasted faintly of brine and her own sweet perfume, and he was suddenly hungry for an even more intimate taste of her. With a fierce effort at control, he drew away.

"Let me shed my clothes," he said hoarsely.

Pressing her back to lie full length on the mattress, he retreated a step to strip off his garments. Selena shivered as the delightful sensations were suddenly cut off. Feeling bereft, she turned her head on the pillow, watching shyly as Kyle undressed. When he was naked, she caught her breath at the marvelous perfection of the powerful length displayed before her eyes.

He was so different from her—earthy and vital and strong, all rippling sinews and bronzed skin...except where his breeches had covered his lean hips and muscular thighs. There he was pale and dark and...splendidly virile.

Kyle saw where Selena's mesmerized gaze had settled, and the touch of it sent raw need quaking through his body. Locking his gaze to hers, he felt himself tremble in anticipation. He was like a callow youth with his first woman, Kyle thought, watching her. His aching arousal was pulsing and erect, his control tenuous and uncertain. He came to her then, wondering as he stretched out beside her if he would have the patience to let her reach fulfillment before him. She was so very beautiful, her skin like gleaming ivory....

Gently his lips touched Selena's hair, while his fingers found the pins in her tresses and let them fall to the floor. He brushed back the damp tangled curtain from her face as his lips moved to her throat. Then slowly he drew her against his taught, tightly muscled length.

The size and heat of him still had the power to shock her, yet she pressed closer, warming her shivering body against the satin of his bare skin. His touch was incredibly sensual, and as he filled his hands with her breasts, a quiver built deep in her stomach. Closing her eyes, she let her head fall back.

"Kyle, please...." she said breathlessly as he continued to stroke her.

"What is it, Moonwitch? What do you want?"

Selena shook her head in frustration. She didn't know what she wanted, only that she was aching with unfilled need.

Kyle knew the answer very well. The quick rise and fall of her breasts, her shallow breathing, the fast beating of her heart all told him. He bent his head.

"Open your mouth to me, love," he whispered, and when she obeyed, he filled her mouth with his caressing tongue.

Selena sighed, her trembling hands reaching up to hold him. Under her clutching fingertips, the muscles of his bare shoulders coiled and quivered reflexively. The feel of his satiny skin, the masculine sea-fresh scent of him was intoxicating. It filled her with a heated glory of wanting, with desire.

Finally, however, Kyle broke off the kiss, letting his lips course over her face, around her ear, into the softness of her throat beneath the sensitive curve of her jaw.

Selena stirred restlessly beneath his tender assault. The heat radiating from his body was drugging her senses. The way his hands molded to the roundness of her breasts was making her feverish. And then his lips joined his hands, capturing the aroused peaks. Over and over his tongue flicked and circled the aching flesh. His devouring mouth dragged across her breasts, pulling at her, nipping softly, tasting her.

Selena moaned and strained toward his touch. Her response aroused Kyle even further, and he fought for control, his corded muscles contracting into hard knots. He was determined to make this good for her, not to satisfy himself until he knew she was satisfied, as well.

He moved his hand slowly up her shivering inner thigh and softly slipped in between. His slow stroking made her gasp. He pressed against the moist cleft, withdrew slightly and pressed again. To his delight and amazement, Selena's hips slowly began to writhe.

Her trembling innocence was incredibly erotic; he longed to bring her to ecstasy. Kyle shifted his weight so that he was kneeling between her thighs, then lowered his head to scatter hot, openmouthed kisses over the taut skin of her belly. In a moment he gently eased her legs apart as his lips moved lower to the triangle of golden down at the juncture of her thighs.

She gasped with shock and grasped at his hair. "No...Kyle.... What are you doing!"

Briefly, he looked up into her startled eyes. "Be still," he ordered huskily, pressing her back upon the mattress.

Shocked to her ladylike core, Selena had no idea how to respond to his scandalous attentions. She lay there, open to him, taut and trembling, not knowing even where to put her hands as his mouth descended again to the silky nest between her thighs. But when he began kissing her again, soft, probing, erotic kisses, she instinctively reached down to curl her fingers in Kyle's hair. He was stirring such sensations in her—desire and heat and staggering pleasure. And panic. Her body gave a sudden leap as his tongue found the center of her passion.

She tried to draw away from him, but Kyle moved his hands beneath her, holding her silken bottom in a relentless grasp as he lifted her hips to make her more accommodating.

"I told you to be still." His voice was deep and soft and utterly determined.

Selena gasped again as he renewed his wicked assault, but she could only let her head fall back in helpless surrender as Kyle stroked her with his tongue, penetrating her warmth. He was arousing a pulsing, heated ache deep within her, one that frightened her with its newness.

How could she allow him to do this to her? Selena wondered dazedly. Yet he was her husband. Her thoughts fled as the throbbing intensified. All she could do was feel. She clutched at Kyle, her fingers tightening reflexively in his thick hair, which was still damp with rain, hardly aware that the hushed moans she heard were coming from her own throat. Her hips writhed as she sought to escape the hot brand of his tongue. Her body pulsed with fire.

"Don't hold back, Moonwitch," Kyle's stirring breath whispered against her. "Let it come."

Frantically, she flung her head from side to side, fighting the blinding tension that was building inside her. And then her entire body went rigid as Kyle at last sparked a slow, devastating explosion within her. Wave after wave of heat shuddered through her, leaving her trembling and gasping for breath.

It was a long moment before the wild beating of her heart slowed and her reeling senses returned to something resembling normal, and another long moment while Selena lay there, wondering what had happened to her. Her skin was flushed and hot now, when it had been chilled only a moment before.

"That's better," Kyle said softly, with approval.

Through a haze of desire, she heard his murmured words. Slowly, she opened her eyes to find Kyle brazenly watching her. His greedy lips were wet, his own gaze smoldering with golden fire. Suddenly shy and acutely embarrassed, Selena averted her gaze.

"No, don't look away. We've only begun." The words were a husky resonance as he eased himself up and covered her with his powerful, muscular body.

He settled himself gently between her thighs, his penetration long and slow, carefully allowing her body to accept his full, hard length, all the while watching her flushed face, the way her breath quickened and her dazed eyes widened with startled desire. He had awakened this prim and proper lady into a tantalizing creature who breathed passion and sensuality, and he wanted to savor every moment of it.

And he did. He held himself utterly still inside her silken warmth, clamping down on his own frenzied need, moving only the fingers of one hand as he teased her erect nipples, letting the heat build again until her soft whimpers and arching body told him she was hot and throbbing for him.

And then he slowly began to move his tautly muscled buttocks, burying himself deeper and deeper, keeping a fierce rein on his own passion until finally Selena's luscious mouth parted in ecstasy and her throaty cry echoed in the cabin.

Then he swelled upward again, letting his control shatter and his own reservations shatter with it as he claimed her fully and filled her with the urgent desire he'd been keeping so tightly in check since his first possession of her that moonlit night on the beach. It was only when his shuddering release was over and his breath was coming in ragged gasps that he even remembered why he had harbored any reservations at all. And by then, he couldn't find the energy for regret. His rock-hard body glistening with sweat, Kyle collapsed on her, barely remembering to protect her from his weight with his arms as he lay against her, spent, sated.

Later, when he could think again, he realized how still Selena had grown. And when he forced his thoughts to focus, he knew her reserve had returned in full measure. Amazing, Kyle reflected, especially when she was still lying beneath him, joined to him in the most intimate way imaginable. Then he remembered his vow to end their marriage. She would be shocked and embarrassed, of course, thinking she had done something shameful with him.

Amazing, Kyle thought again, that he should want to reassure her.

He raised his head slowly, searching her face and seeing the crimson blush on her cheeks. "I guess this means," he said quietly, his gaze filled with a rugged tenderness, "there won't be an annulment, after all."

Chapter Eight

Selena woke late the next morning to the sound of the bosun's shrill whistle piping out orders to the schooner's crew. The sea was now relatively calm. The violent rolling of the ship had ceased, and bright sunlight streamed in the porthole window.

Selena blinked at first to see the strange walnut-paneled cabin, then blushed hotly to remember precisely what had occurred there during the long night. But she was unable to summon an appropriate sense of shock when she realized that she was naked beneath the blankets.

Missing the warmth of Kyle's large body, she raised herself up on one elbow—gingerly, so as not to aggravate the stiffness of her own body and the ache in her bruised ribs. She was alone in the large bunk, which surprised her. She had expected to find Kyle collapsed in exhaustion, if not because of his superhuman efforts during the storm, then because of his similar efforts during their numerous and fierce bouts of lovemaking. There wasn't an inch of her that he hadn't touched or tasted, it seemed. Her breasts were swollen and sensitive, while the hollow between her thighs was tender from his frequent ministrations.

Selena was further surprised when she glanced around the cabin. The wet clothing that had been strewn haphazardly over the floor and furniture now hung neatly on pegs, and her blue sprigged muslin gown had been laid over a chair before the massive desk. She had no doubt, either, that the water pitcher would be filled with fresh water for washing.

Kyle's thoughtfulness brought a soft smile to her lips. At least she hoped it had been Kyle who had straightened the cabin. She was still too new at this business of being a wife to be comfortable with the intimacies they had shared or the thought that one of his crew would guess from the condition of the cabin what had occurred between them.

Wife. The word had a pleasant ring to it...a wonderful ring.

A glow warmed her as she remembered his decision not to seek an annulment. It was what she had hoped for, the chance to prove to Kyle that he hadn't made a dreadful mistake in marrying her. Perhaps their relationship would be different, now that he had accepted their marriage. Perhaps he would come to love her now, the way she loved—

Drawing a sudden breath, Selena slowly sank back onto the mattress. *She was falling in love with Kyle.* Or had fallen. That alone explained this delightful warm glow, this excited quivery feeling. Now she knew why she had been so terrified for him during the storm, why she felt such a fierce yearning to be with him now.

Somewhat shocked by the thought, she stared up at the ceiling. It didn't seem possible. They had been married scarcely a week, and most of that time Kyle had existed in a state of smoldering anger over being forced to wed her. Yet she had been attracted to him from the first. To his strength, his lust for living, his kindness and compassion . . . his passion.

She was still considering this revelation and reflecting on the tenderness of Kyle's lovemaking when she heard the bosun's whistle again. Eager, yet shy of seeing her husband once more, Selena slid out of bed and began to dress.

Kyle wasn't on deck, she discovered when she went above. In the aftermath of the storm, the crew was hard at work repairing the damages to the ship—mending sails, overhauling the rigging, renewing ratlines and clearing the deck of debris. But to a man, they stopped work as Selena passed, tugging caps and forelocks in deference, greeting her with welcome grins.

Their reception surprised and somewhat embarrassed her. Kyle's crew had always been extremely polite and attentive toward her, but there was a new respect in their eyes this morning that indicated word had gotten around about her action during the storm; those who hadn't seen had heard of her daring rescue of the *Tagus*'s first mate. Indeed, Tiny was particularly effusive. For once he had more than a few words to say—all in praise of her—as he expressed gratitude on behalf of the crew for saving Mr. Hardwick's life.

Uncomfortable at being lauded for an action she felt that anyone under similar circumstances would have done, Selena asked where she could find the captain. As soon as Tiny informed her that Captain Ramsey was visiting the first mate, she fled below.

She had raised her hand to knock on Hardwick's cabin door when she heard Kyle's voice through the paneling. It sounded so close that he must have been standing directly on the other side.

"Deuce take it," Kyle was saying, "ten months ago I thought I would live out my days at sea, free to sail wherever I pleased. Then I was saddled with a plantation I never asked for and a wife I never wanted, either."

Selena froze, her heartbeat suddenly too rapid and loud in her ears. It wasn't admirable, eavesdropping on anyone's conversation, but she couldn't force herself to move. She missed Hardwick's reply but had no trouble hearing Kyle.

"Sure, I meant this voyage to be a final spree before I took up my new responsibilities. Last spree, hah! More like last rites. My wedding felt like a funeral, and this bucket nearly became my coffin. You know something? I *wanted* to face that storm. We could have skirted the worst of it, but instead I endangered my ship and my crew."

Hardwick murmured something unintelligible, while Selena took a stumbling step backward, tears welling in her eyes, a tight ache in her throat. She knew Kyle hadn't wanted her, of course, but she had hoped—with all her heart—that after last night they could start anew. It appeared, however, that the passionate night they had shared had done nothing to change their relationship. That devastating night had meant nothing to Kyle.

Her breath caught on a sob. She had been foolish to confuse physical desire with love. Just because a man made love to a woman with such fierce intensity didn't mean his heart was engaged.

A sick yearning in her own heart, she turned away, scarcely hearing as Kyle spoke again. "It would have been entirely my fault if the *Tagus* had gone down. I could have killed us all...."

Blindly, Selena made her way up the companionway stairs, needing to get away, to be alone with her wretched thoughts. And not in Kyle's cabin, where he had aroused her body with such skillful tenderness and broken down every barrier of her reserve, where she would be alone with him if he should find her. She couldn't face it or him. Not until she managed to collect herself and her battered emotions. Not until she had considered what to do.

Below, in the mate's cabin, Kyle was still speaking. "And then that delicate slip of a lady whom I hadn't wanted to marry did something only one man in a hundred would do—risked her life for someone she hardly knew. Do you know, she made me feel *ashamed*? While I was bemoaning my fate, she was off saving the lives of my men. God, I thought my heart had failed when I saw Selena throw herself in front of that wave. If that line had broken . . ."

"We both would have been swept into the sea," Hardwick finished with a grimace, "instead of being bashed by a barrel and speared in the ribs by a foremast yard. I'm supremely grateful to Mrs. Ramsey, I assure you, Captain. Where is she now? Do you suppose you could ask her to call on me, so I can properly thank her?"

"When she awakens," Kyle answered, his tone softening unmistakably. "She was still sleeping when I left her."

Hardwick raised an eyebrow. "I'm sorry my injury caused you such an inconvenience, sir. Maybe you want me to switch cabins with Mrs. Ramsey?"

"Stubble it, mate. You've overstepped the bounds. The arrangement is just fine as it is. Besides, it would cause you serious harm to be moved, no doubt."

"No doubt," Hardwick said with a grin, sitting up with little difficulty to show how unfounded Kyle's theory was. "The men will be relieved. They've been wondering why you've been neglecting your beautiful wife."

A private smile curved Kyle's lips. "I won't be neglecting her in future."

"Good. Maybe you'll quit snapping our heads off, too."

"Have I been that bad?"

Hardwick laughed. "I'll just say that if we hadn't known we'd be rid of you when we reached New Orleans, you might have had a mutiny on your hands. Come to think of it," he added when Horatio chose that moment to squawk, "that parrot's company has been a decided improvement over yours, despite his limited vocabulary. Except for a few coarse words, all he can say is 'Will you dance?' and 'Come to tea.'"

Kyle sent the parrot an amused glance, not bothering to mention how Horatio had learned his new words. "He does seem to be something of a society bird. I'll wager he was raised in a drawing room.''

"I guess you'll soon be getting reacquainted with drawing rooms yourself.''

"Don't remind me," Kyle said with a mock grimace.

"Well, I'll do my best with the *Tagus*, sir.''

"I know. That's why I'm leaving you in command.''

They spoke a while longer about their plans for the schooner, but not even the thought of his impending retirement from the sea could spoil Kyle's sunny mood this morning. It was as if his foul humor of the past week had been washed away by the storm. And somehow, he found himself actually looking forward to his future for the first time since the death of his parents.

It might, Kyle reflected as he made his way back to his own cabin, have something to do with the slender, pale-haired beauty in his bed. Selena had bewitched him with her startling metamorphosis from well-bred gentlewoman to passionate lover. Their lovemaking had been unique in his experience, satisfying him totally yet leaving him longing for more.

He was disappointed not to find Selena where he had left her, for he had entertained some vividly erotic thoughts of joining her in the bunk and arousing her warm, sleepy body from slumber. But since the clothes he had fetched her were missing, Kyle concluded she had gone up on deck.

She wasn't at her usual place under the awning, however, and he had to search the length of the ship till he finally found her at the stern, watching the blue waves of the gulf. She looked so fresh and lovely, it almost took his breath away—the sprigged muslin molding her body in the breeze, the morning sunlight shining in her hair. Kyle purposely had neglected to provide her a bonnet, preferring to see her corn-silk tresses loose or at most, tied with a ribbon. But while her head was bare, she must have found the pins he had tossed haphazardly across the cabin the previous evening, for her hair was bound in a demure knot at her nape.

That tender spot at the curve of her neck looked so appealing that when he came up behind her, Kyle gave in to the urge to taste it. Lightly grasping Selena's arms, he planted a swift butterfly kiss on her silken skin.

When she gave a start and whirled to face him, he grinned with quick, boyish warmth. "So here's where you've been hiding yourself. I didn't expect to find you up this early, after the night you had."

He thought she had simply been startled by his intimate gesture, but Selena visibly stiffened at his words. She didn't seem at all pleased to see him. In fact, she almost looked as if she had been crying, since her eyes were faintly rimmed with red. Yet that could have been caused by the wind. When she quickly averted her gaze, though, his grin faded.

Selena had indeed been startled by his brief caress. Lost in thought, she hadn't heard his approach. She cast a nervous glance around her to be sure no one else had seen his kiss, then turned away from Kyle, biting her lip to keep it from trembling.

The words she had so unfortunately overheard were still spinning in her mind. Kyle didn't want a partner and helpmate. He wanted only what any women could give him—the means to slake his physical lust. And he had done just that the previous night. Her mind burned with the memory of the wild abandon with which she had given herself to him. She wouldn't humiliate herself further by letting him know how much she craved his kisses, his touch.

"I was not *hiding*," Selena replied stiffly, forcing the words past the tightness in her throat. "I believe I've mentioned before that I prefer being on deck to being confined below."

Her tone, her very posture, was cool and aloof. Kyle peered down at her, trying to read her expression. He wasn't sure what he had expected. An acknowledgment of what had passed between them, he supposed.

"You've mentioned it," Kyle responded wryly. "And Hardwick for one is grateful for your preferences. He asked that you call on him, incidentally. He wants to thank you for saving his life."

Selena caught the wry note in his voice and couldn't help comparing it to the tender way Kyle had spoken about her bravery the night before. Had that been a mere pretense? It wasn't that she required him to sing her praises, but she had developed a longing for his good opinion. It hurt dreadfully to think she hadn't truly won it.

Forcibly, she swallowed the lump in her throat. "Mr. Hardwick didn't seem to be seriously injured."

"No, he'll be good as new in a few weeks."

"Then I trust he won't object if I trade cabins with him again."

"Trade cabins?" Sounding mildly startled, Kyle turned her to face him, his brows furrowing as he scrutinized her. "Selena...are you all right? You didn't suffer any injuries other than the bruises I saw, did you?"

She flushed at the reminder that he had seen her entirely naked and at the memory of how he had gently kissed the discolored flesh covering her ribs. At the time, he had seemed to worship her bruises with his lips, as if they were symbols of her victory over the sea. Obviously she had been mistaken.

"I'm fine. I simply think it best if I return to my cabin. I... Horatio will be growing lonesome for my company."

"Horatio...?" he began, but she had already turned and was quickly walking away.

Kyle watched her, his mouth half-open, until she had disappeared through the main hatch. Then he glanced up at the sky. The sun was still shining brightly, he noted with surprise.

How was that possible when the sunlight had suddenly gone out of his day?

He made one more attempt to approach her, that night at supper. As always, she had eaten with his officers, but he thought she seemed even more reserved than usual, and though she didn't ignore him precisely, she never addressed him directly. And even her occasional comments to her other tablemates were cool and scrupulously polite.

When, at the conclusion of the meal, Kyle realized she meant to return to her cabin rather than stroll on deck as she regularly did, he followed Selena to the door and caught her arm as she prepared to leave. He released it immediately when she flinched at his touch, gazing down at her in puzzlement and concern. "Selena, would you mind telling me what is going on? Is there some problem I don't know about?"

Selena managed to return her husband's gaze briefly. For once she was grateful to Edith, for teaching her how to deal with rejection. She was able to answer Kyle's question with scarcely a pause. "Problem? I don't know what you mean."

"The way you're behaving...so stiff and formal. I thought after last night—"

"Am I being stiff? I didn't realize it."

If she sounded cool, perhaps even haughty, then she was glad. Glad that Kyle couldn't see what an effort it was to be so near to him.

He searched her face, hesitating a long moment before he replied. "Would you like to stroll on deck, then? I could accompany you, since Hardwick is unavailable."

"Thank you, but I fear I'm quite weary after being kept up so much of last night. I think I shall retire."

"Well, if there's nothing you need—"

"Your crew is seeing to my needs quite well. Thank you, Kyle...and good night."

She fled, thinking that she'd managed to cover her hurt well—until she reached her cabin and couldn't stop her tears.

Three afternoons later the *Tagus* docked at New Orleans. Selena stood at the rail, eyeing the colorful sights with the first interest she had felt in days. New Orleans differed in many respects from the seaports to which she was accustomed. The Mississippi was far wider than any river she had imagined, for one thing, and far muddier, as well. There were no docks, either, merely a high, earthen levee—to keep the city safe from floods, Hardwick had informed her. The natural wharf was bustling with commerce—piled with crates and barrels and bales and hogsheads and lined with drays and carriages.

The hundreds of boats that lay alongside the miles of levee were also strange compared to the seafaring merchant ships and naval vessels she was used to seeing in English Harbor. These wooden vessels were long and squat, without sails—flatboats and bateaux, Hardwick called them. Or keelboats, if they had a sail. According to him, these flat-bottomed boats floated downriver laden with cotton, sugar, tobacco, leather and furs for exporting to Europe. The ones that were long and narrow like bananas were pirogues, which Hardwick said were used in navigating the bayous.

"'Bayous'?" Selena asked, unfamiliar with the word.

"It's like a swamp that's been overrun by a river," Hardwick explained. "This area is full of them. And until recently the bayous provided a haven for pirates."

"Pirates?"

Hardwick grinned at Selena's tone. "All the notorious ones are gone now, though a few smugglers are still actively engaged in illegal trading."

Relieved, Selena gestured upriver at a big, ungainly boat that sported two tall chimneys and an odd lump at the stern. "What is that one called? I've never seen anything like it."

"That's a steamboat, ma'am. It's powered by steam instead of wind. We'll be seeing more and more of them on the river, I'll wager. Steamboats will never take the place of a good sailing ship, of course, but here on Western waters, they're catching on. They have a great advantage over flatboats, since they're so much faster and they can go upstream as well as downstream. That one's the *Washington*, if I'm not mistaken. She's about the biggest there is. You may even get a chance to travel on her if she's headed for Natchez. Now if you'll excuse me, Mrs. Ramsey," he said as the schooner's gangway was run out, "I'd better be seeing to my duties. The captain will have my head, else."

At the mention of the captain, Selena glanced toward the forecastle, where Kyle was deep in conversation with his cabin boy. She was always aware of where he was on the ship, even though they had scarcely spoken since she'd returned to her own cabin.

Despite the warmth of the day, he wore a pristine white cravat and had donned, over a waistcoat of embroidered silk, a superbly tailored bottle-green coat that molded his powerful shoulders to perfection. When he lifted his high-crowned beaver hat to his head, he looked every inch the gentleman, ruggedly handsome and refined. A man any woman would be proud to call her husband. Or lover.

Selena clenched her gloved hands, fighting the memory that thought aroused. She didn't like to remember their night of lovemaking. Sometimes she forgot for hours at a time the incredibly wanton things they'd done, the pleasures they'd shared. And then an accidental touch or the sound of Kyle's voice would send them rushing back again. Yet he seemed to have dismissed that devastating night so easily—

Just then Kyle shifted his gaze momentarily and met her eyes across the stretch of polished deck, and Selena blushed to have been caught watching him. Her blush deepened when his scrutiny dropped to her breasts. She felt half-naked without the restraints of a corset but had left off wearing it ever since Kyle had refused to help her with her laces. Worse, though, was the way that her nipples hardened instantly whenever Kyle merely looked at her—as he was doing now, his hazel gaze lingering on the spencer jacket that covered her rose-colored gown. She could almost feel the quick strokes of his tongue pleasurably tormenting the bare crests, the gentle tugging of his lips arousing her desire.

Hot-cheeked, Selena turned away and focused her gaze on the bustling levee, trying to remember that she had been comparing the wharves of New Orleans to those of Antigua. At least the sight of stevedores and slaves loading and unloading goods and cargo was familiar to her.

She managed to distract her thoughts momentarily, yet one corner of her mind was still attuned to Kyle. She was relieved to see him shortly leave the ship. He was followed by the cabin boy, and while the lad went off in one direction, Kyle strode off toward the steamship Selena had noticed earlier. To make arrangements for accommodations, she presumed, wondering if those accommodations included her.

It was nearly half an hour later when her attention was directed beyond the levee to the arrival of an elegant chaise drawn by a pair of high-stepping chestnuts. The lone occupant of the carriage was a woman, and even from the distance, Selena could tell she was beautiful. Her figure was voluptuous yet graceful, draped becomingly in an expensive high-necked gown of jonquil-colored silk, while her lustrous Titian hair was secured in a sedate chignon beneath a tall bonnet with a sweeping plume.

"Oh, Lord," said Hardwick softly from close behind her. Selena turned to see him standing frozen as the beautiful redhaired woman secured the reins and stepped down from the carriage. Then, as if recovering from a shock, he leaped into action. Despite the stiffness warranted by his bandaged ribs, he hastened down the gangplank to greet her.

He intercepted her at the foot of the gangway, successfully preventing her from boarding the ship.

The beauty bestowed a charming smile on him and offered her gloved hand for him to kiss. "How good to see you, M'sieur Hardwick," she proclaimed in a lilting tone that was obviously French, belying Selena's initial hope that she was one of Kyle's sisters. "How fortunate that my carriage was passing just at this moment, *n'est-ce pas?* I shall be able to greet Kyle properly."

"He isn't here, Mademoiselle Rouvier," Hardwick said quickly—or at least that was what Selena thought he said. He had lowered his voice so that she could barely make out his words above the normal din of the levee.

The French lady's accented voice carried easily, however, striking a discordant note in Selena's ears, despite its musical quality.

"But of course! M'sieur Kyle does not care to have women on his ship, is that not so? I am an imbecile, me, to have forgotten. *D'accord*, perhaps you will tell him to pay me a call as soon as he is able. I shall wait anxiously, please tell him."

Hardwick glanced uncomfortably over his shoulder, up at the rail, where Selena stood. The red-haired beauty started to follow his gaze, but then she spotted Kyle's tall figure moving through the crowd toward them. With a glad little cry, she launched herself at him, flinging her arms around his neck and pressing her mouth ardently against his.

One of Kyle's sisters, indeed, Selena thought with a fierce stab of jealousy. There was nothing sisterly about the embrace the woman was giving him. Even the most naive of wives would have realized the beautiful redhead was his mistress.

"Veronique!" Kyle said firmly, grasping her affectionate arms and holding them away, at the same time casting an uneasy glance up at his ship. When he caught sight of Selena, he disengaged himself entirely from Veronique's embrace and, taking her by the arm, directed her away from the levee. "Where is your carriage?" Selena heard him say before his words were lost in the general chorus of activity.

Selena followed their progress, unable to tear her eyes away. And although she couldn't hear him, she could tell from the look on Veronique's face that Kyle was telling her about his marriage.

Selena hardly noticed when Hardwick addressed her.

"Perhaps you should return to your cabin, Mrs. Ramsey," he urged, looking highly embarrassed. "I'm sure you'll want to make certain all your belongings are packed."

"I've already done so." She was proud that her voice scarcely trembled.

"Then perhaps you could show one of the men which trunks you want delivered to your hotel."

She had already done that, as well, but to refuse his suggestion of a graceful exit would be to acknowledge the incident she had just witnessed—which a well-bred woman would never do. She would also be denying Hardwick's kindness in trying to spare her humiliation. That he hadn't succeeded wasn't his fault, Selena reflected as she allowed herself to be led away.

Still, she had difficulty regaining her composure, even in the privacy of her cabin. Her cheeks felt hot and flushed, and the ache in her breast wouldn't go away, especially when she remembered Veronique's fervent embrace. She could never behave so boldly with Kyle, Selena thought, forgetting how she had propositioned him that night on the beach. And the redhead's lush figure... Her own figure was willowy at best—no doubt too meager for a man of Kyle's lusty appetites.

Selena's conjecture, however, was very much mistaken; Kyle found her slender body more than capable of arousing him. The sudden tautness of his own body whenever he came near her proclaimed louder than words how much he was attracted to Selena, meager figure or not, and how difficult he was finding it to control his physical reactions to her.

Kyle had been puzzled and frankly astonished that after all the exquisite passion she had shown him, Selena had suddenly turned so cold. Her response had disturbed him, as had the way she'd flinched at his touch.

He wasn't quite sure what had happened, but he didn't like to consider the possibilities. That night Selena had become his wife in more than name only, and the thought that she might have used her body to secure her position and the use of his name was acutely distasteful to him. His instincts told him he was wrong. Another kind of woman might have been so calculating, but while Selena might be cold, he didn't think she was cold-blooded. Yet he couldn't dismiss the thought entirely. The moment he had agreed to accept Selena as his wife, she had retreated into her chilly shell of reserve, making it quite clear she wouldn't accept his attentions.

Perhaps she truly was too prim and cold natured to accept her own passion. But whatever her reasons, it was clear she didn't want him for her husband—at least not physically.

He wasn't going to try to press the issue, though, Kyle decided, at least not yet. He needed time to come to terms with the situation himself. And he needed to determine what he was going to do about his son. He couldn't seek an annulment now, and that left him limited alternatives.

And unlimited frustration.

He was disgusted that their passionate night together had left him throbbing for Selena like a youth hungering for his first woman. Yet there was little he could do to control either the lust licking at his veins or the disquietingly tender feelings that were prodding at his heart. He took refuge in silence, keeping his highly aroused body rigid and tightly restrained whenever it wasn't possible to avoid her.

It was no different when Hardwick shortly escorted Selena to the hired carriage that would transport the Ramseys to their hotel; Kyle sat stiffly in the driver's seat, his muscles taut, his expression wary as he waited for her reaction to what had happened back there on the docks. Selena wouldn't look at him, Kyle noted with chagrin, though as she took her place beside him, he glimpsed that wounded look in her eyes that he had learned to dread.

But if he expected her to take him to task, he was far off, he realized. Selena wasn't playing the betrayed wife. Except for the fact that she placed Horatio's cage between them, she seemed to be ignoring the incident altogether, pretending that it hadn't happened, as she observed the passing scenery of New Orleans.

Somehow her indifference stung him more than anger would have. And it frustrated him that as a gentleman, he couldn't bring up the subject. He wished she would say something so he could at least defend himself.

They were both silent as they drove along the narrow streets of New Orleans, Kyle focusing his attention on the horses, Selena focusing hers on the architecture. The two-story houses stood flush with wooden sidewalks that lined the unpaved streets. Nearly all were built of stuccoed brick and decorated with lacy ironwork, while many possessed galleries.

Kyle finally spoke as they drew up before a large, three-story building on Chartres Street. "Here we are," he said needlessly, "the Hotel des Etrangers. They accept Americans here. When I'm in town I usually stay at a public house that caters to Creoles—a business acquaintance of mine sponsors my visits. But with you along, I thought this would be better."

"It is very handsome."

"Look, Selena, about what happened back there . . ."

When he faltered, Selena looked down at her gloved hands. "She is your mistress, isn't she?"

It was said in a low, calm voice that made the directness of her conjecture all the more startling. Kyle ran a finger along the edge of his cravat, for the cloth suddenly felt too tight. His relationship with Veronique had never been as permanent as that, though he had paid well for the courtesan's favors. "The sea has always been my mistress," he muttered, providing what he thought was a diplomatic answer.

"She is very beautiful," Selena observed, not allowing him to escape the issue so easily.

"Not more beautiful than you."

He meant it, but his hasty gallantry was wasted, for Selena slanted a glance at him that said she clearly didn't believe him. Kyle felt like squirming in his seat. He hadn't meant to expose either his wife or his sometime mistress to such an embarrassment. Indeed, he never intended for Selena to find out at all about his affaire with the beautiful redhead. He had meant to pay Veronique a visit, tell her of his marriage and sever their relationship—in private, not with dozens of bystanders looking on, watching them embrace…including his *wife*, for God's sake. Chagrined by his inability to finesse this awkward situation, he made an attempt at an apology.

"Listen, I'm sorry you had to witness that. I've known Veronique for a long time—"

"No doubt."

At Selena's dry-voiced interruption, Kyle shot her a hard look, suddenly angry at having to defend himself, even if he *had* just been hoping for the opportunity to do just that. "But I've ended the connection," he continued, forcing the words between his teeth. "I have every intention of respecting our marriage vows."

"That is a matter of supreme indifference to me."

This time his heavy brows snapped together. "Look, I wasn't a saint before I met you, I admit it. I've always enjoyed the pleasures of life, and women happen to be one of the pleasures."

Selena raised her chin as she returned his glare. "Must you be so blunt?"

"*I*, blunt? Lady, you take the cake for bluntness. When you deign to speak, that is."

"At least I am never crude!"

"No, you're just the coldest, most unresponsive woman I've ever known," Kyle shot back, ignoring the fact that he had once had her shuddering against him and gasping with passion. "You don't even seem to have the faintest wish to make love to a man."

"I am not," Selena replied stiffly.

"No? I seem to remember you've professed not to want my lovemaking. Maybe I should find a woman who will appreciate my better qualities."

"Maybe you should!"

Kyle would have vigorously continued their public argument, except that he realized a porter from the hotel had come out to serve them and was staring at them goggle-eyed. Determined not to create a further spectacle, he bit back his fury and jumped down from the carriage.

Selena accepted his help alighting with rigid politeness, angry heat still stinging her cheeks. When Kyle thrust Horatio's cage into the gaping porter's arms, she clamped her lips shut, afraid the outrage she felt would spill over into words.

In tight-lipped silence, he escorted her through the arched doors of the hotel, where they were greeted by a smiling proprietor. Kyle immediately requested *two* bedchambers and a private parlor. Originally he'd planned on taking only one room, for he had been willing to give their marriage a chance. But he would be damned if he would plead with Selena for permission to exercise his husbandly rights.

When he had made the arrangements and then tersely informed Selena that he would see her in the morning, Kyle turned on his heel and stalked from the hotel.

Selena wasn't sure where he spent the night. Despite his engagement of a separate bedchamber, she couldn't be sure he chose to use it—particularly when she remembered the redhead's promise to "wait anxiously" for him.

Kyle did not, however, pay a visit to Veronique—although he did send her an expensive gift and a carefully worded note of apology in an attempt to soften the blow of parting. Then he spent the entire night in an exclusive gambling hell playing cards and losing. Feeling plagued by women in general and one in particular, he emphatically refused the feminine companionship that was so willingly offered him. And when he finally returned to the hotel at dawn, he found himself standing in front of his wife's door, glaring at the unoffending portal.

His pride and his passions were waging a terrible war. Selena had no grounds for cutting up stiff over his past association with Veronique. He had explained the situation and asked her forgiveness, and he would be hanged if he would grovel. Selena had no right, either, to deny him her bed. As her husband he was entitled to the physical privileges marriage entailed.

Setting his jaw, Kyle reached for the latch. Then he jerked his hand back as if he had touched a hot coal. He'd never forced himself on a woman, and if he opened that door, that was precisely what would happen.

Kyle raked his fingers through his hair. If Selena was upset about Veronique, how much more resentful would she be when she learned about his son?

He didn't want to think of the answer. He *wouldn't* think of it.

Stalking away, Kyle let himself into the room that was two doors down from Selena's and threw himself into bed—quite alone.

Chapter Nine

Selena didn't see Kyle at breakfast, but she received a curt note from him shortly afterward. It would be another day, his bold, slashing hand informed her, before the *Washington* left for Natchez.

At loose ends, she wandered down to the enclosed courtyard of the hotel, where the lush vegetation reminded her of home. She would have liked to explore the New Orleans shops, but she didn't want to walk the streets of a strange city without an escort or a maid in attendance, and she had too much pride to approach Kyle with such a request. Besides, according to his note, he intended to spend the day away from the hotel, calling on business acquaintances in the city.

Settling herself on a bench shaded by small palms and surrounded by bougainvillea and fragrant white jasmine, Selena occupied herself reading long-outdated issues of ladies' magazines from London and Paris, which a kindly servant provided.

She ate a solitary dinner that evening, and the following morning, the porter came for her trunk and parrot. It was nearly afternoon, however, before Kyle appeared to escort her to the wharf. They made the short carriage trip in silence. Selena was inclined, after so many hours of loneliness and boredom, to initiate a conversation with him, even if it consisted only of polite small talk, but Kyle's grim expression had returned, and she wasn't quite desperate enough to brave his ill humor.

The earthy smell of the river reached her when they were still a block away. And as they neared the throng of people and merchandise that crowded the levee, the steamship caught her eye at once. The great white bulk of the *Washington*'s super-structure stood out from the long line of boats like a clumsy giant among dwarfs, while thin ribbons of smoke curled from the towering black chimneys.

Reluctant to board the strange ship, Selena took Kyle's arm with great unwillingness. She had just put one slippered foot on the gangplank when a hoarse blast from the steamboat nearly startled her out of her skin. With a small cry, she whirled and collided with the hard wall of Kyle's chest. She would have bolted if Kyle's strong arms hadn't closed around her, preventing her from fleeing the ship.

"It's all right," he said gently. "They're just getting up steam. The boat isn't going to sink."

Selena warily eyed the clouds of white vapor above the twin stacks. "Oh," she said lamely before glancing up at Kyle. His hazel eyes were tender, amused.

Flushing at her cowardice and the absurd way she was clinging to him, Selena disengaged herself from his embrace and smoothed the skirt of her gown, then allowed herself to be led up the gangway.

The steamboat's clerk appeared instantly to greet them, es-corting them through a maze of deckhands who were handling cargo to a steep flight of steps. When they mounted the stairs, they found themselves on a second deck that occupied the rear two-thirds of the steamboat.

The entire upper deck, Selena learned from the clerk, was actually one long cabin. It boasted a drawing room, a ladies' dormitory, a common room lined with berths for the accom-modation of the male passengers and three handsome private sleeping rooms, two of which Kyle had taken for their use. The arrangement didn't seem to surprise the clerk; it was custom-ary for well-bred couples to sleep apart. Still, Selena found herself wishing it wasn't so.

She thanked the clerk as she entered her cabin. Before she closed the door, however, she heard Kyle asking about the steamboat.

"Yes, sir," the clerk replied eagerly. "The *Washington* is Captain Shreve's own design."

"Perhaps the captain might be persuaded to allow me a tour."

"Of course, sir, as soon as we get under way."

Of course, Selena thought. Naturally Kyle would want to inspect the boat. A seaman at heart, he would be interested in anything that floated—even a box that made unearthly noises.

She made herself comfortable in her small quarters, removing her gloves and bonnet and setting out her toilet articles. After checking to see that Horatio had plenty of water and seeds, she returned to the small, open gallery that faced the bow. Kyle was already there, observing the activity below, along with a few other of their fellow passengers.

Not wanting to disturb him, she occupied herself with scanning a printed list of regulations that had been posted at the cabin entrance: "Gentlemen" were forbidden to lie down in berths with boots on, the rules decreed, or to appear coatless at the table, or to enter the ladies' dormitory without the ladies' consent.

She was instantly aware when Kyle came to stand behind her.

"I wonder what is allowed *with* consent," he remarked dryly, reading over her shoulder.

Selena glanced up at him with amusement. "I'm afraid it doesn't say."

"I've heard some excellent reports about Captain Shreve, but it's plain he's a river man. On his vessel we males have no rights at all."

"Do you mean to say you're disappointed that you aren't allowed to 'whittle or otherwise injure the furniture'?"

Kyle laughed, a warm, resonant sound that caught Selena's attention. His reply, though, was drowned out by another shriek of steam. Selena jumped and immediately his hands came up to steady her.

"It . . . sounds like an animal in dire pain," she breathed, knowing her tension came far more from Kyle's gentle grip on her arms than from the steamboat's deafening clamor.

Kyle seemed to be aware of the intimacy as well, for something flickered in his eyes and his gaze dropped to her mouth. He was close. So close she could smell the clean, fresh scent of his shaving soap. So close she could see the green flecks swimming in his gold-brown eyes. She wondered with a sudden thudding of her heart if he meant to kiss her.

But disappointingly, he released her.

"More likely one of the sea gods protesting the ruination of a good ship," Kyle said with a twisted grin.

Selena took a steadying breath, trying to recover her composure. "Are you sure it won't sink?"

"Relatively sure. A demasted frigate like the *Washington* wouldn't last two minutes at sea, for she's got a shallow hull and no keel—" Kyle broke off when Selena's blank look told him he was getting too technical. "But she'll be fine on the river," he continued, "where there aren't waves or wind to contend with. And Shreve is reputed to be one of the best pilots around."

Selena nodded, relieved to know Kyle's opinion and even more relieved that he was finally speaking to her again. "Does that mean you've traveled on a steamboat before?" she asked, determined to keep him talking.

"Several, in fact. But they were all designed by Fulton's group.... I suppose I should tell you about that. You should be aware of our American politics if you're going to live here."

Selena thought that particular comment regarding her future somewhat encouraging, so she listened attentively as he told her about the steamboats that the easterners Robert Fulton and Robert Livingston had built, and how Shreve had successfully challenged the monopoly contract with Louisiana that had given them exclusive rights to navigate the Mississippi.

Kyle was about to tell Selena about the sudden boom in the steamboat industry the previous year, when the ship's bell began to clang, followed by the grinding of the capstan as the anchor was weighed.

Feeling the *Washington*'s hull start to quiver, Selena quickly reached out to grab hold of the gallery rail. "What is that noise?" she asked nervously, hearing the slap of the paddles as the giant wheel began to turn.

Kyle gave a rueful shake of his head, as if wondering how she had ever managed to survive the storm at sea, let alone save the life of one of his men. His lips twitching in a smile, he took her hand and directed her attention toward the single water-wheel placed near the stern. The giant wheel worked in a recess, nearly out of sight, so Selena had to crane her neck around the long cabin to view it.

"That's what drives a steamboat," Kyle said gently. "I'll show you more closely when Captain Shreve takes us around. You won't be so apprehensive if you know more about how a vessel like this operates."

Selena wasn't so certain. The clanging bells, the panting engine and the thrashing paddle wheel all combined with the creaking and shaking of the vessel to make her extremely uneasy. But she did accompany Kyle on a tour of the boat. And she discovered he was right; the *Washington* wasn't as alarming as she had expected. Indeed, the boiler that Captain Shreve pointed out was fired from both ends by furnaces similar to those of a sugar works.

Captain Shreve himself conducted them through the vessel. An energetic man of medium build, Shreve was perhaps five or ten years older than Kyle, and he gave the impression that he loved his avocation as much as Kyle loved the sea. Shreve seemed flattered by Kyle's interest and answered all of his questions without reservation, explaining at length about the steamboat's unique design.

Uninterested in the technical details of machinery, Selena let the captains' words wash over her and instead watched her husband. A faint smile curved her lips at Kyle's reaction to the steamboat. He was like a small boy with a new toy. He spent a long time poking his nose into every nook and corner, his face lighting up in an endearingly boyish way whenever he discovered something unusual. Not for the first time, Selena experienced a twinge of sorrow that he had had to give up his ship.

It was only when Kyle mentioned that his parents had been killed in the *Merilinda*'s accident the previous year that Selena began to pay attention once more. Kyle hadn't told her precisely how his parents had died, but the information that he had lost them to a steamboat explosion only heightened her concern about the safety of such vessels and made her wonder how he could be so casual about it. She didn't understand him—but then he really was a stranger to her.

She studied Kyle intently as they climbed the stairs to the high-perched wheelhouse, realizing how little she knew about him. The captain talked about the financial rewards the business had brought him. In one good season, the captain claimed, an owner could return his entire investment and then some. Selena was surprised when Kyle's thoughtful gaze sought her out absently, surprised, too, by the wistfulness in his expression as their eyes met across the short width of the wheelhouse.

When Kyle finished peppering the captain with questions about steamboats and river navigation, he escorted Selena back to her cabin.

"Why did you ask the captain how much a vessel like this would cost?" she asked as they descended the stairway to the passenger deck.

"Because Natchez could use a regular steamboat service to New Orleans. Someone ought to establish one."

"Are you thinking of doing it yourself?"

Kyle's eyebrows drew together for a moment. Then he shook his head, as if he had been dreaming of an impossibility. "No, not seriously. You heard what Shreve said. To build a stern-wheel boat, it takes around fifty thousand dollars in capital, plus ten thousand a year in running expenses."

Yet she could tell that the thought of operating his own steamboat appealed to him. And she didn't believe it was the money that was keeping him from pursuing the opportunity. If rumor was correct, Kyle was wealthy in his own right, not-withstanding the proceeds from the Markham plantation, which would allow him to buy five steamboats if he chose to. So it must be the responsibilities he faced in Natchez that were preventing him from even considering such a step.

But Kyle appeared to dismiss the subject as they arrived at the door to her cabin. "Supper will be served at seven bells...that is, half past seven. I'll return to collect you then." He started to turn away, then glanced down at her. "Do you need any help changing your gown?"

She was immediately conscious of the subtle change in his voice. The tone seemed to ripple over her skin. Selena looked at him sharply. "Thank you, no. I'm not...wearing a corset."

His gaze dropped to her breasts, measuring, lingering. A slow smile curved his lips, as if he could see very clearly what lay beneath the high-necked bodice of her gown. "I know you aren't." The words were an intimate murmur, his gaze a probing visual caress.

At his scorching look, warmth flared in the pit of Selena's stomach. Kyle's eyes smoldered with the same heat she remembered from that stormy night of passion, arousing sensations and images that made her recall other things about that night.... How his mouth had closed hotly over her nipples. How the hard expanse of his chest had rasped sensually against her breasts as he moved inside her. How the weight of his sleek, muscular body had felt between her thighs....

Selena stiffened. It was wholly unnerving the way memories of lying beneath this magnificent man haunted her. Particularly when it was all too likely that he had only recently left the arms of his mistress.

Pressing her lips together in determination, Selena murmured a cool "Good day" and let herself into her cabin. She *would not* allow his scorching looks and suggestive remarks to affect her.

In the narrow corridor, Kyle stood staring after her, wondering how he was going to manage being confined in close quarters for several days with Selena. It had taken the severest restraint just now to resist the temptation of her tantalizing mouth, to overcome the yearning to take her in his arms.

Clamping his teeth together, Kyle dragged his gaze away from her door. He was quite glad he had taken separate sleeping accommodations. There was no way in hell he could share a cabin with Selena and still maintain his distance. The trouble was, even distance didn't help. She bedeviled his dreams, bedeviled his waking hours, bedeviled his thoughts. . . .

In frustration, Kyle plowed his fingers through his hair. What he needed was a good stiff brandy and the width of the Atlantic Ocean between them. Though he had the sinking feeling that even that wouldn't be enough to make him immune to the elusive charms of the frosty, straitlaced lady who was now his wife.

They dined in the common room with the other passengers on board the *Washington*, in a social atmosphere that resembled one of the finer hotels in New Orleans. Kyle found the encounter as difficult as he had anticipated. He was unused to jealousy, and he didn't handle it all well, but the frequent glances his beautiful young wife was receiving from the dozen or so other gentlemen gave him the urge to put his fists to good use.

Yet he could see what attracted their notice. Selena was dressed in an evening gown of blue crepe that fairly shouted taste and good breeding, but the paisley shawl draped demurely across her slender shoulders did little the hide the elegant line of her white neck or the ripe swell of her breasts.

Gazing across the table at Selena, Kyle was struck afresh by her loveliness. It was easy to forget he hadn't wanted to marry her. What was difficult was controlling his physical reaction to her nearness. An exercise in fortitude, he thought grimly. His body was achingly aware of her, even though she occasionally favored him with a distancing glance from those cool blue eyes of hers.

Selena couldn't be said to be enjoying the meal, either. The fare offered a wide variety of meats but few vegetables and none of the luscious fruits she was accustomed to on her island. And she was experiencing a similar physical reaction to the one Kyle was experiencing. A dark blue coat and close-fitting buff trousers hugged the contours of his muscled torso and long, well-defined legs, making her fully aware of his overwhelming masculinity.

But Kyle's unsociable behavior affected her more than his rugged appeal. He seemed determined to ignore her. The few moments of friendly intimacy they had shared earlier that afternoon might never have happened.

The thought lighted a spark of anger in her. Even if Kyle didn't want her for his wife, he at least owed her the common courtesy of civil conversation at the dining table. When she had endured as much of his silence as she could stand, she decided, perversely, to make him talk.

"If you have such a low opinion of steamboats, how do you know so much about them?" she inquired. As polite conversation, it lacked something, but at least she had chosen a subject that she thought would interest Kyle.

He looked up briefly from his rice pudding. "I don't have a low opinion of steamboats. Merely the same prejudice against river craft any self-respecting seaman would hold."

"Oh, I see," she said archly, and when he resumed eating, asked, "Aren't you worried the *Washington* might explode?"

His mouth tightened in a thin line. "Explosions aren't a frequent occurrence, Selena. They get the greatest attention from the newspapermen, but there's more danger to a steamboat from snags and fires. And even those are rare," he lied, not wanting to alarm her further.

"I don't understand how you can be so unconcerned when your parents were killed in an explosion." Kyle looked up sharply, and Selena was sorry to have mentioned it. Kyle's frown showed he didn't like being reminded of the tragedy.

"A careful pilot can prevent most accidents," he answered with obvious forced politeness.

Selena's gaze softened. "I'm sorry about your parents. How did it happen?"

Kyle sighed. "It was never determined. Negligence or sheer stupidity, perhaps. It's possible the engineer weighted the boiler's safety valve but more likely the strikers simply let pressure build to a dangerous level. The *Merilinda* was pulling away from the levee when the boiler went. The ship sank within minutes, with only a few survivors."

"Was it recent?"

"Last fall."

"I suppose your sisters were devastated."

"They certainly weren't happy about it."

There was another silence while Kyle took another bite.

"Are you fond of rice pudding?" Selena said finally.

"Not particularly."

"Is there some dessert you prefer, then?"

Kyle held his spoon aloft as his gaze narrowed on her. "I like apple tarts. Look, why all the questions?"

Selena pressed her lips together in irritation. "I was only attempting to learn more about you."

"I'd rather you spared me the wifely concern."

His sarcastic reply nettled her. What did he have to be angry about? He was the one who had decided to continue their marriage. But it was apparently pointless to attempt a discussion when he was so obviously in a foul mood.

She set down her spoon, and Kyle immediately threw down his napkin. "If you're finished with dinner, I'll escort you to your cabin."

"I don't wish to retire just yet," Selena answered stiffly.

"No?" His gaze raked her. "What *do* you wish to do?"

The suggestion in his tone brought an angry heat to Selena's cheeks. "Have you forgotten there is an entertainment planned for the passengers this evening?"

"You actually *want* to attend an oratory on the evils of alcoholic spirits?"

"It should prove edifying."

"And boring as the devil," he said dryly. "Besides, it won't begin for another hour."

"I'm aware of that. In the meantime, I intend to walk on the gallery."

Kyle clamped his mouth shut, biting back a sharp reply. A solitary evening stroll with Selena was precisely what he *didn't* wish for. It was bad enough having to be near her in daytime or when there were scores of other people present. But at night, even when the moon was missing, Selena was in her natural element. He would find it a living torment. But he couldn't refuse her without sounding like the veriest ogre.

"Very well." Pushing back his chair, he rose abruptly.

"I don't require your escort," Selena informed him as he came around the table to her side.

Kyle shot a glance around the half-occupied common room. "I'm not about to let you walk alone out there. It would be an invitation for trouble." He offered her his arm. "Let's go."

She took his arm with the greatest reluctance, sensing still that air of repressed anger about him.

It didn't leave him when they stepped out onto the gallery; Kyle dropped her arm as soon as possible, almost as if he were afraid to touch her.

He was. His senses were crying out for relief. And merely not touching her didn't supply it. The velvet-black evening was alive with the sounds of the churning paddle wheel, but it was the soft whisper of Selena's sigh that caught his ears; the earthy night smells of the river were primitive and powerful, and so was the odor of burning wood from the steamboat's furnaces, but it was Selena's fragrance that filled his nostrils.

In an act of self-preservation, Kyle went to stand at the rail. Below, the reflection from a boat lantern faintly illuminated the dark water.

To his dismay Selena followed him, coming to stand only a few feet away. Kyle tensed and swore silently.

Trying to distract his thoughts, he stared down at the powerful river that could sweep fallen trees along like wood chips. Yet he was totally aware of the quiet elegance of the woman beside him, the pale luster of her hair. It was like being seduced by moonlight, having to endure her nearness.

Reaching out, he gripped the railing. Hard. But it didn't help to drive away images of how she'd looked naked in his bed. Or the sensation of having Selena's pale, slender body wrapped around him.

Kyle's grip tightened as he recalled fragments of memories from that wild night. Her courage in defying the storm. Her utterly lovely, compelling nudity. The fascinating contradiction of primness and passion. How he had molded her to match his desire. He'd wanted to give to her, to take from her....

"Fiend seize it!"

This time he swore out loud as he struggled to tame his body's fierce, frustrating urges.

Startled, Selena glanced up at him. She was quite aware of the half-savage vibrations emanating from the powerful man beside her, though she wasn't sure of the reason for them.

Summoning a false calmness, she tried to soothe the tense undercurrents radiating between them by asking how long the journey to Natchez would take.

Kyle took a deep, shuddering breath. "With a moderate head of steam," he said at last, getting hold of himself, "and barring any unforeseen circumstances, four days. It's nearly three hundred miles, and the *Washington* will be doing its own wooding."

"Wooding?"

"Cutting and gathering fuel. And I expect we'll be stopping frequently for passengers and to unload freight."

Selena fell silent then, gazing down at the wide Mississippi. But the tension between them only seemed to grow. What was he thinking about? she wondered. His beautiful, red-haired mistress? And then another thought struck her. Was it possible that her own coldness had driven him into Veronique's arms?

An ache lodged in her chest. Perhaps it was her fault. Kyle had called her cold and unresponsive. But how else could she have behaved toward him? She had been raised a lady, taught to exhibit restraint and proper decorum, even in the most trying of circumstances. And her upbringing made it impossible to be other than cool and polite when she was upset. Indeed, she had cultivated such a talent as self-protection against her waspish stepmother. But Kyle would never understand that.

Bleakly, Selena glanced up at him again. He seemed so distant. She longed to recapture the intimacy that had been between them the night of the storm. She wished they could share their thoughts and aspirations and truly talk together, instead of relying on the politely constrained words that usually passed for conversation between them. If only he would show her even the kind of teasing humor he had shown his crew.

Selena bit her lip as she gazed at Kyle. She truly was in love with him. Why else would she be experiencing this painful yearning that was equal parts giving and fear and want? She was finding it harder and harder to retreat into cool reserve when she was near him, especially when memories of his caresses, hot and wild and sweet, kept swirling around in her mind.

She was still reflecting on the tenderness of Kyle's lovemaking when a clanging bell made her jump. Kyle reached out to steady her, and Selena tensed at his touch.

Abruptly, he released her arm. "Why do you flinch, Moonwitch? I seem to recall a night not so long ago you welcomed my touch."

So he did remember that night, she thought. He had seemed to be able to dismiss it entirely. She couldn't, though. When he touched her as he had just now, it made her recall aspects of that night in vivid detail: his warm, hard mouth and the feel of his hands, the rhythm of his sleek, heavy body as he moved against her.

Discomfited, Selena moved a step away, chastising herself for allowing her thoughts to suggest what her body wanted to experience again. "Everything about that night was a mistake," she said stiffly.

"Oh, come now, you enjoyed it."

She slanted a glance up at him. "How can you be so sure?"

Kyle rested a hip against the rail and crossed his arms over his muscular chest. Leaning against the column at his back, he surveyed her dispassionately. "I know when a woman is feigning passion and when she's not. And you—" his glance traveled down her body, assessing her with a detachment that was almost an insult "—my dear wife, most definitely were not."

Selena looked away. If he knew that, why had he called her cold? She suddenly felt a wild urge to prove she wasn't as unresponsive as he said. But she fiercely clamped it down.

"I could make you want me."

The sudden, quiet emotion in his voice startled her. It was a challenge, softly said, and his words possessed a husky resonance that quivered down her spine. Selena found herself clenching her hands to keep herself from trembling.

"I think I will return to my cabin, after all," she managed tightly, her back going rigid at the resulting sardonic smile that curved Kyle's lips.

She took his arm only because courtesy dictated it, trying to ignore the solid play of muscle under her fingers as he escorted her through the common room to the door that led to the private cabins. The corridor was lighted by a single wall sconce and was fortunately too narrow to accommodate two people. Selena was able to release Kyle's arm as soon as they entered.

"Would you like me to come in?" he asked when they reached her cabin door.

Her back still rigid, Selena glanced up at Kyle. In the lamplight, the amber gleam in his eyes was like rich brandy.

"I don't have need of your services," she replied with flawless enunciation. "I can see to my own clothing."

"That wasn't," Kyle murmured, moving closer, "the only service I had in mind." Placing a hand against the bulwark, he effectively barred her from entering her cabin.

He towered over her, his overpowering physical presence so close that Selena felt dizzy. "I can manage without you," she said breathlessly.

Kyle didn't seem to hear. He leaned into her, pressing his body lightly against hers, making her feel his arousal. The hardness and detail of him made Selena's cheeks go crimson.

"Why are you so flushed, Moonwitch?" Casually, he raised a hand to her face. "Your cheeks are hot. Is your body hot, as well?"

Selena gritted her teeth. "How could it be? You said I was cold."

"Not always." His large hand cradled her throat, then glided downward to the ruched neckline of her gown. Curving his fingers over the edge, he slipped them inside her bodice, against her skin, against the warm swell of her breasts. "Not when I do this," he observed in a husky whisper, finding a taut nipple and stroking it with the backs of his knuckles.

Selena caught her breath on a gasp.

"Do you like it when I caress your breasts?"

She closed her eyes in dismay, deploring the stiffness of her nipples beneath his questing fingers.

"Are you shocked, Moonwitch? You shock so easily." Each low, sensuous word stroked her. "Your breasts are beautiful. So full on the underside . . . tilted up at the peaks."

He dragged his knuckles sensuously across the rigid crests, then paused, closing his fingers around a tight bud. It sent an unexpected tremor of pure desire racing through her. "Kyle!" The word was a gasp and a plea as she clutched desperately at his corded forearm. "Someone might come."

"If they do, they'll see me saying good night to my wife. That's what you are, aren't you? My wife?" He bent his head, nuzzling her open lips. "A man has certain rights with his wife."

"No," Selena breathed, trying to avert her face as she realized where his thoughts were leading.

His hand left the bulwark to grasp her chin gently while his lips continued their sensual assault. "I warned you before we were married, you would have to be available to me whenever and wherever I chose."

Selena quivered. He had threatened to take her anytime, anywhere, and she was half-afraid he would make good his threat right there in the corridor. But she couldn't find the will to push him away. His fingers were still wickedly arousing her breasts, while his hard mouth was drugging her senses.

"I could assert my husbandly rights." The husky murmur caressed her lips before he drew her lush bottom lip into his mouth, his tongue outlining its softness.

When she gave a quiet moan of protest, Kyle drew back briefly to stare down at her. His face was taut, his eyes smoldering with a desire so intent it scorched her.

His hand moved across her cheek to nestle in the soft, silken hair just below her ear. But as he bent his head to kiss her, he lost the careful control he had been forcing on himself. The tender persuasiveness vanished, replaced by burning demand. His fingers twined in her hair; his thighs and chest crowded her against the bulwark. Selena could hardly breathe through the heady rush of sensations that assaulted her. Her mouth opened to him, welcoming the fierce, probing thrust of his tongue.

Kyle felt her response. With a low, tearing groan, he wrapped his arms around her, pulling her to him, his mouth fastening on hers with a hunger that seemed to want to devour her, mastering her, robbing her of breath.

Selena moaned in earnest this time as he plundered her mouth. He was searing her with his heat. She was filled with the scent of him, the taste of him, her head swimming, her knees weak.

Her body was sagging bonelessly against his when he finally dragged his lips away and drew a shuddering breath. "I should be getting something out of this marriage."

The muttered words were ragged, shaken, and it took her a moment to digest their import. Then she stiffened in pain. The sound of her own gasping breath was loud in the sudden stillness as Selena stared up at Kyle, regarding him numbly. Was her willing body all he wanted from their marriage? Was lust all he felt for her?

A cold shiver ran down her spine as she remembered the night of the storm, when she had given herself to him without reservation. But what had been such a soul-wrenching, wonderful experience for her had meant nothing to Kyle beyond the gratification of his physical desires. And when they had arrived in New Orleans, he had gone straight into the arms of his mistress.

She wouldn't be such a fool again.

Defiantly, she clenched her fists, her breasts gently heaving as she stared up at him. "Yes," she acknowledged hoarsely. "You could assert your rights. And as my husband, you could command my obedience." She hoped her disdainful tone and rigid body made it clear she wouldn't submit to him willingly.

Kyle drew a sharp breath. His gaze narrowed, meeting Selena's in a deadlock of passion. "*Command*?" Skepticism flickered in his eyes. Then his voice gentled. "Would it be such an onerous duty, then?"

Selena could tell by the husky charm in his voice that he had reverted to his earlier strategy; he meant to batter her defenses with another assault of tenderness.

She tensed in alarm, not sure she could withstand another such offensive. When Kyle lowered his lips to her swollen mouth, she gave a gasp of protest and strained away from him, pressing her back against the bulwark.

"Are you denying that you enjoy my lovemaking, Moonwitch?"

His lips found the vulnerable underside of her jaw, moving down the line of her throat, pressing a kiss tenderly against the pulse that was hammering there.

"Kyle...." A whimper escaped her even as she edged closer to her door in a desperate attempt to escape.

"Can you forget the way my mouth moved over your body? The way I moved inside you? The way I filled you?"

"Please...." Wildly, she fumbled for the latch at her back.

"Would you like me to fill you again, my beautiful Selena?"

The door swung open.

Half stumbling, Selena twisted from his grasp and fled into the safety of her cabin, frantically slamming the door shut behind her, leaving Kyle alone to deal with the painful state of arousal he himself had created.

* * *

They spoke little to each other during the remainder of the journey and certainly never regained the friendly intimacy of that first afternoon. Selena spent a good deal of time watching the boils and whirlpools of the Mississippi, pondering what she should do about her marriage.

A heaviness centered in her chest whenever she considered her future with Kyle. She had driven him into the arms of his mistress, she was sure, and the thought filled her with pain.

But her own unfulfilled yearning for Kyle was somehow worse. She had discovered what it was like to be pleasured by a man, by a considerate and tender lover, and her discovery had marked her physically: a hot, restless longing that she couldn't control; a quickening between her thighs whenever he was near; the tightening of her nipples when Kyle merely looked at her. All these were manifestations of her shameful condition. She wanted to touch Kyle at every turn, to run her fingers through his thick chestnut hair and over his body, to have Kyle possess her the way he had the night of the storm. She had once hoped that he would grow to love her, but sometimes she found herself amending that to a wish that he would simply make love to her again.

She could have brought that about, Selena thought. Kyle might prefer voluptuous redheads like Veronique, but he *was* attracted to her as well—at least to a small degree. He wouldn't have refused her advances.

But she couldn't bring herself to go to him. Not on those terms. Not when he wanted her only for the physical pleasure her body could bring. Not when he would satisfy only her wanton need and not the ache in her heart. She wanted to be his love, not simply the means for him to slake his passion.

Adding to her misery were the conditions on board the steamboat. She had trouble sleeping, for the *Washington* ran on clear nights and always tied up after dark to forage for wood, even when visibility was poor. She never became accustomed to the excessive noise, either—the roar of steam, the cries of the deckhands and shouted commands of the mate, the sounding of signal bells or the explosive exhaust that announced the approach of the boat for miles in advance.

The only positive aspect of the journey was that she had lost much of her homesickness; the yearning she felt for her island had been far overshadowed by her longing for Kyle's love.

Yet as they neared their destination, Selena couldn't help but feel a stir of excitement. She was going to live in a new place, among new faces, with new challenges and adventures. And she had no choice but to be impressed by the virgin wilderness that flanked the river and stretched as far as the eye could see. More and more often she found herself wondering what her new home would be like in this vast, beautiful land that was America.

It was with great anticipation that Selena looked forward to disembarking at Natchez. When the afternoon finally arrived, she was ready hours ahead of time, standing on the small upper deck gallery, with Horatio's cage at her feet.

Eagerly, she studied the towering red-brown bluffs that rose two hundred feet above the crescent of the river. "Is that Natchez?" she asked with excitement when Kyle joined her at the rail.

"That's the Natchez landing at the base of the bluff," he replied. "The town is built above it."

Lifting her gaze to the windswept heights, Selena could see where the abundant forest of papaw and palmetto and pine that hugged the Mississippi gave way to bright green hills. It looked lovely, basking in the afternoon sun.

But as the steamboat grew closer, the scene lost all of its loveliness. The waterfront was swamped by flatboats and keelboats and edged with half-drowned willows and weather-beaten huts perched on pilings. The landing, which resembled a table of muddy ground, was just as congested as the river's edge. Crowds of river men and slaves, bales of fur hides and cotton, herds of livestock, throngs of drays and carts pulled by mules all vied for space.

Beyond, on the steeply sloping mud flat, were two tiers of streets crisscrossed by alleyways and scattered with long, straggling lines of flimsy shanties. Above that, the long, winding road that climbed upward from the landing, hugging the bluff, was lined with more rude huts and disreputable-looking taverns.

Soberly, Selena took in the sight of the wretched wooden buildings and rowdy, hard-faced humanity. As the *Washington* neared the landing, she caught her breath; from the mired earth rose a stinking odor of squalor and musk and decay. She scarcely noticed the blast of steam from the *Washington*'s boiler, for her attention was absorbed by a raucous brawl between two flatboatmen dressed in linsey-woolsey and drab cloth trousers. They were belching and swaying and wielding murderous knives as they tumbled each other in the muck of the landing.

Selena eyed the fighting with dismay. "This is Natchez?" she said faintly, realizing the ugly mud town was to be her new home.

Chapter Ten

"It isn't as bad as it looks," Kyle said quickly, seeing Selena's shocked expression. "I mean, it is—but this is the worst part. The real town is atop the bluffs. This is Natchez-Under-the-Hill."

"I shouldn't like to come here at night," Selena managed in a weak voice as she watched a bevy of scantily clad females spill from one of the taverns a short distance up the nearest street.

"No," Kyle murmured in a wry undertone. "I shouldn't think you would."

They waited until the *Washington* had moored at the landing and the gangway was set before descending the stairs and bidding farewell to Captain Shreve. As they disembarked, however, Selena skeptically eyed the muddy ground at the end of the plank. Her low-heeled slippers would no doubt sink ankle-deep in the reddish muck.

Gritting her teeth, she protectively raised the hem of her gown, preparing to wade through the mess. But before she could take a step, Kyle startled her by scooping her up into his arms. While she clung to him with one hand, awkwardly dangling Horatio's cage from the other, he strode across the landing, his gleaming top boots making short work of the mud.

"*Will* you put me down?" Selena whispered angrily, as he negotiated the throngs of people and merchandise. "This is quite unseemly."

Kyle glanced down at her, the rugged planes of his face creasing in a grin. "Now there you're mistaken, Moonwitch. None of the riffraff here would notice if I decided to dance naked in the street. Although," he amended, "they would no doubt watch *you*."

His grin widened at the high color in her cheeks, but he didn't release her. Instead, he carried her all the way to the livery stables, where carriages and drays were for hire. He stopped short, though, as a bearded, greasy-haired man came reeling out of the stables to block their path. Kyle recognized him as one of the many fur trappers who came to trade hides in Natchez-Under-the-Hill. With straw clinging to his grimy buckskin trousers and fringed shirt, the man looked and smelled as if he had spent the night sobering up in a stall.

"Well, stap my vitals, if it ain't Kyle Ramsey!"

Selena stared at the unkempt trapper, drawing back involuntarily as she caught a whiff of his powerful odor.

"Beaver Joe," Kyle said tersely, reluctant to acknowledge the acquaintance with Selena there.

Swaying, Beaver Joe gave Kyle a black-toothed grin. "I wager Angel'll be mighty pleased to see you. Heard her talkin' 'bout you jest last week."

Kyle stiffened, even more reluctant to have Selena learn about Angel Abbey, who ran one of the higher class bordellos on Silver Street. He started to pass by, but the trapper peered drunkenly at Selena.

"That a new gal yer bringin' in? She's a might scrawny. I dunno if Angel'll want 'er."

"Why don't you keep your tongue between your teeth," Kyle suggested menacingly, feeling his own cheeks redden. "This 'gal' is my *wife*."

The coarse trapper's mouth dropped open. Kyle brushed past him, ignoring his shocked look—and trying as well not to notice Selena's thoughtful scrutiny.

He hired a horse and carriage, and when he had deposited Selena and her parrot in the vehicle and arranged for their trunks to be delivered to the plantation, he climbed into the driver's seat and urged the horse up the steep street. On one side was a precipice; on the other, hugging the bluff, were the shops, barrooms, taverns, gambling houses, slave dealers' sheds and brothels of notorious Natchez-Under, as it was called by the river men.

Selena observed it all in wide-eyed silence, until they came to a two-story establishment that looked more prosperous than the others. Then she quickly averted her embarrassed gaze. A half-dozen women in various stages of undress lounged against the iron railing of the gallery, beneath a huge wooden sign with the words Heaven's Gate emblazoned in red paint.

As the carriage passed, Selena couldn't help but hear the trilling voice that floated down the street.

"Angel, ain't that Kyle with that fancy bit o' muslin?"

Hearing the name, Selena glanced up with a start.

The woman who must have owned it leaned out from the shaded gallery to get a better view. She was built in voluptuous, curving proportions and sported, Selena noted with a sinking heart, a high sweep of flaming red hair.

Kyle muttered an oath under his breath and, without so much as a glance, slapped the reins on the horse's rump and propelled the animal into a brisk trot. His jaw was set tightly, and there was a deep flush under his tan.

The tips of his ears were shading to red, as well, Selena thought, observing him with a sideways glance. "Are there any more?" she asked, grateful that she managed to sound calm.

"More?" His tone was wary.

"Red-haired women in your past?"

He didn't reply, but his ears turned a darker shade. Selena decided she wouldn't care for the answer. She didn't protest when he cleared his throat and began telling her about the town that crowned the bluff, how it had grown from an Indian village to a French fort, then an English, a Spanish and finally an American possession.

Natchez was laid out in squares, its tranquil streets flanked by chinaberry trees and magnolias, its gracious, galleried houses and numerous shops festooned with climbing jasmine. Selena was relieved to see such a stark contrast with the squalor below. The upper town's inhabitants appeared far more prosperous, as well; frequently they passed gentlemen mounted on blooded horses and elegantly dressed ladies driving gigs or riding in well-appointed carriages. Trying to forget that some of those ladies might be intimately acquainted with her husband, Selena decided she would simply have to make the best of her situation while attempting to build a life with Kyle.

Shortly, they left the town behind by way of a narrow, deep-cut road and plunged into a forest of verdant growth.

"Is your plantation near here?" she asked, recollecting that she knew nothing about Kyle's home.

"A few miles."

"What is it like?"

"Montrose?" Kyle shrugged. "Like any other place, I suppose. It's big."

Selena mentally shook her head. If she had been asking about a ship, Kyle would have been able to describe it down to the last shroud and belaying pin.

Rather than taking him to task, though, she settled back to enjoy the ride. The enormous cedars and water oak rising from a tangle of creepers and vines of wild grape gave the feel of being in a deep tunnel—cool and fragrant with the scents of pine and damp earth.

Eventually the woods gave way to fields of cotton. Following the slow lift and fall of the land with her gaze, Selena could see acre upon acre of young plants that were just beginning to flower. It was different than sugarcane, but the bounty of the land made her feel almost at home.

And when some time later Kyle pointed to the crest of a hill and identified the sprawling plantation in the distant clearing as Montrose, Selena was conscious of a deep sense of pleasure. The two-story manor house stood among towering, moss-draped live oaks, its white stucco gleaming in the sunlight. The grace was evident even from so far away.

"It's lovely," she breathed.

Kyle gave her an odd look. "I'm glad you like it," he answered softly, and she thought he sounded genuinely pleased.

Meeting his gaze, seeing the reflective, almost tender, glimmer of amber light in his hazel eyes, Selena wondered wistfully if they might one day have a true home together. She was disappointed when Kyle looked away as if discomfited by his momentary lapse into intimacy. He seemed reluctant to allow any closeness between them or to divulge anything of himself.

"Do your sisters live at Montrose?" Selena questioned, wanting to draw Kyle out.

His lips curved in a wry smile. "Yes, all four of them." Yet despite the persecuted note in his voice, there was no mistaking the real tenderness in his expression. It was obvious he loved his sisters.

"Who did you say was the eldest?"

"Bea—short for Beatrice. She's married to one of our state legislators. When our parents died, she and Thaddeus moved into Montrose to take care of the girls and keep the plantation up, but Bea's expecting her first child soon, and she wants to return to her own home in Natchez in time for the birth."

"That is why you are returning to Montrose? To assume responsibility for your sisters?"

"Someone must. The girls aren't old enough to fend for themselves yet. Lydia just turned sixteen, and Zoe, while mature for her age, is only fourteen. Felicity is ten."

"It's very noble of you," Selena said softly, "to give up your life at sea for them."

Kyle shrugged, as if unwilling to take credit for making a grand sacrifice when he'd had little choice in the matter. But when he lapsed into silence, Selena realized he must be reflecting on how drastically different his new life would be. Not for the first time, she resolved to aid him in making the transition as smooth and painless as possible.

Of course it would help if she could win over his sisters, but for now she would settle for simple acceptance. Kyle was bringing home a stranger, and she was more than a little worried about how the Ramsey girls would react to their brother's sudden marriage. As the carriage neared the plantation, Selena, too, fell silent, wondering what to expect.

They followed a sweeping gravel drive past a shaded lawn and came to a halt before the manor house. Montrose was even lovelier up close, Selena discovered. Fronted by dozens of yellow rose bushes and flanked by magnificent magnolias, it was a harmonious combination of English and French Creole architecture. Beneath a sloping roof, a gallery ran the width of the building, with a broad, cool veranda below that. Delicate iron ornamentation and slender pillars accented the white facade, making the house appear light and airy. Indeed, the entire effect was one of beauty and quiet dignity.

The afternoon was peaceful, as well—heavy with the perfume of blossoms and the drone of bees. Kyle had no sooner descended from the carriage, however, than the peace was shattered by a joyous shriek from within the house. Next, the heavy front door was thrown open, and Selena was startled to see a yellow blur dash across the veranda, skirts flying, and fling herself into Kyle's arms. Felicity, Selena surmised, catching a glimpse of a bright, happy face beneath a mop of brown curls.

The child's delighted laughter mingled with Kyle's as he held her high in the air and whirled her round and round. And when he had done, she gave another breathless cry.

"Bea! Zoe! Come quick! Kyle's here! Put me down, Kyle, do. I'm quite grown up now, and you mustn't treat a lady so."

"A lady, is it, pumpkin? And here I thought only hoydens screeched like fishwives and allowed their ankles to be seen by gentlemen."

"You're not a gentleman," she replied to his teasing as he restored her to her feet. "You're my brother."

Kyle laughed and mussed her hair, doing considerable damage to the yellow ribbon that was threaded through her chestnut curls. But Felicity only grinned adoringly up at him, the freckles that dusted her youthful face standing out vividly against her creamy skin. She would be a beauty one day, Selena thought, observing their warm reunion.

Not so the tall woman who appeared on the veranda. Her plain but lively features resembled Kyle's somewhat, but her hair color was a drab brown like a wren's. She looked to be in her late twenties, and her serviceable gray gown draped a sturdy figure that was swollen with child.

With a glad smile, she hurried down the steps and gave Kyle a fierce hug.

"Lord, don't choke me, Bea!" he complained, but his cheeks were creased in a grin as he held her at arm's length and surveyed her plump figure. "You're looking well."

"Ha, I resemble nothing so much a turnip!" Bea replied good-naturedly. "But bless you for saying so. I'm glad to have you home."

The love in her voice was discernible, even from a distance; it was clear that Kyle and his sisters enjoyed a warm family relationship of a kind Selena had not known for many years. Even the gangly young girl who hung back in the shadows seemed delighted to see him, for when Kyle said "Hello, Zoe" in an infinitely gentle tone, she moved into his embrace without hesitation.

"Welcome home, Kyle," she murmured shyly, standing on tiptoe to plant a swift kiss on his bronzed cheek before burying her nose in his chest.

Watching them together, Selena found herself envious of the obvious, easy affection between Kyle and his sisters. She wished she knew how to gain it herself. Instead, she sat tensely on the carriage seat, waiting to be noticed.

Ten-year-old Felicity was the first to glance Selena's way. "Who's that?" she piped up, once more gainsaying her claim of being a young lady.

"Felicity!" Bea exclaimed. "Where are your manners?"

Nevertheless, Selena felt several pairs of brown eyes scrutinizing her curiously. She was grateful when Kyle moved to stand beside the carriage. Yet he took a long time to answer, clearing his throat first before saying, "This is Selena Markham . . . Ramsey . . . my wife."

There was a stunned silence while all three sisters stared at her, openmouthed.

"Your wife?" Bea echoed, recovering first. "You are *married*?"

Selena felt her cheeks flushing with embarrassment. Yet to her amazement, a delighted smile dawned on Bea's plain face before she turned to scold her brother. "Kyle, you wretch! Why didn't you say so at once?" Instantly, Bea strode forward to clasp both Selena's hands in a warm gesture of greeting. "Hello, my dear, I'm Beatrice. I can't tell you how pleased I am to welcome you to Montrose. I despaired of Kyle ever finding a bride—certainly one as lovely as you. Mercy, you must think us atrociously lacking in manners. Please do forgive us. It's just that we haven't seen Kyle in quite some time."

Selena could have forgiven Kyle's eldest sister anything for showing her such kindness. "Oh, no, of course I understand," she replied quickly.

"Well, I'm not sure *I* could be so generous. Kyle should be hung from a yardarm, or whatever it is they do on those ships of his." With that, Bea shot her brother a frown. "Do help her down, Kyle. Selena should meet her new sisters properly."

Selena thought Kyle might object to being ordered about so brusquely, but as he helped her dismount from the carriage, she saw his lips twitch with a rueful smile.

As introductions commenced, Selena saw again that she had reason to be grateful to Bea, for it appeared that the younger girls meant to follow her example and accept Kyle's marriage.

"You're pretty," Felicity said, beaming as she bobbed Selena a curtsy.

"Felicity!" Bea admonished.

"Well, she is. And I don't see why it isn't good manners to say so."

Selena found it hard not to sweep the precocious child into her arms. "Thank you for the compliment," she said with a smile. "And even if it isn't proper to say so on such short acquaintance, I think you are pretty, too."

"Are you truly married to my brother?"

Selena couldn't help glancing at Kyle. "Yes . . . truly."

Zoe offered a shy smile as she held out her hand to be shaken. "Does that make you our aunt?"

Zoe's shyness touched a cord in Selena, for it was something she understood quite well. "I think perhaps the official connection is sisters-in-law, but I hope it shall make us friends." Meeting the gentle brown eyes, Selena knew they would be friends. Already she felt a surprising closeness with the slender, awkward girl on the brink of womanhood.

And when Bea put an arm around her waist to guide her into the house, saying, "Come, now, Selena, we must show you your new home," Selena's throat unexpectedly tightened with emotion. She had never expected to be welcomed so warmly.

Glancing over her shoulder, she saw Kyle retrieving Horatio's cage from the carriage. "I have a gift for the girls," Selena told Bea as they moved into the house. "That is, if you don't mind."

But once the cover was removed from the cage, there was no question that the parrot had found a home, too. While Horatio ruffled his feathers and squawked "Come to tea!" Felicity jumped up and down, clapping her hands, and Zoe laughed.

It was while the younger sisters were admiring the bird that Lydia came down the wide staircase. The girl was a beauty and quite aware of it, Selena thought. Lydia had the same brown hair and eyes as her sisters, but hers were a darker and richer shade, which contrasted well with the pale pink sprigged muslin she was wearing.

She had far more polish and apparently less warmth than her siblings, as well. When she greeted Kyle, she held out her hand to be kissed.

Selena was surprised at such affectation, but Kyle obviously expected it. Yet there was an unmistakable gleam of humor in his eyes as he executed a courtly bow and introduced Selena.

Lydia's reaction was similar to Bea's. "Your wife?" She shot Selena a startled look. "What about Danielle?"

Shock and disapproval sped across Bea's face, while Kyle's amusement faded abruptly. It was the moment he had been dreading—the moment his past indiscretions were exposed for his wife to see. Not that he had intentionally deceived Selena. He simply hadn't found an appropriate time to tell her. At first he had been too angry at being forced into marriage to think she deserved an explanation. And he was enough of a gentleman to know the subject required delicate handling. Then later, he had been reluctant to hurt her. He could just imagine the wounded look in Selena's blue eyes when he told her his reasons for not wanting to marry her—that he had intended to wed another woman so he could claim his son. Then after her reaction to Veronique, he hadn't wanted to face Selena's censure. Though perhaps, he admitted to himself, he was being cowardly.

Involuntarily, his eyes sought Selena's. There was a quizzical look on her face: puzzled and expectant. So what should he say? Keeping a mistress could possibly be forgiven, as could patronizing a lightskirt; Veronique and Angel were part of his wild past, and he intended to keep it that way—in the past. But how did he explain Danielle Whitfield? How did he excuse his brief but consequential relationship with a woman who was a kind, gentle, *married* lady? How did he tell Selena about his son? And how did he do it in a way that would shield Danielle's reputation as well, without adding fuel to the rumors that had been circulating in Natchez ever since Clay's conception?

Moreover, how did he keep such knowledge from his young sisters? No one except Bea knew for a certainty that Clay was his son; Lydia was only guessing that his interest in Danielle was anything more than compassion for a lonely woman who was struggling to support a crippled husband and a young child. At least he fervently hoped Lydia was guessing.

Kyle cleared his throat, wishing he was back on his ship, where the only tempests he had to deal with were the wind and the sea; where women had no place.

"Will you dance? Awk!"

At the sudden interruption, Lydia dropped her haughty air in her enchantment over the parrot. As she exclaimed over Horatio's cleverness, Kyle sent the bird a look of gratitude; he had never been so thankful for a distraction.

"Stubble it! Stubble it! Blast, awk!"

While the younger girls chortled, Kyle glanced again at Selena. Her intelligent, quicksilver eyes were focused on his face, and he realized he was in deep trouble. She was too perceptive not to have sensed the sudden undercurrents in the hall at the mention of Danielle or to brush off the subject as having no importance.

Surprisingly, Selena raised an eyebrow at him. "Where did Horatio learn that?" she asked with a smile that was a trifle forced.

Kyle realized then that she was giving him a reprieve. She was allowing him the opportunity to sidestep the issue of Danielle. But he should have expected it, he reflected. Selena was too well-bred to cause a scene, especially in front of his sisters.

He met her gaze over the heads of his giggling sisters with a look of fervent gratitude. Later, he promised her silently. When they were alone he would make a clean confession. As his wife, she deserved an explanation.

And Danielle deserved an explanation, as well. He couldn't allow her to hear about his marriage from someone else. He would have to call on her at once and risk the gossip that the call would inevitably create.

And yet he had to consider Selena. A gentleman couldn't simply deposit his wife on the doorstep like a piece of baggage and allow her to fend for herself. Devil take it, how had he ever gotten himself in such a fix?

Hoping he could count on Bea to extricate him, Kyle drew her aside. While Selena was telling the girls how to feed and care for the parrot, Kyle hastily explained his dilemma to Bea. He wasn't disappointed, for she understood at once.

"Of course, I'll help. Kyle, I don't think Lydia really knows what she's talking about," Bea added with a frown. "And even if she does, she has no business discussing it in public, especially in front of Cissy and Zoe. I will speak to her about it—"

"No, Bea, that would only give credence to Lydia's suspicions. Perhaps it would be best to say nothing at all. If you would just see to Selena while I go into town...."

Bea nodded and then stepped in to rescue him, offering to show Selena to her room and help her become settled. When the younger girls had taken themselves off to the parlor in order to further their acquaintance with Horatio uninterrupted, Kyle was free to suggest that he ought to return the carriage to the livery stable. It was a transparent excuse, for a servant could more appropriately have been employed for such an errand. But Selena again showed her breeding by politely accepting his explanation. She was ascending the stairs, listening courteously to Bea's chatter, when Kyle made his escape.

There were two side wings to the house, Selena discovered, the upper floor of one given over to apartments for the master and mistress. It was to this east wing that Bea led her.

"These were Mama's rooms," Bea said, preceding Selena into a bedchamber decorated in creams and golds. "Kyle will have Papa's, of course, now that he's home to stay. His bedchamber is through that door. I hope you'll be comfortable here," she added when she had shown Selena her sitting room and dressing room.

"I'm sure I will," Selena equivocated, though as she glanced at the vast mahogany bed draped with yards of mosquito netting, she couldn't help wishing the Ramseys weren't quite so affluent. In a smaller house, she might have been required to share a bedchamber with her husband.

"Kyle told me about your parents," she said to change the subject. "I'm sorry you lost them so tragically."

A shadow darkened Bea's face. "Yes, well...they were wonderful people. You would have liked them. It was hardest on the girls, but they're recovering. I suppose we should still be in mourning, since it hasn't even been eight months, but Mama detested black. And I can't believe it would be good for the baby if I only stared at somber faces and depressing colors all day long."

Selena smiled, watching Bea gently pat her swollen abdomen. "I imagine you must be very happy."

"Indeed I am! It took me so long, poor Thaddeus had nearly despaired of ever having children. We've been married over three years, you see." She paused as Selena's gaze turned wistful. "God willing, you'll soon be having your own."

Selena felt herself flushing. At the moment, bearing Kyle's children seemed highly unlikely. She could scarcely get him to speak to her, much less share a marriage bed. But she couldn't discuss such a subject with Bea. Turning away, she busied herself with removing her gloves and bonnet and laying them on a small rosewood table.

"I'll send up a maid shortly to help you unpack," Bea said as she lowered her plump, ungainly body into a comfortable wing chair. "I have to confess," she added tentatively, "I was surprised that Kyle married without telling us."

It was an inquiry, Selena knew—phrased tactfully, but still a request for an explanation. "He didn't want to marry me," she replied in a low voice, meeting Bea's eyes directly. And when the plain-faced woman looked at her expectantly, she told Bea the rest of the story, about Antigua and the altercation in the garden and how Kyle had saved her from scandal, leaving out only the fact that she had made love to Kyle on the beach.

"But you care for him?" was all Bea asked at the conclusion of the tale, concern evident in her voice.

"Yes," Selena answered softly, in complete honesty. "I care for him."

Bea relaxed visibly. "Well, then, that's all right. I wouldn't worry about how your union began. I know my brother, and he wouldn't let himself be forced any into anything if he truly objected. Besides, you're underestimating your appeal. Felicity was right. You're so beautiful Kyle probably took one look at you and fell head over heels in love. Now, if you had my looks... It's a wonder what Thaddeus Sidlow ever saw in a plain creature like me."

Selena smiled as she shook her head. It was easy to guess what any man of discernment saw in such a generous, loving woman. "Thank you," she said simply, with gratitude for being accepted so unquestionably. And when Bea grinned in return, Selena knew she had found another friend.

"I'm glad you're here," Bea admitted then. "I worried about leaving Kyle alone in a house overrun by petticoats. He knows nothing about raising girls or managing a household— or running a plantation, for that matter, but with you to help him, I expect he'll do quite well."

"It will be difficult, though, for him to give up his independence."

Bea waved a hand in dismissal. "Kyle may think he wants freedom, but he'll be happy with a family, I know it."

Her smile fading, Selena went to stand at the tall French windows that were opened to the gallery. Below was a garden courtyard, shaded by sweet olive and flowering almond trees and scented with jasmine and roses. Beyond, to her right, she could see the kitchens and house slaves' quarters, which composed a separate rear wing of the house.

"Bea... who is Danielle?"

She felt rather than saw Bea stiffen behind her. It was a long moment before Bea answered, and then her tone was a touch too bright. "Danielle Whitfield? Why, she's one of the citizens of Natchez. Her husband, Jeremiah, was gravely wounded in the Battle of New Orleans—his spine shattered by a musket ball. No one thought he would survive, but somehow he has. It has left him a complete invalid, though, and the doctor thinks it extremely unlikely he will live much longer. Danielle works at Chandler's General Mercantile in town to support him and their two-year-old son."

"That isn't what I meant," Selena said quietly, meeting Bea's eyes.

"I think," Bea said, no longer pretending to misunderstand, "you should ask Kyle."

"Would Danielle have any reason to be upset about our marriage?"

Bea shrugged helplessly. "She can't. She is married already."

Selena turned back to the window. Somehow the knowledge that the unknown Danielle had a husband didn't quite console her.

While her trunks were being unpacked, Bea gave Selena a tour of the main house, conducting her through spacious rooms that were graced with high ceilings, gleaming woodwork, elegant rosewood and mahogany furnishings and polished wood floors covered by plush carpets.

Selena couldn't help but be impressed. There were five rooms on the main ground floor, which included a large drawing room, a small parlor, a music room, a study for the master of the house and a well-stocked library. There were also two rooms in each side wing, which included a formal dining room, a smaller family dining room, a large sitting room and a general room, where the mistress kept accounts and conducted the business of housekeeping. This last was the brightest, since it boasted two windows and opened onto the flagged courtyard, and was also the most functional, with its huge desk and shelf-lined walls. Selena eyed it with approval; she had been raised to manage a large household and knew she would be spending a good deal of time there.

Selena met Bea's husband that evening when the family gathered for supper. Tall and angular, Thaddeus Sidlow had an untidy thatch of brown hair that kept falling into his eyes and a studious air that softened measurably whenever he was near his wife. He obviously doted on Bea. Indeed, his manner was so solicitous that when he stood beside her chair, urging her to add another morsel of chicken to her already full plate, Bea told him good-naturedly to stop hovering over her like a mama bird and take his seat.

Such frankness surprised Selena, and she decided it would probably take her a while to become accustomed to the easy, open ways of the Americans.

She wasn't conditioned to such noise at the table, either. Usually Lydia dined with the adults while the younger girls ate supper in the nursery, Selena had learned, but this evening both Zoe and Felicity had been allowed to join them in honor of Kyle's homecoming. At the moment Felicity was engaged in quizzing her brother mercilessly about his last voyage and giggling at his teasing responses.

Yet despite the strangeness, Selena couldn't help enjoying herself; no one could, she reflected, surrounded by such love and laughter. Glancing down the length of the long table, where Kyle sat at the head, she smiled to see him reach out and tweak his little sister's freckled nose. His obvious delight in the child made her wonder if perhaps Bea wasn't right about Kyle being pleased to have a family. Selena had never seen him so relaxed and content as he was now, his eyes brimming with mirth as he threatened to make Felicity walk the plank.

Watching him, Selena was conscious of a yearning to have him treat her with the same familiarity, with the same high-spirited affection and love. Yet when Kyle glanced her way, she quickly lowered her gaze to her plate, afraid that her longing showed on her face.

She had just dared to look up again when Felicity left off giggling and blurted out an explosive question. "Kyle, did you know Lydia has a beau?"

Lydia, who had sat stiffly through two courses with a pained look on her delicate features as if she were above such childish displays of exuberance, glared at her sister. "Do be quiet, Cissy! You have no idea what you're talking about."

"I do so! I saw you kissing Tanner Parkington in the summerhouse."

Bea let out a soft gasp. "Lydia, you didn't!" she murmured. Kyle's heavy eyebrows had snapped together in a frown. The abrupt silence that followed the revelation contrasted starkly with the lively conversation that had gone before, which led Selena to conclude that despite the easy manners here, kissing a young man could compromise a young lady's reputation as thoroughly in American society as it could in British.

"Is that so, Lydia?" Kyle said at last, a hard note in his tone that Selena recognized. She felt sorry for the girl, if it was true.

Which it seemed to be. Lydia's cheeks couldn't turn any redder, and the glance she gave Kyle was full of guilt.

"Perhaps it is," she muttered, "but Felicity has no right bearing tales."

"In this case, I'm glad she did." Ignoring Lydia's sullen look, Kyle turned to Bea. "Tanner.... Isn't that Parkington's youngest boy?"

"Yes, but he's not really so young. He's twenty now."

"Whatever his age, I intend to warn him away. I won't have him taking advantage of Lydia."

"He didn't take advantage of me!" Lydia protested. "I kissed him back!"

Selena saw Kyle's gaze narrow ominously on his sister. "Tell me, has Tanner found gainful employment since the last time I was here?"

"Of course not! A gentleman doesn't work."

A muscle tightened in Kyle's jaw. "I don't know where you came by that harebrained notion, and I won't dispute it with you, but I don't want him calling here again. Even if his intentions toward you are honorable, he doesn't have a penny to his name. The Parkington plantation is mortgaged to the hilt."

Lydia's expression grew even more sullen, but she didn't argue further. Yet Selena was certain the contretemps wasn't over. She was almost as sure that Kyle hadn't acted very wisely in forbidding Lydia to see her beau. He was only protecting his sister, of course. But such high-handed use of authority was the surest way to arouse rebellion in a girl of Lydia's temperament.

Selena was considering whether to speak to Kyle about it later when Zoe suddenly claimed the attention of everyone at the table by accidentally dropping her wineglass and spilling dark red Burgundy down the front of her blue muslin dress and on the Aubusson carpet.

"See, I told you!" Lydia said darkly. "Zoe isn't capable of eating with the grown-ups. She's far too clumsy."

Selena suspected that Lydia was still smarting from her quarrel with her brother and didn't truly mean to be unkind, but Zoe obviously took the remark to heart. With stricken eyes, the young girl glanced quickly at Kyle, then at Selena.

"If you will excuse me, please...?" she asked, her lower lip trembling as she rose from the table. She fled the room before anyone could say a word.

Kyle scowled at Lydia while Bea struggled to her feet. "I'd better see to her."

"No, please," Selena interjected. "Would you allow me?"

Bea looked surprised, but she nodded at once, and so Selena laid down her napkin and followed the trail of wine drops up the stairs.

She found Zoe in her room, sobbing softly into her pillows. Quietly, she sat beside the girl and placed a comforting hand on her shoulder. "I don't know anyone who hasn't drenched themselves with wine at one time or another," Selena said gently. "I've done it myself dozens of times."

It took a long moment, but Zoe's sobs eventually quieted. Selena reached up to stroke Zoe's hair, and another long moment later she heard her sigh.

"I did so want to make a good impression on you," Zoe said in a muffled voice.

"I know. And I wanted to do the same with you. Do you realize how mortified I was to hear Horatio swearing? I never taught him those words, I promise you. I suspect he learned them on your brother's ship. I should have put cotton in his ears, I suppose.... Horatio's ears, not Kyle's."

There was a pause, then a muffled chortle.

"Zoe, my love, I don't think Lydia meant to hurt your feelings. Indeed, she was probably very grateful to you."

Puzzled, Zoe lifted her tearstained face.

"For diverting everyone's attention from her problems," Selena explained.

Zoe cocked her head, seeming to consider that. "Lydia has been so mean since Mama and Papa died. She used to be *nice*."

"I expect she misses your parents."

"I suppose. I miss them, too, but sometimes I wish I didn't have Lydia for a sister."

"Well, I've often wished I had any kind of sister. I've never had any, or brothers, either."

"You don't have any family?" Her tone sounded shocked. "You must be lonesome."

Selena smiled softly. "Not any longer. That is . . . I was hoping you would be my family."

Shyly, Zoe returned her smile. "Yes."

"Good. Now, why don't you change your gown and splash some water on your face, then come down and join us?"

Zoe glanced down at her wine-stained bosom, then flushed with guilt when she saw the red splotches on the yellow counterpane.

"I expect we can get the stains out," Selena assured her as she rose. "I brought some excellent soap with me from the island."

"Selena?"

She turned as she reached the door, raising a delicate eyebrow.

"I'm glad you've come."

"I am, too," Selena said gently, before leaving the room and pulling the door closed behind her.

She was startled when she nearly ran into Kyle's tall figure. He had obviously been waiting in the hall, listening to her console his sister. But what surprised Selena more was the look in his eyes. Kyle was gazing down at her with the same tender light that she had seen the night of the storm.

She wished he wouldn't. It flustered her to have him looking at her so, as if she had accomplished some great deed rather than simply comforted a weeping child. And his simple words flustered her more.

"Thank you," he said softly, his husky tone vibrating through her, warming her.

She swallowed, her voice suddenly deserting her as she gazed into Kyle's green-gold eyes. She felt herself being drawn into his gaze, into the vital, rugged aura that was so much a part of him. Being this close to him was having a strange effect on her senses. She was too aware of him as a man . . . of his heat, his power, his strength.

She couldn't stay there any longer, Selena thought. Not without doing something foolish, like pressing herself against his muscular chest and raising her lips for his kiss. But when she made to pass him, Kyle reached out a hand to stay her.

"Selena . . . I need to talk to you later."

Disturbed by his touch, Selena looked down and found herself staring at his hands—strong, callused hands that had the power to tame a wildly plunging ship yet could be gentle and caressing and arousing. . . .

Arousing not just herself, Selena remembered, but someone named Veronique. And Angel. And perhaps someone named Danielle.

She wanted desperately to know about Danielle—or rather she wanted Kyle to reassure her that there was nothing to substantiate her jealous imaginings. But she hadn't seen him alone until now. Kyle had missed tea, only returning from town shortly before supper.

Selena took a deep breath, summoning her courage. "Bea wouldn't discuss Danielle. She told me to ask you."

Kyle released her arm as if he had been burned, his expression wary and oddly grim at the same time. "That's what I wanted to talk to you about."

She waited expectantly, watching him, but he didn't say anything more. Instead he looked away, avoiding her gaze. "I don't know how to say this." Finally, after glancing at his sister's closed door, he turned back to Selena, meeting her gaze directly. "We can't discuss it here."

She wouldn't like what he was going to tell her, she could see it on his face. "Where can we discuss it?" Selena asked quietly.

He raked a hand through his chestnut hair in agitation. "Devil take it." Then, "Very well, come with me." Grasping her hand, he pulled Selena down the hall into a deserted bedchamber and shut the door behind him.

The windows were shuttered against the setting rays of the sun, and the unlighted room was dim. Selena had difficulty reading Kyle's expression, but she could see his features were taut with some kind of emotional struggle.

"There just isn't any good way to say this," he muttered, again running his fingers through his hair.

His hesitation was beginning to alarm her. "Perhaps you should just tell me outright."

"Very well. You have a right to know." His voice was so low Selena hardly heard. "Danielle...Danielle is the mother of my son."

Chapter Eleven

Selena stared at Kyle, feeling as if the breath had been knocked from her body. It shouldn't have been so painful discovering that Kyle had a son, some small part of her mind rationalized. She belonged to a privileged class where gentlemen frequently sired children outside of marriage, where ladies turned a blind eye to their husbands' transgressions. She had always believed herself willing to accept this. But somehow it was different now—when it was Kyle. Stunned, sickened, Selena regarded him without speaking. Was it her feelings for him that made such bitter jealousy twist her heart?

"Selena...don't... Please don't look that way."

Shakily, she raised a hand to her temple. Kyle wasn't trying to hurt her, she realized. The rigid muscles of his jaw showed his dismay clearly.

"Look.... I didn't mean to bring it up now.... It came out all wrong—"

He broke off as a soft rap sounded at the door. When Zoe called to them, asking if they were coming down to supper, Kyle muttered a frustrated oath under his breath and answered curtly that yes, they would be down in a minute. Then he peered down at Selena with concern. "Can we talk about this after supper?"

Selena nodded. Perhaps there was an explanation...mitigating circumstances that would make the fact that Kyle had a son less painful to accept. And if not, by then she at least would have had time to collect herself.

She managed to school her facial muscles into a semblance of equanimity as they returned to the dining room, but the sparkle had gone out of the evening for her. Indeed, the whole company was subdued. Lydia quietly apologized to her sister and lapsed into silence, and even chatterbox Felicity, who had caused the initial contretemps, found little to say. It was left for Thaddeus and Bea to carry the conversation. Selena was grateful when Kyle ordered a servant to refill everyone's glass so they could drink a toast to Bea's expected child, for the wine helped calm the turmoil she was feeling.

Kyle had intended just that, judging that Selena needed something to help sustain her nerves. He wasn't fooled by her apparent composure. She had been shocked and hurt by his disclosure, he knew. He hadn't expected that reaction. Anger, perhaps. Scorn, haughtiness, certainly stiffness. Those he could have contended with. But not her look of wounded distress, which made him feel as if he were tormenting something weak and fragile.

Concerned, he glanced at the far end of the table, where Selena was sitting so quietly. She seemed shaken and withdrawn, and the sight tugged at his heart. He wished there had been some way to spare her, but she would have heard the rumors sooner or later. With Bea's help he had managed to keep the knowledge of his impropriety from the tender ears of his younger sisters, but there were a dozen well-meaning citizens in the district who would have made sure Selena heard every sordid word of gossip and innuendo. No, it was better that the story came from him.

He hadn't handled it at all well, Kyle thought, watching her over the rim of his glass. But then, was there any good way to tell your wife that you had sired a child with a married woman you barely knew? Put that baldly, it sounded terrible. But it hadn't really been like that.

And he had been paid for his sin in his own way—and was still paying. Repressing the rumors had meant he couldn't lavish affection on his offspring, which was a father's right. For Danielle's sake, he had struggled to quell his own need to be with his son, his yearning to share the joys and trials of Clay's boyhood, to watch him grow, to teach and guide him.

At least Danielle hadn't suffered too greatly. There had been gossip, but no one had ever been able to prove that Danielle's invalid husband wasn't capable of fathering a child. Jeremiah had supported their story with bitter magnanimity because of his deep love for Danielle, saying he couldn't begrudge her a child when he could no longer be a husband to her.

But now Selena would have to be told the truth. Kyle's fingers tightened around his wineglass. She didn't deserve to be confronted with this, he thought grimly. It wasn't fair to her. It wasn't fair, either, to expect her to care for his sisters. But she would be a good mother to them. He had already come to admire her courage and resilience, and seeing her with the girls, he was learning the extent of her kindness and her generous heart. He could only trust and hope Selena would extend the same generosity to him.

When supper ended, the ladies removed to the drawing room while the gentlemen remained at the table. Over a glass of port, Thaddeus shared all the news and events that had occurred since Kyle's last visit four months ago. Kyle wasn't much interested in how many acts the General Assembly had passed or what issues the legislature planned to address, but he hung on every word, wanting to draw out the interval as long as possible. When it was time to join the ladies, he drained his glass, feeling the need to bolster his courage for the upcoming ordeal with Selena.

He didn't have an opportunity to speak with her at once, however, for when he entered the drawing room, his younger sisters were gathered around Horatio, engaged in an effort to expand the bird's vocabulary. For two hours Kyle had to listen to their giggling attempts to teach the parrot to say "minuet" and "cotillion" and "Scotch reel.." When they finally retired to bed, followed shortly by Bea and Thaddeus, he was left alone with Selena.

The silence hung heavily between them. For a moment Kyle watched her, wondering how to begin. Selena was sitting on the settee across from him, slender back straight, hands folded in her lap, soft lamplight playing on her hair.

She was waiting for his explanation, he knew. When she cast him a brief, somewhat nervous glance, he suddenly realized how important it was to him that she know the truth. He wanted her to understand.

Selena was the first to speak, though. "What is your son's name?" she asked quietly, looking away.

Kyle took a deep breath. "Clayton…but everyone calls him Clay."

"Does he favor you?"

He hadn't expected that question, but he answered it honestly. "A little, I guess. Danielle says so, at any rate. He's a beautiful child. Blond hair and green eyes. I was planning...hoping...to give him my name one day."

"You intended to marry Danielle." It was a statement, murmured in a small voice that wrenched his heart.

"Yes," he admitted helplessly.

"But what of her husband?"

"Jeremiah...isn't expected to live much longer. The doctor is surprised he's lasted this long...." Kyle raked a hand through his hair. He was making a hash of this, stumbling over himself, searching for the right words. "I know it sounds callous to be discussing such things when her husband isn't even in his grave yet, but Danielle has been concerned about how she would manage. I wanted her to know she didn't have to worry, that I was willing to take responsibility for my son...and for her."

Selena looked down at her hands. That was why Kyle hadn't been free to accept her proposal of marriage. She remembered him speaking of a duty he was obliged to fulfill. At the time she had thought he meant his duty toward his sisters. "Danielle...must have been very upset to learn about me."

"I don't know.... There never was anything between us. I knew Danielle, though not well. She had always been a friend of the family. When I came home a few years ago for a visit...she had been through a lot. Her husband had almost died from a bullet wound, and when he managed to recover, he was left paralyzed and in such pain that he had to be kept dosed with laudanum. Danielle had had a rough time nursing him constantly and finding money to pay the doctor's bills." Kyle paused, taking a deep breath. "The last week I was in Natchez, Bea coerced me into attending a revival meeting at a neighboring plantation, and Danielle was there. She was lonely and unhappy and crying, and so I comforted her, and, well...one thing led to another. It only happened once."

Selena didn't need to be given a more explicit explanation of what had occurred between them. She could picture it clearly: a desperately lonely woman weary of struggle and a strong, vital man who was more than capable of momentarily shouldering burdens on his powerful shoulders. Oh, yes, she could understand. She had been in a similar situation with Kyle herself.

"I should never have let it go so far," he was saying. "I suppose I was careless...stupid. I didn't even know about Clay until I returned the next year and Bea told me about the rumors. I wanted to make it right then, but Danielle couldn't marry me. She didn't want to accept money, either, for fear of how it would look, but I discovered a way. By then she was working at Chandler's General Mercantile in town—Orrin Chandler is a friend of mine—and I gave him the money to increase her salary. And I did everything else I could—sent Clay gifts through Bea, talked my father into giving Jeremiah's brother a job here as factor so he could help support them, saw to it that Danielle had a competent Negro woman to stay with Jeremiah full-time. And I've stayed away. That's been the hardest part . . . that I can't claim Clay as my son. I can't hold him or play with him or even visit without providing more food for the town gossips.''

Hearing the note of despair in Kyle's voice, Selena recalled how adamant he had been in his refusal to marry her, how he had almost pleaded with her to intercede with the governor. She had misunderstood his reasons then. Kyle hadn't wanted to marry her, that was true, but it wasn't his loss of freedom that had so disturbed him. It was the loss of his son. And she hadn't given him any way out.

"I ought to regret what happened," he said softly. "And I do—for causing Danielle more hardship. Yet I can't wish the damage undone, for that would mean wishing Clay had never been born. You like children . . . so perhaps you can understand.''

She nodded, her clasped fingers tightening in her lap.

"Selena, maybe I don't have the right to ask this of you—" he plowed his fingers through his hair again "—but if you could manage to overlook Clay's existence, to pretend that nothing is wrong, at least in front of our neighbors, we could manage to avoid a scandal. And I could still see Clay once in a while.''

She finally met Kyle's gaze, her eyes troubled, as his were.

"I can't give him up, Selena," he said with quiet anguish. "He's my son.''

"Of course not. I could never ask you to." Her own voice was husky with emotion. She thought it must have reassured him, for his intense expression relaxed infinitesimally.

"I don't want my younger sisters to know, either. Obviously Lydia has guessed at least a little, but Zoe and Cissy are too young to find out.''

"I . . . I will do my best to see they never have reason to suspect.''

"Thank you." He gave her a faint smile, of relief and gratitude, thinking the words inadequate to express his appreciation for her compassion.

They both fell silent then; there didn't seem to be anything more to say, though Kyle wished there was.

She was so different from any of the women in his past, he thought, watching the lamplight glint on her hair like a silver halo. Observing her quiet, cool beauty, he could hardly remember what he had seen in any other woman.

Kyle shifted in his chair, feeling his body begin to throb as it always did lately when he was near her. He was bewitched by Selena's ethereal loveliness, he knew. Her pale features and deceptive hint of fragility held such powerful allure that he found it harder and harder to remain alone in the same room with her. Making love to her had been like reveling in moonbeams—silver, sensuous rays that bathed him in magic and wrapped around his heart like slim fingers of light.

The thought of going to her now and removing her clothes, one by one, pressing her back upon the settee and burying himself in her enchanting body, beckoned him like a strong spell. And the visual image of Selena naked and writhing beneath him, long, slender legs clasping his hips, her quicksilver eyes liquid with heat, brought him to a pulsing arousal.

Kyle's fingers slowly curled into fists. He couldn't indulge in his inviting fantasies. Selena would be shocked to the depths of her proper little soul. Nor could he make love to her in the more conventional way, in his bed or hers, not when she had so clearly demonstrated she wouldn't welcome his advances. He would have to control his moonstruck lust long enough to finish this conversation and escape.

But it was Selena who took the initiative. After a moment, she rose to her feet.

And yet she knew she couldn't leave it at that. Not when she felt such a burden of guilt for forcing him into marriage. Kyle had made a bigger sacrifice than she knew when he wed her. "Kyle . . . I am sorry you had to marry me."

He shook his head. "No, Selena, don't. There's no point in wallowing in regrets. What's done is done. We're married now, and we'll have to make the best of it." Realizing then how insensitive he sounded, Kyle added quickly, "We didn't have the best beginning, I know, but perhaps now that we're here, we can make a fresh start."

"I would like that," she said softly. And because he had made the first overture, she gathered up enough courage to ask a question that any wife had the right to ask. "Are you coming to bed?"

She wasn't looking at him, though, so he didn't see the flush on her cheeks or realize her discomfort with her boldness. "No, not yet," Kyle said with a sigh. "I need to review the plantation books and see if I can make any sense of them. You go on. I'll see you in the morning."

So much for starting over, Selena thought miserably. And later, as she lay alone in her bed, recalling what Kyle had told her, going over and over the nuances of his voice in her mind, she felt sick at heart. She wanted to believe Kyle's assurances that there was nothing in his relationship with Danielle. But whether or not Kyle had ever loved the woman wasn't the only issue. Danielle shared something with him that she, Selena, couldn't. A son.

And it didn't seem as if she would ever get the chance.

She didn't see Kyle in the morning, or even in the afternoon, for when she came downstairs for breakfast, she learned from the servants that Kyle had gone out to the fields and wasn't expected back till late. She spent the day touring the rest of her new home and becoming familiar with the house staff and their customary manner of operation. Martha, a large-boned, large-bosomed black woman, who had been the head cook before assuming charge of the house staff, was her guide.

The outbuildings were just as impressive as the main house. Selena was pleased to see that the house slaves' quarters were immaculate and relatively comfortable, while the dairy, stables and carriage house were clean and in good repair. There was also a henhouse, a large vegetable garden and a small orchard, all of which were well tended and highly productive.

Martha had saved the kitchens for last. She beamed with pride when Selena admired the giant fireplace with its cranes and pots and the spit where meats were roasted.

"And now," Selena said after inspecting the storage pantries and smokehouse, "if I might see the rest of the outbuildings."

Martha pursed her large lips in surprise. "That be Mista Whitfield's place. I don' wanna be accused of steppin' in his business."

The name Whitfield introduced a jarring note into Selena's otherwise pleasant day. Danielle's brother-in-law, she surmised. She didn't particularly want to meet with him, though she knew she would have to do so sooner or later if he was factor at Montrose. But for today, at least, she would likely be spared that duty, since Whitfield was no doubt giving Kyle a tour of the fields.

"I don't see why Mr. Whitfield would object to you showing me around the plantation, but if he should, I will speak to him."

Martha didn't seem totally satisfied with such an assurance, however. And as they passed the factor's office and the small brick house where he lived, she answered Selena's questions with a wariness that hadn't been noticeable before.

Selena herself was silent as they toured the smithy, carpenter's shop, cotton gin and plantation store. She was intimately familiar with the workings of a well-run plantation, and here, unlike the main outbuildings under Martha's charge, Selena could see evidence of neglect. What was worse, the few slaves whom she saw at work were old men who gazed at her with sullen eyes.

It was a distant walk to the quarters that housed the field slaves, but when she had inspected the small village of wooden buildings set in long rows, Selena was glad she had made the long trek. Here, too, were signs of patent neglect.

"Is Miss Bea aware of the condition of these houses?" she asked Martha.

"Miss Bea ain't been here fo' some time. That be Mista Whitfield's place, like I said."

"I see." And Selena thought she did see. Bea was fully occupied with her house and family and wouldn't have time to ensure that Whitfield adequately carried out his duties as factor.

"That Mista Whitfield, there be trouble with that man that Miss Bea don' know nothin' about," Martha muttered cryptically. "I been in this family fo' twenty-one years, and I ain't seen nothing like it allowed roun' here befo'."

That was all Martha would say about the factor, and Selena knew better than to press her to inform on a white man. But she took such complaints seriously. She contemplated discussing the situation with Kyle that evening, but when he came home, weary from being in the saddle all day, she de-

cided it could wait. She ordered him a hot bath and asked
Martha to hold supper back for an hour.

Then, on second thought, she sought out Bea and asked if
she objected. Bea laughed, however, and said she was pleased
to see Selena slipping so easily into the role of mistress of
Montrose.

Selena knew it was true; she felt comfortable in her new position and was already behaving as if she belonged. Yet she
didn't think the same could be said of Kyle. He seemed dis-
pirited by his first day as master, and even though he didn't say
it in so many words, she suspected he hadn't found any pleasure in being a farmer. Selena would have liked to discuss that
with him, too, but Kyle retired early and was already gone the
next morning when she rose.

She did manage to find out more about the factor from Bea,
however. After setting Zoe and Felicity to work on their lessons in the schoolroom, the two ladies retired to Bea's office,
where they spent the morning reviewing the domestic affairs
of the plantation in detail. Bea and Thaddeus wanted to leave
for their town house in Natchez as soon as practical, and Selena intended to be well prepared to take over her sister-in-law's
duties.

What she learned about the factor did not satisfy her. As she
suspected, Bea had left the running of the plantation entirely
to Gideon Whitfield. Yet nothing Selena had seen convinced
her that he was qualified to manage a large, complex operation like Montrose.

The factor was not the only Whitfield who troubled Selena,
either. She had lain awake most of the night, tossing restlessly, unable to drive thoughts of Danielle Whitfield from her
mind. The thoughts wouldn't go away that morning, either.
Nor would the doubts and fears. Selena couldn't help remembering how her stepmother had successfully conspired to steal
Avery from her and how naive she had been then. This was
worse, though, for she hadn't loved Avery. Moreover, now she
had only a faceless, formless image on which to focus her
fears—like an enemy one couldn't see or fight.

As she reviewed Bea's household accounts, the issue so
preoccupied Selena that she couldn't concentrate. When she
found herself scanning a column of figures for the third time,
she came to a decision. That afternoon, after asking some
subtle questions of Bea, she ordered the gig from the stables
and drove into town.

Upper Natchez was just as neat and pleasant as she remembered, and the shops were just as prosperous. Many of the shop owners followed the Creole custom of bringing their wares out into the street, but Selena scarcely noted the produce a grocer had on display or the bolts of calico and silk a mercer had stacked on a table. At the moment there was only one shop that interested her—Chandler's General Mercantile.

When the gig drew up before the shop, Selena sat there in her seat for a long moment, staring at the storefront window. She recognized her jealousy, but like a tongue probing a sore tooth, she couldn't keep away.

Finally she stepped down from the gig. At the door, however, she hesitated another long moment. The dampness of her palms beneath her gloves had nothing to do with the warmth of the late-May afternoon.

She had dressed in one of her best walking dresses, a gown of lilac lutestring with a high waist banded in deep plum. Armor, she thought with little humor as she took a deep breath and entered the shop.

It took a moment, but when her eyes adjusted from the brightness outside to the cool, dimmer light inside, she could see tables laden with goods—everything from bullet molds and leather goods to cutlery and tinware. After gazing around the shop, Selena glanced beyond a line of barrels to where a waist-high counter stood. Then she spotted Danielle.

Red hair. Of course. The lustrous auburn hair of the woman behind the counter gleamed like the heart of a fire.

Selena's heart sank. Danielle wasn't voluptuous, precisely, but her breasts were full and her features strikingly beautiful. She wore her richly colored hair pinned in a thick knot, and while her brown muslin gown was plain and serviceable, it took on new life when adorned by such glowing locks.

Her head was bent since she was engaged in counting nails. She paused after saying "thirty-seven" and looked up, smiling pleasantly. It was a preoccupied smile, but even so, it was breathtaking.

Selena's heart dropped to the vicinity of her knees.

"I shall be with you in a moment," Danielle said sweetly. "Oh, no—now where was I?"

"Thirty-seven," Selena supplied, wishing she had never come. She turned away, gazing blindly down at a display of candles.

When Danielle reached one hundred and said, "Now, how may I be of assistance?" Selena gathered up a handful of the candles and took them to the counter for purchase. She had to have some pretense for coming.

But her effort was wasted. Danielle glimpsed the pale hair under Selena's wide-brimmed straw hat, and her smile slowly faded. "You must be Selena," she said quietly.

The two women stared at each other for a long moment, brown eyes gazing at blue.

Finally Selena broke the silence. "I had to come...to see..."

She didn't complete the sentence, but Danielle nodded slowly. Selena realized then that words weren't needed, that Danielle understood. The powerful instincts that had driven her to search out her rival were as old as human existence: a female protecting her claim to her mate. And in a strange way, the understanding bonded them together. Selena felt it like a tangible force between them. They were two women linked by the same man.

Danielle spoke next. "I don't know what to say.... Explanations seem inadequate."

"No, there's no need to explain anything. As Kyle says...what's done is done."

"I want to assure you there is nothing now between me and Kyle."

"You—" Selena broke off, her throat tight. "You have a son between you."

Just then there came a scrambling sound from behind the counter and the patter of small feet. Danielle glanced down quickly, then gave a soft cry of dismay. "Clay, no! Come back here this instant."

Even as she spoke, a towheaded child dressed in a floor-length nankeen shirt ran around the corner of the counter. He came to an abrupt halt when he saw Selena, staring at her with bright green eyes. Then he grinned at her, and Selena's heart fell to her feet. She could fight against another woman, perhaps, but not this beautiful child.

And he *was* beautiful, with the same breathtaking smile of his mother and the masculine charm that belonged to his father. In the dimpling creases in his cheeks, in the lively directness of his gaze, Selena could clearly see the young boy's resemblance to Kyle.

Danielle came around the counter then, to place one hand on Clay's small, blond head. Selena didn't miss the significance of the action: a mother protecting her son.

Selena felt the ache in her throat swell further as Clay wrapped his short arms around his mother's knees.

He clung to Danielle's skirts as he pointed at Selena. "Lady?"

"Yes, that is a lady," Danielle said, bending to scoop him up. "Come now, you know you aren't allowed to play in the store."

Selena tore her gaze away, trying to get hold of her emotions, ashamed because they were so unadmirable. It wasn't commendable to be jealous of a two-year-old child just because he could command Kyle's affection when she couldn't. Nor was it commendable to envy a woman her son. But she couldn't deny she would have liked to have claimed Kyle's love or that she would have liked to have Clay as her own.

As Danielle was returning Clay to his authorized play area, a man appeared in the door behind the counter, his arms filled with a large bundle of cane baskets lashed together.

"Danielle, where do you want these?"

Danielle straightened and, for the first time, appeared a little flustered. "The counter is fine. Orrin, we have a customer. This is Mrs. Ramsey, Kyle's new wife."

His gaze shot to Selena.

He was attractive, Selena noted. Perhaps thirty-five, with brown hair and eyes.

He set his bundle down on the counter before nodding to her. "How do you do, ma'am? I'm Orrin Chandler."

He was the proprietor of the mercantile, Selena knew. And a longtime friend of the Ramsey family, according to Bea. Selena murmured a polite reply, watching as Orrin stepped back to Danielle's side and rested a hand lightly on her shoulder. It was the same protective gesture Danielle had used with Clay.

He thought she was going to cause Danielle trouble, Selena realized. Which only confirmed that he knew the truth about Kyle's son. Selena wanted to reassure him, but she wasn't sure of the appropriate way to phrase such a remark.

Orrin spoke before she could think of one. "Is there anything I may do to serve you?"

"No . . . thank you. Mrs. Whitfield has been very helpful."

"Very well." He glanced down at Danielle. "I'll be in the back room if you need me." Orrin turned then and bent down out of view. "Hello, young fellow. Are you keeping out of trouble?"

From the gurgle of laughter that followed, Selena guessed he had tickled the boy's ribs.

"Do you still want the candles, Mrs. Ramsey?" Danielle asked when Orrin had disappeared through the door.

It took a moment for Selena to understand what she was talking about. "Oh, yes...of course." Selena fumbled in her reticule for the American money Bea had given her.

"You don't have to pay now. The Ramseys have a line of credit. I'll just include the price on your monthly bill."

She nodded, watching while Danielle tied the candles together with a piece of string. But when the task was done and it was time for her to leave, Selena hesitated. "Mrs. Whitfield...I want you to know...I would never willingly do anything to hurt you or Clay."

"Thank you," Danielle said quietly, meeting Selena's eyes directly. "I don't think I could be so generous, were I in your position."

Selena went to the door then but turned back before she opened it. "Perhaps you would bring Clay to visit at Montrose sometime."

Danielle tilted her head to one side, an odd look on her beautiful face. "I think you really mean that."

"Yes...I do. I think it would please Kyle. And us being seen together would be the surest way to foil the gossips."

The red-haired woman smiled softly. "Then I will."

"Good," Selena said, returning the smile.

She left then, feeling better for having come. She might not have conquered the jealousy or envy that was gnawing at her heart, but at least now she thought she could deal with them with a semblance of equanimity.

Selena hoped that equanimity was in evidence when she joined Kyle at breakfast in the courtyard the next morning. She had risen at dawn in order to speak to him before he left for the fields.

He looked impossibly handsome, she thought, feeling her heartbeat quicken at the sight. He was dressed in close-fitting knit riding breeches and top boots and a loose-sleeved cambric shirt that showed the magnificent contours of his muscular torso. Distractedly, she wondered how she would manage to disregard the potent virility that he was emanating in such abundance.

He seemed surprised to see her and raised a quizzical eyebrow as he politely rose and held out her chair.

"It was too lovely a day to stay in bed," Selena prevaricated, smiling brightly. As if to prove her point, she took a breath of the fresh morning air. The sharp, cool scent of the sweet olive trees was mixed with the fragrance of cape jasmine and roses.

The small breakfast table had been set up on the shaded portico off the small dining room. From that vantage point, Selena had a good view of the trellised garden in the center of the courtyard and the English myrtle and syringa shrubs that ringed it. She waited till she was served hot chocolate and muffins by a servant before asking Kyle how he had fared the past two days.

"Oh, wonderful." Kyle made a wry face over his plate of beefsteak and eggs. "If you don't count a dozen saddle sores and an aching head from trying to balance cotton receipts. I suppose I'll become accustomed to riding for hours at a time, but I'll never take to account books."

"I could review the books for you, if you like."

"Would you?" Kyle flashed Selena a relieved smile. "I'd be eternally grateful. So far all I've done is mix up bales and hundredweights and come up with figures that make no sense." He hesitated. "That is, if you wouldn't mind. I don't want Montrose to be a burden to you."

"It won't be, I promise. The household is so well run that I have little to do." When Kyle looked skeptical, Selena proceeded to tell him of the efficiency and excellence she'd seen, praising Bea and Martha and their staff. She then asked Kyle if he had found the same with the rest of the plantation and listened attentively as he told her of his impressions.

"The cotton crop appears to be in good shape, but it seems strange to me why all the slaves need to be in the fields. There's hardly a soul in any of the work stations."

That had concerned Selena, as well. "What do you think of your factor?"

Kyle gave her a sharp glance, as if wondering why she would ask. "I don't know yet. I never have liked Whitfield much, I admit, but I felt . . . for Danielle's sake—" Kyle broke off uncomfortably. "I believe he performed his job adequately when my father was alive. Since then he's been driving the field hands far too hard, I think, and he's too ready with the whip. I've already had to warn him once to put it away." Kyle's mouth twisted wryly. "Whitfield responded with some nonsense about God advocating the lash to punish laziness in slaves. He's developed a fondness for quoting the Scriptures, it seems, though I doubt he's interpreting them correctly."

Kyle picked up his coffee cup, his expression thoughtful. "Trouble is, when it comes to farming, Whitfield could be selling me a bag of moonshine. I don't know the first thing about running a cotton plantation—" Kyle grinned at Selena, a self-deprecating smile that was filled with charm "—as you can tell. I expect Whitfield thinks me a gull, and no doubt he's right."

"It might be wise if you found someone else you could ask questions of, someone you could trust to give you an honest account. You could make a better judgment, then."

"You, perhaps? Didn't you tell me you know about growing cotton?"

"I know something about it—my father grew cotton for a few seasons. But I was thinking you should talk to one of the slaves. I could offer you general advice, but you need someone knowledgeable about this particular plantation."

"There is someone... Saul. I only lived here one summer before I shipped off to sea, but Saul was my age. We used to fish together and swim in the creek. I don't know how open he would be with me, though. I saw him in the fields yesterday, and he scarcely spoke a word."

"I wouldn't expect him to be very forthcoming at first, at least not until he realized you mean to be a fair master."

Kyle sipped his coffee, his heavy eyebrows drawing together in a frown. "Come to think of it, when my father was alive, Saul was the plantation blacksmith. It's odd that he's working in the fields now."

"Have you considered that Whitfield might have overplanted?"

"Overplanted?"

Selena hesitated, deciding how to phrase her words so as not to condemn Whitfield unjustly yet to make Kyle aware that he might be facing a serious problem with his factor. "Perhaps Whitfield planted too many acres for the number of people he has available to work the land. That could explain why he has conscripted all of the plantation's craftsmen."

"Whitfield said that at this time of the season, every available hand is needed to thin out the cotton plants."

"This is an important period, but it's no more critical than any other, nor does it require more labor. And it shouldn't be done at the expense of other operations. Focusing all effort on the fields can increase yields for a year or two, but in the long run the plantation will only suffer."

"And you think that's what Whitfield is doing?"

"It's possible, and he may be sincerely trying to increase the plantation's profit. But in my estimation, it's wiser to let fields lie fallow than to overplant. Of course, that is my opinion. You should decide for yourself."

Kyle met her eyes across the table. "But I value your opinion," he said softly. "Have you seen anything else that I should be aware of?"

"Well . . . the field hands' quarters are in a state of disrepair, and the plantation store is lacking some of the most basic goods—like cloth for clothing. There is no school, either—but that can be remedied later."

Kyle's smile was wry. "You should be the planter, not I."

"The most serious problem, however," Selena said soberly, "is that there seems to be no adequate system of justice. My father believed that slaves should have the means of redressing their grievances and the right to complain of a wrong to the master in person. Yet the slaves at Montrose have had only your factor to appeal to."

"What about Bea?"

"She said she had given Whitfield full authority to act as he saw fit. And if there truly were problems with him misusing your people, Bea might never have heard of them. A slave would be too afraid of the consequences to speak up."

Surveying Selena's intent expression, Kyle nodded. "I'll look into it," he promised.

Selena relaxed then and smiled. "Thank you."

"No. I'm the one who should be thanking you . . . for advising me about the plantation. And for making the effort to befriend my sisters. I appreciate you taking the trouble, Selena."

"But I don't consider it trouble."

"Even so, it isn't fair to involve you in our family squabbles."

"No, truly, I mean to enjoy squabbling."

Kyle grinned at her words, the shallow grooves in his cheeks creasing, his eyes brightening with the glimmer of laughter. Selena flushed, not with embarrassment, but with warmth at the feeling of shared intimacy.

"Well, I'm glad you feel that way," Kyle acknowledged. "And as long as you're offering advice, I wish you'd tell me how to tackle the problem of Lydia. Kissing the Parkington lad . . ." He shook his head, grimacing at the memory.

"I don't believe it's wise to make so much of a single incident," Selena said cautiously. "It might be better to discover Lydia's feelings first, to win her friendship so she'll feel comfortable enough to confide in us."

Us. Selena caught herself. She hadn't intentionally used the word, and she wondered if Kyle would take exception. But he merely looked at her thoughtfully.

"Perhaps you're right."

For a moment they sat in companionable silence, Kyle finishing his coffee, Selena her breakfast.

Then Selena roused her courage and spoke again. "I met Danielle yesterday," she remarked casually as she chose another muffin from the bread basket.

Kyle inhaled the swallow of coffee remaining in his cup before losing his grip on the delicate Sevres china. Despite his fit of choking, he made a wild grasp and managed to rescue the cup before it shattered to the flagstones.

Selena looked up to make sure his condition wasn't fatal and then carefully returned to buttering her muffin.

Kyle stared at her between coughs. "And?" he asked warily when he had caught his breath.

"And I liked her very much." Selena glanced up at him. "You were right. Clay is a beautiful child."

Kyle cleared his throat once more, then shook his head, bewildered by her calm tone. "You're not upset?"

"No," she said softly. If it wasn't quite the truth, there was no point in saying so.

"Well," Kyle said, looking at a loss. Not knowing what else to do, he picked up his napkin and dabbed at his shirtfront. He wasn't wearing a coat or waistcoat; with the advent of summer, the days were too warm for the trappings of a gentleman.

"Well," he repeated after another moment. "I had better get to work. Will you excuse me?"

When Selena reluctantly agreed, he pushed back his chair and rose. He stood looking down at her a long moment and then shook his head again. Finally he turned on his heel, walking with long strides along the courtyard to the flagged path that led to the stables.

Selena followed his tall, powerful form with her gaze until he disappeared around the corner of the house. Her expression was wistful, her yearning for him written on her face.

She had brought up the subject of Danielle for a purpose: to clear the air between them. One of the reasons Kyle had been avoiding her, she suspected, was because he felt guilty about his relationship with Danielle. Yet she hadn't succeeded in making him feel more comfortable. Instead, he'd looked at her as if she had thrown a snake on his plate and expected him to eat it.

Selena sighed. At least their discussion about the plantation had been productive. She had made the first attempt at showing Kyle how to go on, had made him aware of a potential problem that needed immediate attention if it wasn't to get out of hand. And she would continue her efforts in the future. Not only because she'd enjoyed the past few moments of companionship, the sense of working together, but because she owed it to him. She was determined to help Kyle meet his responsibilities and to make his life a little easier. Later, perhaps, she could encourage him to channel his tremendous talent into work he enjoyed doing—such as establishing the steamboat service he'd said that Natchez needed.

For now, however, the plantation books awaited her inspection.

Selena gave another sigh. If she couldn't win Kyle's love, she could at least prove to him that she was a capable manager.

Chapter Twelve

"There is no mistake, Bea," Selena insisted. "I've checked my calculations three times, and the result is always the same. The yield from Montrose's last harvest was far lower than it should have been—and so was income."

Bea gave her a worried look. "You truly think someone has been stealing from the plantation?"

Selena frowned down at the open account book in her lap. The figures had so puzzled and disturbed her that she had sought out Bea to discuss her findings. She had wanted to make certain there were no circumstances she was overlooking.

But according to Bea, there had been no disaster that would account for the large drop in output. The plantation acreage was planted entirely with Petit Gulf cotton, which, unlike the former Black Seed strain, wasn't susceptible to the infestations that wiped out whole fields at a time. Yet comparing the weight of bales produced to the number of acres planted showed a large decrease in yield. "I'm certain that not all the income has been accounted for," she replied. "And it looks very much like theft."

"I don't understand," Bea said slowly. "How would that be possible?"

Selena thought over what Bea had told her about how planters conducted business in Mississippi. On plantations not wealthy enough to have a cotton gin, the sacks of cotton balls were taken to a public gin, where they were exchanged for receipts. These cotton receipts were as negotiable as currency and could be assigned over, just as promissory notes were. They were even used to pay bills.

Glancing up, Selena met Bea's gaze. "You said when Montrose's gin was damaged this past winter, nearly a third of the cotton crop was taken to a neighboring gin. That would have presented a prime opportunity for theft. It would have been simple to pocket the cotton receipts. It would also be easy to alter the accounts so the missing revenues would be hard to detect without close scrutiny."

Bea raised a hand to her temple, looking distressed. "It has to be Whitfield. He is the only one with access to the books. And he has been managing Montrose without much supervision since Papa's death. I've been too busy to review the books closely."

Selena's fingers clenched involuntarily around the nib of her pen, indignation and anger filling her at the possibility that Montrose's factor had taken such unscrupulous advantage of the kind and generous-hearted Bea. Eyes flashing, Selena glanced at the far wall of the sitting room, where she had hung the portraits of her parents to help keep her homesickness at bay. Dishonesty is like a pestilence, her father had always told her. It must be rooted out and destroyed.

Struggling with the effort to repress her anger, Selena closed the account book. It wasn't fair to accuse an innocent man. She would have to make certain of her facts before she approached Kyle with her suspicions.

"Theft is a serious charge," she told Bea. "Before I present this evidence to Kyle, I want to inspect the cotton gin to see if it truly was damaged."

Determined to waste no time, Selena made her way out to the enclosed gin lot and entered the building. The wooden cylinder of the cotton gin was in serviceable condition, she discovered, but a number of the slender spikes that encircled the cylinder had been broken off, and the grid was bent where the cotton lint was pulled through to separate it from the seed. Yet the damage wasn't irreparable, Selena noted, wondering why the work hadn't been done.

She was still pondering the problem when she heard shouts coming from outside the building. Hurriedly she went to the door.

The sight that greeted her brought her up short, and for an instant, shocked disbelief held her immobile. Across the yard at the entrance of the plantation store stood a gaunt-faced man, holding a long, rawhide whip. At his feet, sprawled on the ground, lay a young, dusky-skinned woman gowned in the simple cotton garment of a slave.

"Lazy slut!" the white man stormed. "I will teach you to disobey me!" His declaration was followed by a sharp, cutting sound as he sent the whip snaking through the air. The girl's shoulders jerked convulsively, and she cried out as the wicked rawhide sliced through the thin material of her striped cotton gown.

She was heavily pregnant, Selena saw with horror. The girl was clutching her protruding stomach, trying to protect herself from the savage force of the lash.

"Please, Mista Whitfield," she whimpered. "I be sorry."

The factor ignored her plea. "I'll not tolerate indolence!"

He had raised the whip to strike again before Selena found her voice. "Dear God, no! Stop it! Stop that at once!"

He gave a start, glancing over his shoulder at her, but his stroke never slowed. The girl screamed again in pain.

Selena began to run toward them just as a giant black man erupted from the smithy. Before Selena had taken two steps, the huge slave had thrust himself in front of the factor.

He was shirtless and barefoot, wearing dingy trousers of drab cloth, but he was powerfully built. He stood there defiantly, as tall and dark as ebony, his stance menacing, the corded muscles of his forearms bunching as he clenched his fists in challenge.

"Get out of my way, you black devil," Whitfield snarled, "or I'll flay the skin off your hide." With a vulgar oath, he brought the whip whistling down on the black man's shoulders. The dark skin that was glistening with sweat was immediately tinted with blood.

Still running, Selena finally reached them and grabbed desperately at Whitfield's arm, trying to restrain him. "I said stop it!"

Neither her action nor her words made the least difference. The factor wrenched back his arm to fling her away, sending Selena sprawling in the dirt.

Dazed from her fall, she had trouble recognizing the sudden pounding in her head as the clatter of hoofbeats. But from the corner of her eye she caught the sight of Kyle's powerful roan gelding, and she clearly heard Kyle's savage growl as he launched himself from the horse's back. Selena raised her head in time to see him land squarely on the factor.

Whitfield grunted as he hit the ground, crushed by the impact of Kyle's weight, his breath knocked from his body. But he recovered enough to yelp as Kyle's powerful fists rained blow after blow on his jaw.

At the violence, the roan gelding shied in fright and galloped away, while people started to gather about the yard, looking on in shock. Selena clenched her hands, wincing each time Kyle struck the factor, yet feeling a fierce satisfaction at seeing the vicious Whitfield receiving his due. After a moment, though, she realized Kyle meant to pummel the factor's gaunt face to a bloody pulp. "Kyle, no!" she exclaimed finally. "You'll kill him."

Kyle's face was contorted with rage, but his blows ceased with her frantic plea. Breathing rapidly, he pushed himself off the factor's chest, jerked Whitfield up by the lapels and shoved him hard against the wall of the plantation store.

Whitfield was not a tall man, and Kyle towered over him. "All right!" Kyle ground out between his teeth. "Start explaining. I want to know what you were doing striking my wife."

"Your wife?" The factor's eyes slid to Selena. Blood poured from his split lip, and absently he reached up to wipe it from his chin. "I didn't know it was her. But she had no right to interfere in the discipline of a slave."

"She has every right! She's the mistress here." Kyle's voice was as cutting as the lash.

Whitfield cringed in fright. "I was just doin' my duty—floggin' that slave for laziness when that black devil Saul tried to stop me."

A muscle in Kyle's jaw flexed grimly as he glanced over his shoulder at Saul. The tall slave stood protectively over the girl, his giant fists still clenched. Kyle's gaze dropped, taking in the young girl on the ground and her obvious pregnancy. The dusky cast of her skin was tinged with gray.

Kyle's eyes flashed with fury as they narrowed on Whitfield. "Get out," he said, his voice deadly. "You're dismissed. You have two minutes to clear off my land."

The factor stared at him. "But what about—"

"Now! If you want to keep your teeth." Kyle drew back his fist. "I'll have your things sent to your brother's."

Eyeing Kyle's raised fist in terror, Whitfield swallowed hard and nodded. When Kyle released the factor's lapel, he stumbled away. When he was halfway across the yard, though, he turned.

"I was just doin' my duty," he insisted in a shaking voice. "The Scriptures say to cast the unprofitable servant into outer darkness—"

Kyle took a threatening step and Whitfield broke into a run, glancing once over his shoulder as if to make sure he wasn't being pursued. Kyle watched him go, his expression, his entire stance reflecting the same contempt and anger that had filled Selena.

The ensuing silence was heavy with tension, and Selena was the first to break it. "Are you all right?" she asked the girl, her own voice trembling.

Gritting her teeth against the pain, the girl nodded. "Yes'um."

Saul hunkered down beside her. "You sure, Lukey?" he said gently, examining the wounds the lash had made. "You ain't gonna have our baby right here, are you?"

Selena understood then why Saul had risked his life to protect the girl. Yet seeing the tenderness of his expression, she suspected he would have done the same even if Lukey hadn't been carrying his child.

"Those cuts should be tended," Selena said softly.

Saul nodded. "I'll see to it." He helped Lukey to her feet, then turned to Selena. "Me an' Lukey thank you for what you done, missy. You, too, Massa Ramsey."

"I hardly deserve your thanks," Kyle said grimly. "It seems my action was long overdue." Moving over to where Selena was still sitting on the ground, he reached down a hand to help her rise. "Are *you* all right?" he queried, his brows drawn together with concern as she struggled to her feet. He stood there gazing down at her, his hands resting gently on her arms.

The tenderness in his eyes took Selena's breath away, preventing her from answering at once. Kyle was looking at her as Saul had looked at Lukey—in a way that made her feel wanted, cherished. For a moment the rest of the world seemed to fade away. There was only the wonderful light in his eyes that made her hope that they truly had a future together, with children and laughter and love.

The thought flooded her with warmth. Hesitantly, her hand crept to her abdomen. *Kyle's child.* Her heart started beating faster.

But the moment was only fleeting, for Kyle frowned. "Selena? Did he hurt you?"

"No," she replied finally. Kyle was protecting her the way he would his sisters...or any woman, for that matter. "Whitfield didn't hurt me."

But despite her assurances, she was grateful for Kyle's support. Her knees were shaking from outrage at Whitfield's brutality and her own dislike of violence.

She clung to Kyle's arm as she glanced around the yard. There were two dozen slaves looking on, all of them watching her and Kyle. Their shock had turned to approval; she could see it on their faces. They soon began dispersing to return to their chores, but not before Selena realized with instincts honed by long experience that she and Kyle had passed a critical test.

"Do you need me to carry you into the house?" Kyle's concerned voice broke through her intent thoughts.

Selena glanced up at him, a faint flush on her cheeks at the thought of everyone watching Kyle parade her through the yard the way he had at the Natchez landing. "No, I cam manage." Realizing she was still clinging to his arm, she quickly drew her hands back. "That was wise of you to dismiss Whitfield," she said, flustered.

His mouth creased in a wry grin. "He wasn't the best of factors, I can see that now. That was what you were trying to tell me this morning, wasn't it?"

"I had my suspicions. And I wanted to speak with you about another matter concerning Whitfield, but it can wait till tomorrow...at breakfast...." Her voice trailed off as she waited to see what Kyle thought of that suggestion. Perhaps she was being presumptuous, thinking he might want to spend time each morning with her. But they needed to discuss the workings of the plantation, particularly since he was now without a factor. And there was much they could accomplish if only they could work together.

Kyle surprised her by reaching up to brush her cheek with a gentle finger. "Till tomorrow morning, then."

There it was again, that tender light in his eyes. Selena felt her pulse quicken. "Perhaps...you had better go find your horse," she murmured somewhat breathlessly.

"Yes." But he didn't move. His gaze dropped to her mouth, while his voice lowered to a caress. "Moonwitch, you were wonderful just now."

She wanted to reply that no, *he* was the one who had been wonderful for rescuing them, but the way Kyle was looking at her made it difficult to remember her name, let alone what she had been about to say.

He moved closer. Selena caught her breath, holding it as Kyle bent to give her a brief, light kiss on the lips. It was the kind of intimate, companionable gesture a man might give his wife before taking leave of her, and it stunned her.

She stood there long after he was gone, her fingers held to her lips, wondering if there might be more to his feelings for her than simple chivalry, after all.

The next few days proved that her instincts concerning the incident in the yard had been correct. Word spread like wildfire among the field hands about the beating Whitfield had suffered, and to a man, they went out of their way to show their endorsement of the factor's dismissal. Kyle further earned their respect by returning each craftsman to his respective trade and abandoning the acres Whitfield had overplanted. With Selena's help, he also set up a system whereby every slave could have his grievances heard, and he resumed the work schedule the plantation had used before Whitfield changed it—which meant shorter hours and a rest period during the hottest part of the day.

In addition to Selena's tutelage in these matters, Kyle had superior help and advice from another source. Saul's brother, Rufus, was the head driver, and because of Kyle's intervention, Rufus became determined to see the new master succeed. Even Rufus was taken aback, however, when Kyle stripped to his waist and joined the field hands in pruning cotton shrubs. He wanted, Kyle explained, to see just how hard the work really was.

When Selena heard from Martha about Kyle's exploits in the cotton fields, she smiled in relief. She had always known her husband wasn't like the genteel planters of her acquaintance—gentlemen who were afraid to dirty their hands—but it eased her mind to see Kyle throwing his whole heart into the work. She had been worried about how he would fare, for without an overseer, even the best of plantations could quickly go to ruin. Yet Kyle had his people behind him now. Even as inexperienced as he was, his management of the plantation would likely be a success. And as she listened to Martha praise the new master, Selena began to feel more optimistic. Given time, perhaps her marriage to Kyle might eventually become a success, too. That optimism was buoyed by her growing friendship with Kyle's sisters. Selena felt she was making progress with Felicity and Zoe especially, but she entertained hopes of gaining even Lydia's confidence.

And then, several days after the Whitfield incident, Selena's optimism about her future with Kyle was shattered. She was working at her desk one morning when Martha announced that a female visitor had come calling on Master Ramsey.

Danielle, was Selena's first thought, and then she was immediately ashamed of the jealousy that twisted her heart. With fierce determination, she pushed it aside and looked up inquiringly, wondering why Martha had come to her. "Well then, perhaps you should show her to the parlor and send someone to fetch Mr. Ramsey."

Martha shook her head adamantly. "She ain't the kind to let in the house. You best come yourself. I left her standin' on the veranda."

Curious now, and chagrined that Martha would treat a visitor so impolitely, Selena quickly made her way down the hall. Finding the front door closed, she drew it open to admit the caller—and immediately realized what Martha had meant. Like Danielle, this visitor had red hair, but this was a vivid, flaming red, not lustrous auburn. And the gown she was wearing had a shockingly low-cut bodice that barely contained her ample breasts and boasted too many flounces for daytime wear. Her beautiful face was painted with the rouge and kohl of her profession. Beyond her, a one-horse gig sat in the drive.

Selena recognized her at once.

For a moment Selena stared at Angel without speaking. "May I help you?" she said finally, her voice weaker than she would have liked.

Angel lifted her chin proudly, though the gloves she had twisted in her hands showed her discomfiture. "My business is with Mr. Ramsey."

"Please . . . come in. I will send a servant after Kyle."

The red-haired woman eyed Selena warily, but she stepped over the threshold and followed her cautiously down the hall.

What did one do in such a situation? Selena wondered frantically as she led the visitor to the small parlor. She didn't

know how to behave or what to say—but then Angel, too,
seemed nervous. The woman's gaze flitted over the yellow
damask curtains, the French hand-blocked paper and the Aubusson carpet embellished with floral patterns before she
perched carefully on the edge of the brocade settee that Selena indicated.

In the end Selena did the only thing a well-bred lady could
do. "It may be a while," she said from the doorway. "Kyle is
out somewhere in the fields. May I have someone bring you
tea?"

"Tea? Me?" Angel looked shocked. But then she closed her
gaping mouth and drew herself up a little straighter, nodding
primly. "Yes, thank you. Don't mind if I do."

Selena left then and saw to the refreshments, but when she
returned to the office, she couldn't work. She was too conscious of the red-haired woman in the parlor. Finally she went
upstairs to the schoolroom to check on the girls, then to her
own room, where she restlessly paced the floor. She didn't
come down again until she heard a carriage drive away and saw
Kyle striding back across the courtyard, heading for the stables.

That evening, Kyle came home earlier than usual for supper, but he said nothing about Angel's visit, and Selena was
too proud to ask, especially with his sisters within earshot. Just
as she was retiring to bed, however, Kyle announced that he
had business in town and that he would be out late. Feeling ice
spread through her stomach, Selena searched his face. Kyle's
expression remained impassive, showing no indication of his
intentions. She would have liked to demand what his business
was, but she bit back the question and went up to her room
alone.

Kyle followed her upstairs a short while later in order to
change clothes. Shrugging out of his coat and waistcoat, he
tried not to remember the troubled look on Selena's face. He
knew he should have told her what he had to do, but after his
disclosures about his past relationships with Veronique and
Danielle, he couldn't bring himself to admit to Selena that he
would be spending his nights in a bordello. He couldn't lie to
her, either, and so he had pleaded business obligations in an
effort to spare her feelings.

At least Bea had promised to reassure Selena if the subject
came up. He had told Bea where he would be, of course, in
case he was needed, and Bea had understood immediately why

he had to go. Angel was calling in a debt incurred years ago, a promise made by his father, and he was obliged to honor it. And at least it would keep him from having to face this torment night after night.

Pulling off his cravat, Kyle cast a fierce glare at the door that separated his rooms from Selena's. God, he hated that door. How many nights had he spent staring at it and trying not to think of the slender, elusive woman sleeping on the other side? In reality it had only been a week since they had arrived at Montrose, but it seemed like a year.

Now he would be spending those nights at Heaven's Gate, since Angel thought she needed his help to protect her place of business. He planned to return each day to Montrose and carry out his duties as master, but he would have to miss those early-morning conversations with Selena. He didn't want to face her and see that wounded look in her eyes.

At dawn the next morning, he was still gone, so Selena ate a solitary breakfast, missing the intimate moments with Kyle that she had begun to cherish. The same procedure was repeated the following night and morning, and by the third night, despair was eating away at her heart. When Kyle had left for town, Selena made her way up to her room and went out onto the gallery. The air was heavy and warm with the scent of jasmine, but she felt too wretched to enjoy it.

Bea found her there moments later, standing in the darkness, staring down sightlessly at the night-shadowed courtyard. Selena stiffened, steeling herself against the pity she knew Bea would offer. She was sure Bea had heard about Angel's visit. Martha would have told her.

When Bea laid a gentle hand on her shoulder, Selena knew she was right—and Bea's soft words confirmed it.

"Selena...my brother wouldn't betray your marriage vows with a woman like that."

Selena felt her lower lip begin to tremble. Despairingly, she buried her face in her hands to keep the tears from coming. "Oh, Bea, she is so beautiful." The words were dredged from her throat, as if her fears had to be spoken out loud.

"Not as beautiful as you are."

Selena shook her head, unconvinced. How many times had her stepmother, Edith, said that her pallid looks weren't the kind to appeal to men?

After a long moment, however, she got hold of herself and raised her head. "Why is it," she said with quiet vehemence, "that I feel such a violent urge to scratch that woman's eyes out?"

Bea chuckled. "Because you're human, my dear, and your claim on your man is being threatened. And if you have half the gumption I think you do, you'll fight for him."

Wide-eyed, Selena turned to gaze at her sister-in-law, wondering if all Americans were so frank and outspoken.

"Kyle doesn't love her," Bea added soberly, "any more than he loves Danielle."

"He loves his son."

"That's not the same thing at all." She paused, then added gently, "You could make Kyle love you if you wanted to."

Selena gave a weak smile but shook her head. "I don't have the right color hair."

"I think you do. Kyle just doesn't know it yet."

"Very well." Selena took a steadying breath. "I am going into town!"

"Now? At night? Selena, you don't know how dangerous it can be."

"Bea, I can't stand it any longer—not knowing what he is doing with that woman."

"Well, at least take Thaddeus with you. And Saul. They should be able to protect you if there's trouble."

She sounded so pleased that Selena gave her a sharp glance. Bea's eyes were twinkling in the darkness; she could have sworn it.

"I wish I could be there to see it," Bea added smugly. "Poor Kyle doesn't stand a chance."

Neither Thaddeus nor Saul showed as much enthusiasm for driving Selena into town: Thaddeus asked frankly if she had lost her mind, while Saul could be heard to mutter that Massa Ramsey would flay him alive if something happened to her. But Selena remained adamant and got her way by the simple expedient of threatening to drive alone. Shortly she found herself on the road to Natchez-Under.

Both men were grimly silent during the carriage ride, so the sound of revelry was almost a welcome relief to Selena. Even before they reached the bluffs, they could hear the music of plinking pianos and squawking fiddles from the grogshops and

tippling houses below. As they turned downhill and negotiated the steep street, the sounds of bawdy songs and drunken
laughter assailed them—and a different noise, as well. The
shouting and rumbling of a mob.

Saul was driving, and as they approached Heaven's Gate
tavern, he drew sharply back on the reins. In the middle of the
street stood a throng of river men and trappers, two or three
of whom held torches. In the flickering yellow light, Selena
could see that many of the rough men resembled the trapper
she'd met her first day in Natchez. They wore flannel or leather
hunting shirts and homespun jean trousers, and some carried
long rifles. She was glad Thaddeus had thought to bring a
pistol.

Beside her, Thaddeus shifted uneasily in his seat. "Saul,
turn the carriage around, if you please."

"No, not yet," Selena said hastily. She was afraid that if she
left now, she would never find the courage to come again. And
she was concerned about the coarse crowd, wondering if Kyle
was involved in some kind of trouble.

Disquieted, she watched to discover what was happening.
When the throng parted momentarily, she was rewarded with
a glimpse of the man in the center. He wore a long black coat
and buckskin gaiters and carried something that looked like a
book in his hands.

"That's the Methodist preacher who came to town last
week," Thaddeus murmured. "He's planned a shouting revival for tomorrow."

Selena wasn't sure what a "shouting revival" was, but before she could ask, she caught some of the minister's words.

He was conducting an impassioned service right there in
front of Heaven's Gate, Selena realized with surprise. He was
calling to the women in the brothel, begging them to turn from
sin and save their mortal souls. His pleas were accompanied by
choruses of "Hallelujah!" and "God grant it!" by the men
directly surrounding him.

Yet not all the crowd were supporters, it seemed. The itin-
erant evangelist was being heckled by the river men and showered with profanity.

"Thar's trouble brewin'," Saul muttered under his breath,
and silently Selena agreed. She was certain the silver flashes
she'd glimpsed were the reflections of light off steel knives.

Then the crowd shifted again, and Selena drew in her breath.
Beside the preacher stood a man she recognized. The gaunt

face of Gideon Whitfield looked menacing in the shifting torchlight. From the corner of her eye, she could see Saul's spine stiffen, and she herself felt the urge to shiver.

"Repent ye sinners!" Whitfield called with fervor to the occupants of the brothel. "The kingdom of heaven is at hand! Resist the devil, and he will flee from you!"

He was lost from view the next moment. Abruptly, Thaddeus repeated his order to turn the carriage around, but as Saul gathered the reins, the door to Heaven's Gate opened and a hush fell over the crowd. Saul hesitated.

A man stood in the doorway, silhouetted by the light from the taproom. Even at that distance, Selena recognized her husband. Kyle was taller than most of the men, and his dark chestnut hair was visible above the throng.

She heard him calmly suggest that the minister go on his way, but the rest of his words were lost as the assembled rabble closed in. In a moment, though, Kyle raised his voice, speaking loudly enough for the entire crowd to hear. "The fun's over, lads. Miss Angel invites you to come back tomorrow night, when there isn't quite so much excitement."

"Why should we heed you, Ramsey, when the devil has claimed your soul?"

It was Whitfield, Selena thought. His tone was sneering as he turned to address the crowd.

"What do we want to listen to him for? A slave lover! He kept me from givin' proper discipline to a nigra who talked back to me."

"It's true I didn't agree with your methods of discipline," Kyle said with irony.

"You had no right to dismiss me for floggin' a slave!"

"I expect I could have found other grounds for dismissal. I had only to review the account books at Montrose."

Selena held her breath. She had told Kyle about the discrepancies in the factor's accounting, but he had decided not to prosecute Whitfield.

Whitfield's tone turned shrill. "What are you accusin' me of?"

"I don't believe I made any accusations, but if you'd like to make an issue of it, I'll be happy to oblige.... No?" Kyle raised his voice again, glancing over the crowd. "That's enough, all of you! The service is over."

Some of the gamblers at the fringe of the crowd moved, but no one else.

"They're ripping for a fight," Thaddeus breathed.

A heartbeat later a shoving match broke out, and fists began to fly. From what Selena could tell, the clash was between one of the preacher's flock and a buckskin-covered trapper. And Kyle meant to stop it. She watched with dismay as he plunged into the throng to separate the two brawlers.

For a moment she lost sight of him. Nor could she tell from the shouts and jeers what was happening. Then suddenly the crowd fell back, giving her a clear view. The preacher's convert was down, nursing his swollen jaw, while the trapper was facing Kyle in a half crouch, arms outspread. Selena gasped in alarm when she saw the long knife the trapper was brandishing in one hand. The onlookers must have thought the knife dangerous, too, for they were giving the contenders plenty of room.

When the trapper charged Kyle, Selena gave a cry and rose halfway out of her seat before Thaddeus restrained her. "Sit down! Kyle knows what he's doing."

It seemed to be true, for Kyle easily sidestepped his opponent, at the same time thrusting out a booted foot. The trapper went flying, landing on his stomach with a loud grunt and skidding in the dirt for a yard or two. It reminded Selena of the first time she had seen Kyle fighting on the street in St. John's.

The trapper lay there stunned, but after a moment he shook his ragged, greasy head and pushed himself up. The knife was still clutched in his large paw.

When he let out a tremendous bellow and launched himself again at Kyle, Selena clenched her hands so tightly that she could feel her nails pressing through her gloves. But again Kyle managed to avoid the wicked blade, this time catching the trapper by the arm and twisting. His knee came up hard into the trapper's groin, doubling him over. A right fist to the jaw completed the work. The trapper went sprawling backward and lay still, clutching at himself and groaning.

Kyle turned on the crowd with a grim smile. "Make no mistake, you scurvy wharf rats! Next man to challenge me gets his guts rearranged."

He was speaking to the rough men as if he were one of them, which was obviously the correct approach, and Selena felt a pride for him that almost overcame her fear. She shook her head when Thaddeus again ordered Saul to get moving.

"Devil take it, Selena! I'm not going to let you go in there."

"Wait!" She laid a restraining hand on his arm. "They seem to be leaving."

Indeed, the rowdies were dispersing—with some grumbling, to be sure—as they headed down the hill in search of more congenial challenges. The preacher and his flock came uphill, passing within a few yards of the carriage. Selena averted her head, glad she had thought to wear a dark bonnet that hid her face.

When they were gone, a relative silence fell over the deserted street. Kyle had disappeared. The door to Heaven's Gate was closed.

Selena took a deep breath then. "Would you wait for me, please? I shouldn't be above half an hour."

Thaddeus shook his head in disbelief, but he handed her down from the carriage.

Selena felt her heart racing as she made her way to the portico. She raised her gloved hand to knock, then realized it was a public house and reached for the doorknob, instead. Taking another deep breath to steady herself for what she might find, she pushed open the door.

The smoke-filled taproom was nearly deserted. In one corner a small group of men were gambling with dice, in another, with cards. Kyle wasn't in sight, but three women were lounging against the wall to the right. When they spied Selena, one of them straightened and tapped another on the arm. The third, a plump, black-haired woman of indeterminate years, sauntered toward her. To Selena's shock, she wore a lace shawl over a thin shift, and nothing else.

The woman must have recognized her, for she stopped suddenly, her eyes widening like saucers. "Oh, Lordy, we got real trouble now," she breathed.

"I've come . . . to see my husband," Selena said quietly, yet aware that her voice seemed too loud in the sudden silence of the room.

"Yeah, sure." The woman whirled and disappeared through a door, but she could be heard clamoring up the stairs. In only a moment she was back, but not with Kyle.

"Well, I'll be," Angel said slowly from the doorway. "Belle thought it was you when she saw that silver hair o' yours, but I didn't believe her."

A dozen pairs of eyes turned on Selena, and she felt her cheeks flood with color. But she stood her ground. "I would like to speak to my husband."

Angel placed a hand on one hip. "I like you, honey. Never thought I'd say that to a real lady, but you didn't turn me outa your house like I thought you would. So I'm gonna give you some free advice. You turn around and git home. This ain't a place for the likes of you."

"I'll leave when I've spoken to my husband."

Angel stared at her for a moment, then shook her head. "All right, then, come on with me." She turned without waiting to see if she would be followed, so Selena had to hurry to keep her in sight.

Angel led her into a surprisingly opulent bedchamber. A painting of naked cupids hung on one wall, while crystal wall sconces illuminated a huge bed covered with red brocade and strewn with satin pillows. Selena was accountably relieved not to find Kyle there.

Keeping her eyes averted from the painting, she stood awkwardly just inside the door, watching instead as Angel went to a cabinet and withdrew a decanter and two glasses.

"Sit down. We gotta have us a talk." Angel pointed to what seemed to be a small dining table at one side of the room. "You want some peach brandy?"

Selena declined politely as, reluctantly, she seated herself in one of the straight-backed chairs. Angel settled in another and poured herself a large measure of the brandy before beginning.

"I know just what you're thinkin' about Kyle bein' here and all, but you're off the mark. I didn't aim to steal your husband. Just wanted to borrow him for a bit."

"Indeed." It was a ladylike word, infused with a certain amount of hauteur and accompanied by a delicately raised eyebrow. Hearing it, the redhead grinned.

"Now, I told you, it ain't what you're thinkin'. The thing is, my bruiser got his cork drawn the other day—got knocked clean out with a bottle a whiskey. Waste o' good whiskey if you ask me, but it busted his skull. He can't even remember his name, let alone how to use his fives."

"What," Selena said faintly, "is a bruiser?"

Angel stared at her. "Lord, you are a babe, ain't you? Still wet behind the ears. A bruiser," she explained patiently, "is a fella who keeps the peace in gamblin' dens and...er, places like I run. He makes sure the paying customers stay settled down and the broke customers stay out. I got a cousin in Nashville, and I sent for him to come help me out, but till he gets here, I needed a man around the place. That's why Kyle's here. Kyle and me, we're friends . . . from way back.''

Selena didn't want to inquire too closely about the precise meaning of the word "friends." "I'm not sure I understand," she said, instead.

"Kyle owes me, ya see. I saved his little sister a few years back—pushed her down and kept a bullet from partin' her skull when some loose-screw Kaintuck was trying to shoot up Natchez. So Kyle's papa said if there was ever anything I needed, I was to call at Montrose. Well, I needed something.''

"So Kyle is here . . . to help you control the kind of crowd I saw earlier?''

"That's partly it. Someone had to drive away that pack o' Bible pounders. I've got nothin' against religion, ya see, but Silver Street ain't a place to be preachin'. It wouldn't do most of those scoundrels any good to find the Lord, anyhow. They don't have souls to save. But that ain't . . . isn't,'' she corrected herself, "the only reason I needed Kyle. There's been talk of burnin' this place down, and none of my gals feels safe anymore. I can't do business with my gals upset, let me tell you.''

"Well, yes . . . I can see that," Selena admitted.

"But what's got me worried now is *you*. Ladies like you ain't safe down here. You wanna tell me what put such a sap-skulled notion into your head, comin' down here at night?''

"I was worried about Kyle," Selena said quietly. "I thought he might be . . . involved with another woman.''

"Meaning me? Well, let me tell you, he ain't . . . isn't. And he hasn't been fooling with any of my gals, either. Kyle's had women chasin' him since he could fill out his britches, so he can pick and choose who he wants. And he *is* right choosy, let me tell you. He never looked twice whenever I brought a new gal in. Always stuck with—er, but you don't want to hear about that.''

"No." Selena looked down at her gloved hands, her cheeks flaming. Never would she get used to the candid way Americans had of speaking.

"So you came here to drag him back home by his hair?" Angel prodded. "Honey, take my advice, that ain't no way to win a man, especially not Kyle.''

Selena had the miserable notion the woman was right. She had shown incredible naïveté, thinking she could convince Kyle to return home. A babe, Angel had called her. More like a fool. But she had felt desperate. She wanted Kyle at home, with her, in her bed. And she had no idea how to go about getting him there.

But . . . perhaps Angel knew.

Selena cast a surreptitious glance at the beautiful redhead. Did she dare ask for guidance from a woman like that? But yes, she was willing to listen to any suggestions that would improve her chances of winning Kyle. Indeed, she was willing to try almost anything.

Taking a deep breath, Selena swallowed her reserve and her pride. "If I'm not going about it the right way, then what would you suggest?" she queried, at last meeting the redhead's gaze directly. "I do want to win Kyle, I assure you, but I haven't had much success. He hasn't looked at me lately any more than he has your girls."

"I don't believe it," Angel said flatly. "If there's one thing Kyle's not, it's blind. And you're not exactly the kind a man can overlook, anyways. Do you know what kind a price a gal with your looks could fetch here? In New Orleans, it'd be double."

"But it's true. He hasn't . . . not recently."

The redhead gave her a look of patent skepticism. "I was sure it was 'cause of you that Kyle's been so unfriendly lately."

"I don't think I'm the reason. Kyle isn't . . ." Selena hesitated, knowing she was blushing to the roots of her hair. She didn't know how to say this. "He isn't . . . sharing my bed."

Angel's mouth dropped open. "But you're his wife!"

Selena briefly described the circumstances of their forced marriage. At the end of the story, Angel looked relieved.

"Thank the Lord. I thought maybe Kyle took sick—brain fever or somethin'. At least nothin's happened to his . . . er . . . private parts." She had the grace to look embarrassed then and took a swallow of brandy to cover up her blunder. "All right, let me figure a minute. There oughta be somethin' you can do." She thought for a moment, tapping her fingers against her cheek. "Seems to me, the thing you gotta do is seduce him."

Selena's eyes widened. Seduce Kyle? Four weeks ago the suggestion would have shocked her; never would she have considered such a thing. But then, she wasn't the same person she was before her marriage. Indeed, from the moment she had met Kyle, she hadn't been the same. Even so, she wouldn't know the first thing about seducing a man.

"I'm afraid I wouldn't know how," she said forlornly.

Angel chuckled, shaking her head. "You got instincts, don't you? Even if you are a fine lady. Now listen to what I'm gonna tell you...."

She leaned forward with a confidential air. Ten minutes later, Selena was the one shaking her head. She was too shocked to be embarrassed. "I don't know.... I'm not sure I can do it."

"Sure you can. You jest let nature take its course, and Kyle'll do the rest."

The redhead rose from the table and went to the door. With rising panic, Selena latched on to the one excuse that might save her. "Angel, I can't! Not tonight. I left Thaddeus waiting outside."

"Thaddeus Sidlow? He hasn't been around here in an age. Well, I'll just invite him in. The girls'll keep him entertained."

"No! I mean...Bea would prefer that Thaddeus go straight home, I'm sure."

Angel grinned at her. "Then I'll send him straight home. If what you got planned works the way I think it will, you won't be gettin' outa that bed till long past daylight, anyways. Now, you get ready—and mind what I told you." And then she was gone.

Selena stared at the closed door for a long moment. Then, with unsteady hands, she reached for the ribbons of her bonnet.

Chapter Thirteen

Kyle came too soon. Selena wasn't ready, having only just removed her gown.

When the knock sounded on the door, she snatched up the wrapper she had retrieved from Angel's wardrobe and held it up before her, trying to cover her corset and shift.

Kyle must have been intimately familiar with the room's proprietor, she noted, for he didn't wait but a moment before he strode into the room.

"Angel? Belle said you wanted—"

He stopped abruptly, arrested in midstride, his words cut off in midsentence. "Sweet heaven." He breathed the words as he stood there staring at Selena. She had snuffed out all but a single candle, and her skin glowed pale and lustrous in the dim light.

Seeing her unbound hair falling in a silver cascade over her naked shoulders, Kyle drew a quick breath. For a space of a dozen heartbeats, he didn't move. Then slowly, he pushed the door shut behind him and propped his left shoulder against the door frame, as though he needed the support.

Selena returned his gaze, wide-eyed and uncertain. This was going to be much harder than Angel had suggested.

It was a long moment before Kyle slowly let out his breath. "I suppose," he said softly, "you're going to tell me what this is all about."

"I ... I came to keep you company." Selena could feel herself flushing. "Angel thought you might be in need of some ... female companionship."

Kyle didn't reply at first, knowing full well what Angel's idea of female companionship was. He shook his head, not trusting his ears—or his eyes. It couldn't be Selena standing there, issuing him a provocative invitation for the use of her body. "Let me see if I've got this right.... You're here to provide me with a woman for the evening?"

"Yes."

"You're going to *service* me?" He couldn't believe it. Not his prim, proper wife—though just the idea made him harden with arousal.

Selena's color deepened at the crude word, but she was committed now. She couldn't retreat. "Yes, if that's what you want."

"You're too much a lady."

"Well, perhaps... I mean... I think I could try...not to be a lady."

Kyle stared at her. This wasn't the first time she had set him on his ear with her unpredictable behavior, but he still couldn't believe what he was seeing. And now that he had started to recover from the shock of her presence in a bordello, he began to feel an undercurrent of anger beneath his skepticism. Anything could have happened to Selena in this notorious town. If it wasn't for that, he might even be able to find this incredible situation amusing.

"How did you get here?" he asked with sudden seriousness.

"I came in the carriage."

"Alone?"

"No, Thaddeus accompanied me."

"I'll wring his neck," Kyle muttered.

"No, please.... I asked him to bring me."

Incredulously, Kyle shook his head. He couldn't quite work out what his wife was doing in a bordello, but he certainly wasn't going to turn down what she appeared to be offering. If, of course, that was really what she was offering. It was hard to believe, so unlike the cold-blooded woman he had convinced himself she was.

"All right," he said. His mouth curved in a faint smile as he crossed his arms over his powerful chest. "I'm waiting."

Selena stood unmoving, unsure how to respond. The intent way Kyle was looking at her made her forget every point of Angel's sage advice. His hazel eyes were narrowed on her body, reflecting the glint of candlelight. She felt undressed, naked, vulnerable, even though she was partially clad. "I don't know what to do," she said in a small voice.

"Drop," he replied helpfully, "whatever that is you're clutching so desperately."

She hesitated for a moment, then obediently let the wrapper fall. It was all she could do to stand there motionless under Kyle's inspection. Her corset came to the top of her hips, her shift to midcalf, but her shoulders and upper bosom were bare, and her legs were clad only in dark silk stockings. Kyle's bold stare assessed her frankly, raking her with practiced detachment, openly speculating.

When his gaze focused intently on her barely covered breasts, an uncontrollable blush covered Selena's entire body. Which was absurd, she realized. Kyle had seen her without her clothes on; indeed, he had thoroughly explored her body with more than his gaze. Selena bit her lip in consternation. She was making a terrible mess of this. Kyle would send her packing if she couldn't do better than act like a frightened innocent.

"What comes next?" he asked dryly, as if to underscore her thought.

Give him a drink o' brandy to turn him up sweet, Angel had said. She could at least do that much. Seeing the skeptical smile that hovered around the corners of Kyle's mouth, Selena went to the table. She could feel his eyes following her, and when she had poured him a full measure of the peach brandy, she carried the glass to him, using both hands because they were so unsteady.

He accepted her offering silently and raised it to his lips, watching her all the while. Uncertain what to do next, Selena looked up at him, searching his rugged features. There was a maddening hint of amusement in his eyes, as if he found her efforts to please him humorous. Selena stiffened her spine.

Kyle held the glass to her lips and murmured, "Now your turn." She stubbornly took a quick sip of the brandy, realizing he had expected her to refuse. The potent liquor burned a fiery trail all the way down to her stomach.

Kyle startled her then by cupping her throat with his long fingers, tracing the rippling path the brandy made as she swallowed. Selena closed her eyes and shuddered, partly because of the unaccustomed spirits, mostly because of the delicate massage Kyle's fingers were giving the soft underside of her jaw.

"I think," he murmured with a warmth that bathed her heightened senses, "I'd like to know how peaches taste on your lips." He pushed away from the door, where he had been lounging, and bent his head.

Yet to Selena's surprise and dismay, he didn't kiss her. His mouth hovered just above hers, heating her lips, caressing them with his breath and the heady fumes of peach brandy, making her feel hot and shivery.

Use your instincts and Kyle will do the rest, she remembered. And her instincts told her he was too far away. Impatiently, she strained toward him. She was bewildered when Kyle drew back, just out of reach. Opening her eyes, Selena stared at him.

But he wasn't even looking at her. Or rather, he was, but it was her bosom he was scrutinizing so intently as he slowly reached up and curved his fingers around the top edge of her corset. Gently he tugged, gliding his hand from left to right as he drew the stiffened buckram of the bodice downward.

Selena caught her breath, her entire body tensing. The tips of her breasts were hard and aching under Kyle's warm fingers, and she realized that she quite desperately wanted him to continue touching her there. She remained perfectly immobile as he drew down the lacy edge of her chemise, exposing the erect peaks.

She saw his reaction in his gaze. His eyes changed, the teasing glint darkening, turning into something both primitive and powerful. Without a word, he dipped a forefinger in the brandy and slowly lifted it to touch a taut nipple.

Selena gasped at the ice-hot sensation, her hands clenching involuntarily.

"Do you like that, Moonwitch?"

His voice seemed to come from far away, penetrating her dazed mind. But she couldn't find the breath to speak. His brandy-drenched finger moved to the other nipple, just barely touching, slowly circling the rosy aureole. "Come now, lovely lady. You'll have to tell me what you like."

"Yes," Selena said mindlessly, this time clenching her jaw against the powerful ripples of heat that were streaking from the aching tips of her breasts to gather lower, between her thighs.

Any minute now she will pull away, Kyle thought distractedly, and found himself praying he could hold out till then. His blood was racing with sexual frustration, the tension in his body making his pulse pound. It was pure torture to have Selena standing half-naked before him. He ought to end this,

Kyle knew, before she did—if he wanted to retain any vestige of male pride. Yet he couldn't resist the lure of her pale breasts, the tight buds that were alert and beckoning. Lifting a softly swelling weight in his hand, he bent against his will. His tongue flicked the brandy-wet nipple, tasting peaches and warm woman.

He intended to draw the taut peak gently into his mouth but found himself urgently suckling, instead, rolling his tongue around the bud, biting it softly. He felt a fierce satisfaction in Selena's muted gasp of pleasure but knew that if he kept it up, he would soon be groveling at her feet.

Keeping himself in check with superhuman effort, Kyle drew away. "Give me your mouth," he said almost harshly.

She looked startled, but she complied, raising her lips for his kiss. With a grim determination, Kyle took her tantalizing mouth with his, forcing himself to divorce his thoughts from Selena's luscious body and what it was doing to his. He was determined to keep control of the situation—if it killed him. She couldn't really—after so many cold days—be offering her body to him like this.

His kiss was hard and hot and slow, almost lazy, and Selena melted under the heat of it. Her body, of its own accord, pressed against Kyle shamelessly, seeking the intimate contact, quivering as the fabric of his shirt rasped against her unrestrained breasts, as his vital hardness caressed her belly. She found herself longing to feel his skin.

She was supposed to remove his clothes, Selena remembered vaguely. She drew back slightly, and with trembling fingers she loosened the buttons of his shirt one by one and parted the edges of the fine cambric. Then she slowly reached up to touch a taut cord in his neck. He flinched as if burned but didn't move away.

Determined now, she trailed elegantly tapered fingers down Kyle's chest. The muscles covering his ribs felt hard and sleek, the slight matting of hair, soft yet springy. She felt his muscles contract harshly with tension as she drew her fingers over the hard ridges of his stomach. Looking up, she met his heated gaze. And then her fingers boldly moved lower.

His sharp intake of breath was audible, and so was the sound of her heartbeat as she attended to the buttons in the front of his trousers.

"Selena," Kyle breathed, the word a warning and a plea for mercy, neither of which she acknowledged.

He was full and hot, throbbing beneath her touch, and the silken feel of him roused a desire in her that was incredible for its acute intensity. Angel hadn't mentioned that, Selena reflected. Nor had she mentioned what Kyle's reaction would be—only that he would like it. So why was Kyle closing his eyes, as if he were in pain? Perhaps she wasn't doing it right.

Trying to recall the brief lesson she had been given in the art of pleasing a man, Selena dipped a finger in the brandy and repeated what Kyle had done to her: touching him with the slightest of pressures, drawing the tip of her finger slowly along the full length of his heated shaft.

Kyle shuddered and made a grab for her ministering hand, holding it away.

"Don't you like that?" She looked up at him, a question in her blue eyes.

"Of course," he said in a strangled voice. "But I'm warning you, if you keep it up, you won't be going home tonight."

As a threat it lacked substance, since it was precisely what Selena had hoped for. Taking courage from his reply, she did what she never thought she would find the nerve to do: slowly she knelt before him.

"Lord," Kyle rasped when he realized her intent.

Selena was more than a little shocked by her own brazenness, but she reminded herself that this was Kyle, her husband. Cheeks aflame, she leaned forward to taste his pulsing erection with her tongue.

"Lord," Kyle said again in a breathless whisper, his hand coming up to ride her head. But then he became completely still as he submitted to the shy explorations of her mouth, afraid to breathe, afraid he would frighten her away. Her touch was unpracticed and tentative but all the more tantalizing because of it. And it was driving him over the edge.

Unable to bear the throbbing tension any longer, Kyle grasped Selena by the arm and drew her to her feet. His fingers tightened as he stared at her incredulously. She didn't seem about to turn modest on him. Her flesh was soft and pliant beneath his fingers, her eyes warm and liquid with desire. Kyle shook his head. Every time he thought he knew how Selena would behave, she startled him afresh with some new action. But he was going to quit trying to figure her out. And he was going to quit fighting her seductive advances. For days he had suppressed his intense desire for her, and he was going to accept what she seemed to be willingly offering.

Without a word he strode over to the table, pulling Selena behind him. When he had set down the glass, freeing his hands, he proceeded to undress her, first loosing the laces of her corset, then helping her out of the thin chemise. He discovered he had trouble breathing as he surveyed her then. It was erotic: the slim nude body garbed only in stockings and slippers. The sight added inches to his arousal.

When she bent to untie her garters, he stayed her with a touch of his hand. "No, leave it. I want you just the way you are."

Selena caught the flare of undisguised lust in his eyes and abandoned the dictates of her well-bred conscience. "Shouldn't you take off your clothes?" she asked.

Kyle's glance slanted sideways, flickering over the table. He hesitated, struggling with his inclination to lay her there and bury himself quickly in her body. But she wasn't a tavern wench or any of the countless doxies he knew who would have enjoyed such a lusty coupling. She was his wife, a lovely, totally feminine lady. Clamping down fiercely on his urges, he strode over to the bed and sat down on the edge to remove his boots. Then came his shirt and finally his trousers.

Selena, much to her shame, found herself watching Kyle's every movement as he shed his clothing, drinking in the way the candle flame cast a golden luster over the smooth expanse of flesh and sinew. His coppery body was breathtaking, powerful and sleekly muscled. And his straining magnificence held a fascination for her that was almost hypnotic. She couldn't look away.

He settled himself on the bed again and met her gaze across the room. His amber eyes reflected the light of the candle, glowing with the same warmth. "Come here," he said softly.

She couldn't have disobeyed if she tried. She went to him at once, quivering as he lightly grasped her hips to draw her between his powerful thighs. His hands were warm against her cool flesh, the gleam in his eyes hot and smoldering.

He had wonderful hands, Selena thought dazedly as he began to caress her. All bronzed sinews and rough calluses. They moved slowly over her slim waist and flat stomach, stimulating, arousing, making her breath come too rapidly. Then he cupped her breasts in his palms, running his thumbs lightly over the nipples, and she stopped breathing entirely. He tugged gently on the peaks till they were distended and hard and Selena was ready to plead with him for release.

Moonwitch

Desperately, her hands came up, her fingers tangling in the soft thickness of his hair. "Kyle...please." She wanted him to take her nipples into his mouth, as he had done before, but he wouldn't oblige. Instead, he splayed his fingers and ran his hand down her body, sliding it intimately between her legs.

He caressed the heavy satin of her inner thighs with the subtle eroticism of an experienced lover, discovering all her tender, most responsive places, while his lips danced moist kisses over her breasts. In only a moment Selena was quivering and throbbing with aching need.

But then Kyle slid from the bed to his knees, letting his tongue swirl over the taut skin of her abdomen. When his lips moved lower, she gasped.

"Kyle...."

"Hush, I want to taste you."

She knew she should have protested, but reason fled as he buried his tongue in the curls between her thighs. Letting her hands fall to his shoulders, she braced herself for his tender assault. In this room there were no barriers, no inhibitions. Just Kyle and herself, naked and wanting. He was her lover, rugged and untamed, and she was his woman, her body straining toward him with a woman's longing.

She could feel him reveling in her body's heated response, and she abandoned herself to his touch, glorying in the strength of his muscles bunching beneath her hands. And then his mouth opened more, pressing harder against her. She whimpered when she felt the soft probing of his tongue, stunned that she could be so aroused by such a caress. Then a tremulous wave of desire racked her body so fiercely that she sagged against him, her quivering legs unable to support her weight.

Kyle caught her as she fell, and turning, lifted her onto the mattress. Tenderly, he gazed down at the trembling, sexually aroused woman on the bed. He had never seen a woman more ready to be loved. Her delicate skin gleamed pale and rich in the candlelight, a striking contrast to the lush red brocade counterpane and the dark stockings that ran halfway up her thighs. And the contrast was no less erotic than her unconscious pose. Her thighs were slightly parted, and she lay bare and open to his gaze.

Sweat broke out on Kyle's body in anticipation, despite the breeze coming through the open window. He had been denying himself, making the pleasure last, but the waiting was over.

Excitement flared through his senses as he stretched out beside her. His lips came down on Selena's, insistent and urgent, his tongue sinking roughly into the depths of her mouth. And while his mouth ate hers greedily, he shifted his weight and settled himself between her legs, thrusting with one long, continuous motion into her pulsing, silky sweetness.

Selena felt the hard pressure of his hips on her inner thighs and gasped at the bright flare of sensation that shot through her as he filled her. He was enormous and hard and fiery hot, and she wanted him with a fierceness that shocked her. She arched against him, clasping him with her long legs, drawing him deeper as she clutched at the flexing muscles of his back. She held his powerful body so tightly that she felt the thud of his heart against her breast.

Kyle's searing flesh branded her as he took her almost violently. She felt the passion building like a raging inferno, hot and wild, until at last her world erupted in a white-hot blaze that was too bright to bear. At the crest of her rapture, she cried out his name in ecstasy and heard Kyle's groan of pleasure as his body shuddered with the same fierce delight.

It was some time before she regained her senses and became aware of the heaviness of Kyle's weight and his harsh breathing in her ear. Not that she cared. The sharp edge of pleasure was receding slightly, leaving her languid and dazed.

Kyle recovered even more slowly. Eventually, he rolled onto his side to relieve Selena of most of his weight and pulled her with him, holding her close against his hard muscles, one of his sinewy legs still draped across her. A sheen of perspiration covered their bodies, and the night breeze was cool against their damp flesh.

Closing her eyes, Selena lay cradled against Kyle's chest, listening contentedly to the steady rhythm of his heart, which mated with his languorous breathing. She liked feeling the naked heat and strength of him, liked breathing the clean male scent of him, which mingled with the musk of their lovemaking.

Kyle lay sated and unmoving, his thoughts scattered and fleeting yet centered around the woman in his arms. It was incredible the way she could torment and satisfy his senses at the same time. Even now, exhausted from the gratifying climax, he wasn't immune to her tantalizing attractions. Her lips were parted slightly and her breath rippled across his skin, arousing his desire with a speed he hadn't thought physically possible.

Still weak from the violence of his first brutal release, Kyle eased his shoulder from beneath her cheek and pushed himself up, resting his weight on one elbow to gaze down at Selena. Her silver hair was splayed in disarray over the red counterpane, her exquisite face flushed. Her lips were swollen and glistening from his kisses, her nipples still puckered and aroused.

A heartbeat later, she opened her eyes drowsily. Seeing where his gaze was focused, Selena pulled away in embarrassment, bringing one arm up to cover her naked breasts. Kyle caught her hand gently and held it away. "No, let me look at you."

His eyes roved over her slim body, lingering at the juncture of her thighs, where he had found such a haven of pleasure.

Selena's hips shifted slightly in involuntary reaction as she fought the urge to squirm under the heat of his gaze. "Kyle...should you? I'm not sure it's right."

His mouth curved in an intimate smile. "Yes, it is right, Moonwitch. You're my wife. And I don't want a prim and proper lady in my bed." When a blush tinged her cheeks, Kyle chuckled. "Don't be upset, sweetheart. You weren't acting the lady a minute ago. I distinctly remember you screaming with pleasure."

Her eyes widened in disbelief. "I didn't scream."

"Liar." He said the word softly, with a secret light of laughter in his eyes.

Selena's blush deepened and he reached up to trace the outline of her ear with one finger. "It makes a man," he added with gentle amusement, "feel powerful to hear his woman scream."

"Kyle...please." He was teasing her, she knew, but still she couldn't quite feel comfortable with it.

He stopped, his gaze gentling as his fingers played in the wisps of her hair. "You enjoyed our lovemaking, Selena, admit it."

She hesitated. "Well...yes." But she said it in such a shy voice that it made Kyle all the more determined to overcome her reticence. Her reserve, her shyness challenged him.

Deliberately, he trailed his fingers down her lustrous, bare skin to the pale triangle of down and watched her eyes flutter shut, her lips part in anticipation. The pattern of her breath changed as her hips rose slightly to strain against his hand.

Kyle smiled softly, delighting in her unconscious sensuality.

He bent his head, pressing his lips against the quickening pulse at her throat. He would make her lose her inhibitions, he vowed. He would lead her to discover the depths of her own passion.

It would be a fair exchange, he thought as he nuzzled his face deep into the satiny skin between her breasts. She was teaching him to manage a cotton plantation. He would teach her the meaning of pleasure.

Chapter Fourteen

Selena woke to the sensation of Kyle's hands on her breasts and his body curved around hers, pressed against her back. He was warm and hard, his rising maleness stiff and insistent against the backs of her thighs.

Drowsily she opened her eyes, disoriented for a moment by the delicious warmth. Sunshine streamed in the open window, flooding the strange red room with brightness. When she saw the clothing scattered over the floor, though, she remembered the activities of the previous night and blushed. Turning her head on the satin pillow, she glanced up at Kyle, seeing the golden flecks in his eyes that danced like warm sunlight.

"Morning, Moonwitch," he said huskily.

She returned a soft smile.

Kyle raised himself onto one elbow, his gaze roaming over her face. "How is it that you're even more beautiful in daylight?"

"How," Selena demurred, "does one answer a question like that?"

A grin curved the corners of his mouth. "By kissing me."

He bent his head then and gave her a long, leisurely kiss that set her pulse racing. "Do you know," he said at last, murmuring against her lips, "that we've never made love in the daytime?" And before she could answer the question, he lowered his head and brushed his lips against her nipple. The bud was tender and sensitive, so that even the lightest touch aroused her. Selena drew in her breath and arched her back involuntarily.

His tongue flicked out to continue the delightful torment. "Don't you think," he mused, "that we should remedy the oversight?"

Selena's eyelids fluttered shut, and when she responded with a breathless "Yes," it was the last coherent word she spoke for a long while.

It was even longer before she found the energy to slip out from under the muscular arm that Kyle had thrown over her in exhaustion and leave the bed to wash and dress.

She found the water pitcher half-full and performed her ablutions with haste, for Kyle was watching her shamelessly. He had pulled himself up to lounge against the headboard, making no effort to hide his nakedness.

To her own shame, Selena found herself stealing surreptitious glances at Kyle. He looked starkly masculine and gloriously rugged with that growth of dark stubble shadowing his jaw. The sight made her skin tingle with remembered pleasure. And when Kyle met her eyes knowingly, holding her in a lazy gaze, she realized he was quite aware of how his nudity was affecting her.

He remained silent as she donned her chemise, but when she picked up her corset, Kyle shook his head. "Leave it. I want my woman to be a woman, not some trussed up goddess."

Selena cast a startled glance at him. "Very well," she said doubtfully, and obediently let the corset drop to the floor. When Kyle grinned with a quick, boyish warmth, Selena felt her heart flutter. She returned his smile shyly, realizing how much she wanted to please him.

Their intimate glance was interrupted, however, when a thumping knock sounded on the door. Selena had only enough time to snatch up Angel's wrapper before Angel herself came bustling into the room.

The redhead was carrying a tray piled with food, and she grinned broadly as she surveyed Selena. "I brought you two lovebirds some breakfast. Thought you might be in need of a little sustenance after so much exercise."

Selena's cheeks turned the color of the brocade counterpane, but Kyle answered with an easy grin of his own. "Angel, my love, you know just how to win a man's heart."

"Sure hope so. Otherwise, I'd be outta business, now wouldn't I?" As she set the tray on the table, Angel's glance took in Kyle. He had modestly covered the lower half of his body with a sheet, but his rock-hard stomach and well-muscled chest were exposed to her appreciative gaze. "You know it's past noon?"

"Is it?" His tone was bland.

"Yeah, and I gotta have somethin' to wear." Angel went to the wardrobe and pulled out a high-necked dark blue gown. "Can't go around in evenin' attire on a Sunday. Wouldn't be proper."

"I suppose," Kyle said, casting an amused glance at where his wife stood rooted to the floor, "we should thank you for the use of your room."

"Don't mention it. It's the least I could do after the way you ran off those Bible pounders."

"All quiet downstairs?"

"Downstairs, yes, but not up here, I reckon. Lord, a body can't get any sleep with all the caterwaulin' goin' on."

Her pointed reference to the cries of ecstasy coming from the room made Selena's face flood a deeper shade of crimson, but Angel appeared not to notice. With a swish of skirts, she crossed to the door. Before she left, though, she turned to wink at Selena. "You just keep it up, honey. I'd say you're doin' fine."

Ready to sink through the floor, Selena stood still even after the door closed, her face burning. She couldn't look at Kyle.

She heard his soft chuckle behind her as he got out of bed. "Why are you so embarrassed, Moonwitch? I'm the one who ought to be mortified. Seduced by my own wife in a brothel! It's a good thing my crew isn't around to witness it. They would roast me alive. Now come and eat breakfast before it gets cold."

Selena ventured a look at Kyle, and her embarrassment turned to shock. He meant to eat without any clothes on, she realized. And he seemed totally unconcerned by his nudity, for he flashed her a teasing grin as he held out a chair for her.

When she hesitated, his grin deepened. "Selena," he murmured, laughter in his eyes, "it's a little late for modesty between us."

She took her seat then, trying to appear unconcerned, as well. But she was grateful when he settled himself across the table instead of next to her.

Kyle kept up a stream of light conversation as he served both their plates, and listening, Selena realized she had never seen him so cheerful.

Eventually his good humor began to affect her, too, and she started to relax, despite the savage splendor of the bare, bronzed chest facing her. Halfway through the meal she was even responding to Kyle's bantering remarks. By the time Kyle pushed away his plate, Selena's guard was down. She wasn't at all prepared for his suddenly serious question.

"Well, now—" he leaned back in his chair and clasped his hands over his flat stomach "—do you mean to tell me what brought you here?"

"I . . ." Selena looked away, deploring her regrettable tendency to blush. "I was worried about you . . . when you didn't come home."

"So you came down here to spy on me?"

"No, of course not!" Her eyes flew back to Kyle's. When he raised a teasing eyebrow at her, Selena grew indignant. "Very well, I admit I wanted to know what you were doing here. But I didn't intend to spy. I didn't plan to stay, either. I was merely going to talk to you and make sure you weren't pursuing other women. But Angel thought that would make you angry. Seducing you was her idea."

"I didn't think it was yours," Kyle said wryly. When Selena remained silent, he shook his head. "I can't believe Thaddeus actually brought you to a place like this."

"I'm afraid I didn't give him much choice."

"What did you tell him?"

"That you needed some clean socks."

"Socks?" Kyle stared at her a second, then threw back his head with a shout of laughter.

"I know it was a feeble excuse, but that was the only one I could think of at the time. I didn't want him to know why I was concerned."

Kyle's laughter slowly died as he surveyed the soft flush on her cheeks. Was it possible that she might be jealous? Any woman's pride would suffer over a roving husband, but Selena wasn't the type to let her emotions show. Yet her distress seemed genuine. It was almost as if she truly cared. He was conscious of the pleasure that thought engendered.

"I hope you know now," he said softly, "that I wasn't pursuing other women."

"Well, yes. I saw you last night fighting those men. And Angel explained the rest to me. I think you might have told me, though."

"I didn't want to upset you." He paused, then glanced down at her breasts, where her wrapper had fallen open. Through the thin linen of her chemise, her rosy nipples were clearly visible. "Actually, I rather like the way it turned out. I was getting bored with my own company. That doesn't mean, however, that I want you coming here again. As much as I'd enjoy having you, it would be too dangerous."

Selena nodded, though she barely comprehended what she was agreeing to, Kyle's hot gaze was so distracting. It required a great effort to remain still and submit to his perusal without either covering herself or baring herself further.

Kyle must have realized her dilemma, for he grinned. "Come on," he said with a murmur of laughter. "Get dressed and I'll take you home before we wind up in bed again."

She obeyed unwillingly, reluctant to end the pleasant interlude, and Kyle was fully dressed by the time she had finished buttoning up her gown. She was beginning to pin up her hair when she felt his hands warm on her shoulders and the press of his lips against her nape. "Leave your hair loose," he whispered. "I like it better that way."

Selena shuddered, loving the way his hands and mouth felt on her body. His caresses were addictive. And it seemed as if he, too, were addicted to touching her, for his hands glided around her to cup her breasts.

"Wanton," he said with a chuckle when she arched shamelessly against his palms, but there was unmistakable approval in his voice.

Perhaps she was wanton, Selena reflected as they went downstairs to take their leave of their hostess. She had thrown herself at Kyle and practically forced him to make love to her. But she didn't regret it. At least now he wasn't avoiding her. Far from it. When she was seated before him on his big roan horse, Kyle wrapped an arm securely around her waist, settling her firmly against his body.

And the closeness between them this morning wasn't merely physical. Their hearts and minds seemed to be touching, as well. As they left both towns behind, Kyle continued to tease her with an intimacy that would have shocked her a month before. He roasted her particularly about Angel's parting comment. The redhead had told Selena that if she ever required a job, she knew where to come. But while Kyle jested about Selena's ability to become a prime attraction, his threat to flay her alive if she so much as put a toe inside Heaven's

Gate again held a possessiveness that warmed her. As they rode along the sun-dappled road beneath sentinel oaks and venerable cedars, Selena relaxed against him, enjoying the solid play of muscles at her back and the strong beat of his heart.

Only when they were in sight of Montrose did reality intrude on their intimacy. Selena felt Kyle suddenly stiffen, and she followed his gaze to where a gig had drawn up before the house. A woman and child were seated in the carriage, while Bea stood beside them, deep in conversation. In spite of her best intentions, Selena felt her heart sink. Then she firmly yanked it back up again. Danielle was part of the legacy she had inherited when she married Kyle.

"I didn't plan this," Kyle said quickly, as if worried about her reaction.

"I know," Selena answered with determined serenity. "I did. I thought you might like to have some time with your son, so I invited Danielle and Clay to visit."

Kyle placed a finger under her chin, turning her face toward his. He searched her eyes for a moment, then shook his head. "You," he said in soft amazement, "are the damnedest woman."

She wasn't certain but she thought it might be a compliment. She couldn't mistake the approval in the tender smile Kyle gave her. It was reward enough, she decided, for her efforts to quell her jealousy.

The meeting wasn't awkward at all after the first moment, for everyone took their cue from her. When she greeted Danielle warmly and shook her hand, treating Danielle for what she was—a close family friend—they all relaxed.

After that the visit took on the air of a holiday. Selena shook Clay's hand, too, which made him giggle, and then proposed a picnic, saying she had promised Felicity one.

"Pic-nic," Clay parroted, clapping his hands.

Danielle smiled. "I don't think he knows what a picnic is, but I'm sure he would enjoy it."

Selena returned Danielle's smile, then glanced at Kyle. "Perhaps you might take Clay for a ride while I locate your sisters. Would you like that, Clay, to ride on a horse?"

The child obviously knew very well what a horse was, for he began to jump up and down with delighted shouts of "Horsey! Horsey!"

So while Kyle took Clay up with him in the saddle, the ladies went into the house to find the younger girls and arrange for the food to be prepared.

To one side of the plantation buildings, at the edge of a dry bayou, was a latticed summerhouse half-hidden by a line of cherry laurels and overgrown with yellow jasmine and wild azalea. The women spread quilts on the grass in the shade but neglected the food in favor of playing a game of blindman's buff to entertain young Clay. Everyone but Bea joined in, and soon the air was ringing with shrieks of laughter.

Half an hour later, Felicity got caught by Kyle. When he proceeded to tickle her breathless, an argument ensued.

"Not fair!" Felicity cried, trying to escape. "Kyle cheated!"

Merrily, Lydia defended her brother. "No, he didn't, Cissy. You're just miffed because you got caught."

"But he peeked, I saw him."

Still holding Felicity, Kyle feigned a wounded expression. "I did not 'peek.' Could I help it if something got in my eye and I had to raise the blindfold?"

Zoe chimed in with laughter in her soft voice. "Kyle, you have to play fair. You have to chase us again."

"Play fair? I suppose you think I should pay a forfeit." He made a threatening face at Felicity. "Very well, then, I'll give you a kiss."

She chortled as he planted his lips on her cheek, then screeched as Kyle rubbed his jaw against hers. "Ouch, your face is scratchy."

Chuckling, Kyle released her and made a grab for Lydia, who laughed and scurried out of his way. Selena, who had paused to watch the dispute, wasn't so lucky.

"I think I could learn to like this game," Kyle acknowledged as his powerful arms snaked around her waist. His mouth swooped down, but his kiss landed on her lips, not her cheek, and lasted far longer than was proper.

"Not fair, Ramsey," Thaddeus protested. "You're supposed to be *paying* the forfeit, not receiving it."

When Kyle allowed Selena to come up for air, she was flushed and breathless. He grinned at her, his cheeks creasing with wicked dimples, and went sprinting after Clay, who squealed with delight. "Come, young fellow," Kyle said as he scooped Clay up in his arms and adjusted his blindfold. "You can tell me when I'm getting close." And the game got under way again.

Their play finally ended when Thaddeus, as the blindman, tripped over a vine and wound up with flowers in his hair. Yet the laughter never stopped, even when they finally collapsed on the quilts, for as soon as Thaddeus began complaining about his loss of dignity, Horatio squawked unsympathetically and told him to stubble it. Felicity had begged to be allowed to bring the parrot along, which proved a delightful diversion.

"Sub-ble it," Clay echoed, pointing to the bird. Danielle grimaced and caught her son's hand, while Bea shook her head.

Pulling Clay onto his lap, Kyle ruffled the boy's blond hair. "I wouldn't say that if I were you, lad. Your mama wouldn't approve. You'd best stick with 'Come to tea.'"

"Tea! Pretty corset, awk!"

Kyle flashed a grin at Selena. "Someone really ought to teach that bird to keep his tongue between his beak." Then he reached over and tweaked Zoe's nose. "What about it, puss? Should Horatio take lessons in the schoolroom with you?"

"Oh, Kyle." Zoe smiled shyly.

Leaning back on his arms, Kyle eyed the parrot with speculation. "I'm hungry. I wonder what roast parrot tastes like."

That brought a shriek of protest from all his younger sisters, and they hastened to lay out the food to keep Kyle from eating their pet.

After stuffing themselves on roast chicken and lemonade and peach cobbler, they sprawled lazily on the quilts, and even then the laughter continued.

Selena watched them all quietly, contentment flowing through her like warm wine, like a drug, the happiness and friendship so potent that it made her heart ache. She felt as if she truly belonged; this was her family, her life.

Her gaze fell most often on Kyle. He was lounging beside her, allowing his youngest sister to tug on his arm in an effort to make him return to their play. When Felicity poked at his jaw and asked Kyle why his face was so scratchy, his deep-grooved dimples flashed.

Rubbing the dark stubble on his chin, Kyle glanced up at Selena, his gaze locking with hers. "I forgot to shave this morning. I was otherwise occupied, if I remember correctly."

A soft blush crept to her cheeks. There was laughter in his eyes, and tenderness, and something more that looked very much like gratitude. When he reached beside him to curl his hand over hers, her heart did a sudden flip-flop. She could feel the warmth, the strength of his fingers as they smothered hers. Her blush deepened as she returned his gaze, the memory of his hands waking her body that morning rippling through her.

Minutes passed as they looked at each other while the laughter and chatter of the children faded. Kyle couldn't tear his gaze away. He was too caught up in watching Selena, in surveying her cool beauty, in contemplating her warm lips and unbound hair with remembered pleasure. She never ceased to amaze him. The startling way she had shed her decorous behavior and become a creature of passion, the kind of woman every man dreamed of having in his bed. The way she had welcomed Clay and Danielle. Far from wresting him from his child, Selena actually seemed to understand his need to be a father to his son. More than that, she seemed determined to bring them together. How very grateful he was to her—

"Clay, come back here this instant! You aren't to play there." It was Danielle, calling after the toddler, who had wandered away. The inquisitive child was nearing the edge of the dry bayou, where an earth slide had resulted in a sharp drop-off of some forty feet.

The possible danger drew Kyle from his pleasant musings.

"I'll fetch him," Kyle offered. With a last brief look at Selena, he climbed to his feet and went after his son. Then he and the youngsters returned to their games, while Thaddeus took Bea back to the house to rest.

Selena and Danielle were left to observe the play. Neither of them spoke for a time.

"I can't thank you enough for giving us this day," Danielle said at last, watching Kyle perch his giggling son on his powerful shoulders. "Clay's had too little joy in his life."

Conscious that some of the cheer had suddenly gone out of the warm afternoon, Selena met the other woman's dark eyes, seeing the sadness there. "I'm so sorry about your husband," she said gently. "I understand he is very ill."

"Yes. Jeremiah is dying." Danielle's voice was low and husky with emotion. Her eyes misting, she looked away toward the giant magnolias and the majestic, moss-draped live oaks of Montrose. "It has been hard…watching him die. Ours wasn't a love match, but we had a good marriage…before Jeremiah was wounded. He's a good man."

She began to cry quietly, silent tears spilling from her eyes. "Do you know what the hardest part was? Living with the knowledge that I betrayed him. He never condemned me, not with words. But the hurt look in his eyes when I told him I was going to have a child . . . I've had to live with that.''

Selena's own throat tightened. She wished there was something she could say in comfort. Watching Danielle, she could see how Kyle would be driven to console such a beautiful woman; a shaft of sunlight was striking her auburn hair, turning it to fire, while her unhappiness was enough to melt a heart of stone. Yet that consolation had taken the most intimate form possible. Selena flinched at the image of Kyle and Danielle together. It made her heart ache to think of it. Even so, she reached out to touch the other woman's shoulder in sympathy.

Danielle started then, as if suddenly realizing to whom she was speaking. ''Oh, I beg your pardon,'' she stammered, choking back her tears. ''I had no right . . . It was unforgivable . . . Kyle is your husband.''

''Danielle, it's quite all right.''

''No, I'm sorry.'' She looked appalled. ''I didn't mean to bring that up. But you should know what happened. You see, I was so wretchedly miserable, and Kyle was there—''

''I understand. You don't need to explain.''

Danielle hesitated, wiping her eyes. ''I should never, *never* have let it happen. It was a sin.''

''No,'' Selena replied with quiet vehemence. ''Such a lovely child couldn't be a sin.''

Danielle turned to look at her son. ''He's the joy of my life.''

Selena followed her gaze. Kyle was lying back in the grass now, letting a chortling Clay bounce on his chest. ''I would like to have a son,'' she said softly. ''You are very lucky.''

Danielle met her eyes, offering a watery smile. ''I think Kyle is the lucky one . . . to have you. You're so . . . serene . . . and comforting. I imagine you hear a lot of confessions.''

''No,'' Selena said with a laugh. ''Not really.''

''Well, thank you for listening to mine. I feel rather foolish.''

''Please . . . don't.'' Selena pressed her hand. ''I should like us to be friends.''

''Yes,'' Danielle agreed. ''I should like that, too.''

It was early evening when the picnic finally ended. While the younger Ramsey girls gathered the quilts, Kyle carried his sleepy son back to the carriage. Selena and Danielle followed more slowly.

"Did you receive the invitation to the ball Bea is giving for us week after next?" Selena asked Danielle. "If you can come, we would be delighted to welcome you."

"I don't know.... Jeremiah doesn't like me to remain at home because of him, but the neighbors are so critical...."

"If your husband doesn't object, I should think that the neighbors have no right to criticize."

"Well, we shall see," Danielle said with doubt in her voice.

Clay was already curled up on the seat when they reached the carriage, but when Kyle handed Danielle into the gig, the child opened his eyes and flashed one of his dimpled smiles as he pointed at Selena. "Moon lady."

Selena was at a loss, but Kyle understood and laughed; Selena's hair was loose and flowing, framing her face in a silver halo. "Clever lad," he murmured while his arm came around Selena's shoulders, drawing her close.

His intimate gesture startled Selena, at the same time filling her with delight and pleasure. She didn't want to place too great a construction on his casual embrace, but it buoyed her spirits after her unsettling conversation with Danielle.

She was able, therefore, to project a measure of equanimity when she said goodbye to their visitors. Danielle might be the mother of Kyle's son, but *she* was his wife. She was the one who shared his life and home. If only, Selena found herself wishing as they walked back to the house together, she could share his nights. Kyle had committed himself to protecting Heaven's Gate and would be returning there shortly.

He was explaining that it would likely be another three weeks before Angel's cousin arrived from Nashville, when they entered the hall behind his younger sisters. The girls had been chattering happily, but they fell silent abruptly upon realizing Montrose had another caller.

A handsome, blond young man was standing at the door to the parlor, hat in hand, looking as if he had been waiting for some time. He wore the white broadcloth suit of a planter, and the intense way he was looking at Lydia made Selena suspect this was the young man who had been seen kissing her in the summerhouse.

Her suspicion was confirmed when she saw Kyle's lips tighten. "Parkington," Kyle said with a curt nod of greeting.

The young man cleared his throat, his fingers curling nervously over the wide brim of his hat. "Mr. Ramsey, sir, might I speak with you?"

Kyle glanced at Lydia, seeing her pleading eyes. "Very well," he replied tersely. "I'll see you in my study." He ushered Tanner Parkington into the room, closing the door behind him.

Although curious as to why the young man had requested an audience, Selena followed Zoe and Felicity upstairs to freshen up. Lydia loitered in the hall, anxiously watching the study door. She was still there when Selena came down again.

Just as Selena was about to suggest they wait in the parlor, however, the door opened and Tanner Parkington emerged. His shoulders were slumped in defeat and disappointment flickered in his eyes. He met Lydia's gaze with a despairing shake of his head, then tipped his hat to Selena with a quiet "Good evening, ma'am," and let himself out of the house.

Lydia, her cheeks pale, marched directly into the study to confront her brother. "You said no, didn't you?" she demanded of Kyle. "Tanner offered for me and you refused!"

Selena followed in time to see Kyle eye his sister narrowly. "I refused my permission for him to pay his addresses, yes," Kyle acknowledged. "In the first place, you're too young to be considering marriage—"

"I'm not too young! I'm sixteen!"

"And in the second, he doesn't have the means to support a wife."

"What does that matter?"

Kyle raised a skeptical eyebrow. "Lydia, that kind of irresponsible question just proves my point. What do you propose to live on? For that matter, *where* do you propose to live? Tanner's father is losing his plantation."

"I don't know," she declared stubbornly. "We'll live in a slave cottage if we must."

"Romantic," Kyle responded wryly, "but hardly practical. You'd regret it the first time you had to prepare a meal or had to wash your own linen. And heaven forbid when you discovered you couldn't purchase a new gown that caught your fancy."

"I tell you, I don't care about those things!"

"Well, I care about you living in poverty." When Lydia didn't reply, Kyle's voice softened. "I told Parkington I would reconsider if he finds gainful employment. If he can prove he's willing to work to provide you with a secure future, I'll allow him to call on you in the presence of Bea or Selena. Until then, I don't want you associating with him."

"Call on me? *Call* on me?" Lydia wailed. "But, Kyle, I love Tanner! I want to *marry* him."

"Lydia, my beautiful little goose," he said patiently, "you don't know the first thing about love."

"I know more about it than you do!"

Kyle's gaze flicked to Selena, then back again. "That may be true. Very well," he offered, "I'll make a pact with you. In a year or two, if you're still of the same mind and Tanner has a reasonably steady income, you may marry him with my blessing."

Lydia's bottom lip trembled. "How can you be so cruel? You don't care if my heart is breaking! I wish you had never come home!" She burst into tears then, and whirling, ran from the room.

Kyle raised his eyes to the ceiling. "Females!" he muttered. When he caught sight of Selena watching him from the doorway, his gaze narrowed defensively. "Do you think I made the wrong decision?"

"No, I expect you were right," she answered softly. "Young girls sometimes have difficulty being practical, though, when they're in love."

"I'll wager you never found it hard to be practical."

Selena winced. She wasn't sure why she found his assessment so painful, except that it implied she wasn't capable of letting her heart rule her head. Kyle thought her too reserved, too cool, she knew. She wanted to remind him that she was learning to shed some of her inhibitions, to tell him that she was willing to change in order to please him, to become the woman he wanted her to be, but she could see by the way Kyle was plowing his fingers through his hair that his mind was still on Lydia.

"Would you try and talk to her?" he asked in frustration. "You'll probably have better luck than I in making her see I've only her own interests at heart."

"Yes, of course." She turned to go.

"Selena?"

"Yes?" She paused, meeting his gaze. The sudden gentleness in his eyes made her breath catch.

"Thank you for today," he murmured. "For giving me Clay...and you."

She felt a glow of pleasure start somewhere in the vicinity of her heart and spread downward through her body. "Yes...of course."

"I'll see you tomorrow, when I return from town."

"Yes, of—" Realizing she was about to repeat herself for the third time, Selena merely nodded and returned a soft smile. But as she left Kyle and made her way upstairs, she found herself hoping that Kyle's words might actually be signaling a turning point in their marriage.

The hope bolstered her spirits as she attempted to soothe Lydia's broken heart.

"Kyle is a horrid beast!" Lydia proclaimed as soon as Selena entered her room. "Other girls marry at my age."

Selena repressed a smile as she closed the door behind her. "He only wants you to be well provided for," she replied.

Lydia gave her a look that labeled her a traitor. "You don't understand, either! I *love* Tanner."

"I think I do, Lydia. I was in love at your age." Selena paused as a surprising realization struck her; she hadn't thought of Edward or her first betrothal in weeks.

"But marriage is a serious undertaking," she continued gently, coming to sit on the bed beside the weeping girl. "You should be very certain of your feelings before making a commitment to spend the rest of your life with a man." Hypocrite, her conscience scolded as she recalled her hasty marriage to Kyle.

"What happened?" Lydia demanded with a sniff. "When you were in love, I mean?"

"My betrothed was killed in a storm at sea."

"Oh. I'm sorry."

"I was, too. For a long while I grieved for him...and I didn't think anyone could take his place in my heart. When my father pressed me to marry someone else, it didn't seem to matter that I wasn't in love. My father was a wonderful man, and I wanted very much to please him. But it would have been a dreadful mistake. I was fortunate to have discovered that before it was too late."

"Do you love Kyle?"

Selena hesitated only a moment. "Yes," she said before realizing another truth. What she had felt for Edward had been a girl's love—adoring and starry-eyed and throbbing with idealistic devotion. What she felt for Kyle was far deeper—the love of a woman for a man.

But her consoling words seemed to have the opposite effect from what she had intended. Lydia's lower lip began to tremble. "I want someone to love," she whispered, her tears falling again. "I don't have anyone. Not since Mama and Papa died."

"Oh, Lydia...." Selena's throat tightened as she felt the girl's misery. It went far beyond the disappointment of losing a beau; anguish and desolation lay naked in her dark eyes.

With a murmur of sorrow, Selena gathered her close. Lydia gave in to the grief then. She buried her face in Selena's shoulder and wept brokenly. "It isn't fair," she sobbed in a muffled voice. "Why did they have to die?"

Silently Selena pressed her cheek against Lydia's shining chestnut curls, rocking her slowly, knowing mere words would never be enough to ease the pain.

Selena kept a close eye on the troubled young beauty during the next few days. Lydia seemed withdrawn and subdued rather than defiant, acting more like her younger sister, the shy, serious Zoe. Felicity, on the other hand, was the same precocious whirlwind as ever. Of the three, she appeared to have had the least difficulty adjusting to their parents' death. Yet Selena noticed that even Felicity would occasionally suddenly touch her sisters on the arm, as if to reassure herself that they were still there.

Having lost her own parents, Selena could sympathize entirely. She had no trouble remembering her own pain and loneliness, which she tried to explain to Kyle the morning after her discussion with Lydia.

His expression was troubled as he listened to Selena's account of the conversation. "Is Lydia really in love with the Parkington boy?" he asked finally.

"She's convinced of it, but I'm not certain. I think the biggest problem is her grief over your parents' death. What she needs most—what all the girls need—is understanding and love."

"We can give them that."

We. The word warmed her; it rang of duty and companionship, of shared responsibility between husband and wife. Yet Selena had to look away, certain that her feelings for Kyle would be written in her eyes for him to see.

Her yearning for Kyle, however, was matched by her yearning to help the girls through their difficult period, and in the following days, Selena made every effort to show them they were wanted and loved. She found it a joy to assume the supervision of their lessons—directing their study of English, history, ciphering and botany, and the more genteel pastimes of drawing, music and needlework—because it gave her an opportunity to become close to the girls. It wasn't long before she realized she was growing to love Kyle's sisters nearly as much as she loved him.

She was also beginning to settle in at Montrose. She took great pleasure in executing her duties as mistress of the plantation, and she enthusiastically aided with preparations for the ball that Bea was holding to welcome her and Kyle to Natchez. And during those early summer days, she met many of their neighbors.

The social life in Natchez, Selena discovered, was genteel, well regulated and indolent. The planters, in their broadcloth suits and broad-brimmed straw hats, spent their time hunting or fishing, paying morning calls, playing whist or chess or lounging the day away under a spreading oak, while their wives followed a similarly leisurely schedule. The gentlemen were all horsemen, always with riding whip in hand, while the ladies drove about in gigs.

Selena's life at Montrose wasn't as slow or pampered as that; she approached her responsibilities as mistress there with as much seriousness as she had in Antigua. But it was a life she knew, and she felt as if she belonged.

Her favorite part of the day, though, was the time she spent with Kyle. It became a custom to meet him at breakfast every morning when he returned from town so that they could discuss the plantation's operation. The topics ranged from how to repair the cotton gin and save the ten percent toll that the public gins charged for those services to developing a training system for their slaves. Selena wanted to expand their proficiency in wood carving, blacksmithing and a dozen other trades to make the plantation more self-sufficient.

Her first priority, however, was teaching their slaves' children to read and write. In Mississippi there were laws against educating slaves, but she and Kyle talked at length about ways to get around that, and Selena was pleased to know she had his full support. She was even more pleased to see his genuine concern for the welfare of his people. She had expected Kyle to exercise justice and honesty in dealing with his slaves, but he proved to be a staunch champion of their freedom, as well.

"The Negroes at Montrose," Kyle told her one morning over the breakfast table, "may be as well-off as anyone can be under bondage—at least now that Whitfield is gone—but they still have scarcely more rights than cattle. And I still find it difficult to stomach owning another human being. What would you say if I wanted to free our slaves?''

''I would say,'' Selena replied thoughtfully, ''that it is a compassionate and noble ideal, and then ask if you were a rich man.'' When Kyle raised an eyebrow in query, she explained. ''Most of the capital of a cotton plantation is tied up in slaves, so if you freed them all immediately, you would lose thousands of dollars. But worse, you risk losing the plantation entirely. When cotton is fetching a good price and profits are high, you can afford to pay your field hands a wage and support their children. When times are poor, there isn't enough money to pay wages. Yet you still have to feed and clothe your people—unless you're prepared to let them starve. Under such circumstances, a plantation couldn't survive more than a few years. Then everyone loses—owner and worker alike.''

''But didn't you tell me you had freed some of your slaves in Antigua?''

''Yes, any slave who wished to do so could work out his emancipation. But we did it more slowly. Service was more like a term of indenture. Each person was credited with a regular wage, depending on his contribution, and when he had earned a sum equal to his purchase price, he was given his freedom.''

''Could we do it here?''

''Of course.''

Kyle grinned. ''So when do we start?''

We. There was that word again. Kyle's growing acceptance of the responsibilities of the plantation gratified her, but the shared endeavor of meeting those responsibilities together made her heart swell.

After that, their discussions centered on establishing a fair wage system and formulating replies for the time when the neighboring slave owners protested, as according to Bea, they were sure to do.

Kyle was quick to grasp the intricacies of the accounting procedures, which surprised Selena a little, until she remembered he had commanded his own ships for most of his adult life. She was quite surprised, however, at how quickly he was learning the business of planting. Without a factor to oversee the operation, he was having to spend most of his time in the fields, but it had the advantage of giving him firsthand knowledge of the operation.

And in spite of his avowed dislike for farming, Kyle seemed bent on succeeding. Often he stayed out in the fields during the dinner hour, and always he was the last to return in the evening. Concerned that he was driving himself too hard, Selena made sure someone carried him a nourishing meal at midday and that a bath was waiting for him when he came home hot and tired.

One of these latter occasions—the first after their passionate night of lovemaking in Natchez-Under—marked a definite change in their relationship. Kyle called her into his dressing room on the excuse that he needed someone to scrub his back, then shocked her by pulling her fully dressed into the large tub with him. Selena flushed furiously, but after his tender and totally thorough assault on her lips and breasts, she was clinging to him with breathless passion. She scarcely noticed the discomfort of squeezing herself into the tub as she straddled Kyle's powerful body or her wanton moans of pleasure as he surged upward into her delicate warmth.

After that, Kyle made use of every opportunity to involve her in other scandalous situations—which Selena protested only halfheartedly. It was as if he were determined to break down her inhibitions, to make her respond to him without shyness or reserve.

He took her again when he had just stepped out of his bath, this time on the floor, soaking the carpet. He made love to her in the kitchen pantry, a dozen servants within the sound of their voices. He lured her into the deserted summerhouse and took her standing up, her back pressed against the intricately carved paneling. Even on horseback, he found an opportunity to arouse her. Selena never suspected his purpose when Kyle invited her to go riding and then drew her up before him on his horse. But as they rode deeper into the woods, his hand found its way beneath her skirts and worked its magic, bringing her to a climax so shattering that the roan gelding nearly bolted.

But he never came to her bed. The primary reason, she knew, was that he was still spending his nights at Heaven's Gate, yet Selena sensed he was also holding back part of himself from her. They were lovers, but not husband and wife. Not in the fullest sense. She wondered if he was engaged in a silent rebellion, as if by avoiding her bed, he could avoid admitting the finality of their marriage. But she wouldn't allow herself to despair just yet. The intimacy between them had deepened into something resembling friendship, and it wasn't inconceivable that she might someday win Kyle's heart.

It would help, however, if she could spend more time with him. One day shortly before the ball, she decided to aid her cause by taking Kyle his dinner herself. That morning he had expressed the intention of clearing a huge stump that littered one of the fields and had taken the gigantic Saul with him. When Saul returned at noon alone, Selena discovered Kyle's direction and rode out to meet him.

She was glad for the protection of her wide-brimmed straw hat. The hot June sun was bearing down on the ripening cotton plants and filling the air with the heavy smell of baking soil. She came upon a sweating group of field hands about to begin their own dinner, led by Rufus, the head driver. Rufus lifted his shapeless hat in greeting and grinned when Selena asked where Master Ramsey was working, pointing toward a distant clump of oaks.

She found him wielding an ax, and her heart leaped at the sight. Kyle had stripped off his shirt, and the hot sun glistened on his naked shoulders and the flexing muscles of his back. Selena pulled her mare to a halt, feeling a deep, secret pleasure in watching him. He was a highly physical man, earthy and sensual, and as vital as the land he had engaged in combat.

Her horse nickered then, making Kyle glance over his shoulder. For a moment his eyes locked with hers, and then his mouth curved in a slow smile, as if he knew she'd been admiring his body.

"I've brought your dinner," Selena said, flustered.

With an easy swing, Kyle sank the ax into the stump and came forward to meet her. "You look good enough to eat yourself." The heat smoldering in his gaze as he surveyed her gown of cherry-colored muslin emphasized his appreciation, but he didn't reach up for her as she expected. "Can you dismount on your own?" he asked, wiping his palms on his breeches. "I'm too dirty to touch you."

He wasn't, to her mind, but in the interest of modesty, she let his comment pass. She hadn't yet lost enough of her reserve to tell him that his half-savage state gave him an air of raw strength or that she found the musky male scent of his body more arousing than even the sight of him, since she associated it with their lovemaking.

When she had slipped down, Kyle took the reins from her and led the mare to a nearby oak. While he retrieved the flask of lemonade and bundle of food she had brought, Selena settled herself in the shade and removed her hat.

She caught the flicker of pleasure in Kyle's eyes as he joined her. Since that morning in Natchez-Under when Kyle had claimed that he preferred her hair loose, she had worn it down in the daytime. Now it was dressed simply, pulled back from her face with combs.

He surveyed her with appreciation, then unwrapped the linen napkin and applied himself to his meal. They chatted amiably while he ate, and when he was done, Kyle put his hands behind his head and lay back on the grass with a contented sigh. "Those apple tarts were the best I've ever tasted. I can't believe they came from Montrose's kitchens. Not even Martha can cook like that."

"It was my mother's receipt. I showed Martha how to make them."

"Your talents are limitless, Moonwitch." Glancing up at her, Kyle flashed her a slow grin. "I didn't realize what a bargain I was getting when I married you."

It was said in a teasing voice, but it made Selena's heart ache. She wanted to do more for him than bring him apple tarts. "Kyle," she said gravely, "do you remember when we talked about Natchez needing a regular steamboat service?"

"Um-hmm."

"If you were to establish one, how would you go about it?"

"Hypothetically? If I had the necessary capital, I'd commission a shipwright to build a couple of steamboats after Shreve's design. Then I'd get the legislature to grant a charter and hire a commission agent to handle the business of arranging cargos."

From his ready answer, she knew he had already given it some thought. "How much capital would it take?" she asked.

Kyle frowned up at the oak branches above his head. "I'd guess about a hundred thousand dollars. But I don't have that kind of money on hand."

"What about my dowry?"

"The money from the sale of your plantation? I couldn't use that."

"Why not?"

"Because I'd feel like a blasted fortune hunter, that's why." He shook his head. "No, if I wanted to start my own steamboat service, I'd sell one of my ships and try to come up with the rest from private investors."

"Why, if your ships are making a profit? And wouldn't private investors demand a say in how the service was run? It would be better if you were solely in control."

"You have a point."

"Then why don't you use my dowry? It's rightfully yours, anyway. You could treat me as an investor, if your conscience won't let you act otherwise."

Kyle's eyes widened in mild shock as he turned his head to stare at her. "You're really serious."

"Yes. It would suit you far better than being a planter, wouldn't it?"

"Of course it would."

"So why don't you do it?"

He shrugged uncomfortably. "Because, I'm needed here."

"It would be necessary to hire a factor, of course, but Rufus is capable of seeing to the harvest, and I can handle the accounting."

He stared at her a long moment before he slowly began to chuckle. "You've been waiting a long time to propose this, haven't you, Moonwitch?"

The color in her cheeks deepened, but her blush only confirmed Kyle's suspicion. Shaking his head in amazement, he reached out to take her hand and carry it to his lips. "Do you know the surprising thing? A month ago I would have jumped at the chance to become involved in such a venture, but now... No, Moonwitch. I greatly appreciate your offer, and I may take you up on it someday, but not now."

"Why not?" Selena queried, disconcerted by the gentle touch of his lips, by the bemusement and affection in his hazel eyes.

"Because I'm just now beginning to make progress with the plantation. With your help, I've remedied some of the damage Whitfield caused—and even made the operation better than it was under my father's rule. There's a kind of pride in that...." Kyle shifted his glance, gazing thoughtfully up at the sky again. He hadn't released her hand, and the pressure of his fingers was friendly and warm.

"It isn't as onerous as I expected," Kyle said seriously. "Running a plantation isn't so very different from commanding my ship or dealing with my crew. You've made me see that...." He laughed softly then and slanted a glance up at her.

"Next you'll be turning me into a farmer. Imagine, *me* a farmer." His eyes danced with rare delight as his gaze locked with hers. "Is there anything you can't do?"

Yes, Selena thought silently. I can't make you love me. And I wish with all my heart that I could.

Chapter Fifteen

Friendship, not love. That was all Kyle seemed to be willing to offer her—although there were times during the following week when Selena felt an occasional glimmer of hope that she might be wrong. Frequently Kyle treated her with the same affection he showed his sisters and looked at her with the same tender light in his eyes.

She wished it was love. If only she could truly be Kyle's wife, if only she could win a place in his heart, she thought she would be totally content. Still, her life was good. There were moments of quiet happiness and shared laughter, days filled with work and play, with neighbors and family concerns…the squabbles that Kyle had taken for granted but that Selena was learning to cherish.

And she was needed. The girls needed her, and so did Kyle, even if he had refused her dowry, even if he was beginning to stand on his own where the plantation was concerned. His ability to apply the skills and knowledge he had learned at sea to the operation contributed greatly to his success, and his growing expertise with the plantation meant he didn't have to depend on Selena so heavily or seek her advice quite so often.

Yet her new family *did* need her, Selena was convinced—if only to intervene in their disputes. That conviction was confirmed when one of their squabbles broke out the day before the ball, when the ladies of the Female Charitable Society came to call. Lydia had argued that Zoe and Felicity shouldn't be allowed downstairs, but Bea allowed the younger girls to appear briefly to meet the six ladies of the society and the Presbyterian minister, Thomas Henderson.

Bea had invited them all for tea with the intention of introducing Selena and involving both her and Kyle more deeply in community affairs. Unfortunately for Kyle, the ladies brought with them the same traveling Methodist preacher who had been trying to close down Heaven's Gate—a starkly dressed gentleman named Denby. Not only was Kyle required to receive the man, but he was forced to listen politely when Denby managed to corner him. By the time the tea tray was brought in, Kyle's expression was one of boredom, exasperation and desperation.

Intent on rescuing her husband, Selena joined the two men in time to hear the Reverend Denby make a solemn pronouncement.

"I am pleased to say that Mr. Gideon Whitfield has chosen to take up the cloth. He will accompany me when I leave this good city, to assist me in teaching the word of God."

Bea, who was close enough to overhear the conversation, gave Selena a skeptical look that clearly said, "God begins in the heart, so what is Whitfield doing spreading His word?"

Selena thoroughly agreed but wouldn't say so in front of the reverend. Just as she was about to murmur a noncommittal reply, however, Denby raised a pinch of snuff to his nostrils and lapsed into a sneezing fit so violent that it threatened to shake the house down. Immediately the chatter ceased while the curious guests turned to stare.

Selena was worried for the poor gentleman. Not only were his eyes streaming with tears, but he couldn't catch his breath. Indeed, he couldn't even stand without Kyle's support. When eventually Denby's sneezing slowed, Kyle retrieved the snuffbox from the floor, where it had fallen. His gaze narrowing, he dipped a finger into the box and gingerly tasted the remaining contents.

"What in blazes!" Kyle swore. "This is pepper!" His murderous gaze swung to the door. "Felicity," he added in that same awful tone. "I'll flay her alive."

In four strides he was across the room and out in the hall. Selena quickly followed. She was able to deduce enough about what had happened to make her fear for Felicity's skin, if not her life.

The young girl was crouching at the head of the stairs, peering between the rails of the banister. She gave a yelp when she saw her furious brother coming after her. Leaping to her feet, she made a dash for the safety of her bedchamber.

Kyle was faster. He took the stairs two at a time and caught Felicity by the scruff of her gown's neckline as she reached the door. "Oh, no you don't, you little wretch."

"Kyle, don't hurt her," Selena pleaded breathlessly as she climbed the last steps.

"Hurt her! I'm going to string her up by her thumbs. Denby could have choked to death."

"I'm sure Felicity didn't mean to put him in danger."

"Confound it, Selena! What she did was more than a harmless prank."

Selena glanced down at the hall below, noticing the attention they were attracting; two of the ladies had left the parlor and were staring up at them. "Perhaps we should discuss this elsewhere."

Kyle looked as if he might like to give vent to an oath, but he clamped his jaw shut. Marching Felicity into her room, he shut the door after Selena, then folded his arms across his chest and glared at his sister. "All right, you shameless little hellion. How do you explain yourself?"

Felicity gave him a frightened glance. "I just wanted to have some fun."

If anything, Kyle's expression became more savage.

"Kyle," Selena said gently, forestalling his explosion.

"Very well. I'm still waiting, Felicity, for you to give me one good reason why you would serve such a trick to a guest."

"Because Reverend Denby is a prig. He patted me on the head and told me I was a pretty creature."

There was a pronounced silence while Kyle considered her answer. Both Felicity and Selena watched him anxiously. His lips were still pressed in a tight line, but a muscle flexed in his jaw, as if he were trying to bite back humor. "You might be right, pumpkin," he said finally in a dry tone, "but not even a prig deserves a noseful of pepper."

"I won't do it again, I promise."

"I trust not. Or you'll find yourself with a dose of your own medicine."

"I think, Felicity," Selena observed to change the subject, "that you owe Reverend Denby an apology."

.Felicity nodded eagerly.

"And," Kyle added, "I want your promise that you won't play any more tricks."

Felicity gulped. "I won't, but..." She gave Selena a desperate look. "What if I already have?"

Selena experienced a sinking feeling. "Felicity, what did you do?"

"I . . . left Horatio's cage open."

Kyle raised his eyes to the ceiling as if praying for patience, while Selena bit her lip. "I'd better check on him," she said worriedly.

Leaving Kyle to deal with his sister, Selena hastened downstairs. She didn't need to search for the parrot, however, for she could hear his raucous squawks coming from the parlor. It would have been dreadful enough if he had strictly been issuing his usual invitation, but her worst fears were realized when she caught what he was saying. Mortified, Selena hurried into the room, where she found Horatio perched near the ceiling on the punkah fan, overlooking the crumpets and cucumber sandwiches. He was flapping his feathers as he entertained the guests, his lively curses drawing titters and shocked gasps from the company.

Cheeks aflame, Selena scooped up a handful of blueberries from a dish and offered it to the bird.

"Blast it! Awk. Blast it!" Horatio replied, but after a moment, he fluttered down to perch on her arm and devour his feast.

Managing a polite disclaimer, Selena turned to make her escape with the parrot and found Kyle watching her from the doorway. He looked at her with laughter in his eyes but responded to her unspoken plea by launching into an apology to the company for the bird's scandalous behavior. Intensely grateful, she gave Kyle a strained smile as she passed.

She found Horatio's cage in her office, where she had left it, and when she had restored the parrot to his home, Selena took a deep breath and returned to the parlor, reluctant to face the guests after such a scene.

Much to her chagrin, those same ladies were present the next evening at the ball. Selena had strong reservations about the occasion. She dreaded meeting countless strangers and being subjected to their critical scrutiny. Yet when the day arrived, she was relieved to find she had already met many of them, and that they seemed to accept her with genuine goodwill.

The ball was a great success, if one judged by the numbers of guests that had been pouring into Montrose all day and who now overflowed the house. The only drawback to an otherwise perfect evening was the heat, Selena thought as she glanced around the crowded drawing room. The candlelight that blazed from a myriad of wax tapers looked lovely gleaming off silver dishes and polished floors, but it added greatly to the warmth.

The gathering was less formal than those she was accustomed to, indeed was a study in contrasts—lavish elegance vying with rustic simplicity. In the drawing room played an orchestra of violins and tambourines, while in the courtyard, a grizzled old black man performed a Virginia jig upon a gourd fiddle. The ladies' costumes, too, presented a view of a disparate society. The planters' wives had arrived in carriages, bedecked in jewels and lace, yet their less affluent female neighbors had ridden on horseback, dressed in calicoes and were carrying their ball gowns in bundles.

Kyle, in an elegant forest-green coat, was a contrast all to himself, Selena thought as her eyes sought him above the heads of the guests. Rugged yet graceful, he possessed a strength and vitality that was incredibly appealing to her heightened senses.

His blatant masculinity appealed to the other females present, as well, Selena was aware. More than once she caught another lady favoring Kyle with a discreet glance, looking at him sideways with fluttering lashes and a pretty blush. He returned their interest with an open friendliness, his teasing remarks no different from his interactions with his sisters, the aristocratic dowager who had conferred her presence on the ball or even Angel. Indeed, Selena was beginning to realize that Kyle accorded highborn ladies the same treatment as the lowest of tavern wenches—he treated both simply as women.

Yet she couldn't help experiencing an ungovernable jealousy at all the attention he was attracting, especially when she observed an ebony-haired beauty fawning over Kyle during an entire set of dances. When the set ended, Selena realized her concern was much too obvious, for it was the first thing Bea mentioned when she joined her.

"Don't pay Miss Jenkins any mind," Bea advised. "She's one of the dozens and dozens of ladies who have pursued my brother to no avail."

"I'm not concerned," Selena said untruthfully. "Like I, she hasn't the right color hair."

"Well, you put her in the shade. You look exquisite—as I'm sure I've already told you."

Selena smiled gratefully at the compliment. In deference to the poorer guests, she had eschewed jewelry and chosen a bandeau that sported an ostrich plume as her only adornment, yet her empire-waist lutestring gown, the shade of dusty violets, bespoke wealth and supreme good taste. She thought she looked attractive, but in the face of such competition from the other beauties present, she needed the reassurance.

Bea gave her that and more, swearing that Kyle had only danced with Miss Jenkins out of duty. Yet Selena was grateful when he turned the dark-haired beauty over to a new partner.

When her own partner claimed her for the next dance, she made a determined effort to bring her jealousy under control, trying not to gaze at her husband above once a minute. Even so she found it difficult. She was far more aware of Kyle than she had ever been of any man. He had awakened her physically to a lush world of pleasure and desire and sensation, of aching need and passion. A thousand times a day Selena found herself wanting to touch him, to slip into his arms and fit her lips and her body against his, and she found it a torment not to be able to do so now.

More incredible, though, was his ability to rouse her with merely a glance. Kyle had only to caress her with those glowing hazel eyes to remind her of past moments when he had been buried deep inside her, and she would start to quiver.

Still, it was only lust. Her plan to make Kyle fall in love with her, she knew, was no further along than it had been several days earlier when she'd met him in the fields. Since then they'd had little chance for intimacy other than their early-morning conferences. And she hadn't spoken to Kyle at all this evening, not since the first dance, when, as the guests of honor, they had opened the ball together.

It was with the hope of drawing Kyle away from the company for a moment or two of privacy that Selena refused the next dance and threaded her way through the crowd. She found him conversing with an elderly couple, but no sooner had the couple wandered off to partake of the buffet supper than they were joined by the Reverend Denby.

Selena tried not to show her disappointment. She was politely inquiring of Reverend Denby whether he had recovered from his ordeal with the pepper, when a hush fell over the crowd. Turning to see what was causing the problem, Selena spied Danielle Whitfield standing in the doorway to the drawing room. Her chin was lifted slightly, and she clung with the slightest pressure to Orrin Chandler's arm, as if she were determined to brave the wolves but needed his help to do so.

Selena's heart twisted the way it always did when she saw the beautiful redhead. Danielle was garbed in a plain gown of gray cambric, yet she was as lovely as ever. The wealth of sadness that shone in her eyes only added to the impression of enduring strength and touching vulnerability—the epitome of womanhood. Selena had thought her own ball dress attractive, but she felt colorless and faded in comparison to Danielle's vibrant beauty.

She would have preferred to slip away to a dark corner and hide but was obliged to play hostess; Bea wasn't in the drawing room at present, and the guests seemed to be awaiting her response with bated breaths, in anticipation of a scandal. They wouldn't know of her tentative friendship with Danielle, Selena realized.

Aware that all eyes were on her, she summoned a gracious smile as she swept across the room to greet the newcomers. When she pressed Danielle's hand fondly, the collective sigh in the room was audible. And when Kyle appeared at her side the next moment and slapped Orrin on the back in a hearty welcome, the company resumed their interrupted activities—with only a few guests looking disappointed that a scandal had been averted.

After the furor had died down, Selena suggested Kyle fetch them some sangaree or lemonade and then watched as he gallantly offered Danielle his arm and escorted her from the room. His head was bent close to hers as he listened attentively to whatever she was saying.

They make a magnificent couple, Selena thought as she watched them leave together. She was surprised to find herself trembling.

"That was well-done of you," a masculine voice observed gently.

Startled, Selena looked around to find Orrin still beside her, his brown eyes sympathetic and compassionate.

"Danielle told me," he continued in that same quiet tone, "how kind you've been to her. I confess I didn't believe her, but I can see how greatly I was mistaken. I'd like to offer my apologies for that and to say how grateful I am for your refusal to shun her. Not many women would be as generous as you've been."

"It was nothing," Selena murmured, looking away.

"If it's any consolation, I know how you feel. I've loved Danielle for years—but I was always too late. First her husband . . . then Kyle. I can't deny that for a while I tried to hate Kyle, but he was too good a friend."

Too discomfited to reply, Selena nodded in silent understanding. She would have liked to be able to hate Danielle, too, but it was impossible to dislike someone who was so genuinely gentle and good.

Orrin sighed, echoing Selena's heartache. "I can only stand as Danielle's friend and give her what support I can," he declared quietly.

She met his gaze then. "I think any woman would call herself fortunate to claim such friendship."

They shared a smile, which cemented the tentative bond between them and made Selena feel as if she had found another ally in the sea of strangers she had been tossed into.

Several of Orrin's friends joined them then, and a moment later Selena felt a slender hand slip into hers. She turned to find Zoe giving her a shy look. Both older sisters had been allowed downstairs to join the company, though Zoe didn't have permission to dance. Felicity had been banished to her room as punishment for her misbehavior the previous day.

"Felicity must be lonely up there all by herself," Zoe said softly. "Would it be all right, do you think, if I take her some sweets? These are her favorites."

Selena smiled to see the plate Zoe was holding. It was filled with jellied peaches and blancmange. "That would be very kind of you," Selena admitted. She understood quite well how the young girl would feel being left out of the festivities. "Shall I come with you?"

They went upstairs, hand in hand, and delighted Felicity with their surprise. Settling themselves on the bed, they kept her company while she enjoyed the treats. It was only a short while later that a soft knock sounded on the door.

When Felicity called "Come in," they were all surprised to see Kyle step into the room.

Felicity scrambled to her feet. "I've been very good, Kyle—I have." She looked very young and vulnerable, standing there in her nightdress in the glow of lamplight, looking up at him.

His glance shifted to Selena and Zoe and the half-eaten plate of food, then back to Felicity. "I see I'm too late." With an endearing grin, he held out the plate he was carrying. It was filled with jellied peaches and blancmange.

Felicity laughed and flung herself into her brother's arms, then pulled him toward the bed to join the impromptu tea party.

When he'd settled himself, Kyle met Selena's gaze over his sisters' heads. "So this is where you've been hiding."

His comment made her heartbeat quicken; it sounded very much as if he had been searching for her. She returned his gaze with a soft smile, watching as he began to tease his sisters, and contentment wrapped around her.

How different this was from her life the past few years, Selena reflected. She had never thought of herself as being disadvantaged, yet she was a little shocked now to realize how very barren and cold her existence had been since her own parents' deaths—the dearth of warmth and affection before Kyle and the girls had come into her life. This was what she had been missing: this feeling of being a family. This feeling of love. If only they could bring Lydia into it....

"I greatly fear we're in danger of spoiling these two baggages, Moonwitch."

Her thoughts interrupted by Kyle's observation, Selena smiled. "I don't think so."

"Well—" he glanced around him "—perhaps we should return to the ball."

"Yes," she answered with reluctance, not wanting to break the spell.

As Kyle kissed both his sisters, wishing them a good-night, Selena found herself yearning for him to do the same to her. She wanted him to put his arms around her, to hold her, to love her. She wanted it so fiercely her heart ached. Glancing up at Kyle as they descended the stairs, Selena wondered if she dared tell him so.

As they reached the lower floor, she gathered her courage and slipped her arm in his.

Kyle raised an eyebrow at her. "Is something amiss, Moonwitch?"

Selena hesitated as she looked up at him, feeling strange to be purposely seeking a man's attention, even a man who was her husband. "No.... I just wondered if you meant to rejoin the dancing."

"It's too warm to dance. It's hot as hades in here."

Selena took a deep breath. She had watched Miss Jenkins enough to have an idea as to how she should proceed, but she couldn't quite bring herself to employ the coy play of eye-lashes. Instead, she stroked his sleeve, and the light brush of her gloved fingertips conveyed its own subtle but unmistak-able message. "It's cooler in the courtyard," she murmured, her voice taking on a husky catch that was also unmistakable.

Kyle's slow, knowing smile brought a becoming flush to her cheeks. "Well then, madam wife," he responded with amused formality, "may I hope you will oblige me with a stroll in the courtyard?"

The glimmer in his eyes was more than amusement. Selena nodded wordlessly, conscious of the now familiar quickening between her thighs.

The courtyard was cooler, they discovered, but it also was nearly as crowded as the house, filled with guests who had also been seeking respite from the heat. Disappointed, Selena re-signed herself to merely enjoying Kyle's company rather than the intimate moment she had hoped for. She was surprised and gratified when, without words, he took her hand and led her away from the heat and the crowds and the noise, till the laughter and music of the ball became only a murmur.

Fingers clasped, they strolled beneath the majestic magno-lias and moss-shrouded oaks, between draperies of swaying gray lace that had silvered in the brilliant moonlight, wending their way without conscious thought toward the distant sum-merhouse.

Selena felt her body tightening with excitement as antici-pation flared through her senses. A soft breeze scented with jasmine fanned her face, but her rapid heartbeat was at odds with the gentleness of the evening.

Kyle, however, was feeling all the tautness slowly draining from his muscles. All evening he had been fighting the urge to plant his fists in the face of every man who merely looked at Selena, and it was a relief to be able to relax his guard and to consider his fierce reaction. He wasn't accustomed to jeal-ousy; perhaps that was it. His solution had been to stay away from Selena to avoid the distraction she always presented by mingling with the other guests, but it hadn't worked, for she had never been far from his thoughts.

Nor was jealousy the only emotion he'd experienced re-cently where Selena was concerned. A smile touched Kyle's mouth as he recalled his frustration yesterday at her determined rescue of Felicity from his wrath, his delight in watching her struggle with that infernal bird, his pride when he had witnessed her greeting Danielle this evening. Not one woman in a hundred could have shown as much aplomb or been so gracious to someone she had every right to spurn.

Pride, that was it, he realized with faint surprise. He was proud that Selena belonged to him.

He let the thought linger in his mind, and when they reached the line of cherry laurels that bordered the summerhouse, he paused and turned to survey the land he had inherited against his will. The full moon was working its magic, weaving a spell of radiance and splendor and peace. Even the din of the cicadas seemed hushed.

Kyle let out his breath on a sigh, conscious of a sense of contentment, a sense of being where he belonged. Drawing Selena back against his chest, he slipped his arms around her slender waist, noting with intense pleasure that she wasn't wearing a corset. He held her that way for a long while, keeping her warm woman shape pressed to him, drinking in the unearthly beauty of the scene—a beauty, he thought, like Selena herself. Tantalizing and elusive.

"Clay had it right when he called you 'moon lady,'" Kyle murmured against her hair. "The first time I saw you in the moonlight, I wondered if some sorcerer had been at work. You looked like a moonbeam come to life."

Selena closed her eyes, trembling as his touch rippled through her. It was the closest Kyle had ever come to saying that he cared for her. She could have stayed there forever, savoring the closeness between them, she thought. And yet she wanted more than that from him. Her body ached with a hunger so feverish and intense that she felt weak. Vaguely, she wondered if Kyle felt the same torment. Perhaps he was waiting for her to take the first step. Well, she would. She no longer had any shame where he was concerned; her reserve melted whenever he touched her.

Turning in his arms, she gazed up at him with silent yearning. "Kyle," she breathed, her voice a whisper and a plea.

He knew what she wanted. Only a man with ice in his veins could have failed to detect the sensual longing in her eyes and voice—or failed to be affected. Yet he wanted to hear it from Selena's own lips. He wanted her to admit that she craved his possession, his touch.

Kyle lifted his hands to her shoulders, feeling their long, graceful swell beneath his palms. With piquant slowness then, he bent and kissed the corner of her mouth. "What is it, Moonwitch?" His own voice was warm and husky and only half teasing. He let his lips trail a wealth of light kisses along the curving line of her jaw to her ear and heard her soft intake of breath as he tugged on the sensitive lobe. "What do you want?" he prompted as Selena arched against him.

"You," she answered breathlessly, clinging to him.

"Very well, I'm yours. What will you do with me?"

"Kyle." The word was at once plaintive and commanding, an imperative demand for fulfillment. And he had every intention of seeing that the lady was fulfilled.

Breaking their embrace, Kyle grasped Selena's hand and pulled her after him, past the cherry laurels and up the two steps to the summerhouse. Pausing in the warm, pulsing darkness, he let his eyes adjust to the dimness. In the slender shafts of moonlight that spilled through the latticed walls, he could see the outline of a wrought iron bench. "Will this do?" Kyle said as he drew her toward it.

Selena's glance was quizzical but trusting as he settled himself on the bench and pulled her down to sit on his lap. She felt him rising hard against her, and a shudder of desire streaked through her in response. "I don't know.... What if someone comes?"

"Then we'll hear them.... That is, unless they hear us first—which is probably more likely, the way you carry on when you're in the throes of passion."

"I do *not* carry on."

Kyle flashed her a slow grin. "You do, Moonwitch. And I love it." As if to emphasize his point, his hand slipped behind her head, carefully, so not to disturb the neat coil of her hair, and drew her down to meet his searing kiss.

It was long yet urgent, his tongue delving into her mouth to communicate his desire, his fingers stroking her bare arms above the edge of her long gloves. Selena melted against him. She loved the feel of his hands caressing her skin, the gentleness behind the strength when he ran his work-roughened palms over her body, as he was doing now so expertly. But it wasn't enough. Too many layers of clothing separated them.

She knew Kyle must have thought so, too, for he suddenly pulled his lips away. "I want to taste you, Moonwitch. Give your nipples to me...now."

His husky command shocked and thrilled her. Obediently, with trembling hands, Selena complied, drawing down the low-cut bodice of her gown, baring her breasts to her husband's hot gaze.

"That's good," he murmured, "but not good enough."

When Selena stared at him in bewilderment, Kyle met her gaze with a bland expression that was at odds with the smoldering gleam in his eyes. "I can't reach, you see," he murmured helpfully. "Offer your breasts to me."

Feeling her cheeks flood with color, Selena hesitated. But desire overcame modesty, and a heartbeat later she cupped her fingers under the swell of her breasts, pushing them up, craving the heat of his mouth.

But when he bent his head, he turned his lips aside, instead, brushing the sensitive right nipple with his cheek. The peak was already hard and distended, and the rasping contact sent a streaking heat shuddering through Selena. She whimpered in spite of her vow not to make a sound.

"What do you want me to do next, Moonwitch?"

"What . . . do you mean?"

"Do you want me to kiss your breasts?"

She did, but she couldn't make herself say so.

"Do you want me to touch you there with my tongue?" Unhurriedly, Kyle flicked his tongue over the taut bud. Selena clenched her jaw at the exquisite torment. "Come now," he chided when she didn't reply, "do you want me to suck on your nipples?" With deliberate slowness, he closed his lips over the tip and tugged.

"Kyle . . . you're tormenting me."

"Do you want me to—"

"Yes!" she gasped.

"Then say it."

"Kyle . . ."

"Say it."

"Yes . . . I want . . . you to . . . kiss me there."

And finally he did, his lips and tongue and even teeth carrying out the delightful torment he had promised, giving her as much pleasure as she could possibly stand. And except for a soft pant or two, she endured it all in silence, conscious of his accusation—until his sensitive fingers found their way beneath her skirts and discovered the warmth of her below. When he cupped the rise of her silky curls at the juncture of her thighs, Selena quivered, and when his hand moved between her legs, seeking and caressing, her hushed moan was audible in the quiet darkness.

"See," Kyle murmured, a smile in his voice, "you do carry on."

Selena opened her eyes abruptly. It stung her pride that he was so right.

"Perhaps," she countered with breathless indignation as she met his gaze, "I could make *you* carry on."

He cocked his head in speculation, his eyes glimmering. "I imagine you could. You're certainly welcome to try."

It was a challenge Selena couldn't ignore. Stiffening her spine, she proceeded to remove her gloves, one finger at a time.

"This looks serious," Kyle commented with mock alarm. "Are you declaring war?"

"Indeed," she answered without hesitation, and let her gloves fall to the floor. Slowly then, and with great daring, she looped her arms around his neck, leaning forward and deliberately pressing her breasts against his chest.

But when she would have kissed him, Kyle drew his head back. "What if I surrender first?"

"No, I won't allow it."

Startled by the husky determination in her voice and the seductive smile on her lips, Kyle stared at her. Selena had been a gently bred lady when he married her, a mere innocent, but just now her eyes held a woman's promise, provocative and fascinating.

He had tutored her better than he knew, for while Selena's soft lips played with his, her clever fingers sought and found his rigid arousal beneath his pantaloons, curving around the pulsing crest. With exquisite slowness, she stroked him, watching with satisfaction as Kyle closed his eyes and let his head fall back in surrender. It was gratifying to see him clench his jaw in an effort to control himself, to feel his powerfully muscled body tremble at her touch.

It wasn't long, either, till she gained her original objective. Several moments later, when her delicate fingers slipped even lower to cup the softer flesh at the base of his magnificent shaft, Kyle groaned.

"Selena, love," he said on a gasp, "if you keep this up, neither of us will be able to return to the ball without changing clothes first, and then all our guests will know precisely what we've been up to."

She should have been worried, but instead she laughed, a low, husky, triumphant sound, too pleased with the sudden discovery of her new powers to abandon her sensuous assault just yet. It was left to Kyle to retain a vestige of discretion and sanity for both their sakes.

With struggling determination, he grasped Selena's waist and lifted her up, settling her again in one skillful motion astride him. And as her wide-eyed gaze focused on his face, he thrust upward slowly, seeking the very depths of her sensuality. Her lips parted in a soft gasp while her back arched, bringing her tantalizing breasts closer, the rose-pink nipples excited and turgid. Kyle could almost hear his wildly beating heart quicken in response.

Fighting his urgency, he inhaled a sharp breath and surged upward into her clinging heat, luxuriating in the feel of her hot velvet pulsing around him, all the while wondering at the incredible, overwhelming desire he felt for her. How was it possible that with all the women he had known before, this passion he felt with Selena was so achingly new? How could she arouse such hot longing and compelling delight in him, such searing pleasure and lavish satisfaction, without even trying?

He watched the quicksilver light play over her delicate features and pondered the questions in one small but insistent corner of his mind—and came to one definite conclusion. He was skilled enough to make Selena's body want him, but that wasn't enough for him any longer. He wanted her to *need* him, to ache for him the way he did for her.

Suddenly Kyle was all seriousness, no longer feeling the slightest urge to prolong what was torment for them both. He took her mouth, his kisses violent and hot, with the same demanding intensity that he took her body. Crushing her soft, silken curves into him, he rose to meet her restless ardor, pressing her hips fiercely down as he swelled within her. And as the first convulsive shudder shook him, and he felt her fingers tighten on his shoulders in frantic response, Kyle captured Selena's cries of delight with his mouth, aware even in his turbulent passion of the need for circumspection. Still, he couldn't suppress his own rasping groans as she carried him with her to the sublime, dizzying heights of ecstasy.

A long, exquisite moment later, Selena collapsed on his chest, panting softly, sated and fulfilled. His own breathing labored, his racing heartbeat echoing hers, Kyle basked in the same repleteness. His hands gently stroked her back as he held her close, his cheek against her hair, his own body languid with sensual pleasure and contentment.

It felt natural and right to hold her like this—the thought floated through Kyle's mind when he could once again think. Odd that once he'd wanted to be free of Selena. He understood now that he'd never be free of her...that he didn't want to be. Somehow, without his ever realizing it, Selena had become immeasurably important in his life.

Yet even as he contemplated this new notion, the murmur of voices reached him. One was female and pleading; the other male and determined.

They were rapidly growing closer, Kyle realized with a silent oath. Selena heard the voices a moment later and went rigid in his embrace, but when she tried to sit up, Kyle's arms clamped around her. It was too late now to make a graceful exit, and any mad scramble to settle their clothing or alter their compromising position would only draw attention.

"Don't panic," Kyle whispered as he slid Selena off his lap to the bench beside him and quietly began adjusting the bodice of her gown.

He was fastening the buttons of his pantaloons when he recognized the voice of his sister Lydia. When he realized the other was Tanner Parkington's, Kyle stiffened in outrage. It was one thing for him to bring Selena out here; she was his wife. It was quite another for an impoverished youth to seduce his innocent sister after he had been warned away.

Kyle clenched his fists as fury surged through him, but when he would have leaped to his feet, Selena's hand sought his arm and stayed him. In the moment that he'd hesitated, she had realized the young couple were not bent on lovemaking but rather on arguing. And when they paused just outside the summerhouse, silhouetted against the moonlit sky, she could clearly make out the subject of their argument.

"You don't love me," Lydia was saying petulantly. "You don't really want to marry me."

"Of course I love you," Tanner replied, an edge of frustration in his calm voice, "and of course I want to marry you. How can you doubt it? You're the most beautiful girl I've ever seen, and the kindest, and the sweetest—"

"If you did, you would at least consider running away with me."

"Lydia, please, be sensible. We can't elope. Your brother was right. I couldn't support you, not yet, not until I find steady work. I couldn't even offer you a place to live. My uncle has taken my family in only begrudgingly, but he would balk for sure if I tried to foist a wife on him."

"But I wouldn't be at all expensive. I can be frugal, Tanner, I can!"

"I know you would, my love, or at least you would try, but I couldn't allow you to make such a sacrifice. Perhaps it's my pride, but I want to be able to give you things—pretty gowns and whatnot. It won't be long, I promise."

"It will," Lydia replied, sounding near tears. "Kyle said a year at least, and then only if you have an income. And you told me how difficult it is for a gentleman to find employment."

"Well, it isn't for lack of trying. I just haven't had any success yet. It would be easier if I had a trade. All I know is planting. But I'm considering trying to apprentice out as a carpenter."

"That could take years!"

"Lydia, don't cry, I beg you. Come here."

There was a soft sniff as Tanner put a comforting arm around Lydia's shoulders. Within the summerhouse, Selena felt Kyle tense beside her, and again she pressed his arm in warning.

Kyle didn't move, but he ground his teeth as he watched Lydia lift her face to Tanner's. "Tanner, will you kiss me?"

"Lydia, I can't. It's not honorable. I shouldn't even be speaking to you. We're betraying your brother's trust as it is."

"I don't care. And you wouldn't either, if you loved me. Maybe you'll be sorry if I find someone else to marry."

Tanner grasped her shoulders. "No, you've got to promise you'll wait for me." The urgency in his voice must have communicated itself to the girl, for she sighed heavily and murmured "Oh, Tanner," before burying her face in his shoulder. A moment later, she suddenly drew back. "I know!" she exclaimed, sounding hopeful. "*I'll* find a position. Perhaps Mr. Chandler would allow me to work in his store like Mrs. Whitfield does."

"No, I won't have it," the young man replied, putting a period to that notion at once. "Just try a little to be brave, my love. We'll find a way. Now come, I'd best return you to the ball before you're missed. We've already been gone too long."

"No one will miss us. Everyone is either eating or dancing, and they'll continue for hours."

"Lydia," Tanner warned.

Lydia sighed again but took his arm obediently and allowed him to lead her away from the summerhouse. When they were gone, Selena glanced uneasily up at Kyle. She was surprised to find his expression thoughtful.

"You don't mean to call him out, do you?" she asked.

Kyle met her gaze. "As it happens, I was considering something quite different. What would you think about offering him the position as factor of Montrose?"

"I think," Selena said with a slow smile, "such a solution would benefit you both."

Kyle nodded. "As a planter's son, Parkington has the farming experience I lack. And he has far greater sense than I credited him with."

"And honor, as well. He would make Lydia a good husband."

"Oh, no you don't, Moonwitch. I'll admit I like the lad, and he seems to deal with her better than I do, but I'm not willing just yet to give him Lydia's hand. He'll have to prove himself first."

Selena shuddered. "Thank heaven he is too much a gentleman to elope with her."

"I don't know about that. If Parkington were willing to consider an elopement, I might give him my blessing, just to get Lydia off my hands."

"Kyle, you don't mean it!"

"No." He smiled in fond remembrance. "Actually, Lydia surprised me, offering to find a position herself. Perhaps there's hope for her yet."

"Well, at least you don't mean to take Mr. Parkington to task for merely refusing to elope with her."

"I couldn't—" Kyle's grin was full of mischief and affection as he reached out and ran a languid forefinger along her collarbone "—for then I'd have to acknowledge being here with you. And if you think your parrot raised some eyebrows, you can imagine the scandal if it became known I'd been ravishing my beautiful wife."

Selena thought about protesting his choice of words, but when Kyle's finger dipped between her breasts, the thought fled. "When must you return to town?" she asked, holding his gaze.

"I promised Angel I would be there tonight when the ball ended."

"But you don't have to go just yet?"

Her tone was breathless and entirely unreserved, with even a hint of eagerness. Kyle's eyebrows lifted. This was his totally modest, straitlaced wife? "No, I don't have to go just yet," he said, amused.

"Good." Sliding her fingers through the heavy, dark waves of Kyle's hair, Selena leaned forward and ran her tongue lightly over the surface of his lips. "Because I seem to remember an unsettled question as to which one of us 'carries on' the loudest."

Kyle laughed, and the laughter stayed inside him as he surrendered gracefully and gave himself over to the lovely siren in his arms.

Chapter Sixteen

Late June, the beginning of full summer. Long days of sweltering shade and lingering twilight. The smell of fresh-scythed grass and baking earth, of waxy magnolias and sweet, sweet jasmine. The night sounds of croaking frogs and chirping cicadas. The melodic trill of a mockingbird. Selena grew to love the now-familiar scents and sounds of her new home, in spite of the merciless heat that was unrelieved by the trade winds she was accustomed to on her island.

Life at Montrose was quieter after the ball. Or perhaps, Selena decided, it merely seemed so with Bea and Thaddeus gone. They had departed two days afterward for their town house in Natchez to a chorus of sobs and regrets, even though they would only be a few miles away.

Selena missed Bea's good-natured chatter, for while she had the plantation and the girls to occupy her time, she saw little of Kyle. During the week following the ball, he was busier than ever. When he'd offered Tanner Parkington the position as factor, the young man had accepted with such eagerness that Kyle thought he might have to restrain Parkington physically to keep him from sleeping out in the fields. And in addition to establishing Parkington as factor, Kyle still had nightly duties as guardian of Heaven's Gate.

And yet the moments Selena did share with him gave her hope, for amazingly he seemed entirely willing to forget he had been forced to marry her.

Selena was fervently looking forward to the time when Kyle could at least spend his nights at home. But as it happened, the day Angel's cousin arrived from Nashville to assume responsibility as chief bruiser at Heaven's Gate, Jeremiah Whitfield passed away.

When Bea sent a note to Montrose informing them, Selena drove into town to offer her help.

"Danielle is taking it as well as can be expected," Bea whispered in greeting. They were sitting with several other neighbors in Whitfield's small, shabby front room, which doubled as parlor and kitchen. "She looks paler than usual but seems to be holding up."

Selena agreed when Danielle emerged from the back room, where she had been helping to lay out her husband's body. Her white skin seemed so translucent as to resemble fine porcelain, contrasting starkly with her black gown and the deep red of her hair and giving her the kind of unearthly beauty that was usually attributed to saints and martyrs.

But in this case Selena had no difficulty repressing the jealousy that she sometimes felt in Danielle's presence, for her heart was aching with sorrow and pity.

"I am so very sorry about your husband," Selena murmured as she pressed Danielle's hand.

"No, please...." Danielle replied. "No one of compassion could have wished him to linger."

"Is there anything I can do to help you?" Selena asked. "Would you like me to take Clay for a few days?"

Danielle shook her head. "Thank you, but I think everything is being done. Orrin Chandler is looking after Clay. But I would be grateful if you would—" She broke off, her voice suddenly choking with tears. "If you would attend the funeral."

"Of course," Selena replied, realizing her presence would help lay to rest any rumors about Danielle and Kyle. She wished there was more she could do. But Danielle wasn't friendless; she had neighbors and distant cousins who had gathered around her to lend comfort. And to insist on providing support when it wasn't needed, Selena knew, would make the situation more awkward.

She and Bea stayed only a short while longer before taking their leave. Selena gave Bea a lift to her home and then drove on alone.

She met Kyle on the road just outside of town. He was riding his big roan gelding, and his expression was grim as he drew up alongside the gig. It was obvious he had received the message she had left for him about Jeremiah's death.

"How is she?" Kyle said without preamble, the intensity of his tone made harsher by protective concern.

A heaviness centered in Selena's chest as she met Kyle's gaze. "Danielle is fine."

"I intend to call on her."

"Of course. It would look odd if you stayed away."

"How is Clay taking it?"

"I don't know. I didn't see him. Orrin is keeping him, I understand."

"The devil he is," Kyle muttered, his jaw hardening.

Selena searched his face, wondering if he meant to challenge Orrin for the right to keep Clay. She thought such an action might only cause more difficulty for Danielle, but this didn't seem the time to argue with Kyle. Selena nodded mutely when he told her not to hold dinner for him, and she silently watched him ride away.

Orrin must have prevailed, however, for Kyle returned to Montrose without his son. Selena could only guess how Kyle felt about it, for he didn't share his thoughts with her, and indeed, remained grimly uncommunicative for the two days before the funeral. But she knew it was troubling him and wished there was something she could do to help ease his pain.

The morning the ceremony was to be held, she found Kyle in his study, staring sightlessly out the window at the moss-shrouded oaks of Montrose.

He didn't acknowledge her entrance or even her presence when she came to stand by his side. When he didn't speak, she lightly touched his arm. "Kyle, what is it?"

For a moment she didn't think he would answer. When at last he did, she could hear the quiet anguish in his voice. "Clay is over two years old, Selena. Do you know how many hours I've spent in his company? A score. Less than two days. Orrin spends more time with my son in a week than I've spent in his entire life."

Selena hesitated, not knowing how to offer him comfort. "What do you mean to do?"

"I don't know." He shook his head in despair. "The only option I have is to adopt Clay."

Selena digested his declaration in silence. "I'm not sure that would work," she said finally.

"Why not? It's a reasonable solution. I'm much more capable of providing for Clay than Danielle is. I would continue to give her financial support, of course, so she won't have to worry on that account."

"Even so, I don't think she would accept your offer. I very much doubt she would be willing to give up her son. Clay is all she has now."

Bowing his head, Kyle shut his eyes. He didn't want to hear the truth. He didn't want to be told he could never be a father to his son, even if his reasons for wanting Clay were selfish ones. "And what of my responsibility to Clay? Should I just dismiss that?"

"I think," Selena said softly, "you must do what's best for the child."

Kyle raised his gaze to stare out the window. However much he didn't want to listen, he knew she was right. He couldn't take the boy from his mother, even if his claim had the practical aspects of wealth and a stable home to bolster it. Besides, Danielle would never consent to giving up Clay. And to fight her for him would publicly brand them both. He couldn't do that. But God, it hurt.

Selena felt the grief he was going through. Forcing herself to wait, she watched Kyle trying to come to terms with the situation, a heaviness squeezing her heart.

The heaviness, however, became a sudden hollowness in the pit of her stomach as a different thought struck her. Danielle was free to marry again—or would be, after a proper period of mourning. If Kyle had been similarly free, he would have been able to claim his son through marriage.

That realization must have occurred to Kyle, Selena reflected.

Miserably she searched his face, but she saw nothing in his expression to suggest that he wasn't bitterly regretting his marriage to her.

"Kyle...I'm sorry. If you hadn't married me, you would be free to make Clay your son, as you once planned."

He shrugged heavily. When he finally met her gaze, there was a bleakness in his eyes that tore at her heart. "Well, I'm not free. So don't even think of it."

The quiet words did nothing to quell the ache or dispel the cold knot that had formed in her stomach.

The service for Jeremiah Whitfield was held in an old Spanish parish house, since Natchez didn't yet boast any

Protestant churches. His body was laid to rest in the town's burying ground. There were numerous damp eyes and grieving faces among the attending crowd, for Jeremiah had been well liked and pitied for the terrible tragedy that had befallen him. And the sight of his beautiful widow garbed in black with the small, bewildered boy clinging to her hand was enough to wring tears from granite.

Selena watched Danielle and Clay as the final prayers were said, unable to tear her eyes away, her heart aching for them and for herself, as well. But her attention was focused on Kyle. She was conscious of the tension emanating from him as he stood beside her, as if he were forcing himself to remain dispassionate and detached. His eyes remained on his son.

Just then, as Danielle scooped up a handful of earth and sprinkled it over the coffin, Clay whimpered and broke away from his mother with a cry of "Papa!" He ran through the crowd, short legs churning, and with a sob. launched his small body at Orrin's knees.

Without hesitation Orrin bent and caught the weeping boy up in his arms, holding him close and murmuring soft reassurances as Clay hid his face from the crowd.

Like the other mourners, Selena had been watching the child, but then she glanced up at Kyle and caught the naked pain on his face. Her heart twisted for his agony, but she knew there was nothing she could do. Kyle had to accept for himself that he was losing his son to another man.

The service over, Kyle drove Selena home in the gig. His grim mood had, if anything, intensified, and he spoke not at all for the first part of the journey. Selena didn't press him, for she could sense his simmering anger waiting to boil. Yet the presence of such powerful emotions dismayed her. Danielle was so heartachingly beautiful, it wasn't beyond possibility that Kyle had fallen in love with her, despite his denial. At the very least, his feelings for Danielle were augmented by his despair over his son.

The thought only intensified the hollow, sick feeling in the pit of Selena's stomach.

It wasn't helped, either, by Kyle's abrupt announcement when they were halfway to Montrose.

"I intend to return to town this afternoon," he said in a low, fierce tone. "I want to comfort Clay. A boy needs his father."

When Selena didn't answer immediately, Kyle shot her a dark look. "If you mean to suggest that I'll be promoting a scandal, you can save your breath. I'm not going to let that stand between me and my son."

As if the thought further roused his fury, Kyle slapped the reins against the bay horse, startling the animal into a dancing gait. "God, I'm sick to death of the sanctimonious gabblemongers in this town, always thinking they have the right to throw the first stone."

"I wasn't thinking of the scandal," Selena replied, her throat tight. "I was considering Danielle's feelings. This is not the time to be fighting with her over her son."

"Fiend seize it, he's my son, too! My only son."

Selena stiffened. Given a chance, she, too, could provide Kyle with sons. "You seem to have forgotten," she retorted, heat rising to her cheeks, "that you have a wife now who can give you children."

"I don't want other children! I want Clay."

The angry words were like a blow. And they brought sudden tears to Selena's eyes. Clenching her teeth to hold them back, she averted her face and stared blindly at the passing scenery.

When Kyle glanced at her a moment later, he swore softly, as if he had just realized what he'd said. "God, I didn't mean that," he ground out. When she didn't reply, he hastily drew the bay to a halt and turned to her, grasping her arm. "Look, Selena, it was a stupid, childish thing to say. I lost my temper. This situation with Clay is driving me insane, but that's no excuse to lash out at you."

She shook her head. "It doesn't matter," she said quietly, choking back her tears.

"Yes, it does matter, of course it matters."

"Very well. I accept your apology."

"Selena...." He hesitated, placing a finger under her chin to make her meet his gaze. "Look, I know this isn't fair to you, and I don't mean to put you through this. I just don't know how to deal with losing Clay."

Selena nodded, not trusting herself to speak.

"I have to return to town. I need to discuss the future with Danielle, to decide what we'll do about Clay."

"Kyle...." Her voice was so unsteady that she swallowed. "No matter how much it hurts, you can't take him away from Danielle."

He looked away, raking his fingers through his hair. "I realize that."

"I understand how painful it is to accept," she insisted quietly. "I know what it's like to lose someone you love."

After a moment, Kyle nodded and released her arm. He didn't reply, but inside he knew she was right. He could never have Clay as his son; he would have to accept that. He had to let go. Gathering the reins, he set the horse in motion and didn't speak for the remainder of the brief ride.

He was too wrapped up in his own suffering to realize he'd left Selena prey to her doubts and fears. When they reached Montrose, he handed her down from the gig and ordered his roan saddled. Selena watched him ride out, a wretched knot of despair lying cold and hard in her stomach. If she could be sure it was only his son Kyle was longing for and not Danielle, she might have found his leaving easier to bear.

He hadn't returned by the time she retired for the night. Restless and aching, she lay awake in the darkness, staring at the canopy above her bed, watching the shifting shadows made by the flowering almond outside the window.

She heard him come in sometime before midnight. Without meaning to, Selena listened intently to the quiet sounds he made as he moved around his room. The slight noises eventually ceased, yet the heavy silence felt tense and alive.

Nearly half an hour later she heard the slight click of the latch as the door to her bedchamber slowly opened. Hesitantly, she sat up, hardly daring to breathe as she pushed aside the swaths of mosquito netting. Kyle stood without moving in the doorway, fingers of moonlight playing on his rugged features and reflecting from the dark green brocade of his dressing gown. His dark hair was tousled, and there was a rough shadow of a beard on his jaw. It was the first time since their marriage that he had come to her room at night, but though she could hope, she couldn't be sure of his intent. His eyes, like his expression, were inscrutable.

Her own eyes wide with uncertainty, Selena watched as Kyle quietly shut the door behind him and crossed the room to her bedside. She could feel her heart pounding in slow, sharp pulses as he stared down at her.

"You were right," Kyle whispered, "about Clay. I have to give him up, no matter how much it hurts."

The pain in his voice was soft and throbbing. Wanting to offer comfort, she reached up to give him her hand.

Yes, he thought, help me ease the hurt.

His fingers curled over hers, warm and pleading, like the dark message in his eyes. Without releasing his grasp, Kyle slowly sat beside her.

"Selena." He said it like a caress. "My wise, understanding Selena." And when she moved into his arms, he gathered her against him with a tenderness that stirred hope as well as desire and longing in her heart.

With a sigh, Selena pressed her cheek against the tightly curving muscles of his chest, where his dressing gown had parted. He was naked beneath, and she could feel her cool flesh warming against the satin of his bare skin. She wanted to ask him about Danielle, but she couldn't bear to hear the answer and destroy this moment. Instead, she closed her eyes, listening to the vital rhythm of his heart mate with his breathing.

But Kyle's heart wasn't as tranquil as the steady tempo suggested. Indeed, it ached...for the loss he had sustained...for the woman in his arms. Selena was so very beautiful—her slender, white body bare except for the gauzy film of her nightdress, her pale hair kissed by moonlight. That image had burned itself in his memory weeks ago, indelible and strong. It was that image he remembered first whenever she was away from him. That was what had sustained him tonight during the long hours while he struggled with the bitterness of losing his son. Selena was right. He had to consider Clay's best interests and not his own selfish needs. That knowledge had kept him from returning to town. Instead, he had gone to the fields, where he had tried to work out his frustration physically—to dull the grief that was tearing at his insides.

It hadn't helped, nor had the hours of hard riding afterward. Yet it was only after he had returned home that he realized he was searching in the wrong direction for the wrong remedy. He had only to look close to home to find what he sought. Selena. She could assuage his pain. She could heal his aching heart. She could give him the solace he so badly needed.

He had been slow to realize it...unforgivably so. He had spoken in bitterness and anger, wounding her without meaning to. If he had driven her away, it was only what he deserved, Kyle told himself savagely.

Yet he didn't mean that. He was quite certain that the despair he had felt over losing any chance to be a father to his son would never match the bleakness he'd feel if Selena turned away from him.

Disquieted by the sudden thought, Kyle drew back, searching her face, trying to measure the effect of his earlier ill-considered words. Her expression was expectant, waiting, and he was caught in the quiet, solemn depth of her calm blue eyes. You understood all along, didn't you? he asked silently. You understood and cared.

"I didn't mean what I said this afternoon," he murmured. "About not wanting other children."

Selena held her breath, watching him.

"And I don't want to be free of you simply so I can claim Clay." Still holding her gaze, Kyle carried her hand to his lips, brushing his mouth over each finger in turn. "I want you, Moonwitch. Very much."

Not "I need you" or "I love you," but "I want you," Selena thought. But it would have to do.

When she tried to move into his embrace, once more, though, Kyle held her away. "Selena, it was true once," he said urgently, wanting to explain. "I never wanted a wife. I only wanted the sea...the freedom and challenges it gave me."

He saw something like sorrow flicker in her eyes before she quietly replied, "I know."

"But I've since come to change my mind. You've made my life here bearable...no, much more than that. Happy. You've made this a home." That also was true, he reflected. She had made his life far easier, more comfortable with her gentle touches and quiet, determined ways. He still missed the sea sometimes, but his yearning for freedom was fast fading... because he had found something even more fulfilling.

But he faltered when it came to explaining that to her, for he couldn't find the right words, never having felt anything quite like what he was experiencing...this swelling in his heart, this burgeoning ache that was such a profound mixture of tenderness and desire.

But explanations weren't what Selena wanted from Kyle anyway, nor praise for her domestic abilities. She wanted reassurance that she had no reason to be jealous of Danielle. And she wasn't sure Kyle could give it.

"No, please," she said, her voice low and hushed. "Don't talk. Just hold me...kiss me."

He took her mouth, trying with the gentle play of his lips to express what he was feeling. And Selena responded in kind.

When his kiss questioned, asking forgiveness, hers answered and gave it. When his tongue sought hers, stirring and soothing, she matched him with an abandoned intimacy. Yet when his kiss deepened, promising pleasure and lavish sensuality, hers did more; it vowed peace. Kyle accepted her unspoken pledge cautiously, his body trembling with the powerful sensations it engendered.

His vulnerable response restored some of her shaken confidence. With love for him welling inside her, she reached up to hold his face with her slender hands.

He could think of only one thing. Yes.... Yes, touch me, Moonwitch, with your cool hands and quicksilver passion. Take me inside you, into your serene world of shadows and silver-bright light....

His breathing altered, and his lips moved to her hair as he drew off her nightdress. When he had shed his dressing gown, he joined her quickly, wanting and finding the fulfillment she'd promised; her mouth was welcoming, her body completely yielding to his as he possessed her.

And Selena quivered in turn as she dissolved into throbbing, impassioned need. He filled her completely, moving over her, within her, unraveling the hard knot of doubt and pain.

Later, as they lay entwined, their skin damp and clinging, their heartbeats gradually slowing, Kyle finally let his drifting mind focus on the turmoil that had raged inside him from the first time he'd met Selena.

He'd once thought it was his son he was fighting for. But he'd been fighting against himself, Kyle realized suddenly. Against the admission that he needed and wanted Selena.

Yet to be truthful, it had never been much of a battle. He'd lost it the moment he'd kissed her on the streets of St. John's.

And having admitted that to himself, he could at last accept what he'd been too stubborn or too blind to see. His heart was irrevocably committed to Selena. He loved her.

Kyle's mouth fashioned in a twisted smile as he finally recognized the powerful emotion he'd been unable, perhaps unwilling to name. He had never thought he would find love; he'd always expected it to be something tantalizing and elusive, like Selena herself. Instead, it was like a tempest at sea, and it frightened him . . . both the force of it and the power it held over him.

The trouble was, fear at sea could be deadly. He would have to face it, Kyle knew. But that he could handle. What scared the blazes out of him was the possibility that Selena didn't return his feelings.

He tensed, his arms tightening around Selena as he remembered what she'd said about losing someone she loved.

"What was his name?" Kyle murmured suddenly in the silence.

Selena's head moved on his shoulder as she lifted a puzzled glance. "Whose name?"

Feigning nonchalance, Kyle raised a lock of her silken hair to his lips. "The man you were betrothed to."

"Edward."

Kyle took a deep breath. "You said you loved him."

"Yes," she answered after a brief nod.

Kyle longed to ask how much she had loved this Edward, but he couldn't frame the question. He wanted to know precisely how deep that love had been and how it compared to what she felt for him...if she felt anything at all. He wanted her to soothe the savage jealousy that was raging in his breast. But his own feelings were too new, too raw and tender to risk rejection.

And so instead of pressing her, he merely held her close in a wordless embrace.

"Why did you ask about Edward?"

Her tone was tentative, questioning, but he only murmured a disclaimer as he moved his lips gently against her hair. "I was curious."

Yet even as he said it, Kyle made a vow to himself: he would make her forget, if he could, the man she had loved. And with that vow came the fragile hope that he might someday succeed in winning Selena's love for himself. Until now it hadn't really been a fair test. He had never attempted to woo Selena or to earn her regard. He had done nothing to prove himself worthy of her. Indeed, at the beginning of their brief marriage, he had virtually ignored her in his effort to keep his distance and maintain his sanity.

But all that would change.

He would pursue her with every skill he possessed, with every ounce of charm and gallantry he could muster. He would court Selena properly, the way she deserved....

Hearing her soft sigh, Kyle shifted his weight to gaze down at her, at her quicksilver eyes, which were searching his so intently. And as tenderly he brushed back the cloud of pale hair from her face, he renewed his vow. He would make Selena love him. And then he would ask her to share his bed, his children, his life.

July, the onset of full summer. How could such a short span of time make such a difference in one's life? Selena wondered as she reread the letter from her friend Beth in Antigua.

Beth had written a lengthy epistle full of news from the island, including a postscript that said Selena's stepmother, Edith, was expected to snare Avery Warner any day—a just reward, Beth declared, since they deserved each other. Yet only now, while Kyle was out in the fields and the girls had scattered to pursue their own amusements, had Selena found time to pen a reply.

Her thoughts, as they had countless times during the past week since the night Kyle had come to her bed, soon turned to Kyle and her marriage, to her happiness, which ran quiet and deep. Her days were filled with small pleasures—pleasures that were sharpest when shared with Kyle . . . a glance, a smile, a brushing of hands. Her nights were filled with ecstasy.

For long moments at a time she was even able to dismiss her misgivings about Danielle as mere imaginings. Indeed, it was only when Kyle was away from her that her doubts about their marriage returned to assail her. He wanted her physically, Selena was certain. He had proved that very thoroughly with his passionate lovemaking during all the wonderful nights he had visited her room. Yet she couldn't dispel the haunting fear that Kyle's feelings for her could never go beyond physical desire.

Accordingly, she had examined in minute detail, over and over again, every word Kyle had said that first night. He had declared he wanted her for his wife, admitting his appreciation for her domestic skills. She made his life bearable, he'd said, even happy. But he had also asked her about Edward. The question had puzzled Selena at the time, yet the longer she considered it, the more it disturbed her. Had Kyle perhaps been trying to tell her something? Had he mentioned her love for Edward to prepare the way for his own revelation? Had he meant to admit that he loved Danielle, but then lost the courage?

The possibility nearly drove her to distraction. She should never, Selena realized, have allowed Kyle to introduce such a disquieting subject and then suddenly drop it. She should have pressed him to explain. Even knowing he loved Danielle would be better than living with this dreadful uncertainty.

And yet she couldn't bring herself to ask the question that would end it, for with the end of uncertainty might also come the end of hope.

She couldn't forget, however, how easily Danielle Whitfield seemed to draw men's love. That thought had been uppermost in Selena's mind when she'd faced her duty and called at the mercantile to inquire how Danielle was faring. It concerned Selena to see her looking so pale. Danielle appeared subdued and saddened by her bereavement, yet she was facing her loss with a courage Selena couldn't help but admire. So in spite of her jealous misgivings, Selena felt genuinely sorry when Danielle again refused any offer of help from her.

At least Danielle had Orrin Chandler's support. Orrin's affection for the beautiful widow was quite apparent, yet her behavior was always so circumspect that Selena couldn't tell if Danielle returned his feelings. And she didn't feel, under the circumstances, that she had the right to ask about it.

Orrin's unhopeful pursuit of Danielle wasn't the only relationship that concerned Selena, either. She had been worried that Lydia might somehow prevail on Tanner Parkington to elope, after all, and so she'd never relaxed her vigilance.

It seemed, however, that Parkington was too honorable and too intelligent to jeopardize his future by plunging them into a scandal, for he barely made time to speak to Lydia. Indeed, the young man was taking his responsibilities as factor so seriously that he was in grave danger of offending his love.

Selena had been in the hall outside the schoolroom when she overheard Felicity taunting Lydia about it.

"Well, that's no reason to snap at me," Felicity protested after she had just been called "a little beast" by her elder sister. "You're just miffed because Tanner Parkington is paying more attention to our cotton fields than to you."

"He is not!" Lydia retorted. "Tanner loves me."

"I don't know what you see in him, anyway. I think he's boring."

"No one asked your opinion."

"Well, I'm never going to fall in love and allow some man to break *my* heart."

"You needn't be concerned that any man would be interested in breaking your heart. No doubt you'll remain a spinster all your life."

"Exactly! I don't intend to marry," Felicity announced airily. "I mean to manage my own plantation."

"Girls can't manage plantations."

"They can so! Selena did. She told me."

"Oh, why don't you just go away, Felicity?"

Zoe spoke up then in her soft voice, reminding Felicity that she had lessons to finish, and so it wasn't necessary for Selena to intervene in the dispute or even to mention that she had overheard it when she entered the schoolroom a few minutes later. Yet the knowledge that Lydia was discussing her affaire with Tanner openly and no longer keeping it a secret relieved Selena and gave her reason to hope that at least one problem at Montrose would eventually work itself out.

After she had finished her letter to Beth, Selena's thoughts turned to another matter: Kyle's interest in steamboats. The previous day, when Bea and Thaddeus had come to dinner, Thaddeus had mentioned that in the next session the members of the legislature planned to address the need for a regular steamboat service for Natchez. It would be a perfect opportunity, Selena realized, for Kyle to pursue his venture.

She was aware that Kyle had given up the idea of starting a steamboat company, at least temporarily, for the sake of the plantation and his sisters, but she desperately wanted him to be happy in his chosen occupation. Despite his success with the plantation, despite his avowal that he was growing accustomed to working the land, Kyle wasn't a farmer. What he needed was interests and challenges outside his plantation and family.

And perhaps she had another more selfish reason, Selena reflected. Kyle had refused her dowry out of a sense of honor, because he didn't want to feel like a "blasted fortune hunter," or so he'd said. Yet she still wasn't certain he wanted to remain married to her. It would provide some measure of compensation, Selena decided, if she could supply the means that enabled him to pursue his dream. And in some twisted application of logic that originated more in her heart than her head, she rationalized that if Kyle accepted her dowry, he would be committing himself to her fully.

That night, as they lay together in the warm darkness, Selena renewed their last discussion about steamboats by bringing up the subject of the legislative session. She was surprised when Kyle seemed less than enthusiastic about attending.

"The legislative session?" he murmured. He found it difficult to focus his thoughts on business after the passion they had just shared.

"You remember what Thaddeus said. Tomorrow the assembly plans to discuss the need for a regular steamboat service."

"Selena . . . it isn't really crucial that I go."

"That wouldn't be wise, would it? If you aren't there to show your interest, the legislature may grant a charter to someone else. Besides, even if you mean to wait for a year or two before you purchase any steamboats, wouldn't it be better for you to be in on the discussions at the start?"

"Yes, I suppose so."

"Well, then, why don't you attend?"

Kyle hesitated, not wanting to admit the real reason for his reluctance. How could he woo and win Selena if he was away pursuing steamboat ventures? "Do you know how guilty I feel," he prevaricated, "always leaving you here alone to shoulder the burdens of the plantation?"

"Kyle, it isn't a burden, truly. And I don't want you to defer your venture because of me, certainly. I know how you feel about it—" Her tawny brows drew together in a puzzled frown. "You haven't changed your mind about investing in a steamboat enterprise, have you?"

"No."

"Then I don't understand your indifference."

Because I'm busy courting you, blast it. Can't you see that? Kyle wanted to say. Every day for a week he'd spent all his free time with her, and every night he had come to her room. But he seemed to be making little progress in winning Selena's affection. "The legislative session may last all day," he murmured, watching the moonlight play on her beautiful face.

"Shouldn't you leave early, then?"

Am I doing something wrong? Like not acting enough of a gentleman? Or too much? he wondered. "I expect so," he said finally. "And I suppose while I'm there I ought to contact an agent to discuss arrangements for shipping our cotton after the harvest begins."

"Good."

Kyle gave a sigh. He had hoped Selena felt the same bliss he'd felt during the past week, but it seemed as if she were anxious to be rid of him. Trying to bite back his frustration, he gently placed a finger under the delicate curve of her jaw. "Are you sure you will be all right here with the girls?"

"Yes, of course." She sounded mildly exasperated as well as amused. "It's only for the day."

He didn't like to be reminded how easily she could manage without him. He wanted her to need him, to miss him when he was away, to count the hours they were apart, as he did. He wanted her to ask him to stay.

"At least young Parkington can be relied on to help you," Kyle said lamely. "He's proving even better a factor than I'd hoped."

"Kyle, we'll be fine. And Tanner needs the opportunity to demonstrate his capabilities without your supervision."

He gave up. "Very well, I'll go to Natchez tomorrow." He pressed a tender kiss on her brow and gathered her close, trying not to dwell on his dissatisfaction or his deepening worry that he might never win her love.

They were both silent for a moment while the warm night surrounded them and their separate thoughts.

Beside him, Selena took a slow breath. Now was the time, she realized, to ask him about Danielle. "Kyle?" But when he glanced at her, Selena faltered. She couldn't do it. She couldn't come right out and ask, "Do you love Danielle?" She didn't dare, for fear of what his answer might be. "I hope the session goes well," she murmured, instead. "I want you to be happy."

Hearing the wistful note in her voice, Kyle took heart. "Do you, Moonwitch?" His eyes glowed with golden fire as he slowly bent his head again. "Not more, I think," he said against her lips, "than I want happiness for you."

Her breathing quickened in response, even before he slid his hand up the quivering sleekness of her belly to mold the fullness of her breast. When she arched against him with unconscious abandon, Kyle responded with conscious delight.

Slowly, without words, he roused her, intending to show her just how much she meant to him, how much he needed and wanted her love. His hands skimmed her body, touching, caressing, claiming for his own the alluring, eloquently lovely lady who had wrapped herself around his heart.

Shortly after Kyle left the next morning, Saul's wife, Lukey, was delivered of a strapping baby boy. Selena was present both at the birth and later, when Saul was allowed into the cabin to hold his son.

Seeing the tenderness light Saul's dark face as he gazed at his wife and child, Selena couldn't help but remember his fierce protectiveness when he had thrown himself in the path of Whitfield's lash. The memory made her wonder if Kyle would ever feel the same kind of deep love for her, and thinking of Kyle naturally led to thoughts of Danielle, as usually happened of late.

That afternoon, Selena was inventorying supplies in the plantation's store when she was surprised by a visit from the subject of her jealous thoughts. She looked up from contemplating bolts of cloth to find Danielle standing in the doorway.

"I hope you don't mind the intrusion," Danielle said quickly. "I wouldn't let Martha fetch you, for I didn't want to take you away from your duties."

In spite of her recent thoughts, Selena gave her visitor a smile. Then she saw Clay standing behind his mother's skirts and realized they must have come to see Kyle. "Kyle isn't here, I'm afraid," Selena admitted. "He went into town today and probably won't be back till late."

"That's all right.... That is, you said I could call. But I don't want to impose," Danielle added in a small voice.

Danielle had come to see her? Selena felt a moment's surprise and then a fierce stab of guilt at the lukewarm welcome she had tendered. She should be giving comfort, not standing here wrapped up in her own concerns and jealousies.

"Good heavens, it isn't an imposition," Selena insisted, abruptly dropping her bolts of cloth and coming forward to take Danielle's hands. "Indeed, I'm delighted to see you. With Bea no longer living here and Kyle away, I've been rather lonely. I would be grateful for your companionship. Please, won't you come back to the house with me? We can have tea."

"Well, actually...I thought I might help you here, instead...if you'd like." Glancing around the store, Danielle flashed a self-conscious smile. "Orrin said I needed a rest—he wouldn't let me work at the mercantile today. But really I prefer to keep busy."

"Of course.... I would appreciate your advice." And she meant it, for Danielle's knowledge of merchandise and dried goods was extensive. More than that, Selena understood quite well Danielle's unspoken need—that occupation could keep one's depressing thoughts at bay.

Just then Clay tugged on Danielle's skirts. "Mama, Raysho."

Laying a gentle hand on his blond head, the auburn-haired woman looked a question at Selena. "Clay has been asking every day to see your parrot. Do you think he might be allowed?"

Selena smiled down at the child. "Horatio will be delighted to have you pay him a visit. He has missed you most dreadfully." When Clay gazed up at her and gave her his heart-stopping grin, Selena could see very well why Kyle had been so reluctant to give up his son.

Danielle had brought along the elderly black woman who had been Jeremiah Whitfield's nurse and now helped with Clay. When the servant had taken Clay into the house to view his friend the parrot, Selena asked Danielle how her son was faring.

"Quite well, actually. He still doesn't realize why Jeremiah is no longer lying in his bed."

"And you?" Selena asked gently. Danielle herself still looked pale and a bit weary.

Her lips sketched a smile. "I'm recovering. Jeremiah had been ill for so long. I don't think he wanted to live." She paused before adding, "I wanted to thank you, Selena, for all the support you've given me. That's really why I came today. And I thought it might give us the opportunity to become better friends, as you once suggested."

Selena's acknowledgment was automatic, but even as she found herself agreeing out loud that a deeper friendship between them would be welcome, she had difficulty keeping her misgivings from showing in her expression.

It wasn't that she disliked Danielle; in truth, she liked and admired the red-haired woman a great deal. It wasn't even that Danielle had borne Kyle a son; Selena thought she could have overlooked that indiscretion if she could be assured Kyle's feelings for the beautiful widow went no deeper than appreciation.

It was Kyle himself who stood between them. Selena knew she wasn't being fair to let her doubts about Kyle color her view of Danielle. Yet she wasn't certain she could be generous and unselfish enough to develop a cordial, intimate acquaintance with the woman who might very well have captured his love.

Still, her innate sense of justice demanded that she try, and so during the next several hours as they worked together in the

store, Selena made a sincere effort to cultivate their friendship.

She succeeded better than she'd anticipated, for by the time
tea had been served in the small parlor, she and Danielle had
passed beyond polite chatter and social conversation and were
almost on what might be called intimate terms. When the talk
turned to children, Selena told Danielle about the new baby
who had been birthed that morning on the plantation.

Clay's nurse had taken the boy outside to play in the courtyard, and the windows were open to catch the slight breeze.
The child's gurgles of laughter and the pattering of his feet
could be heard at intermittent intervals.

After a time, however, Danielle looked up from her cup with
a frown. "I don't hear Clay," she said, cocking her head to
listen. "I hope Zelda didn't take him to the summerhouse.
Ever since the picnic, he's been begging to go there again. But
I warned her to keep Clay close . . . so he wouldn't explore."

"We can go and check on him, if you like," Selena offered.

But no sooner were the words out of her mouth than she
heard what sounded like a distant cry. Both she and Danielle
froze. Selena couldn't be sure of the direction since the parlor
opened onto the courtyard and not the front of the house, but
she thought the sound might have come from beyond the east
wing.

When the ominous sound was followed by another muffled
shout that was clearly a shriek, Selena felt dread quicken
within her. Both women leaped to their feet, but Selena was
two paces ahead of Danielle as they raced for the courtyard.

By that time a dozen people had appeared there to investigate the commotion, but there was no sign of Clay. They ran
on, reaching the east end of the house just as his nurse burst
from around the corner. Her black face was a sickly shade of
gray, and she was sobbing for breath.

"Masta Clay . . . Masta Clay," Zelda cried, nearly incoher-
ent as she stumbled into Selena's arms.

"Zelda!" Selena demanded, dread clutching at her stomach as she gripped the black woman's wiry arms, "What happened? Where is Clay?"

"Masta Clay . . . he fell from the cliff."

"Dear God, no." The anguished moan had come from
Danielle. Desperately she caught up her skirts and started
running again toward the summerhouse, while Zelda kept

wringing her hands and moaning, "That poor chil', that poor chil'."

Selena bit back the urge to follow both examples and instead shook the servant's shoulders. "Zelda, please . . . tell me how badly Clay is hurt."

Taking another gulping breath, she nodded. "I don' know. He didn't move. . . . Oh, missy, I feart that poor chil' be dead!"

Chapter Seventeen

A soft smile curved Kyle's mouth as he left the jeweler's shop in Natchez with his purchase. The stunning set of sapphires and diamonds had cost him a small fortune, particularly since he'd requested the order be rushed, but he considered the expense well worth it; Selena would look exquisite in the fabulous necklace with its matching earrings and bracelet.

He had thought long and hard about what to get for her. He'd never given her a gift—unless he counted the wedding band that he'd been forced to bestow on her—and he wanted badly to make it up to her. Yet his sudden generosity was more than a desire to court her properly. He would have given her the moon if he could have managed it.

The thought lent a wry twist to Kyle's smile. He was beginning to resemble a love-struck swain. But that was precisely what he was, he reflected. And nothing he could give Selena seemed good enough—even the jewels he'd ordered the last time he was in town.

They were the best he could do, though. Tastefully designed, they exuded a quiet brilliance much like Selena herself did. Yet what if she didn't like them? Selena rarely wore jewelry and shunned ostentatious displays.... His smile fading at the possibility, Kyle slid the small parcel into his horse's saddlebag and swung himself up in the saddle.

He had only ridden halfway down the street when a vendor selling roses caught his attention. Perhaps Selena would prefer flowers to jewels.... On impulse, Kyle tossed a coin to the vendor and scooped up a bouquet, laying it across the saddle. Then he turned his horse toward Montrose and spurred the animal into a canter. He was anxious to be home. The hours without Selena had seemed like an eternity, and even though his discussions had proved worthwhile, he had begrudged every moment. Just like the endless nights he had spent away from her while he guarded Heaven's Gate.

Never again, he vowed. He would take Selena with him when he traveled to Louisville to commission his new steamboats. Perhaps they would even make it into a wedding trip....

His mind was occupied with such pleasant thoughts when he reached Montrose that Kyle at first didn't notice the commotion in the distance, beyond the line of cherry laurels. He was startled from his reverie when he recognized the powerfully muscled black man running toward the summerhouse, a coil of rope slung over each shoulder.

"Saul!" Kyle shouted as he spurred his horse to catch up. "What's amiss?"

Saul was breathing hard as he grabbed the roan's bridle, but he managed a reply. "Missy Whitfield, her boy fell from the bluff yonder."

"*Clay?* It was *Clay* who fell?"

Saul nodded. "Zelda said he was dead, but I dunno."

Every muscle in Kyle's body went rigid.

"Your missus tole me to fetch some rope. She done gone with Missy Whitfield to the bluff."

"Then come on, man!" Kyle exclaimed, reaching down to grasp Saul's arm. Within him fear warred with cold urgency as he hauled Saul up behind him on the powerful roan. Frantically he dug in his heels, aiming the horse at the summerhouse. The bouquet of roses he'd been holding slid to the earth to be ground into the dust.

Was that movement she detected? Selena wondered as she craned her neck over the edge, trying to see through the tangle of pine and wild grapevines at the bluff's side, peering at Clay's small, white face. Then, unmistakably, his eyelids fluttered. She caught her breath as hope stirred inside her. "Danielle, he's opening his eyes!"

"Thank God...."

Selena murmured her own grateful prayer as on her knees she inched closer to the edge.

The earth slide wasn't really a bluff, nor was it very high as bluffs go, but it was a great distance to a two-year-old child. Clay had fallen about twenty feet, his descent only stopped by the exposed roots of a papaw tree. His small body appeared to be wedged in the roots, while below him there was a further twenty-foot drop into the dry bayou, which was strewn with branches and rocks.

"He moved his arm."

"Please ... Selena, do something." The words were a sob.

"Yes, we'll rescue him."

One glance over her shoulder at the auburn-haired woman's stricken face, though, told Selena she would have to take charge. Danielle was too debilitated by terror to be of any help. Worse, she appeared prepared to step off the bluff to her death in order to save her son. Forcibly Selena reached up to clutch Danielle by the arm and hold her back.

"Mama," Clay suddenly wailed from below, trying to squirm free.

As Danielle gave a terrified sob, Selena's grip tightened. "You can't go down there!" she declared, her own voice shaking. "You'll be killed. We have to wait for a rope."

When the young child began to wail more loudly, Danielle gave Selena a look of frantic entreaty.

"Wait!" Selena urged as she climbed to her feet. She cast a desperate look around her, wishing fervently that someone would come with the rope she had called for.

Her heart leaped as she saw her husband gallop up with Saul clinging behind. "Kyle, thank God.... Clay's alive," she told him as both men sprang down from the horse, "but he's caught."

"Please help him," Danielle pleaded.

"Yes," Kyle answered simply. He was instantly in command, Selena realized, watching as he moved swiftly to the edge of the bluff. It was the air of authority that had made him such an effective ship's captain, the reason his men had been willing to follow him without question. Unhesitating, exuding confidence and skill ... demanding and receiving instant obedience. Selena was infinitely glad to have him in charge.

Kyle took in the situation at a glance, deciding what Selena had already concluded: the limbs of the papaw tree would make rescue difficult.

"We can't lower a rope to him," Selena began. "Even if he could manage to put it around his waist, the tree—"

"I'll have to go down for him."

"Perhaps you could lower me.... I'm lighter—"

"No, I'll do it. I've been climbing ropes since I was Clay's age." He was already retrieving one of the coils of rope and making a small loop at the end, tying it off with a knot.

"Kyle, are you sure? Not even Saul could bear your weight."

"No . . . but a half-dozen people could. Saul? I need you to form a line with everyone here to lower me down. Can you see to it?"

"Yassuh!"

"You stand at the front. Get a good grip on the rope. Don't pay it out or you'll end up with burns. Start back from the edge and walk forward slowly."

Saul spun around and started pointing at the house servants who had come to watch. "You, Martha, plant yourself right there, and you, woman . . ."

But even as Kyle positioned himself at the edge and slipped his foot through the rope's end loop, another problem made itself known.

"Clay!" Danielle cried. "Don't move! You'll fall. . . ."

Selena knelt beside her and immediately realized the danger. Clay had managed to stand up and was trying to climb up the steep wall of dirt and vines.

"Please, darling," Selena added her pleas to Danielle's, trying to keep the fear from her own voice. "Be still. We'll come down and fetch you."

She flung a glance at Kyle. He had shed his coat and was testing the rope for tautness as he lowered himself over the edge. His tone quiet and efficient as he called up orders to Saul, he slid downward through the undergrowth toward the tree where his son clung.

Clay saw him coming and turned, arms raised, but his small foot slipped on a root and he fell, nearly tumbling to the gully floor below.

Kyle uttered a sound that might have been an oath or a prayer, while Danielle shrieked. Selena, her heart in her throat, watched helplessly as the child hit his chin on a root and burst into fresh tears. Danielle followed suit.

"Danielle!" Selena murmured frantically, thrusting the weeping woman behind her, "You're only frightening him. Clay, please love, stay right where you are."

I have to talk to him, Selena thought. Give Kyle time to reach him. But Kyle was being lowered with such deliberate slowness that her nerves were screaming.

"Clay, did you hear that?" Selena said desperately. "Horatio is calling to you. You must be very quiet to hear him."

She thought the child understood her, for it seemed that his cries lessened fractionally.

"Did you hear what Horatio said, Clay? He wants you to come to tea. Of course, I think what he really would like is a picnic." Kyle was nearly there...a yard to the right of the tree. "When you come up here, you can give him a cracker. Would you like that?" She held her breath as Clay raised his tear-streaked face to her, his attention diverted.

"Please God," Danielle sobbed. "Just spare my son."

"Please Kyle, just a few more feet," Selena whispered, digging her fingers desperately into Danielle's arm. "Beside the tree now. Please, hurry."

Kyle made his move then. Reaching around a limb, he grabbed for Clay, wrapping a hand around a small arm, dragging his son against his chest as he clung to the rope.

The boy let out a wail, while above them Danielle buried her face in her hands.

"Thank you, God," Selena breathed, her voice little more than a croak.

"All right, pull us up...slowly." Holding on to the rope with one hand and to his wailing son with the other, Kyle shielded the child's small body from the worst of the underbrush as they were slowly pulled up the bluff. They finally reached the top.

"Far enough, Saul! Here, take him," Kyle rasped as he half pushed, half lifted Clay toward Selena.

Throwing herself to her stomach, she stretched as far as she could to reach down for him. When her fingers closed over the small arms, she pulled the whimpering child to safety and gave him to his terrified mother.

"Oh, thank God, thank God," Danielle sobbed over and over again, clutching so desperately at Clay that she was in danger of smothering him.

Selena remained where she was on the ground, not trusting her weak knees to support her. She was panting for breath as if she'd run a great distance, and her heart still thudded in her breast.

Kyle, too, was breathing hard as he dragged himself over the edge. He scarcely gave Selena a glance as he got to his feet and drew the weeping Danielle into his embrace.

"Danielle, it's over," he murmured. "It's over." The ragged note of relief in his voice was apparent as he pressed his cheek against her hair, offering strength and comfort to the trembling woman.

Trembling herself, Selena averted her gaze. The sight was too intimate, too painful to bear.... Kyle with his arms around Danielle, their son between them.

It was her worst fear confirmed.

She was almost grateful for the sound of galloping hooves, for it provided a distraction from the tormenting sight. As Orrin Chandler came charging toward them, Selena struggled wearily to her feet. Her racing heartbeat had slowed, yet the place where her heart was supposed to be located felt achingly hollow.

She watched with only vague interest as the man on horseback drew his mount to a skidding stop.

"Clay?" Orrin said at once, taking in the scene.

Kyle looked up briefly. "He's going to be fine."

And it was true, Selena reflected. Already Clay had ceased crying, attesting to the resilience of youth. Perhaps in a few weeks or months he wouldn't even remember his brush with death. But unlike Clay, she wouldn't recover... not from losing Kyle. And it seemed apparent, when Kyle spoke again, that that was indeed what had happened.

"Take Selena back to the house," Kyle told Orrin quietly. "I'll see to Danielle."

The words seemed so final, communicating an unspoken message. *Keep away, I protect what is mine.*

Selena glanced at Orrin, wondering if he would object. But although she saw for a moment what might have been her own despair reflected in his eyes, he merely nodded.

She scarcely heard Kyle ordering Saul to bring the carriage around. When Orrin urged his horse closer, she silently accepted his assistance in mounting. But as they rode away, Selena couldn't prevent herself one final look. Gazing over her shoulder, she saw the three of them—her husband, Danielle and Clay—framed like a painting done in rich oils. The afternoon sunlight glinting off Danielle's vivid, dark hair, and in the backdrop, the fertile cotton fields of Montrose stretching the distance....

Couple with Child, she would call such a painting.

The image branded itself in her memory, haunting her.

The three of them belonged together, Selena thought wretchedly, misery stabbing at her. And what was more, she had no place in their lives. She had been fooling herself to think Kyle could ever return her love. He wanted his son—far more than the physical relationship she could provide him as his wife. He didn't really need her at all. He could easily satisfy his physical needs with any one of a dozen women, as he had done before their marriage. His plantation was operating smoothly, the plans for his steamboat enterprise would be under way eventually. As for a mother for his sisters and companionship for himself, Danielle could provide that—perhaps better than she herself could.

Selena wasn't allowed to dwell on her morose reflections, however, for she was required to explain to Orrin, who had come to accompany Danielle back to town, what had happened on the bluff. And when they arrived at the house, she was greeted by scores of tense, waiting faces, all worried over the fate of the young boy who had captured their hearts with his dimpled grin.

Selena reassured them all that Clay was safe, thanked Orrin for his help, then escaped into the house. Kyle's sisters followed her upstairs to her room, though.

"Did Clay really fall off the bluff?" was the first question Felicity asked. "Why, he could have broken his neck."

And so Selena had to explain again that Clay seemed to be unhurt, but that no doubt he would be examined by a doctor. Kyle was taking the child and his mother home. She stumbled over the words, her voice quavering.

Felicity seemed to think Clay's fall a great lark, but Lydia looked pensive. Zoe, on the other hand, seemed more concerned for Selena.

"Selena, are you quite all right?" Zoe asked in her quiet voice.

"Yes," Felicity piped up. "You look wretched."

"I think perhaps we should leave Selena to herself," Lydia suggested, showing an unexpected thoughtfulness and clear evidence that she was growing up.

In appreciation, Selena gave her a smile that was only slightly forced. When she was alone, she went into her dressing room and caught a glimpse of herself in the cheval glass. No wonder the girls had commented about her appearance, she thought dismally. Her sprigged muslin gown was stained with mud and grass, her chin was smudged with dirt, and her hair, which had been neatly braided and coiled on her head earlier in the day, had lost its anchoring and hung in pale wisps around her face.

But it was her expression that was most startling. Her face was drawn and weary, her eyes despairing. She looked precisely what she was: a woman facing a bleak future. A future without Kyle.

Selena's throat tightened as she remembered the scene on the bluff. She'd come to a decision as she watched him embracing Danielle. She would free Kyle from their marriage. Indeed, that was only solution to this wretched situation. Kyle had originally wanted an annulment, and perhaps he could still obtain one, since he'd been forced to marry her. And if that was no longer possible, there were other ways he could gain his independence and therefore his son. If he asked the legislature to grant a bill of divorcement, she wouldn't stand in his way, Selena vowed. She wouldn't force him to stay in a marriage he had never wanted.

Resolving to tell him so when he returned, Selena wearily washed her face and then changed her gown. She was putting a final pin in her hair when she heard a timid knock on the door.

Selena tensed, afraid that it might be Kyle. Despite all her noble intentions, she wasn't quite ready to confront him. But when she bid entrance, it was only Felicity who peered around the door.

"Selena, a peddler is here! You must come see the beautiful ribbons he has brought. If you like, I'll buy you some with my pin money to cheer you up."

Selena was beyond cheering, but she didn't have the heart to refuse such a generous gesture. Fetching a purse filled with coins from her office, she accompanied Felicity out to the plantation yard.

The aging, unkempt peddler was engaged in retrieving wares from the hickory-withe panniers of his two pack mules and laying them out on a blanket. Zoe and Lydia were already there, as were Martha and a number of other house servants, all inspecting eagerly the strange assortment of goods—knives and handmade powder horns, thimbles and items of women's apparel.

When Felicity asked the peddler if he had any more ribbons to show them, he gave her a gap-toothed grin and shuffled over to his swaybacked mare, where he proceeded to search through his saddlebags. Felicity followed, dragging Selena along with her.

The peddler had to dump a number of items on the ground to find what he was looking for, and the young girl grew impatient. "What is this?" Felicity asked, picking up a small earthen jar.

"'Tis a pot of kohl, and not for a young lady like yerself."

"Why not?"

"Felicity," Selena said gently, "kohl is a cosmetic for the eyes."

"Oh, paint." The girl nodded wisely. "You mean it is only for females of questionable virtue."

Selena was relieved that she needn't respond, for Felicity was already examining the other wares. With a curious look, the girl held up a small packet of dried leaves. "Is this a cosmetic, too?"

"'Tis a dye called henna," the peddler answered. "Guaranteed to turn the hair red."

"So that is how it is done." Felicity made a face and let the packet drop. "Personally, I don't see why anyone would want red hair."

Her disdainful words struck an aching chord in Selena. When Felicity turned away to show her sisters the new ribbons, Selena eyed the henna leaves with a bitterness she couldn't repress. Perhaps if her hair had been red, Kyle would have found her more appealing.

The thought sent an irrational surge of anger whipping through her, slicing through her despair. One last effort, she thought with wounded fury. She would make one final attempt to win Kyle's interest before she gave him up to Danielle.

Clenching her jaw, Selena picked up the packet of hair dye. "I should like to purchase this," she told the peddler, not allowing herself time to reconsider. "What is the price?"

The old man's shaggy eyebrows drew together in a startled frown. "You want to buy the henna?"

"Yes," Selena said defiantly, meeting his puzzled gaze.

And when he told her the price, she didn't hesitate, but counted out the required coins with a determination born of desperation.

* * *

The sun was nearing the horizon as Kyle returned to Montrose. Saul came out of the smithy to meet him as he drove into the stable yard.

"Yes, Clay's fine," Kyle answered in response to the slave's question. "A few scratches, that's all."

Saul shook his head. "Amazin' the way chil'ren can git bounced on their heads and come up askin' for more."

"I know." Their gazes met in agreement as Kyle handed over the reins. "Saul, I'm grateful for the help you gave me today. I won't forget it."

The black man grinned. "You already done enough for me, Massa Kyle. But you oughtta do somethin' 'bout that bluff."

"Tomorrow we'll fence it off," Kyle said wearily as he climbed down from the carriage. He had spent the past several hours fetching a doctor to examine Clay and comforting both the child and his mother. Now all he wanted was to find Selena. "Do you know where I can find the mistress?"

"She was here more'n two hours ago, but I ain't seen her since," Saul replied. "You want I should see to the hosses?"

"Please. Give them a rubbing down, and then go back to your supper." He turned to go, but then hesitated. "I understand congratulations are in order. A boy, was it?"

Saul's mouth split into a wider grin. "Yassuh, Massa Ramsey. A fine boy. An' the best part is, he's gone grow up to be a free man."

Kyle essayed a smile before making his way to the house, his urgency communicating itself in his long stride.

Inside the stable, Selena nearly panicked. She had been saddling her mare when Kyle arrived, so she had overheard most of his conversation. When she heard Saul coming into the stable, she dashed to the far end of the barn and slipped into an empty stall. She couldn't face Kyle. Her attempt to turn her silver-blond hair to a fiery auburn had ended in disaster, while the desperate courage that had driven her to douse her head with the henna dye had totally deserted her. Now all she wanted to do was weep—and hide. She intended to seek refuge with Bea, if Bea would take her in.

She waited with feverish impatience for Saul to finish tending to the horses. If Kyle was intent on finding her, he might return at any moment. She had left a note for him—which seemed foolish now—saying she was visiting Bea.

Finally, though, Saul completed his task and left the barn. Selena returned to struggle with the heavy sidesaddle, all the while listening for the sound of familiar footsteps.

They weren't long in coming. Desperately, Selena glanced around the stable, searching for a safe place to hide. Catching sight of the ladder that led to the loft, she scurried up it with a speed she hadn't believed herself capable of. She had barely scrambled through the straw to the far corner when Kyle entered the barn.

Selena could hear every beat of her heart in the silence that followed. Kyle was inspecting her mare; she could tell. Then he was searching each of the stalls. She could almost see him looking around, wondering what had become of her.

"Selena?"

She held her breath, not daring to breathe.

"Selena, I know you're here. You didn't pass me on my way to the stables, and your mare is still in her stall. And the wisps of straw floating down from the loft give you away."

Her shoulders slumped. She had been found out. "Please go away," she replied, hoping she could convince him to leave.

As orders go, it lacked both power and conviction, and Kyle didn't obey. In only a moment he had climbed the ladder to the loft. He paused, though, when he spied Selena. The heat in the loft was sweltering, yet she had huddled her arms about her, hugging her knees, as if she were terribly cold. Kyle's gaze narrowed in concern. Sunlight was spilling through the chinks in the shutter, the final rays before sunset, yet he couldn't make out her expression, for the brim of her bonnet shielded her face from view.

"Selena, is something the matter? Are you hurt?"

"No. I merely want to be alone."

Her voice was soft and shaky, and it only increased his concern. "Very well," he agreed, crossing the loft, bending low to avoid hitting the rafters. "You can be alone when you tell me what's wrong."

Sinking down beside Selena to his knees, he gently grasped her arms, making her lift her face. Then his mouth went slack as he stared at her. "Good God, what happened to your hair? It looks pink!"

There was no denying it was an odd color. What had been silver tresses was now a faint shade of orangey-pink that contrasted strangely with the plum-colored muslin of her gown.

Selena felt Kyle's shocked gaze search her face, but she wouldn't meet his eyes. She wanted to sink through the loft. Fortunately, though, pride momentarily came to her rescue, and her trembling chin came up. "I dyed it."

"I can see that, but . . . in heavens name, *why*?"

"I was under the impression you liked red hair."

Kyle chuckled softly as he loosened the ribbons of her bonnet and slid it off her head. "I'm partial to red, yes, but I never much favored pink."

"Don't make sport of me!" Her eyes filling with tears, she buried her face in her hands.

Immediately Kyle swallowed his choked laughter. "Selena—" his fingers closed again around her arms, this time urgently "—please, will you tell me what this is all about?"

It was the final humiliation, having to confess. But it didn't matter any longer how she humbled herself before him. After this she wouldn't have to face Kyle again. She wouldn't be seeing him again. She started to explain, but her throat was so tight she found it hard to speak. "I thought . . . if I had red hair . . . you might want me. But I must not have applied the henna correctly. I was supposed to steep the leaves—"

Kyle understood only the first half of what she had said. "Might want you?" he echoed. "Of course I want you."

Sadly, Selena shook her head. "You don't want me as your wife. You don't love me—"

She suddenly found herself in a fierce embrace as Kyle wrapped his arms around her and drew her close. "You wonderful, brave, generous, incredibly beautiful female," he breathed against her hair. "How could you think that? Certainly I love you. How could I not love you?"

Selena's breath caught in her throat. "You . . . never said so."

"That's only because it took me a while to realize it," Kyle said tenderly. "And then I was afraid to mention it until I was sure I stood a chance of winning your regard. I do love you, my darling Selena. Very much."

She wanted desperately to believe him, and yet the image of him holding Danielle wouldn't go away. "But Danielle . . ."

"What about Danielle?"

"The way you were holding her this afternoon—"

"I was comforting a hysterical woman, Selena. Danielle doesn't have your courage, your inner strength. She couldn't cope with losing Clay, not after all she's suffered. She was frightened."

Selena hesitated, remembering the child lying there so still and quiet. "I was frightened, too."

"So was I," Kyle declared fervently. "I thought... But it didn't happen." Sighing, he raised his hand to stroke her hair with a possessive gentleness. "Do you know how many times in the past few hours I've thanked God you were there? Doubtless you saved Clay's life, Selena."

"But I didn't do anything."

"You did. You kept your head, talking to him about that damned parrot. I couldn't have reached him in time otherwise."

She shuddered in Kyle's embrace. "No, it was you. If you hadn't come in time—"

"I have every confidence you would have thought of something, my brave, beautiful Moonwitch."

Hearing the smile in his voice, Selena drew back to search Kyle's rugged face. Sunbeams highlighted his thick hair with gold and increased the sharp clarity of his eyes, making it impossible for her to deny the love she saw there. She took a steadying breath, daring to believe. "I thought I had lost you," she whispered, her voice nearly breaking.

His mouth curved with quizzical amusement. "Is that why you were leaving?"

"I thought I would stay with Bea until you could obtain a divorce."

Kyle's expression turned instantly sober, but Selena continued, determined to give him a final chance to reconsider. "Then you would be free to marry Danielle...and claim Clay as your son."

Kyle held her gaze intently. "I suppose I should be grateful for your unselfish offer, but I'm not. Besides, your plan wouldn't work. In the first place, I don't want to marry Danielle, and she doesn't want to marry me. She and Orrin are far better suited, and I imagine she's already come to that conclusion. They'll be married after a decent interval, no doubt. And in the second, I *can't* marry Danielle. I already have a wife—whom I love very much."

"But... what about Clay?" Selena said helplessly.

"I admit I would have liked to make him my son legally, but as you pointed out, it isn't possible. I've come to terms with that. Besides, Orrin will make him a good father. I'll settle a sum on Clay that he'll inherit when he's older. And it isn't as if I'll be giving him up entirely. He can come and play here with our children when we have them.''

''Our children?'' Selena breathed, still not sure she wasn't dreaming.

''Yes.'' It was Kyle's turn to be humble. He took her hand, gazing down at her slender fingers as if afraid to meet her gaze. ''I haven't been much of a husband to you, Selena. I don't know if I can be, but I mean to try my damnedest. I intended to court you properly and win you, if I could—that was what I was trying to do this past week, though it didn't seem to be working.'' He hesitated, glancing up at her with a plea in his eyes. ''Tell me it's not too late, Moonwitch.''

''No,'' she whispered. ''It's not too late.''

''I'm not what you deserve. I'm not nearly good enough for you—''

''Oh, Kyle.'' She murmured his name on a sigh as she pressed her cheek against his solid chest. ''You're everything I want.''

''And do you think you could come to love me someday?''

She heard the uncertainty in his tone, felt the tension in his body, and her heart melted. ''I love you now. I have for a long time.''

Kyle hesitated, still tense. ''More than...what was his name? The man you wanted to marry.''

''Yes, more than Edward. I was so young then...a mere girl.''

His sigh was one of relief as his arms came around her. ''You can't imagine how jealous I was of him.''

''Yes, I can. I felt the same way about Danielle...and Angel...and that red-haired woman in New Orleans.''

''It sounds like you didn't trust me.''

The laughter was back in his voice, and his teasing unfortunately reminded Selena of the tormenting jealousy she had endured during the past month or more. She stiffened, pushing against Kyle's chest with an indignant look. ''How could I trust you with so many women chasing you?''

''Selena, my love,'' Kyle said with a smile as his mouth slowly descended, ''I promised to be faithful—'' he nuzzled her open lips in a tantalizing caress ''—and I have been, body and heart.'' His tongue slid inside her mouth, seeking hers.

Pressing Selena down into the straw then, Kyle proceeded to kiss her with a tender, arousing passion that left her breath erratic and her body throbbing.

He was breathing hard, too, when he finally drew away. "How," he said with weak laughter as he propped himself up on one elbow, "could I ever look at another woman when I have you?"

Too dazed to move, Selena murmured a contented sigh in answer. She felt Kyle brush an escaping tendril back from her face.

"How could I not love you?" he repeated quietly. "You've shown me how to run this plantation, you've been a mother to my sisters, you've made it easy for me to be with Clay.... I do love you, Selena. Every night for the past week I've tried to show you how much."

Her eyelids fluttering open slowly, Selena gazed back at Kyle, watching his eyes, the green flecks swimming in a sea of gold. "I thought it was just physical desire."

"No." Kyle shook his head solemnly. What he felt for her wasn't merely lust. It hadn't been that for a long time, perhaps from the first. And yet passion was an integral part of his love for her. Quite aware now of his body's throbbing hunger, he traced the delicate curve of her jaw. "Do you have any idea what torment I endured night after night, sleeping apart from you, knowing you were so close?"

"Then why did you avoid me for so long?"

"Because every time I got near, I couldn't manage to keep my hands off you. And you let me know very clearly you wouldn't welcome my advances."

"That was only because you said you didn't want me."

His brows drew together in a frown. "When did I say that?"

"On your ship...that morning after the storm. I overheard you telling Mr. Hardwick."

"I remember telling him how brave you were for saving his life," Kyle said, puzzled, "and that I was looking forward to being married, after all."

"I wish I had known."

The creases in his cheeks deepened as his mouth curved in a teasing grin. "Serves you right for eavesdropping."

"I wasn't eavesdropping when I saw you kissing Veronique," Selena replied archly.

"I didn't kiss her, she kissed me."

"Perhaps. But what about that night, and the next one? You didn't return to the hotel."

"Yes, I did, only it was late. I stayed out playing cards. I never saw Veronique again."

She traced the lines of laughter around his eyes, feathering her fingers over his bronzed skin. "Truly?"

Kyle's expression softened. "Yes, truly."

"Well, I didn't know that. And I was jealous. Especially after discovering that Angel and Danielle were also part of your past."

"And that's just where I intended them to stay, in my past."

"But when we arrived here, you never came to my bed."

"Selena, I told you why. I thought you didn't want me to. Besides, you never came to my bed, either."

"It wasn't my place to make advances."

Kyle chuckled at her prim reply.

"Well, how could I?" she protested. "You had told me I was passionless, and you blamed me for depriving you of your son and for taking away your freedom—"

"I never blamed you—at least not after I got used to the idea."

Boldly, Selena encircled his neck with her arms. "Kyle, you know very well you didn't want to marry me."

She felt the laughter rumbling in his chest. "That's only because I couldn't see what a treasure I was getting. I've since come to realize that the smartest thing I ever did was kiss you on the streets of St. John's."

"Truly?"

His smile was an endearment. "Truly."

Her arms tightened about his neck, never wanting to let go. Happiness, joy, delight were welling in her, filling her because this rugged, vital man belonged to her, every glorious inch of him. Quivering with the feeling, Selena drew back. "Kyle," she said with sudden urgency, "make love to me."

"Here? Now?" His eyebrows rose in feigned shock, though the passion in his eyes was compelling and tender.

"Yes, now." Her body, alive to the promise in his eyes, yearned for him.

"Aren't you worried someone will hear?"

"All the servants are at supper, and the girls will have eaten. They decided to feel sorry for me and allow me some solitude."

"I don't know, Moonwitch." Kyle glanced around him skeptically. "I've always thought straw overrated. As a bed it leaves much to be desired."

"I don't care. Kyle, please...."

"You know," he observed with amusement, his fingers stealing to her bodice and deftly baring her breasts, "I always did have one major problem. I never could resist you...."

"I'm glad."

His husky laughter caressed her nipple as his lips came down to capture it, and Selena quivered, her senses flaring with sensation, the intensity of pleasure she felt in his burning touch heightened by the certainty of his love.

He aroused her slowly, with a skill that left her trembling and breathless, and undressed her with reverence, as if it were the first time. Unashamed, Selena watched as Kyle removed his own clothes, glorying in the beauty of his powerful, bronzed, totally masculine body. And when he came to her, she clasped him to her breast with a possessiveness that his glowing eyes told her he shared.

"I want so much to give you a son," she murmured, and the glow in Kyle's eyes deepened to a golden flame as his mouth came fiercely down to claim hers.

Her hands roved over him, caressing the broad, damp expanse of his back with the muscles rippling under smooth skin, the tightly contracted strength of his buttocks and waist, his satiny, powerful arms, until he was trembling as violently as she.

"Selena," Kyle breathed at last as he slid deep inside her welcoming warmth. "My woman, my lady, my love."

Yet deliberately he held back, gazing down at her delicate, enchanting face. No longer was he aching because fate had deprived him of his son; he had Selena and a lifetime to spend loving her and their future children. No longer did he feel the restless need to roam the seas in search of challenge and adventure; he was home. No longer would he struggle against the chains of obligation and duty that bound him to the land and shackled his precious freedom; he had found freedom in her arms. His heart was soaring with a bliss so profound that he felt dizzy.

Giddy with the same joy, Selena arched against him as he moved within her, clutching the taut sinews of his arms, giving herself over totally to the passion that was hot and wild and sweet. And when together they found their own heaven, her cry of ecstasy mingled with Kyle's hoarse groan of fulfillment. Still, he lowered himself to her, dropping his face into the warm, wet hollow of Selena's throat as he lay against her, spent, shuddering.

It was a long time before they returned to earth, to the pulsing, sweltering heat of the loft. Selena made a small murmur of protest as Kyle eased his weight from her, but he pressed a conciliatory kiss on the damp, flushed skin of her temple and gathered her close, relaxing with a sigh of exhaustion. The last rays of sunlight glinted off the spinning dust motes as they lay together in sated silence.

"I think," Kyle said sometime later, his voice still husky with passion, "I take the honors for noise this time."

Selena roused herself enough to lift her gaze to his face. Seeing how contented he looked, she traced a provocative finger from his lightly furred chest to the hard, flat plane of his stomach, smiling when she felt his muscles tense. "I like it when you 'carry on,'" she observed with deliberate smugness. "It makes a woman feel powerful, knowing she can make her man groan."

At her echo of his onetime remark, Kyle put his head back and roared. She was a constant source of delight to him.

"No doubt," he said wickedly when he could talk, "the uniqueness of the situation had a hand in arousing me. I've never made love to a pink-haired woman before."

Selena's cheeks flushed scarlet at the reminder. Wanting to hide, she buried her face in Kyle's chest.

"I'm flattered, Moonwitch, that you would want to gratify my whims, but I happen to like you the way you are."

"I'm never going to live this down," she muttered ruefully.

"It isn't that bad, I suppose. Only a very *pale* pink."

Selena groaned in mortification.

"I expect the color will fade," Kyle assured her, abandoning his teasing.

"When?"

"I don't know. Did you try to wash it out?"

"I rinsed out the dye."

"We'll scrub it with lye soap."

"What if that doesn't help?"

"Then you can wear one of those turbans that are all the rage. You'll be considered a leader of fashion. And I'm certain you'll look every bit as beautiful as usual. Now why don't you forget about your hair for a moment. I have a proposition to discuss with you." He slipped a finger under Selena's chin, making her lift her gaze. "What would you say to taking a trip to Louisville? Not now—the harvest will soon be under way. But next spring, before planting begins."

She hesitated. "Louisville?"

"It's a town upriver from here that is fast becoming a major steamboat center, according to the gentlemen I spoke to today. It already has a reputable firm of shipbuilders and a major engine manufacturer. They suggested I commission our steamboats there."

"Then you really mean to do it?" she asked, sounding pleased. "How many do you plan to build?"

"Two, to begin with." Kyle rested his palm against her cheek, his thumb tracing the outline of her lips. "And I intend to christen the first one *Moonwitch*."

A slow smile lighted Selena's eyes, reflecting her joy. Seeing their gentle sparkle made Kyle recall the gift he had brought her. Later, he promised himself, his own eyes gleaming as he pictured Selena decked in sapphires and diamonds and nothing else.

"And since," he continued, "I'll have to travel there anyway to inspect the construction, I thought we could make it our wedding journey. I haven't had you to myself since our marriage, and the idea rather appeals to me."

"It appeals to me, as well. But what about your sisters?"

"My sisters be hanged," Kyle said with a grin. "They can manage without us for a few weeks. We'll ask Danielle to come and stay with them—or someone else, if she makes you uncomfortable."

"Danielle never made me uncomfortable. It was the idea of you and her together that I found so objectionable."

"Well, I'm giving up red-haired women altogether."

"I'm gratified to know that," she replied, her eyes shining with love in the gathering dusk.

"And tonight, you'll sleep in my bed, where you belong."

Selena caught her breath as Kyle's hand moved down her throat to stroke the delicate line of her collarbone. "Then you don't mean to avoid me any longer?"

"Moonwitch," he said with a murmur of laughter as he bent his head, "just try and keep me away."

*   *   *   *   *

Harlequin romances are now available in stores at these convenient times each month.

Harlequin Presents **Harlequin American Romance** **Harlequin Historical** **Harlequin Intrigue**	These series will be in stores on the 4th of every month.
Harlequin Romance **Harlequin Temptation** **Harlequin Superromance** **Harlequin Regency Romance**	New titles for these series will be in stores on the 16th of every month.

We hope this new schedule is convenient for you. With only two trips each month to your local bookseller, you will always be sure not to miss any of your favorite authors!

Happy reading!

Please note there may be slight variations in on-sale dates in your area due to differences in shipping and handling.

HDATES

Don't miss one exciting moment of you next vacation with Harlequin's

FREE
FIRST CLASS TRAVEL ALARM CLOCK

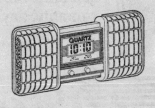

Actual Size
3¼″ × 1¼″h

By reading FIRST CLASS—Harlequin Romance's armchair travel plan for the incurably romantic— you'll not only visit a different dreamy destination every month, but you'll also receive a FREE TRAVEL ALARM CLOCK!

All you have to do is collect 2 proofs-of-purchase from FIRST CLASS Harlequin Romance books. FIRST CLASS is a one title per month series, available from January to December 1991.

For further details, see FIRST CLASS premium ads in FIRST CLASS Harlequin Romance books. Look for these books with the special FIRST CLASS cover flash!

JTLOOK

HARLEQUIN'S "BIG WIN"
SWEEPSTAKES RULES & REGULATIONS
NO PURCHASE NECESSARY TO ENTER OR RECEIVE A PRIZE

1. To enter and join the Reader Service, scratch off the metallic strips on all your BIG WIN tickets #1-#6. This will reveal the values for each sweepstakes entry number, the number of free book(s) you will receive and your free bonus gift as part of our Reader Service. If you do not wish to take advantage of our Reader Service but wish to enter the Sweepstakes only, scratch off the metallic strips on your BIG WIN tickets #1-#4. Return your entire sheet of tickets intact. Incomplete and/or inaccurate entries are ineligible for that section or sections of prizes. Not responsible for mutilated or unreadable entries or inadvertent printing errors. Mechanically reproduced entries are null and void.

2. Whether you take advantage of this offer or not, your Sweepstakes numbers will be compared against the list of winning numbers generated at random by the computer. In the event that all prizes are not claimed by March 31, 1992, a random drawing will be held from all qualified entries received from March 30, 1990 to March 31, 1992, to award all unclaimed prizes. All cash prizes (Grand to Sixth), will be mailed to the winners and are payable by check in U.S. funds. Seventh prize will be shipped to winners via third-class mail. These prizes are in addition to any free, surprise or mystery gifts that might be offered. Versions of this sweepstakes with different prizes of approximate equal value may appear at retail outlets or in other mailings by Torstar Corp. and its affiliates.

3. The following prizes are awarded in this sweepstakes: ★ Grand Prize (1) $1,000,000; First Prize (1) $25,000; Second Prize (1) $10,000; Third Prize (5) $5,000; Fourth Prize (10) $1,000; Fifth Prize (100) $250; Sixth Prize (2,500) $10; ★ ★ Seventh Prize (6,000) $12.95 ARV.

   ★ This presentation offers a Grand Prize of a $1,000,000 annuity. Winner will receive $33,333.33 a year for 30 years without interest totalling $1,000,000.

   ★ ★ Seventh Prize: A fully illustrated hardcover book published by Torstar Corp. Approximate retail value of the book is $12.95.

   Entrants may cancel the Reader Service at anytime without cost or obligation to buy (see details in center insert card).

4. This Sweepstakes is being conducted under the supervision of an independent judging organization. By entering this Sweepstakes, each entrant accepts and agrees to be bound by these rules and the decisions of the judges, which shall be final and binding. Odds of winning in the random drawing are dependent upon the total number of entries received. Taxes, if any, are the sole responsibility of the winners. Prizes are nontransferable. All entries must be received at the address printed on the reply card and must be postmarked no later than 12:00 MIDNIGHT on March 31, 1992. The drawing for all unclaimed sweepstakes prizes will take place May 30, 1992, at 12:00 NOON, at the offices of Marden-Kane, Inc., Lake Success, New York.

5. This offer is open to residents of the U.S., the United Kingdom, France and Canada, 18 years or older, except employees and their immediate family members of Torstar Corp., its affiliates, subsidiaries, and all other agencies and persons connected with the use, marketing or conduct of this sweepstakes. All Federal, State, Provincial and local laws apply. Void wherever prohibited or restricted by law. Any litigation within the Province of Quebec respecting the conduct and awarding of a prize in this publicity contest must be submitted to the Régie des loteries et courses du Québec.

6. Winners will be notified by mail and may be required to execute an affidavit of eligibility and release, which must be returned within 14 days after notification or an alternative winner will be selected. Canadian winners will be required to correctly answer an arithmetical skill-testing question administered by mail, which must be returned within a limited time. Winners consent to the use of their names, photographs and/or likenesses for advertising and publicity in conjunction with this and similar promotions without additional compensation. For a list of major winners, send a stamped, self-addressed envelope to: WINNERS LIST, c/o Harlequin Reader Service, 3010 Walden Ave., P.O. Box 1396, Buffalo, NY 14269-1396. Winners Lists will be fulfilled after the May 30, 1992 drawing date.

If Sweepstakes entry form is missing, please print your name and address on a 3" ×5" piece of plain paper and send to:

In the U.S.	In Canada
Harlequin's "BIG WIN" Sweepstakes	Harlequin's "BIG WIN" Sweepstakes
3010 Walden Ave.	P.O. Box 609
P.O. Box 1867	Fort Erie, Ontario
Buffalo, NY 14269-1867	L2A 5X3

Offer limited to one per household.

© 1991 Harlequin Enterprises Limited   Printed in the U.S.A.

LTY-H191R

COMING NEXT MONTH

#63 THE SILVER LINK—Patricia Potter
American army scout Tristan Hampton sought adventure in
New Mexico, but he found much more in the arms of fiery
Spaniard Antonia Ramirez. Their hearts told them they were
lovers; their people told them they were enemies—and bitter
hatred threatened to destroy their perfect love.

#64 CONTRABAND DESIRE—Lucy Elliot
Union officer Quinn Erskine made it clear that a refugee slave
camp in war-torn Tennessee was no place for the refined
Elizabeth Whitley. But Elizabeth's undaunted determination
to help the refugees was a light in the darkness of war, and her
love was a fire in the darkness of Quinn's heart.

#65 HIGHLAND HEATHER—Ruth Langan
Spirited Brenna MacAlpin swore never to marry an
Englishman, despite Queen Elizabeth's orders. But her English
captor, the ruggedly handsome Lord Morgan Grey, soon had
her longing to exchange one vow for another.

#66 FORBIDDEN FIRE—Heather Graham Pozzessere
Marissa Ayers already regretted being a party to the deceit she
would bring to Ian Tremayne's household. Still, when she'd
pledged to masquerade as her friend, Marissa never dreamed
that Ian was not expecting a ward...but a wife.

AVAILABLE NOW:

#61 BRADEN'S BRIDES
Caryn Cameron

#62 MOONWITCH
Nicole Jordan